LEGACY OF EVIL

LEGACY OF EVIL

Peter Harrison

The Book Guild Ltd
Sussex, England

Although based on the author's research and containing some real characters, *Legacy of Evil* is a work of fiction.

This book is sold subject to the condition that it shall not, by way of trade or otherwise, be lent, re-sold, hired out, photocopied or held in any retrieval system or otherwise circulated without the publisher's prior consent in any form of binding or cover other than that in which this is published and without a similar condition including this condition being imposed on the subsequent purchaser.

The Book Guild
25 High Street,
Lewes, Sussex

First Published 1997
© Peter Harrison, 1997
Set in Baskerville
Typesetting by Raven Typesetters, Chester

Printed in Great Britain by
Antony Rowe Ltd, Chippenham, Wilts.

A catalogue record for this book is
available from the British Library

ISBN 1 85776 164 2

*To my wife Erny
in appreciation of her continuous support*

1

1942

It was raining heavily as the Mercedes picked its way through the Munich streets on that late November evening. The officer in the back seat peered past the driver's head and watched the flag fluttering above the pointed star on the radiator top. He felt his swollen neck, which seemed worse than the previous day. As if liver problems and then nasal difficulties were not enough ... He had undergone extensive treatment in Zemmering only six weeks before, but his early return to North Africa before the treatment was complete had not helped. Those six weeks had been the worst in his life for his morale, and now being openly castigated by his Führer had further depressed him.

His aide sat silent at his side. The Field Marshal, he rightly judged, wasn't in a talking mood. Like almost all his staff, the aide respected and liked him, and wondered what had happened in the personal interview he had had with the Führer – the interview for which he had flown over 2,000 miles at a critical stage of the campaign.

The car pulled up at the Haupbahnhof and the driver sprang out to open the door. It had been a privilege to be assigned to drive the most famous officer in the Wehrmacht during his brief visit to Munich. Field Marshal Erwin Rommel returned the salute and walked into the dimly lit station whilst the driver arranged for a porter to carry the luggage.

Rommel stood under the clock and checked his watch by

it. He was a stickler for time, in keeping with his military upbringing. He turned to his aide. 'Did you check the car left Ulm on time?'

'*Jawohl*, Herr Field Marshal, in plenty of time. They should arrive any moment now. I chose the driver myself and he has exact orders.' He had hardly finished speaking when a Mercedes staff car without insignia pulled up in front of the station and Rommel, momentarily putting aside his rank and 51 years, ran to greet the passenger in the back of the car.

'Lola – oh, my darling Lola, it's so wonderful to see you!' He kissed and hugged her. 'Come on – we must find our compartment on the train and settle in before the Reichmarschall arrives. This is no ordinary express, this is his personal train, with all the trappings, I have no doubt. We have about half an hour together before he arrives and I must be ready to receive him.'

The two angular figures were ushered along the platform by the aide and a railway official and shown into a large compartment with a sitting area and twin beds made up for the night.

Twenty minutes later Rommel stood by the train, looking impressive in a fresh uniform. The car which drove to the station didn't stop at the concourse. With the two motorcycle outriders ordering the barrier to open, the sleek limousine went straight onto the platform and Rommel raised his arm in salute as Reichmarschall Hermann Goering emerged, dressed in a pale grey silk suit with dark lapels. 'I'm so pleased you are travelling with me to Rome, Rommel. So much to talk about. Is your wife with us?'

'Indeed she is, Herr Reichmarschall, but I thought you might like to talk with me privately after this morning's meeting with the Führer.'

'Not at all, my boy, not at all – what could we conceal from your wife, eh? I've known you all these years and never met Frau Rommel.' He strode along the platform, smiling at the station staff and acknowledging salutes. 'Let's dine together. The food in my dining car is very good – better than North Africa, eh? Though I'm told that Montgomery keeps a fine mess gong even when you give him a hard time. No – you fetch Frau Rommel from your quarters and meet me in the dining car in twenty minutes, eh?'

Rommel walked through the corridor of the train and back to his compartment. 'The Reichmarschall wants us to dine with him tonight – in twenty minutes. I had forgotten you'd never met him. He's a strange man, as you will see, with an annoying habit of saying "eh" at the end of a sentence. It drives me mad but I suppose I've bigger demands on my sanity than that at present.' Rommel looked out of the window as the train jerked forward and moved slowly out of the station.

Hermann Goering greeted Lucie Maria Rommel warmly. 'My privilege to meet the lovely wife of our national hero – the first officer in the Third Reich and destined for high office after the war.'

Rommel's creased face broke into a wry smile; that wasn't the impression he had gained from the Führer at yesterday's meeting, or even the milder session that very morning. Goering continued his chatter and led Frau Rommel into the dining room and the waiters stiffened to attention. The three sat down and Goering kept up his talk of how he saw life in Germany after the victory over the Allied forces. Goering leant forward to make a point over the table and Rommel noted his gold watch encrusted with diamonds. On his ring finger was a gold ring with an enormous single diamond. Rommel shuddered inwardly at the vulgarity but Lola's eyes lit up and Goering noticed.

'You like my ring and watch, eh? I love beautiful things; this stone must be one of the most valuable in the world. Wherever I go I collect lovely things, not just because of their value but because of the pleasure they give me – I have an outstanding picture gallery at my home as well as many statues. They call me the Maecenas of the Third Reich.' The Reichmarschall sat back in his chair and laughed. 'Balbo, when he was in Cyrene, sent me a statue of Aphrodite – but the Field Marshal here, he has no love for the arts, I believe.'

'I'm a simple soldier, Herr Reichmarschall – I stick to my soldiering as my life and my hobby,' Rommel answered. Goering rocked with laughter. 'Then I have a piece of art which I, as head of the Luftwaffe, can present to a distinguished soldier – something of artistic beauty which even a simple soldier will appreciate.' Goering felt in his pocket and handed Rommel a Fluggenführerabzeichen, the Luftwaffe Pilot's Cross, in diamonds and slapped him on the shoulder. 'Don't take too much to heart what the Führer said. He is under great strain.'

Rommel took the cross, placed it on his side plate and kept his eyes on it as he spoke. 'The fact is, Herr Reichmarschall, that he called me a coward and a defeatist – and said that had I been on the Russian front I would have been shot. That is so hurtful that I cannot put it out of my mind. I served the Führer at a distance in the early and mid thirties, and since the beginning of the war on a closer front, even being in charge of his personal safety. I cannot see any justification for such accusations.'

Goering looked Rommel in the face, his eyes shone showing his trust. 'The Führer wants to see results in North Africa, and he believes you are the man to produce them. Bear in mind that only last month after El Alamein, when General Stumme was killed, the Führer telephoned you in hospital and asked – not commanded – you to return to take command of the Afrika Korps. Does that not convince you of his confidence in you?'

'But you know, my dear Rommel, you do provoke the Führer when he is under strain. You think you are being realistic and honest when you point to problems; he sees it as being defeatist. Be like Bormann – tell him what he wants to hear. That's the secret of Bormann's success. Keitel as well, he plays "*Yes man*" to his own definite advantage. Another thing: you always give him the military salute rather than the salute of our beloved party.'

Rommel started to reply but Goering waved his hand and continued. 'Raeder is the same. As head of the German navy he should be a party member but he's as stubborn as you – he infuriates the Führer with his salute. Even when the *Bismarck* was launched at Hamburg, Raeder and indeed his immediate staff all saluted in the naval fashion. It irritated the Führer and he talked to me about it over dinner – "lacking in commitment to the cause" were the words he chose.'

Goering leant across the table and his hand grasped Rommel's arm. 'It would be, how shall I say, expedient for you to support the National Socialist Party and to be less direct with the Führer – but I see you will not accept my advice.'

Rommel looked out of the window as the train was slowing into a station, but with blackout regulations there was no telling where it was. 'Herr Reichmarschall, if the Führer wants results he must send me supplies. I cannot build a house without bricks. If we had the same supplies of petrol and arms as Montgomery, we should be back in Alexandria by now and the Suez Canal would be ours before Christmas.'

Goering leant forward and his left hand with watch and ring pointed at Rommel. 'You heard what the Führer said – you are to receive our complete support. We are on our way to Rome to ensure that the Italian forces keep you in fuel and armament supplies. You can rely on me – indeed you can build a house on me. You can have your precious bricks. Now let us talk of more interesting things; we are boring your wife.'

Goering finished his dinner of duckling and sat staring out of the window. He had been talking incessantly since the start of the meal and Rommel welcomed the pause. The door at the end of the carriage opened and Rommel's aide de camp came to the table and saluted. 'Excuse me, Herr Field Marshal, but there is a signal for you from OKW. There is worse news from North Africa.'

Rommel raised his hand and took the signal. He read silently and his face furrowed. 'We will have to stay only a short while in Rome, Sneider – the Führer's direct instruction is that we return to the front.' Turning to Goering he was surprised to see the Reichmarschall looking at a photograph in his wallet.

'Isn't it beautiful? This is the Aphrodite from Cyrene I told you about. Whenever I hear bad news I look at it and realise there is still beauty around us – but you don't appreciate art, do you, Rommel!? You are the thorough professional soldier – no art and no politics. Yet Balbo, who gave me this, can be head of the Italian air force and a lover of art at the same time!'

Rommel looked at his superior quizzically. 'I believe a soldier can be both, Herr Reichmarschall. It is just that I am not personally involved in art. The colonel here, for example, as well as being my aide on this trip (for as you know, my personal aide, Hoffner, is ill) has a fine appreciation of the arts.'

Goering's eyes narrowed. 'Look at this picture, colonel – an Aphrodite from Africa, indeed the only North African statue in my collection, eh.'

The colonel looked at the picture and drew a deep breath. 'It is indeed beautiful, indeed magnificent, Herr Reichmarschall – I have never seen anything so lovely. I would love to see it personally.'

'So you shall – one day. A true lover of art should share his joys. I understand there are many beautiful collections in North Africa, one in particular which is in the hands of the Jews. So, with the Field Marshal's agreement I will give you a special assignment when you return to the front, which will be...' He turned to Rommel and the Field Marshal added, 'In a week or so.' 'Very well,' Goering went on. 'Tomorrow morning at ten you will report to my carriage before the train gets to Rome and I will give you a letter of authority and my precise instructions, eh.'

Colonel Sneider raised his arm in salute and Hermann Goering raised his tie and studied his diamond pin. 'We must always appreciate beautiful things in life, even when life is hard – always remember that, Rommel. I want to be remembered as a man of artistic talent... not just as a soldier and a politician who did so much for the fatherland. I am to have a bust of my head sculpted in Italy. One day every German home will have a replica.'

The dinner was over and Goering suggested they took some brandy before retiring. They sat in a semicircle at the end of the carriage and Frau Rommel asked if she could be excused as she was tired. The two men rose as she left the carriage and Goering patted Rommel on the shoulder. 'A fine German lady – you must be very proud of her. After the war she will stand you in good stead when you achieve even higher authority.'

'I hope so,' Rommel replied, 'but first we must win, and I cannot overemphasise the matter I raise today about supplies and the unreliability of the Italians. Italian troops are not to German standard. I regard them as incompetent soldiers headed by imbecile officers.'

Goering shook his head. 'Rommel, we have enjoyed a good meal and good conversation in charming company. Let's not spoil it with such matters.' Brandy was served for Goering but Rommel declined. 'Of course, your liver – I forgot. Please excuse me,' Goering waved his hand over his face.

Ten minutes later Rommel took his leave of the Reichmarschall and retired to his compartment, where his wife was already in bed reading a book. 'How's the megolamanic?' she grinned.

'I think Goering is a twentieth-century Louis the Fourteenth – unable to distinguish between what is for the good of his country and what is good for him personally,' he said as he put out the light.

Lola put her hand across and held his. 'One day all this will be over, Erwin, one way or another, and we can live a civilised life together.'

Rommel sighed. 'It's the way it will end – the needless waste of life – that worries me.'

The etched lines in the face seemed even more pronounced as Erwin Rommel kissed his wife farewell on Rome's station two days later. 'Remember what I said, Lola – I'll soon be back.'

She held his hand. 'You're doing all you can, darling – no one could expect more of you.'

The train jerked and moved slowly away. The Field Marshal waved until it was out of sight and then, heavy hearted, walked to where his aide stood beside the Lancia staff car. 'OK – let's get over to the airport.' The driver closed the doors behind the two officers and the car was soon in the traffic wending its way around the Colosseum. Neither spoke. Rommel's thoughts were absorbed with the events, or rather non-event, of the last 24 hours. Only yesterday morning they had arrived in Rome and gone in separate cars to the Hotel Excelsior.

Rommel had arranged lunch with Field Marshal Count Cavallero, who was responsible for the supply situation in North Africa. Rommel had not bandied words. He had a low opinion of Italian soldiers and an even lower opinion of the officers. In North Africa he had been continually frustrated by their lack of heart for battle and appalled by the fact that the several senior officers had arrived in Africa with a carload of mistresses. This was too much for the puritanical Rommel but if they had commanded their troops effectively he would have overlooked the matter. Now to have to rely on Cavallero – whom Mussolini had promoted to Field Marshal to enable him to talk to Rommel and Kesselring as an equal – to keep him in essential supplies was a matter of complete frustration. Count Ugo Cavallero had kept up his talk of 'doing his very best' and 'fully appreciating the situation' and Rommel had slapped his hand down on the elegantly laid table and raised his voice. 'The Führer assured me that we would receive the new Nebelwerfer Multiple Mortars and Tiger tanks. Tell me when, exactly when, will we receive them, at what port and in what quantity? To these questions would you please give me direct answers.'

That evening at six, irritated by the Italian's evasive reply, Rommel had sought Goering at the hotel, only to be told by his secretary that the Reichmarschall was out on a search for paintings which he wished to purchase to take back to Germany and then he was going to inspect a model railway. Rommel arranged to see Goering at seven thirty but when he arrived at the fourth-floor suite, the valet told him that the Reichmarshal was preparing to go to a fancy-dress party and did not want to be disturbed.

Rommel muttered to himself as he thought over the situation, and Colonel Sneider glanced at him, noticing the intense disgust on his face as he sat despondently huddled in the back seat of the car. Sneider made no comment.

The following morning at breakfast in the columned dining room Rommel had gone to the Reichmarschall's table, leaving Lola in their corner. Goering had listened to Rommel for a few moments and then waved airily. 'My good Field Marshal, I admire and respect your concern for supplies but you have heard from the Führer himself that you will get all you require and I have given you my assurance. Now I really must ask you to leave me in peace as I have a busy day. I've acquired a Monet and I am going to personally organise its packing and transportation – it's a special technique, you know. eh.'

Rommel brooded over the conversation as the car approached the airport and then, turning to his aide, asked, 'And what did the Reichmarschall command you to do for him in your special interview, Sneider?'

Colonel Sneider gave a wry smile. 'I have been made personally responsible for obtaining art treasures from North Africa for the Reich.'

Erwin Rommel, loyal soldier and diplomat, made no comment, and the car turned into the air base where the Junkers was ready for take-off.

2

Captain Otto Grieb wished it was evening. The sun had blazed down on him for nearly an hour and a half and his open Kubelwagen was as hot as hell. In pre-war years his annual holidays had been spent sunseeking, and he had driven down to the French Riviera or Spain in his Frazer Nash open-topped sports car to swim, eat and enjoy a healthy and varied sex life in an enjoyable climate.

Now he had all the sun he needed to last a lifetime and he longed for the officers' mess – a decrepit warehouse in the centre of the tiny town of Zarzis – and a few stiff drinks, even if it was that revolting Zibib brew. One day this goddamned war would be over and he would be drinking whisky once again in his beloved Hamburg. Maybe – once the British had been defeated, as the Führer had always said they would be – whisky would be cheaply available, for he had read somewhere that huge stocks lay in bonded warehouses in England and Scotland. It seemed to Grieb a worthwhile reason to invade, just to get hold of that golden store.

His reflections were interrupted by a couple of Arabs and donkeys blocking the road ahead. He sounded the horn and the Arab drivers moved their stock to the side of the narrow track.

'What an arsehole of a place, this desert!' he said aloud, and the car shuddered as it hit another of those potholes which fill with dust to confuse even the most experienced desert drivers. He accelerated onto a wide track and the fine dust off the road billowed up from the car's tyres.

Shabib oasis came into view on his left and he knew that within 15 minutes he would be back in the mess. Wars were OK for professional soldiers, he mused, but no life for a 24-year-old jeweller who wanted to get back to his homeland and develop the business he had taken over from his father. Then war had broken out in September '39 – three bloody years ago, and it seemed never-ending. Otto Grieb was no arch patriot – all he wanted to do was perform his duty to the satisfaction of his superiors, stay alive and get back to Germany just as soon as he could.

Grieb parked in the sandy patch outside the mess and, returning the salute of the sentry, he wandered across the compound and into the warehouse which called itself an Officers' Mess.

'A large Zibib on ice!' he called to the steward, and shrugged his shoulders when he received the reply that there was no ice – the refrigerator in the bar had broken. 'Like everything in this pisshouse,' he commented to a subaltern as he ran his eyes around the room. Gerdt Schichlinger, a major in the company adjacent to his own and a friend since they had met four months ago, raised his eyes.

'Heard the news about the enemy advance?' he queried. 'Montgomery has pushed past Benghazi and reports are through that we've lost a lot of troops – equipment bogged down in sand, so they say. Christ, what a bloody war!'

The two walked to the window and drank slowly their warm and strong-tasting local brew. 'There's a new divisional commander arrived – big stuff from Berlin, supposed to take command and inspire the likes of us. Got one of those Abwehr guys under him but Christ knows why. Name? The commander? Oh yes, Zimmerman – supposed to be a tough bastard but I guess you have to be tough to survive this hell-hole and keep those bloody Italians at bay, all yelling that Libya is their country and they should command. As if any-one wants the bleeding place!'

Half an hour later the two men finished their drinks and

walked around the compound before shaking hands and bidding one another goodnight.

Grieb slipped under his mosquito net and picked up a book – he had already read it three times but the desert was hardly the place to hold a well-stocked library. He was in the middle of the first paragraph when the light failed. Was it a generator failure or a warning of enemy aircraft? He didn't know and didn't much care.

Colonel Gunter Sneider lit another cigarette and walked towards the window. He was soldier – a professional soldier who had joined the army in '31 and seen his Führer become Chancellor of Germany. He had witnessed the rise of the Third Reich from the mess which Germany had become by the early thirties. Herr Hitler's leadership, his binding together of the German people in a common cause, had inspired him and he respected his leader in a totally uncompromising way. The Weimar Republic had been conned with the Treaty of Versailles after the first war and Adolph Hitler had recognised that and grasped control in 1933. Whatever the Führer did he believed in implicitly. One day Germany would rule the world, and when the major positive step was taken to invade Poland in the autumn of '39, Sneider believed that this was the true beginning of world domination by the Fatherland. Of course there had been weaknesses – indeed the British had virtually captured North Africa due to the incompetence of the infernal Italians. Rommel had made that clear to him. He was the first, as a soldier and a perfectionist, to appreciate that not all the armies had fine soldiers led by experienced and dedicated officers. The recruitment of some officers, particularly those who had not been committed members of the Hitler Jugend had illustrated that. But his few weeks' service as aide to Field Marshal Rommel himself was an honour he would always cherish.

His thoughts were interrupted by a knock on the door. He took the top secret scroll from the orderly and opened it. His face fell at the news. Montgomery had made another major advance and the 21st Panzer Division had been forced to fall back. He was ordered to fall back to Gabes and to service a supply depot there with transport to the front line.

The signal was signed by General Messe and finished with the salutation 'Fight on – and win! Those are the Duce's words.'

Sneider poured himself another whisky. What the hell does he think we are trying to do here – build sandcastles? he thought. Rommel was right about Italian generals: cinema commissionaires, all piss and wind, insisting on control on Libyan soil.

* * *

Grieb opened the door as instructed and saluted. Gunter Sneider motioned his subordinate to sit down and passed him a cigarette.

In his early thirties – probably a professional soldier and loving every minute of this goddamned war, Otto thought to himself. A typical *Junker* officer, a product of the Prussian military machine. Been away with Rommel so probably angling for promotion.

The colonel took no time in coming to the point. 'I have a task for you – come down from Group HQ. Very high authority – seems unnecessary to me but there must be a reason for it. Do you know the island?' he queried.

'You mean Djerba?' Grieb asked.

The colonel nodded and went on. 'Outside the small town of Houm Souk is a synagogue, although why in Christ's name those Jewish swine want to live on an Arab island I don't know. High Command has instructed me that they have to be rounded up and sent up to a camp in Sfax. Alongside the synagogue is a villa – pack of Jews living there, wealthy Jewish family all tied up with the synagogue no doubt. General Zimmerman will make his headquarters there. It's close to the airfield for good communication. You are assigned the task of arresting everyone; shoot anyone who offers the slightest resistance. The place, indeed both places, are full of valuables and these are to be sequestered on behalf of the Reich. This action must be fast – no heavy articles, just pictures, statues and any trinkets of their...' he hesitated for a word, 'belief. So, Grieb, you will send two trucks and a small detachment of men under your command. The Jews are to go to Sfax, the valuables are to be returned here for forwarding to Berlin, and this must be done tomorrow. Any questions? Good. Then see to it.'

Otto Grieb stood and saluted. He left the room and strode slowly across the sandy track to the officers' mess. Christ Almighty, another shitty job, he thought. OK, they may be a pack of stinking Jews but they're not doing anyone any harm over there on the island. There they are, at this moment living over there – tomorrow their whole world will be shattered, and what the hell will happen to them at Sousse.

Before leaving Germany he had been involved in rounding up Jews in Austria and sticking them in cattle trucks to go to concentration camps in Germany. He had never seen a concentration camp but he had heard from fellow officers that the inmates had a bad time of it. He had heard stories which he wished he hadn't.

Well, he mused, his was not to argue ... He was a mere machine in this fucking war and it didn't do to argue with senior officers. Entering the mess, he tossed his cap on the broken-down settee which, as it had no purpose other than to hold coats and hats, took up more than its fair share of room. One of his young platoon commanders was just leaving the adjacent toilet and Otto greeted him.

'Fritz, tomorrow we have an assignment – round up a pack of Jews outside Houm Souk and take 'em to Sfax. Meet me at my office at 7 o'clock and let's get this over before it gets too hot. With any reasonable luck we can take a break at the club at Gabes on the way back.'

Otto Grieb's day was a busy one, for endless signals were coming through from the front, and more and more demands for replacement vehicles. It seemed crazy to him that with a crisis situation at the front line someone should be concerned about a pack of harmless Jews on an island fourteen kilometers away – but life was full of strange priorities and he had long since given up trying to apply any natural thought to such military decisions. He spent the evening drinking the foul local beer and returned at eleven, feeling the worse for wear.

It was five o'clock when he was awakened by his batman, and he swore under his breath. He was needed urgently at battalion headquarters – a signal had been received which needed his urgent attention. He shaved, showered under a bucket device he had designed himself, dressed quickly and strode over the sandy path to Battalion Headquarters. The signal was a demand for yet more transport in the front line – indeed he resolved to take the full company forward. He called Colonel Sneider's office and received orders to prepare for a move by 1100 hours.

It was the entrance of young Fritz Scholtz which jogged his memory – Christ, those bloody Jews. He picked up the field telephone and again called Colonel Sneider's office for orders. Adjutant Weissman answered. Yes, the arrests must go ahead – he must delegate someone to do it.

Otto called Fritz Scholtz from the far side of the ramshackle room. 'Fritz, I've got myself tied up on his transport requirement in Tripoli. I want you to get over to that synagogue outside Houm Souk, arrest those Jews, pack up all their trappings and take them over to the POW camp at Sfax. There is a large villa adjoining the synagogue wall – going to be used as Divisional Headquarters. Apparently the contents are valuable, really valuable. Orders are to remove all contents, pictures, ornaments and the like, and bring them here. They are to be handed over to the CO personally, OK? You should be back here mid-afternoon so you should spend the night here. Then tomorrow move forward to meet up with us at this rendezvous at the front line. Get it! OK – it's over to you. And Fritz – only take one truck and eight men – we need everything we can get up where the action is.'

The journey from Zarzis to the island of Djerba is an interesting one. Although officially regarded as an island in fact it is linked to the mainland by a mile-long causeway. The south Mediterranean has a minute tide but when there is, by

Mediterranean standards, a high tide due to low barometric pressure, the causeway is covered by water 15 centimetres deep.

The morning of 2 December was the usual hot dusty one which makes the North African climate boring when you have been there as long as Lieutenant Fritz Scholtz – the best part of a year. Using a three-ton truck and eight soldiers, 21-year-old Fritz sat alongside the driver as the truck made its way over to the island across the causeway. Fritz recalled that he had read or been told that the causeway was built by the Romans, but why they wanted to connect to a barren island not more than ten by sixteen kilometres was a puzzle. In reality he knew he was trying to keep his mind off the unpleasant task which lay ahead – and he knew that Grieb had been only too pleased to delegate this dirty assignment.

Once over the causeway the truck wound its way along the dusty track towards Houm Souk and then, checking with his map, Fritz instructed the driver to bear left along an even smaller track which led to the synagogue and its surrounding houses. His destination came into view and he was surprised by its size and impressive appearance. A terracotta wall surrounded the synagogue and an arched gateway crowned with the Star of David was the obvious entrance. A large opulent villa overlooked the place of worship.

The truck drove straight into the courtyard and Fritz and the troops dismounted. With fixed bayonets they entered the main building, rounding up only three worshippers. After a thorough search through the surrounding accommodation, the total complement of the establishment stood in a frightened group in the courtyard. Fritz Scholtz counted them – 11 in all, including 3 children. It amazed him, he had expected a larger number – about 25 – and he had been just a little concerned that he only had a small attachment to carry out the arrest.

None of the prisoners could speak German but any talking was unnecessary. The actions of the soldiers spoke louder than words and within ten minutes the Jews were loaded into the truck. Scholtz kept his eyes away from them. He sensed their terror and that was more than enough.

Scholtz wanted this over as quickly as possible. He hadn't bargained for children being involved and the frightened look on their faces disturbed the young officer. 'Get the trappings out of there,' he barked, and two troops disappeared into the main building.

Five minutes ticked away and Scholtz fidgeted with impatience. Two of the women were weeping and one of the small children had started screaming. It was affecting him badly and he knew it. This wasn't soldiering – this was bullying and he hated it.

Four soldiers carried articles of worship out of the synagogue and Scholtz threw them in a sack. 'Put the stuff in there,' he ordered, and the troops tossed various items into the neck, held open by a young corporal. Three other men were at the villa and Scholtz shouted over to them, revolver in hand in case there were hidden occupants. In the hallway stood a tin trunk and inside was the most dazzling collection of gold items, sparkling in the bright sunshine which came through the open doorway. Scholtz drew a deep breath and raised one cup into the air. Encrusted around its base and halfway up its side were jewels he could not recognise but which were obviously valuable.

'*Mein Gott*,' he breathed, 'this is unbelievable – unbelievable.'

He closed his lid. 'Did you put these in that trunk?' he asked the corporal.

Corporal Voss nodded. 'Sir.'

'Then go easy. We don't want them spilling out.'

One of the two male prisoners in the truck shouted in protest and Scholtz returned to the job in hand. 'Get it all in the front,' he commanded, and the precious load was lifted into the driver's cab. Scholtz squeezed in beside the treasure trove, pushing the heavy trunk between him and the driver. 'Let's go,' he ordered, and the truck sprang into life and drove out of the gateway and down the steep hill towards the causeway, swaying and jolting in the ruts.

Where the camel cart came from no one knew. One

moment the truck was moving quietly through a grove of palm trees and then it appeared, crossing the road, laden with water melons on the way to market. The driver stood on the brakes and the truck's wheels locked. The vehicle slid on the dusty path and hit the cart amidships. Scholtz and his driver were thrown against the windscreen and for a minute or so they sat there dazed. Steam was rising from the engine and Scholtz looked in the driving mirror to see that his nose was streaming blood. The young driver was mopping a large gash over his left eye. The steam cleared a little and revealed the demolished cart with the driver sitting on the sand, blood running from his mouth. The camel had broken free from his crude harness and stood within the shade of the palms, regarding the scene with uninterested eyes.

Handkerchief over nose, Scholtz jumped from the truck and walked to the back. No one was hurt; bruised and shaken perhaps, but certainly no more than that. Scholtz ordered the troops to get out of the truck and signalled them to sit on the ground, while he worked out the next move. Steam from the bottom of the radiator showed that the vehicle was immobilised. Shortly he was joined by the driver, whose eye still continued to bleed profusely. He was obviously in much pain. Scholtz cursed the fact that they had no radio, for they were in the middle of no man's land and the only good factor was that Zarzis and home camp lay less than four miles away. The only course of action was to march his prisoners there and obtain replacement transport. A further idea occurred to him. He would need some method of carrying the heavy treasure trove, and his eye fell on the solemn camel. Instructing two of the soldiers to catch the beast, he motioned to the assembled company to form a line. 'When you have the camel, take it to the front and load up that trunk,' he barked.

The camel was not keen to be returned to useful service and protested by tossing its head and refusing to move. Making clucking noises which they had heard Arabs make to urge their camels forward, they moved the ungainly animal to the front of the truck.

Scholtz turned around impatiently as one of the assigned troops addressed him. 'What is it now?'

'*Mein Herr*, it is extraordinary – it – the trunk – has gone?' Scholtz spun on his heel and ran to the vehicle door, which was open. It was true – the inside of the cab was empty. Scholtz shouted for the driver, who came at the double.

'The trunk – where the hell is it? What have you done with it?'

The youngster stammered an inaudible reply but it was obvious to Scholtz that he was as surprised as anyone. Scholtz looked around him as if expecting the offending article to reappear on the sand. His eye fell on something bright and sparkling about five paces away towards a dune. He ran over and picked it up – it was a large ring in the shape of a star with a variety of stones mounted in it. At least he had the direction in which the trunk had been carried. Shouting at his driver to come with him, Scholtz ran up the dune, revolver in hand. From the top of the dune he could see a rock-strewn area, down to a small clump of palms and a track behind. Together they ran down the slope into the palms. Nothing could be seen. For the next half-hour they searched through the area but drew a complete blank. Whoever had taken the trunk had disappeared as if they had never been. 'This is impossible, just impossible,' he muttered to himself.

Scholtz was worried. Questions were bound to be asked at headquarters. He wished that this little assignment had been carried out by his superior. How on earth could he report this and to whom? As he made his way slowly back to the truck with the driver, a thought struck him. He liked and respected Grieb. If he could get back to Zarzis within the next couple of hours maybe Grieb would still be there. It was a long shot but he felt Grieb would help. Putting his hand in his pocket he felt the gold ring. It made him feel uncomfortable yet he couldn't bring himself to throw it away.

Scholtz was not to have a lucky day. The sight which greeted him at the wrecked truck made his stomach heave. Seven soldiers lay stretched on the sand, their heads badly beaten. Of the prisoners there was no sign. His feet were like lead as he sat on a large lump of rock at the trackside. My God, what the hell do I do now? he thought.

The driver sprinted up the dune once more but no sooner had he reached the top than a crack of rifle fire broke the silence and he staggered forward and fell, holding his thigh. Scholtz ran for cover beside the broken-down vehicle and waited. Nothing happened. Scholtz shouted to his driver to stay still but the answer came back, 'It's just a flesh wound, sir, nothing more. Hurts like hell but I can walk. What do we do now, Sir?'

'We're taking a walk back to base – get over to me now and let's move along.'

It took them just under two hours to reach Zarzis and they staggered exhausted into the camp. Scholtz's nose was caked with blood, his back dripping with perspiration. He went straight to Grieb's quarters and the driver went to the Medical Centre.

Grieb sat in silence as events were told. Scholtz had taken a shower and had done a patch job on his nose – at least he could breathe reasonably now. But he ran out of breath from time to time as he told Grieb what had happened since he had left that morning. Grieb interrupted only once – to press Scholtz on whether he had personally observed all his men after the accident had occurred. Had one gone off to relieve himself, he asked. Scholtz was adamant – no one had left the scene of the accident. The stuff had just disappeared into thin air.

Grieb listened to the end of the story and lit another cigarette, blowing smoke rings in jerks into the roof of the tent they had chosen for their meeting. 'I don't believe those women and children killed our troops,' he opined. 'And another thing, I'm amazed there were only eleven people in the Jewish community. You yourself said you were surprised about the small number for a good-sized complex. The Commandant originally ordered two trucks to go, and when I told you to take one, all we could spare, I thought you would have a tough task fitting all the bastards and their junk into one. It doesn't make sense – there must have been others, and that camel cart also – it was all too obvious.' Grieb paused for thought. 'I believe you were ambushed and then the trunk was taken. The fact that your men were killed by clubbing is interesting – it was silent. But your driver was shot. Whoever killed your troops took the rifles and then used one on your driver when he silhouetted himself on the dune ridge. It's the only explanation.' He sat contemplating and Scholtz awkwardly put his hand in his pocket where his fingers closed on the ring. He took it from his pocket.

'That's all we have of the loot,' he sighed.

Grieb took a deep breath and held the ring to the light. His heart jumped with excitement. As a trained and experienced jeweller, he knew a valuable piece as soon as he saw it. 'Christ Almighty! This is a beauty. It's worth a fortune – it's one of the most beautiful pieces I have ever seen.'

Grieb made an instant decision to send the convoy on ahead with his second in command. He himself would personally supervise the rounding up of the escaped Jews who now roamed the island of Djerba. He must get over there quickly. Ordering Scholtz to go with him, he shouted through the window at a corporal to muster eight men, and packed a Mercedes scout car to the hilt.

Within 20 minutes the Mercedes was speeding across the causeway towards the island. It would be like looking for a needle in a haystack, he mused, for even an island so small contained a number of hiding places where a community could hide individually or collectively for some time.

They drove straight for the scene of the ambush, for Grieb was now convinced that that was what it was. The bodies lay in the afternoon sun, made even more macabre by the presence of flies around their faces, and Grieb turned them over to face the ground. It made him feel sick to see them. He instructed the soldiers to dig a mass grave – a shallow one and quickly whilst he and his subordinate officer made a reconnaissance of the area. The Mercedes was a four-wheel drive so it was comparatively easy to ascend the dune and drive down towards the palm clump where Scholtz had searched earlier in the day. Nothing was to be seen so they drove out the far side of the clump and over a wide stretch of gravel and sand. Grieb was able to drive quite quickly over the firm surface and after a mile stopped on the top of a short rise. He raised his Zeiss binoculars and carefully scanned the horizon. He froze to a position.

'Look,' he said, grasping Scholtz's arm. 'See them – look.'

He passed the powerful instrument to Scholtz. There, not more than 500 metres away, two figures crouched beside a ridge of sand. Grieb jammed the lively go-everywhere vehicle into gear and it sped towards the figures.

The car was spotted immediately it began its approach, and the figures broke cover and started to run towards a dense palm wadi a few hundred metres away. They had a strong advantage for the vehicle was running into deeper and deeper soft sand and its speed dropped dramatically as it tussled with the terrain. Grieb and Scholtz jumped out and unclipped the rifles which were housed in the sides of the body. Both were experienced shots and at 300 metres the targets were not difficult to hit. They saw the two figures fall on the sandy waste – and they rushed through the soft sand towards them. The softness of the sand ceased, in the strange way it does so frequently in the desert, and the last 100 metres was over a hard surface. They need not have hurried. The two fugitives lay motionless on their faces near a hole. Blood between the shoulder blades of one and at the centre of the other's back told the story. Scholtz turned the bodies over – they were Jews, no question about that. Their black clothes and beards made them officials of the synagogue – rabbis perhaps. Neither of the two Wehrmacht officers had had much experience of Jews before.

'I guess these two took the trunk and hid it somewhere in this area,' Grieb commented. 'Whilst you and your driver were looking around, their colleagues killed your troops. So what we need to know now is where the hell is that trunk?'

For an hour the two officers walked the area, prodding the ground wherever they saw the sand had been disturbed. It was a frustrating and fruitless task for the desert kept its secret and there was no clue where the cache lay. Darkness started to fall in the rapid way it does closer to the equator and they decided to abandon the search and return to the troops.

Six minutes later the wrecked lorry appeared in view with the men. Their burial duties were performed and they sat around smoking.

Grieb slowed the vehicle and looked at Scholtz. 'Let's keep the events of today to ourselves. One day this fucking war will be over and this desert will still be here. We can come back and find that trunk. What's in there will keep us comfortably – and I mean comfortably – for life. We'll tell the men the shots they heard were at a group who got away. They don't know about anything being taken from the trunk – the original guys you had with you are now there...' He jerked his thumb downwards to the sand. 'So let's stay dumb about this – it's one way to go through this sodding war with thoughts of a comfortable future.'

They piled into the Mercedes and 15 minutes later they were in the camp and making their way to the officers' mess for a dose of the inevitable Zibib. After the second glass Scholtz looked piercingly at his colleague. 'You know, Otto, there is someone we overlooked – the driver. The trunk had gone and he is well aware we went off to look for the Jews and the trunk. He can talk and questions might be asked. He didn't know much but he sure as hell knows more than the next.'

Otto Grieb flicked his ash onto the carpet in annoyance. 'We'll talk with him in the morning, in the convoy. He can drive my vehicle – he only has a small wound and he's fit enough to drive. I'll assign my regular driver to another task.'

3

The following morning the assembly parade was at 0500 hours and by the time an hour had passed, the convoy of 17 lorries, heavily laden with ammunition loaded the previous day, was throwing up a giant cloud of dust as it moved towards the Libyan frontier. Otto Grieb eyed his newly appointed driver with a large plaster over his eye. He was a fresh young man of no more than 19, Grieb thought. Grieb asked him for his theory about what had happened on Djerba the previous day.

'I believe there were a number of Jews who for some reason or other weren't at the synagogue – maybe in the fields or something. They saw what happened and hatched a quick plan. All in all our guys must have been there around twenty minutes to half an hour. Somehow they drove the camel and cart into the path of our vehicle and caused the accident. Then whilst we were sorting ourselves out and getting the prisoners together one group of Jews took the trunk. When the Oberleutnant and I went after them this split our ranks and the remaining Jews made a surprise attack on our troops – crept up on them with batons of some kind and beat them to death. The prisoners ran off and we returned. Well, you know what we saw, sir.' He was obviously curious about the sequel to the story. 'Did you and the Oberleutnant see anything when you returned, sir?'

Grieb recounted how they had seen two figures and opened fire but the range had been great and they had escaped.

'Then they must have hidden that loot – to return to collect it later,' replied the driver.

Grieb concealed a sigh of relief. 'Yes, I guess that's what happened,' he commented in what he hoped was a nonchalant manner, 'and those bloody Jews will open up their synagogue again and go on using their expensive trappings.'

They passed by a desolate pile of stones which marked a *bir* (well) and stopped to draw water with a canvas bucket and a long rope. The water might have suited a dehydrated camel but did little for thirsty troops.

A large truck was revving up as the driver took advantage of the break to make an engine adjustment. That was probably why they didn't hear the Blenheims come low into the attack. Before they had the chance to take advantage of the sparse cover the whole world around them was full of the howl of the attacking planes, the crack of bombs bursting on the hard surface and the squeal of splinters through the air.

It took them a full three minutes to start to return the fire. The rattle of machine-gun fire and the dust, the infernal dust, made it impossible to see anything but one's immediate surroundings. Grieb, from a hump of sand hardly qualifying to be called a dune, spotted a light machine-gun with the gunner lying dead beside it. Grabbing the gun, he fired into the air at the swooping aircraft but the dusty haze made the exercise futile. A sudden explosion of a truck some 30 metres on his right threw him sideways and the weapon toppled off its bipod. As he scrambled to reassemble the unit the noise stopped and a deathly silence descended on the area. A silence penetrated by the crackling of burning trucks.

The Blenheims, six in all, made three sorties over the target and 15 minutes later a shattered Otto Grieb crept from a dune to see what remained of his precious convoy. Most vehicles had exploded with their volatile cargo. His own vehicle lay overturned and badly crushed, with the roof collapsed into the main bodywork. The first body he discovered was his driver, and as he staggered towards his car he summoned the survivors around him by whistle. The first truck behind him was blazing and a few metres from it the body of Fritz Scholtz lay face upwards in the blazing sun.

* * *

Grieb saluted on entering the room. A quick look at the stern, rimless-spectacled figure sitting behind a barrack table which served as a desk told him that all was certainly not well. He had been told 15 minutes before that Colonel Sneider wished to see him immediately. The orderly who brought the message had placed special emphasis on the 'immediately' as if he sensed trouble. Grieb had promptly returned to the lavatory, made himself ready for the interview and told himself, with little conviction, that it was probably about the advance of British forces and plans for supplies for the counter-offensive.

The figure at the desk continued writing and then looked up to study Grieb's figure with a cold stare. He wasted no words. 'Tell me exactly what happened at Houm Souk.' The colonel looked down again and continued writing.

Grieb swallowed and started to report how he had delegated Scholtz to the assignment when he, Grieb, had to set up supply lines to the front. He told how Scholtz had made the arrest of a small number of Jews, had packed a few gold cups in the trunk and driven off. He reported the incident of the camel cart, the disappearance of the trunk, how Scholtz had left with his driver to find the missing goods and the discovery of the assassinated troops on his return. 'Scholtz reported to me that little of any value was found – just impressive-looking articles with peeling gold plate,' Grieb concluded.

'Why did you return with Scholtz later in the day?' The question was clipped and the questioner did not lift his eyes from the pad.

'I wanted to see the site of the action myself, sir, to supervise the burial of the dead and to attempt to track down the missing Jews and the equipment which they had carried away.'

Colonel Sneider lay back in his chair and lit a cigarette.

For what seemed an age he said nothing but stared at the stained ceiling of the Arab house which served as his office.

'And you were not successful,' he said softly.

'Sir, we completed the burial of the dead and circled the area by vehicle. During our search we found two Jews who were challenged – but they were a good distance from us, several hundred metres. They ran off and disappeared in the dunes. Presumably they had hidden the valuables and will return to pick them up later, maybe days later. We couldn't find anything.'

'And that completes your story – except for the unmentioned fact that an incident report was not submitted because on your return you had to move quickly to the front line.'

'That is correct, sir.'

Grieb wished he too could sit and smoke. The atmosphere was most certainly becoming colder and he could feel a bitter taste in his mouth as his superior leaned forward to slowly and deliberately stub out his cigarette in the terracotta bowl which served as an ashtray.

Grieb's eyes fell casually on the bowl and he froze. On the sand in the bowl, flanked by several cigarette butts, lay the ring Scholtz had shown him.

'It is beautiful, isn't it. Pick it up and examine it yourself. Maybe it's a trinket but on the other hand it may be worth something. Take a look.'

Grieb saw his hand trembling as he stretched across the desk and took it. A tiny Star of David was inset in the major stone and the gold setting had been slightly twisted. 'It is beautiful, Herr Colonel, and I suppose it must be of some value.'

'Some value!' The normally quiet, steady voice became an unbridled one. 'Some value, you lying bastard – you're supposed to be a jeweller, are you not?'

Grieb blinked. 'I was, sir, but four years....'

'Four years my arse. You are a trained jeweller who came from a family of jewellers. That's why you were given the assignment, to avoid bringing back crap. I understand your fellow officers have had watches and similar items valued by you – is that or is it not correct?'

'It is correct, sir.'

'That ring, of "some value", as you put it, was discovered by the burial party disposing of the body of Oberleutnant Scholtz. The corporal in charge recognised the filthy Jewish symbol and felt it his duty to report the matter to the platoon commander, who took it to the adjutant. That is how it is in my possession. The question I now put to you is simple and you will answer it immediately and truthfully or I will have your hide on the wall. How did Scholtz come to be in possession of that ring?'

Grieb's throat was so dry he could hardly croak an answer. 'I believe he must have taken it from the synagogue, sir – put it in his pocket rather than put it in the trunk with the other–'

'Valuable items,' broke in the colonel.

'Yes, sir.'

'Yet you reported that Scholtz had said the rest was worthless religious junk. Gold plate, you said – as if Scholtz could tell.'

'In his opinion it was.'

Colonel Sneider raised himself slowly from his chair and walked across the room to a trestle-table covered with papers and books. From behind a book he produced a bottle of whisky and a glass and carefully poured himself a large drink. 'Those were my words: worthless junk. Not Sholtz's. That is what you would have me believe, is it not?' The colonel inhaled deeply.

'I will tell you exactly what I believe happened, Captain Grieb. I believe that you returned to the site of the ambush late that afternoon and that your search for the missing Jews was successful. You discovered the "treasure trove" and buried it. The only witnesses were the Jews, who you shot. Your idea was to return when the Wehrmacht has driven the British out of North Africa for good – and you would have a fortune awaiting you to use in our victorious fatherland after the war.'

Grieb swallowed. 'Sir, with respect, that is not correct.'

'We shall soon discover whether it is correct or not. In the next few days you will be closely interrogated by a member of the Abwehr who is highly qualified in determining, how shall I put it, truth from lies. His methods are primitive but his results outstanding. In the meantime you will be confined to your quarters under house arrest.'

Colonel Sneider rose and went to the door. Opening it, he spoke in a muted voice to someone outside. Looking up, Grieb saw his fellow officer Gerd Busch approach him.

'Captain Grieb, you are under house arrest – you will accompany me to your quarters.'

Grieb rose and walked slowly to the door. He turned to speak but Sneider waved him away. 'Write down what happened and things will change – I don't want to speak any more.'

Under normal circumstances the conversation in the officer's mess that evening would have been about Grieb's arrest. But the circumstances were not normal. Following Montgomery's attack on the night of 23 October 1942 at El Alamein, the German forces had been able to hold the thrust initially by means of well-placed mine-fields which the New Zealand Division and British 51st Highland Division had been unable to penetrate except in one place. General Stumme had moved his 21st Panzer Division to the north believing that the attack would strengthen there, away from the treacherous Quatara depression of cliffs and shifting soft sand. Stumme was now dead. Rumour had it that he died at the hands of his own driver.

Now the British, New Zealand and Australian forces had driven three corridors through the German defences and Rommel had returned from a visit to Germany and, after a detailed investigation of the situation, had given the order to retreat. There was a rumour that the Field Marshal's health was deteriorating rapidly.

There followed a dramatic turn of events in yet another part of North Africa. On 8 November a strong Anglo-American force under General Eisenhower had landed in Morocco and by the 11th had captured Casablanca. The 13th was indeed unlucky for the Wehrmacht. News broke that Tobruck had fallen and British troops were heading for Benghazi. For the Italians to have lost Tobruck to the British in January 1941 had always been a constant source of annoyance to the German High Command. Now it was German forces who had been forced to surrender and were fast retreating towards Tripoli. The situation was deteriorating daily.

The gap between the American forces in Algeria and the British, Australian and New Zealand forces in the south was closing steadily.

The officer's mess was a simple structure – a large marquee with a faded swastika draped over one wall. Trestle-tables and benches gave an air of temporary existence. Indeed the atmosphere which prevailed that December evening was one of poor morale and frustration. Most officers had brought up supplies by convoy from Zarzis some 300 miles away and suffered heavy losses by British aircraft on the way. Now there was rumour of some supplies having to be taken back to base camp, leaving a forward camp of supplies for the retreating forces.

Adjutant Weissman entered the room without removing his hat and belt, as was customary on coming into the mess. He quietly drew aside the four company commanders, who were talking in various parts of the marquee. The five left without a word.

Conversation died and the only noise was the diesel generator which provided lighting to the austere quarters. Fritz Schlacker, a young moon-faced *Oberleutnant* broke the silence.

'Weissman has bad news – see it in his face. I'll tell you what I think: that bloody Eighth Army is so close on us now we'll be belting hell for leather back through Tunisia only to find the Americans in Morocco come across and we'll be in a trap – right here in the bloody sand dunes.'

'Rommel's lost his grip,' commented another young officer. 'Been back in Germany on sick leave – he's a sick man and, however brilliant a general he is, if his health isn't up to it he's buggered. We're sitting here as cannon fodder trying to supply an army which is on the run – with the Italians saying that it's their country and they want command.'

'Gentlemen!' The voice cracked like a whiplash across the room. 'You will not talk in this way – our army is regrouping not retreating, and remember that the Italians are our allies. We are here to work, to fight together.'

The voice was that of the adjutant, who had silently entered the room. Weissman was a short, stocky officer with piercing eyes. Mess rumour had it that before the war he was training in his father's undertaking business in Bremen. True or not, Weissman always seemed to be around at times of trouble or misfortune. He exuded gloom.

'Now, gentlemen, you will attend your company commanders in fifteen minutes to receive your orders for tomorrow.' Weissman's piercing eyes shone through his rimless glasses.'And recall my orders: no more talk such as I have just overheard.'

Thirty minutes afterwards the officers returned to the mess, knowing that the next day they would be transporting three-quarters of their supplies back to a supply base at Achae – a place they had left only less than a week before on their way to the front line from Zarzis. The front line was now severely holed and the Axis armies were retreating rapidly.

Otto Grieb lay looking at the ceiling. Could it be raining – surely this hot hell-hole didn't have relief like this? But rain it was. The tent leaked like a sieve; it was intended to keep out the sun and nothing else. He looked at his officer guard, Schackler, who had relieved Busch late in the evening. Conversation was somewhat sparse as Schackler wasn't too happy, wondering how fraternising with a prisoner would be regarded by his superiors. He liked Grieb – they shared the same cynical view of military service – but he thought silence would be the discreet course of action. He was himself bursting with curiosity to discover the truth about Grieb's alleged offence. He had overheard some discussion in the bar about Grieb stealing some synagogue valuables he had been sent to sequester on behalf of the Reich. It puzzled him because he had understood that his friend Scholtz had gone over the causeway to the island to round up some Jews so that Grieb could concentrate on the supply move forward. He also felt it better to avoid the subject as Grieb was considerably senior in rank to him. Although it was usual for an officer under house arrest to be guarded by an officer of equivalent rank, the shortage of officers due to casualties made this impossible. Just what was he supposed to do with this guard duty, he wondered. A right bitch-up if ever there was one. As it was, Grieb seemed content to stare at the ceiling and smoke.

But Grieb was far from relaxed. The thought of an interview with the Abwehr was making his stomach turn. Was it just a bluff on the part of Sneider, who was known for his sense of drama? The morning would tell. He turned over and tried to sleep.

At first light he asked Schackler if he could relieve himself and Schackler agreed.

'I'll have to be with you, I think,' commented the young man.

'OK – you can come and hold it for me, if you like,' sneered Grieb, and the two men left the tent and climbed the soft dune. The sun was starting to rise, giving the desert a salmon and cream glow.

Neither of them saw what happened. The roar of aircraft engine and stutter of machine-gun fire shattered the still night air of the desert. Sand jumped around them in spurts as they rolled flat. Three times the Hurricane attacked and each time Grieb believed that each lull was the lull before his life finished. At last silence fell and he looked up. Schackler lay on his back, his eyes wide open and blood running from his lips and neck. Burning trucks and collapsed tents were everywhere. He could just make out the figure of Weissman, his left hand grasping his shoulder as he shouted commands. Someone was backing up a truck to the officers' mess tent, which had collapsed at one end, resembling an oversized camel on its haunches.

Grieb crawled to the top of the dune and rolled down the

other side. This was his opportunity to work out what he wanted to do, and it didn't take him long to come to a firm conclusion. He would stick it out and wait for the British forces to arrive. From the base of the dune he ran down a narrow wadi, which after half a mile divided into three. Choosing the centre one, he ran on until he found a shallow cave in the side of the escarpment and threw himself into it. For the first time in months he felt free of the shackles of military discipline and free from all the strain of the war he despised so much. Now he was on his own and all he had to do was kill time in this lonely spot.

He didn't have long to wait; 35 minutes later the hungry and bleary-eyed German officer walked towards the first British Sherman tank with a white handkerchief in his hand. He hadn't known what to expect but he was pleasantly surprised. His English was sufficient to understand that he was required to get into the tank, where he was given water and then tied to the superstructure of the hull.

The young subaltern in command spoke German and Otto Grieb assured him that he was a willing prisoner.

The active war of Otto Grieb was over. He wasn't sorry.

4

1988

The change in engine note wakened Adrian Franklin. He straightened himself in his seat and listened to the announcement, which he could recite by now in many languages. Yes indeed, be would put his seat in an upright position and fasten his seat belt. He looked out at the myriad of lights which twinkled in the mild evening. Why was it that lights, when viewed from the air, always seemed to twinkle? Some boffin must be able to explain it, he mused. It wasn't that important; what was important was the fact that one of those lights was 37 Blenheim Gardens, SW1, and home.

Home? Well, it depended how you looked at it. Where Lorna lived was home in his life. Few men had his good fortune to have a daughter who was so young, vivacious and with a happy family unit – a unit prepared to accept a 50-year-old who had suddenly found himself alone.

The 'No Smoking' sign was now on and the final announcement made. Two more minutes and they would touch down at Heathrow. The British Airways flight from Rome would soon be discharging its passengers into the frenzied atmosphere of the airport building. Lorna would be waiting for him, and perhaps young Sam, now three years and as lively as the proverbial cricket, would be there too. He had taken the toy tank as cabin baggage, for whatever else might go astray, the gift for Sam was an essential. No three-year-old could accept the vagaries of airline baggage.

Twenty minutes later he was waiting at the carousel. His

bags appeared and he loaded them onto a conveniently placed trolley and pushed his way past the watchful eye of Customs. His luck was out and a youthful official called him aside. My God, how young these guys looked, he thought; what was the cliché about policemen appearing younger as you got older? Now it could be applied to officialdom generally.

In answer to the young man he read the card then gave all that was needed of him. He had been in Rome for 11 months; purpose – well, it was none of his damned business, but 'pleasure' would do. Pleasure – he gave a grimace – pleasure to try to recover from the loss of Ann, who after 28 years of marriage had decided to 'do her own thing'. Enough of that – live for today.

Yes, he had 40 cigarettes too many. Yes, he had a small bottle of whisky in addition to the allowance and he had bought a couple of pairs of shoes in Italy. It all seemed rather petty and he desperately wanted to get out of the place.

Everything was finally in order and Adrian hurriedly pushed his trolley round the corner. Yes, there they were, Lorna and Sam. He rushed forward and the next few minutes were spent in the warm welcome which everyone who has been away for several months savours.

The car journey into London took the usual age – traffic seemed much worse whenever he returned but the Rome traffic had conditioned him to a large degree. Sam's endless questions dominated the conversation: how could you raise the tank's gun, why did it have letters on its side, did it fire real bullets and could it float in water? The atmosphere was full of excitement, yet there was something not quite right. He knew his daughter well enough to know when all was not well. Somehow she was reserved, distant. Something was undoubtedly worrying her and he wished he could get an idea what it was.

The car was parked and the bags carried into the house. Lorna helped him move the three suitcases and the inevitable plastic bags of overflow goodies into the bedroom where he had lived for six months prior to his break in Rome.

He took a bath and changed and was just finished in time to say 'Goodnight' to Sam and tuck him up with a promise that tomorrow would be spent experimenting with the treasured tank.

In the sitting room he lit a cigarette and poured himself a large gin and tonic in the crystal glass he loved so much. The fire burned brightly, not for heat but for what Ian always called atmosphere. Ian? He should surely be home shortly, and Adrian reflected that throughout the journey no reference had been made to him.

Lorna came into the room. She had slipped into a casual kaftan and looked beautiful. But her face had a sad and worried look.

Adrian didn't have to wait long to discover the cause of her anxiety. 'How's Ian?' he asked.

Lorna looked her father straight in the eye. 'You're not going to believe this,' she replied. 'Indeed I wonder if I really do. But the straight truth is Ian's disappeared.'

The ticking of the grandfather clock sounded loud for the next ten seconds. 'Disappeared?' he repeated with a lump in his throat. 'What on earth do you mean?'

Lorna prodded a log which was crackling in the fireplace and poured herself a large Scotch. 'It all started around two months ago,' she said. 'Ian and I went to a house sale – what the Americans call a garage sale. Someone was moving house and just wanted to clear out all the junk. We saw the ad in the paper and thought it would be fun. We wanted some garden tools and ornaments for the terrace, so it seemed a good opportunity. So on the Saturday morning we went along there with Sam. It was the usual scene – the dealers were there fighting over anything of value and we managed to pick up a good lawnmower and a bunch of garden implements for quite a reasonable price. I took Sam to the toilet and while I was away Ian bought a bookholder – one of those large shelves with a stand at each end – and a mixed lot of books. I think they went for five pounds or so and he couldn't resist the temptation. We loaded up all our purchases and took them home and that evening Ian sorted out his books –

throwing one or two away but putting the remainder in the bookshelves. For the next few days Ian was engrossed with one of the books – he took it to bed and read late until I complained about the light. Next day he took it to work with him and in the evening he was reading it again. He's a keen reader but I had never known him to be that absorbed in a subject.'

The moment seemed right to interrupt so Adrian did so. 'What was the subject?'

'The North African campaign of World War Two,' she replied, 'by an author I had never heard of – Collingson, I think. He's keen on history but this subject seemed to really dominate his interest over a week. At the weekend Ian seemed very quiet, and when I awoke around 3 a.m. on Saturday, he was awake and I asked him what was worrying him. He wouldn't tell me much about it but he was convinced that it contained information which he said was "truly amazing". He thought it might have been a hoax, but there was something which could change our lives. He wanted to find the original owner and said he would make some telephone calls in the morning.

'The next day I was going off for a week or so. You probably don't remember Sara Brice – she and I have been friends for quite a few years. She was expecting her fourth child and her mother was going to run the house and look after the children, but her mother became ill so I agreed to go up to Birmingham and help out for a while – I expected to be away for about a week. Sara has always been good to me. Anyway, I took the train to Birmingham with Sam, and Sara drove us to her house at Four Oaks. I called Ian when I arrived but when I telephoned a couple of days later there was no reply – I guessed he was eating out a lot. As the week wore on I still couldn't contact him, even late at night, and I must admit that I did get very concerned. The company said he had taken a few days off.

'After ten days I came back by train with Sam. I came back on a Saturday morning – arriving here by taxi at one. Ian is usually in for lunch then, but the house was empty. His car was in the garage. His briefcase and the book he was reading when I left were gone. I waited until late that evening and then I became very worried indeed and called the police. They came round and asked all the questions which I'm sure they have in standard form when husbands or wives disappear – all based on the assumption of a family bust-up, which we certainly hadn't had. Ian was placed on the missing persons file and they said they would let me know if they heard anything. That was six weeks ago and I haven't heard a word from Ian and frankly I'm desperate – I'm worried out of my mind. The company has been on to me endlessly as Ian was setting up the marketing of a new Japanese product and they need him urgently.'

Lorna stopped talking and gazed into the fire. 'Dad, what do I do? Where do I go from here?'

Adrian lit another cigarette and inhaled deeply. 'Look, my love,' he said, blowing a ring cloud into the air, 'I have nothing to do, no job to go to, and I think there is some simple explanation. I propose to get to the bottom of it. First thing is to get hold of a copy of that book and then read it thoroughly to find out what grabbed Ian's interest so intensely. However, there is one point I don't understand at all...' Lorna looked up quickly. 'Why did he want to find the owner of the book rather than the author?'

Adrian awoke early the next morning and decided to take a walk after his shower. The road was scattered with people walking to the bus or underground and he turned into the newsagent to buy his copy of the *Telegraph*. Whenever he stayed with Lorna he preferred to pick up his paper from the shop rather than have it delivered.

The white-haired lady who had run the shop for at least the past five years looked up in surprise. 'Why, if it isn't Mr Franklin. How nice to see you back again. Did you enjoy your trip abroad – to Italy wasn't it?' She hesitated and her face illustrated her question without uttering a word. She was bursting with curiosity to know if there was any news of young Mr Ian Lacey, who had disappeared without a trace. But

Adrian wasn't falling for the bait. Bidding her good morning, he left the shop and crossed over the road to the park. A comfortable bench on a sunny morning is just the place to make the traditional grim news of wars, strikes and economic crises look a little rosier. However, Adrian was in no mood to concentrate on his paper. The question which predominated his thoughts was: What the hell happened to Ian – walking out on a good marriage, lovely wife and son? It just didn't tie up at all.' Adrian always became deeply concerned when people acted out of character, and this was really out of character for serious minded, career-orientated Ian, who managed to balance his private and work life so that at 35 he had made a success of both.

First things first – and the most important point was to get hold of the book. He had made a note of the title the previous evening and as soon as the public library was open he would be there.

At 10 a.m. the library opened and Adrian questioned the young bespectacled woman about it. Yes, they had a copy, and Ian settled himself down in the reference section for some quiet reading. He called Lorna and told her he was on the first part of the research and not to expect him back until late afternoon.

He read carefully but quickly. The book told in graphic terms, from the view of an eyewitness, of the German activity across North Africa.

There were several interesting anecdotes. One dealt with the writer being lost in a sandstorm, or *Khamsin*, for several hours and then not being able to get his truck free from the loose sand. Another story involved a German officer who offered money to the author to avoid being taken prisoner, but one of the staff officers accompanying the author had been involved in Bank of England security work and recognised the money as counterfeit. Then there was the writer's personal interview with Montgomery, who had found him asleep at the wheel of a gun tractor.

Nothing, however, appeared to relate in even the slightest degree to Ian, who had not even been born when the North

African campaign took place. He may have been interested, but why the sudden disappearance?

The sun came out and started to shine brightly through the window, reminding Adrian of the months he had spent in Rome. He kicked himself that he had not left an address where Lorna could have contacted him about the dramatic turn in her life. He had wanted to get away from it all, to try to prepare for a new life. He had adored Ann – he still did – and he had become totally confused devising theories about why she had left after so many years of marriage. So isolation had seemed a good idea at the time – time to think, time to adjust.

He flicked the book through once more and then booked it out with the librarian after a certain degree of hassle about not being a local householder. He would read it through at home again; but what this copy lacked was the name of the owner Ian had mentioned. Why was that so important, he wondered once more.

When he arrived home the house was empty and he let himself in with his own key. He sat in his favourite chair and contemplated. Suddenly he sat upright. Of course, why hadn't he thought of it before? The way to the original owner was through the purchaser of the house – the house where the sale had taken place.

Twenty minutes later Lorna returned and Adrian presented her with his burning question. Yes, she remembered exactly where the house was but didn't recall the name of the people. In any event they would have left as the sale was to clear it for moving. Maybe the new owners could help by giving the sellers' new address.

The drive to Richmond was slow with the late afternoon traffic nose to tail along the Cromwell Road, and it was nearly five thirty before Lorna's Ford Fiesta pulled up at a late Victorian house which a faded sign announced as Starlings. Lorna stayed in the car to look after Sam whilst Adrian walked up the small overgrown garden to a heavy oak front door.

The door was answered by a middle-aged woman with hair

tied tightly in a bun – a character in keeping with the house, Adrian thought.

After introducing himself Adrian started to tell the story of Ian's mysterious disappearance. As the tale progressed it seemed less and less likely, and once or twice he thought he noticed a flicker of disbelief in Mrs Fenton's face.

'Yes – I think I understand now,' she said when he had finished. 'Indeed I may be able to help you trace the previous owner. Mrs Girdler moved to Windsor. Her husband died, you know – a military gentleman, I believe. She found the place too large and she disposed of many of her personal effects.' She paused. 'However, you are not the only person interested in Mrs Girdler. I had another gentleman here only a few weeks ago asking the same question about the previous owner.'

Adrian looked up sharply. Could it be Ian? He asked the woman to describe him.

'He was elderly, bald, medium height,' she recalled. 'Yes, and he had a slight accent – not English. He didn't give a name – he merely asked me if I had the address of the previous owner as he wanted to contact her over an important matter.' The woman opened a roll-top desk and produced a small address book. She wrote carefully and passed a piece of paper. 'That's Mrs Girdler's address, but I don't have her telephone number.'

Adrian thanked her for her help and returned to the car. It had become a paperchase, he commented to Lorna. The next step would certainly have to be Windsor.

By seven thirty they had reached Windsor and found the small cottage on the edge of the Great Park. Mrs Girdler turned out to be an elderly lady of small stature but a jolly, roly-poly face – a motherly figure if ever there was one. She invited Adrian into the sitting room without hesitation – Lorna and Sam again waited outside in the car – and he marvelled that people could be so trusting in times when attacks on elderly people were so frequent as to scarcely make the headlines.

He swiftly outlined the purpose of his visit. Mrs Girdler

poured him a cup of tea from a pot which she had just made and fetched another cup for herself. She sat down carefully and thought. Yes, she remembered the rack of books which had been on the mantelpiece of her husband's study. The books, however, she could not remember – they were all military books or books on antiques and obviously not to her personal taste. 'My husband was a military man, you understand, Mr Franklin, and he liked to read about such things. To me the past is the past so I didn't want to dwell on it. I'm sorry I don't know the book in question, nor can I give you any help about where my husband purchased it. Books were his passion. He was always reading or working on corrections. He was a quiet man – just liked to be left with his reading and writing.'

Adrian joined Lorna and gave his report; little seemed to have been achieved. He had Mrs Girdler's telephone number in case something new turned up and he had given her Lorna's number.

Dinner was a simple affair that evening. So much time had been spent on the research that there was none left for cooking. Sam went to bed, happy with the thought that he had seen Windsor Castle again, and Lorna and Adrian tucked into a cold supper and a bottle of white wine.

After dinner Adrian stood in front of the fire and drew deeply on a cigarette. The subject of Ian was in the forefront of both their minds and there seemed no point in pretending otherwise. Adrian walked over to the bookcase and looked at the array of titles.

A thought struck him. 'Could you pick out any of the other books which were in the sale?' he asked.

Lorna paused. 'I may be able to – just maybe,' she replied. Her eyes ran over the shelves and slowly, thoughtfully, she picked out four. 'Yes, I'm sure these were among them,' she commented. 'There were at least a dozen but I'm sure these were in the holder we brought home.'

Adrian took them to his chair and started to flick through them – three were on military history and one on birdwatching.

Half an hour later 14 books stood in three pillars on the

sitting-room floor. So there must have been 15 books in the purchase. Adrian started to categorise them. Three dealt with birdwatching, seven were on antiques, one on stagecoach routes of the eighteenth century and three were on military history. Adrian picked up the first and slowly flicked it through. Suddenly his eye caught a pencilled mark in the margin – on page 67; *Heinz Harmel*. He flicked through the book and on no less than 20 times he came across pencilled notes in German. Why on earth should a retired army officer write in the book in German? He looked at the faded cover: *Operation Market Garden*.

Adrian deliberately ran through the other books – in all the military books margin notes appeared in pencil, and a few in ink, and what was particularly irritating was that he was not able to interpret them.

He picked up the telephone and called Mrs Girdler. She was surprised to hear from him so soon and he explained what he had been doing that evening. Could she cast any light on why there should be markings in German, he asked. He heard her take a short breath. My husband would never, never deface a book. It would be totally out of character – it must have been someone else.' She went on to say that Mr Franklin mustn't hesitate to call her if anything new developed – she would do all she could to help.

Adrian turned in early but found it difficult to sleep. Where on earth was Ian and how did the books and their pencilled margins tie up with his disappearance? He would get the translations done tomorrow and he would also contact Ian's office – maybe someone there could throw a light on the whole mysterious affair.

* * *

The day started with Sam's tank advancing across the landing and Adrian looked at his watch – seven fifteen. Maybe it hadn't been such a good idea to give his grandson the toy. It could have been worse, like a drum, he mused – but adults rarely considered the consequences of the presents they bought for young children.

He studied himself in the mirror as he finished shaving. Not vanity, just curiosity whether the strain of the last few months had started to show. In theory he should have some extra wrinkles, he thought. But now, he saw his dark weather-beaten face and greyish hair and realised that for the first time for weeks he had a sense of purpose, a job to do: he was going to discover the truth about Ian.

Adrian Franklin was not a man easily put off. For over 20 years he had been employed by a major construction company and in his final eight years had been Sales Director with a staff of 70 under his control. He had gained the reputation of an autocrat who nevertheless produced results, and he had enjoyed his life with the company and the travel that it entailed. With his redundancy money he had financed a small advertising agency which had been running for several years under the direction of a close friend. The partnership had not worked out and Adrian had discovered that having a friend as a business partner was neither good for the friendship nor the business. The financial loss was not substantial and Adrian had just extricated himself from the partnership when Ann had decided to take flight with her young lover. Adrian's Roman holiday had been a direct result, for his redundancy money would certainly last for another couple of years if no job presented itself. He could live cheaply.

In the kitchen Lorna was battling with bacon and eggs and he settled himself down with young Sam to the typical English breakfast he had not experienced for some time. Sam's presence meant that conversation around the subject occupying their minds was precluded and small talk was the only order of the day.

Adrian left the house shortly after nine and took a taxi to a translation bureau off the Fulham Road. He had used the bureau frequently in the past and knew them well. He described what he wanted – a brief idea of what the pencilled notes contained.

'It's simple, Mr Franklin,' the bright bespectacled young woman replied as she flicked through the pages. 'They are notes made by someone who obviously had good knowledge of the subject matter and is correcting the author's comments. Here, for example, it says, "To north of Elst road", here is "2nd Brigade" – the note writer is disagreeing with the author. Probably whoever wrote the notes was present at the battle of Arnhem or was a student of the subject.' She took another look. 'Here in the book on the D-Day landings the same writer feels a mistake is made in the names of the beaches and that they have been confused – especially the reference to "Easy Red". His note says that Omar Bradley did not choose that beach – it was, as he puts it, an alternative thrust on them by what he calls "excessive and unexpected resistance".'

Next Adrian took a taxi to Phoenix Marketing, the small company where Ian had worked as Project Manager for the past five years. The building was sandwiched in a narrow alley off Wigmore Street and Adrian decided to take a coffee before visiting them. He reflected that he had no appointment and wished he had checked with Lorna about whom he should see.

As he sat on the uncomfortable stool with his coffee he surveyed his progress so far. What exactly had he established? Someone presumably had written notes in the book on the North Africa campaign. The information had been sufficiently important to Ian for him to seek the writer of the notes. But why? Why? What was the importance of the notes? The jigsaw had pieces which would not fit together.

Adrian finished his coffee and entered the tall office block which housed Phoenix Marketing on its sixth floor. A friendly blonde receptionist greeted him and he explained his mission – he would like to speak to the Managing Director on the subject of Ian Lacey. While she telephoned through, Adrian waited patiently, his eyes wandering across the walls, which displayed the wide range of products, from fertiliser to bathroom towels, from cordless telephones to cough syrup, which Phoenix marketed on behalf of the clients.

Mr Jules Fairson was not too enthusiastic to have the matter revived all over again. He had already told all he knew about Ian Lacey to the police. Ian had a promising career with the company, was highly regarded by all the staff and had just started work on a new project when he had stupidly vanished. Only explanation was another woman. Lacey had always had an eye for a pretty girl and had been on intimate terms with his secretary in the past. No, in Jules Fairson's view there was no question about it – sex was the reason and that was that.

Adrian listened intently. 'This secretary of his – is she still with the company?' he asked.

'No,' came the answer, 'she was with us until a year ago and then left. Anyway, she isn't here now, so if you'll excuse me, Mr Franklin, I must return to my work.'

Adrian didn't like Mr Fairson, and had the strong feeling that it was mutual.

Mr Fairson's secretary saw Adrian to the lift and waited with him for it to arrive. She looked at him shyly. 'Mr Franklin, if you want to speak to Betty, I have her number.'

'Betty?' Adrian asked.

'Yes,' the girl replied, 'Mr Lacey's secretary. She is living with a man in town somewhere. Here's her number – she was a good friend of mine when she was here.'

Adrian thanked her, returned to street level and took a taxi to Blenheim Gardens, where Lorna and Sam greeted him. He spent the next half hour telling Lorna what had happened, whilst Sam absorbed himself in tank exercises across the floor. He diplomatically skirted around Ian's alleged sexual involvement with his secretary.

It was evening when Adrian called Betty. She was guarded and wanted to know his business exactly. Was it his imagination or was it the telephone – but he thought she gasped when she heard who he was. Maybe it was the reaction of a young girl being called by the father-in-law of a man who had seduced her. An unusual situation, Adrian mused. Perhaps she was anticipating an accusation of breaking up the family.

He arranged to meet her at lunchtime the next day, at a coffee shop close to Knightsbridge Green. She worked at

Harrods and would be free between twelve thirty and one thirty.

Adrian replaced the receiver, still feeling that there was something strange in the call.

Betty Silvester was certainly not more than 21 years of age. She came into the coffee bar nervously and Adrian recognised her by her description on the telephone. Blonde and not more than five foot four, with eyes that had a piercing look. She was dressed well – perhaps expensively. Adrian concluded that she came from wealthy parents. She had that air about her – an air that Harrods would appreciate.

Adrian ordered coffee and an apple pie each and for five minutes they exchanged pleasantries. Betty was obviously worried about the reason for the meeting. Eventually Adrian asked her point-blank, 'I take it you know about Ian's disappearance.'

She nodded.

'Do you have even the slightest idea why he should have vanished like that?'

Whatever he anticipated, he couldn't have been more surprised at her answer.

'You are not aware of one thing, Mr Franklin, and I may as well tell you straight away. Ian telephoned the Saturday morning that he disappeared – he wanted the telephone number of our Technical Director at home. Mr Davies is ex-directory, and I was his secretary for a short while. As it happened I did have the number and I gave it to Ian. He told me that he had discovered something extremely thrilling but he wanted some technical advice – I really didn't know what he was talking about and I was about to go out. Anyway, following the break-up of our relationship, I've kept away from Ian so the telephone conversation was short. I would rather he didn't call me at home because – well, you know about us, I take it?'

Adrian nodded.

Betty paused to light a cigarette and blew a smoke cloud into the air, staring at it thoughtfully. She lowered her eyes.

47

'Frankly, Adrian – you don't mind me calling you by your first name, do you? Frankly, I'm puzzled and worried. When I heard he had vanished – from a friend at Phoenix Marketing – I called Mr Davies and he told me that Ian had been over and discussed finance. What do you make of that?'

Adrian put the question squarely to her. 'Did Ian make any reference to a book he was reading – a book on the North African campaigns of World War Two?'

'No,' she replied. 'What on earth has that to do with Ian?'

Adrian shrugged his shoulders. 'I wish I knew,' he replied.

The coffee bar was filling up and the noise of a piercing steam processor was drowning their conversation. Adrian thanked Betty for her help and jotted down his number for her. He had a strong feeling that she could have helped him further if only he had known the right questions to ask.

Roland Davies was enjoying an early pre-theatre dinner when the telephone ran. He cursed it soundly. Why on earth did that wretched thing always have to ring at the beginning of a most enjoyable meal? Davies enjoyed his food, indeed he enjoyed what is generally known as the good life – and the house certainly reflected his love of luxury, backed by quiet good taste.

The caller was one Adrian Franklin – he had never heard of him but the subject matter certainly caused him to sit upright in his William and Mary high-back. Yes, he had received a call from Ian Lacey and had seen him at home on the Saturday afternoon of his alleged disappearance. No, he didn't want to have a visit from the unknown Mr Franklin and what was his interest anyway?

Adrian explained his situation – his daughter losing her husband without any explanation and –

'Look, Mr Franklin,' Davies interrupted, 'the company has already had the police asking questions about Ian Lacey and I've told them all I know. Lacey was a dreamer – total lack of responsibility. He had a good sales mind but that didn't make him a good all-round businessman. He ran himself into a fearful financial mess – probably due to his womanising. He came round to see me about borrowing money – several thousand pounds. I told him that I was in no position to help him, gave him a drink and then he left.'

'Of course he was depressed,' he said in answer to Adrian's question, 'but frankly, if I was to finance everyone I discovered who was short of ready funds, I would soon find myself in Carey Street. Mr Franklin, I have a dinner getting cold so I really must go. Let me advise you on one point – don't waste time on Ian Lacey. He's either gone to ground because of money or because of some woman. Take it from me, Mr Franklin – I know Ian and I know I'm right.'

'Apart from money, did Ian ask about anything else – either to do with the company or privately?'

'Not really,' came the reply. 'He rattled on about the various projects he was working on and how he expected some big commissions which would get him out of financial difficulties. I reminded him I was the Technical Director not the Financial Director, and he left it at that.'

'Have you any idea why he came to you?' Adrian asked.

'None.' Davies sounded sharp in his reply. 'I do have a reasonable amount of capital and I assume he wanted to tap some. I suppose my lifestyle does show that I'm not hard up. That's all I can offer you in the way of ideas, I'm afraid.'

Adrian pressed on. 'I was told, Mr Davies, that Ian wanted to talk to you at home on a technical matter. Could you tell me more about that, please?'

'Quite simple. I am a consultant to Phoenix Marketing on a variety of products. After the importation of goods from around the world I do the adaptations and development for local conditions. Lacey was responsible for the marketing, he felt I was delaying final approval for a group of products, a few of which were sure quick sellers. Lacey wanted to get his hands on some commission cheques as soon as he could. Naturally he wanted to know when some tests would be completed and he could start his long-delayed marketing drive. I told him. Now I really must go, Mr Franklin.'

The conversation was clearly at an end and Adrian

replaced the receiver and walked slowly to the kitchen, where Lorna was preparing dinner and young Sam in his pyjamas was having his late-night glass of milk. Adrian loved cooking and he helped Lorna until he was chased out of the kitchen with orders to take Sam up to his room and read him a story. Picking the youngster up, he carried him to his bedroom, where the sun cast weak evening beams of light from the skylight windows.

'What's the story for tonight?' he asked the boy.

Sam thought for a moment. 'Tell me a story of Treasure Island, Poppie,' he said.

Eventually a story which bore little resemblance to Robert Louis Stevenson's original classic was finished and Adrian switched off the light and bade Sam goodnight.

He strolled into the sitting room and poured himself a large gin and tonic. The fire was alight and he sipped his drink, watching the dancing flames consuming the logs which the Lacey family always preferred to give atmosphere to the home. Strange thing for a home-loving man to walk out on all this – but stranger things have happened, he thought. All the same, there was something which didn't fit – didn't fit at all.

5

Ella Grieb wished it would rain. She sat on the terrace of the small villa with the wide picture window open. It was too hot to do anything – and what was there to do anyway. Retirement in Marbella on Spain's Costa del Sol (it was that all right) had seemed a good idea when Otto was alive. They had been able to go places and see things, had even been able to go down to Gib, now that the frontier had opened, and he had shown her where he had spent three long years as a prisoner. Better forgotten, Ella had thought, but Otto had liked living in the past.

Since Otto's death there had been a void in her life and many times she had wished she was back in Hamburg. In the past few months the situation had changed. Henry would be back soon and, if the temperature dropped, they would walk together down to the beach and take a meal at the Europa beach bar, where the food was good. In any event, it would save her from cooking. Cooking was enough of a chore even in the best of weather, but in this heat she regarded it as torture. Ella had adapted well, speaking fluent Spanish, joining local organisations, enjoying Spanish food and making many local friends. The hot weather and bullfighting were two areas she could pass over – she could do without either and hoped she would adapt to the former.

Ella decided to kill time, until Henry returned, by writing to Franz. Franz would be 24 next month and she wanted some idea of what he would like as a present. She had thought about it over the last few days, but she hadn't reached any conclusion. It was easy when he had been a boy but now, as a young man, it had become more difficult. Otto had always been full of good ideas on what to give their son but now she had no one with whom to discuss the matter. Henry hadn't even met Franz, so he couldn't contribute much in ideas. One day soon they would meet, she supposed, but it wasn't really a meeting she contemplated with relish. There was always the chance that they wouldn't hit it off – sometimes the chemistry between people just doesn't work. Perhaps Franz would feel that it was too early for his mother to get involved with another man – after all, she had been a widow for less than two years. Being married to Otto for over 20 years had been good. However, when you find yourself alone in your forties, you realise the debit side of marrying a man 25 years older than yourself. Still, they had a comfortable, if not lavish, life and the last few years since his retirement they had enjoyed the life in a warm climate with agreeable neighbours.

Ella was halfway though the letter when Henry arrived. She kissed him and asked him how the day had gone on the boat. He frowned in that characteristic way of his, his whole face creasing and expressing his mood. She looked at him and her heart turned over. There was no denying the charisma of the tall, slim Englishman with his undoubted touch of class.

'The goddamned electrician who was supposed to spend the whole day didn't show up. That meant that guy I had booked to do the carpentry could only do a small amount in the aft cabin and then spend the rest of the day on trivial items. Marcel, of course, downed tools like a shot at two o'clock. I did a bit on my own but I'm no craftsman, so I went and had some light lunch at Duke's bar. Met up with some nice people. They're here on holiday from England. We had a good afternoon but I'd rather have had *L'Anticipation* at sea.'

Ella concealed a wry smile. Ever since she had met Henry at a friend's dinner party, *L'Anticipation* had lived up to her name. At that time Henry had lived on board and spent all his time working on the ten-metre yacht which was his pride and joy. He had spent the spring and early part of the summer sailing in the Mediterranean and then in July he had put in to Puerto Banus to carry out repairs and have modifications done by a company which had been recommended to him. Things hadn't progressed as he had hoped so he had engaged freelance labour working under his supervision. The task had proved long and frustrating.

Ella poured him a large single malt whisky and gave herself a small one on ice. 'I've just had a brilliant idea, the best one of the day,' Ella said.

Henry looked at her over his glass. 'Tell me.'

'I'll stand you for dinner at Los Monteros if you'll make yourself look respectable before we go.'

Henry grinned. 'You're on.' He downed his drink and left the room.

Ella put her drink down on the desk and continued to write. A drink helped with a difficult letter. Just what would be the reaction of Franz – probably the realistic Franz would put it down to his mother's whim of fancy which would soon pass. She wrote about the weather, the day she had spent recently in Granada and the fact that she had taken her first golf lesson. She finished by asking him what he wanted for his birthday and then turned to see Henry, blue-blazered and regimental-tied, with a strong smell of Aramis.

'I can see I'll have to compete for you this evening,' she laughed, and went through to the bedroom to change.

When she emerged, Henry rose and took both her hands in his. 'I'm the one who will have to compete.' He studied the kaftan, a deep green with gold edging, and his attention was drawn to her necklace. 'That's beautiful. Where did you get it? Not Germany, I'm sure – does it have a special name?'

'It's the hand of Fatima,' Ella answered. 'I'm not sure of the exact story, but Fatima was an Arab religious figure of the seventh century. Egyptian, I believe, whose hand was supposed to bring luck to whoever it touched; held flat, it warded off evil. Sounds like you need some luck with your boat troubles, so I'll touch you with it.' She drew out its long chain and pressed the hand on his cheek. 'Now you'll get your luck.'

Henry laughed. 'I surely do need it. But where did you get that necklace? It's so lovely.'

'It isn't all that valuable. Otto bought it for me in Tunisia at some market stall. We used to go to Tunisia quite a lot on holiday and one year this caught our eyes.'

'I've never been to Tunisia. Is it good? Must be, I suppose, as you went there so much.'

'I love it, but we started going because of a strange obsession of Otto's. He was there during the war – actually he was taken prisoner there – and there was an incident regarding some hidden treasure t—' She hesitated, seeking the word in English.

'Trove,' added Henry.

'Yes, that's it, a treasure trove. Here's the taxi now – I'll tell you about it over dinner.'

Henry swirled the armagnac around the bottom of the goblet and studied it intently.

'You know,' he sighed, 'that's about the most extraordinary story I have ever heard – and believe me, I've heard some stories. Good God, lying there under the sand in some little island off Tunis...'

'Tunisia, actually,' Ella chipped in. 'It's in southern Tunisia, about four hundred odd miles south of Tunis itself.'

'OK,' Henry continued, 'in this little south Tunisian island there could be a hell of a lot of loot, a veritable Aladdin's Cave – unless of course someone else, another officer who was around at the time, got in there first, so to speak.'

Ella sighed. 'It all came to nothing – Otto never found anything after all that searching. Such a waste of time and money. It's there all right, but exactly where...'

Henry called for another armagnac and a Tia Maria for Ella, and asked for the bill. He presented his Visa card and the waiter disappeared to the back of the restaurant. A large, noisy group were leaving from the far end. A broad-shouldered, florid-faced man, wearing a leather jacket and adorned with a gold bracelet, broke away from the crowd and made towards them.

'Well, well, well. If it isn't Charlie boy himself,' the arrival greeted Henry.

Ella looked at Henry in surprise. He had gone as white as a sheet and half rose from his chair.

'I-I – just glad to see you, Royce, r-real glad,' he stammered.

'Been keeping clean, I hope – nothing like it. Be good now. Like your tie – army ain't it? 'Spect it's the Brigade of Guards. Not Boy Scouts, for sure. Nothing too good for Charlie Singer.' Tapping Henry on the shoulder the large man left, just as the credit card and docket were placed in front of him by the waiter.

Henry signed and got up. As he took Ella's arm to guide her out of the room, she asked 'Henry, who on earth was that? Looked like a nasty thug.'

'I forget his name – just someone who I knew a long, long time ago. You're right, he's bad news and I'd rather he went his way and I went mine – OK?'

* * *

'I'm really in two minds over letting you see these,' said Ella. 'It's all so personal and I wonder whether Otto would have liked me showing them to you. After all, they were – well, are – part of our private life together.'

'I feel he would want someone to continue the search – to complete his work, his commitment,' Henry replied. 'It's not as if they are love letters – just notes on your research together in Tunisia. Maybe it will all be a dead loss, but there's no harm in seeing if I can find something both of you overlooked.'

Ella handed over the worn school exercise books and Henry returned to the small patio, where the sun was streaking in. With a packet of cigarettes and a bottle of whisky, he read through the afternoon, occasionally making a pencil note.

Halfway through, he broke off to make a sandwich and, as he munched it, he looked out of the window across to Incosol and Los Monteros. Christ, that had been unfortunate last night – the very last person he wanted around at that moment was 'Royce' Rollason, so nicknamed because of his surname and his love for expensive cars. Royce could make a lot of trouble. He had been big trouble in the Scrubs – rumour had it that he had connections at a very high level and had received a light sentence in return for favours to his friends. Another rumour of a previous associate who had double-crossed him having an unfortunate rapid encounter with a motorway pool of liquid concrete had made many of the cons keep well clear of Royce. Still, he might be on the Costa for the sun – but in his heart Henry felt otherwise.

Three hours later he put down the exercise books and gave himself a big neat malt. Sipping it, his mind went over what he had read. 'Interesting,' he said to himself and, calling to Ella, told her he was slipping out for cigarettes at the corner store.

Walking briskly in the warm evening, he turned off the Avenida Ricardo Soriano into the bank, where he drew out some small coins, and then crossed to the bus station, where he settled into a telephone kiosk and dialled the international code 07, followed by a number he took from his hip pocket.

Ella lay awake. It was so hot and the humidity was high for Marbella, so that it had become rather like a South-East Asian evening. She turned and looked at her watch on the bedside table – eleven minutes past two – the worst time to wake for anyone even slightly affected by insomnia. She turned back and looked at Henry, who was breathing heavily and letting out a long slow whistle like a steam valve. Her thoughts turned to the evening at Los Monteros. After they returned, having had a good deal to drink, they had had some more brandies and yarned a great deal. They had made love when they went to bed, a pastime where Henry really excelled, anticipating her every move and being so gentle. Then she had dropped off to sleep, naked in his arms.

Tonight was different. The fine afternoon, the blistering heat, had made her tired and she had dozed for two hours in the uncomfortable evening humidity. Now fully awake, she found herself worrying about the brief encounter with Royce – he had called him that, but a few minutes later he said he didn't know his name. And why had Royce called Henry 'Charlie Singer'? Certainly Henry had pretended he hardly knew him but that wasn't the impression Ella had formed. What did he mean by 'keep clean'? It had a sinister undertone. Henry had looked so white, so scared – and really, what did she know about Henry? She knew only what he had told her – Marlborough College, commission in the Coldstream Guards and then two years with his father's company, which was bought out, leaving him with enough money to buy *L'Anticipation* and lead an easy life. He had been divorced but had no children and didn't want to discuss that particular chapter in his life. But, come to think of it, he didn't really discuss any chapter. Had she been right in letting him see Otto's notes? The more she thought about it the more uneasy she became. But two in the morning, she argued with herself, wasn't the best of times to make judgements – everything was distorted and problems were magnified. Eventually she dozed off.

After breakfast Henry took the BMW and made off for the boat, dressed in his jeans and smock. Ella kissed him on both cheeks and helped herself to another cup from the Cona. Her doubts came up again. She picked up the telephone and dialled a number in England.

Colonel James Slattery had known Ella since she was a little girl and, although an ardent atheist, he had somehow been chosen by her parents as her godfather. He had come to know Otto and liked him, pulling his leg about being on the wrong side during the war. Otto had always taken it in good heart and the two had become firm friends.

Jimmy Slattery was delighted to hear from Ella. Sure, he would check him out – Henry Southon, ex-Captain,

Coldstream Guards. 'Sure, I'll speak to my friends at Sandhurst and the Army Records office, see what they know about the fellah – leave it to me, Ella.'

Since his retirement, Jimmy Slattery had been bored stiff. He had tried to take on all kinds of voluntary work but had been exhausted by what he regarded as well-meaning idiots. Doing some checking around would make an interesting day and he could speak to chums at Sandhurst and the Guards Club with a purpose.

At midday Colonel James Slattery called Ella Grieb. His message was affable but brief. Captain Henry Southon, aged 35, was killed in a car crash whilst holidaying in South Africa in 1985. Ella slowly put down the receiver.

* * *

Royce Rollason jabbed out another cigarette in the sand-filled ashtray of Villa Lamorna. The Filipina maid, whose services on occasion extended beyond that normally required of a domestic, brought him another coffee and, he grunted his thanks.

'Tony! Come in 'ere a minute. I want to bounce something off yer,' he called back through the picture window.

A muffled voice from the back told him that Tony was otherwise engaged in the toilet and he would have to wait. Royce didn't like waiting. He liked people jumping to his orders, and that hadn't happened since he'd moved out of the East End and down to warmer climes, where few knew of his reputation and fewer cared.

Royce prided himself on being a real professional, a graduate of the world of crime. He had come up the long, hard way, going to an approved school at the age of 12. At 16 his interest in cars had led him to Borstal, simply because they were other people's cars he was interested in. At 22 he had heard the judge at the Old Bailey describe him as 'someone from whom society must be protected' and then he had vanished from his usual hunting ground for eight years. He had never got over that – eight years in the Scrubs was a long time for a young man with an appetite for young women, especially as he wasn't the one who had hit the old lady. He had just held her down on the study floor to keep her quiet. It was old Flooky Forster who had actually hit her – just a bit too hard, that's all. Royce Rollason felt the world had not shown him justice.

Dartmoor was another matter. Those six years had been worth it. He had come out to a considerable fortune, which the good bank in Luxembourg had kindly looked after for him; they had given him interest and he had made a good deal on the exchange rate into the bargain.

Now, nearing 60, he had retired. He really felt that 21 years in a lifetime was enough for anyone to spend as a guest of Her Majesty. It wasn't that he wanted to go straight; he wanted to break his boredom by acting as consultant to the amateurs of the game – late entries or 'noovos' as he called them. Such a noovo was Charlie Singer, otherwise known as the Tenor. Tenner was just about his value, Royce had observed to Tony Trappins and Steve Smyley in the car the previous evening, and had laughed at his own joke – which he had initially made in the Scrubs on first meeting Charlie.

Tony joined him on the balcony. 'What do you want?' he asked bluntly.

'Can't get over that bum Charlie Singer sitting around here on the Costa, all dressed up and with a fancy bird – older than 'im, I guess, and that's not 'is style. Could be 'e's down 'ere havin' a break, but 'e's tanned, so 'e's been 'ere some time. That car we saw 'im get last night – I got its number an' it's German plates. That makes me uneasy too – 'e's up to something, an' I want to know what it is an' if it's good. You know me, Tony – just one or two nice consultancies a year, a nice cut of the action and no risk, no risk at all at my age.'

Tony nodded; he knew. His span behind bars couldn't rival Royce's but he didn't want to increase his score – five years behind Royce was fine with him. He didn't have that kind of competitive spirit.

Royce raised his enormous frame off the chair and put his arm around Tony. They made a ridiculous pair together; the giant, burly Royce, wearing open-neck white shirt and gold chains contrasted sharply with the thin, pinched, middle-height Tony Trappins, with his clipped moustache, looking all the part of an Italian waiter from a cheap café – which is what he was, until he discovered that taking from well-off people paid better than serving poor ones.

'I want to know what that runt is up to. I don't want investigations going on around 'ere. Lot of discomfort and I'm onto a nice little number at the moment – just consulting y'know, just introductions. Charlie's a noovo and a poor noovo. Find out what 'e's up to, Tony, and then we'll decide what to do next.'

It was early evening when Tony returned. It had not taken him long to trace a red BMW with a black soft top and German plates. It was parked alongside the quay at Puerto Banus and Tony had it under observation whilst he took a beer at a nearby café. The waiter had been able to put him wise on the driver.

'He comes here every day,' he had told Tony, 'working on his boat, the *Anti-ception*.'

Tony laughed at his mispronunciation, but Royce wasn't in laughing mood.

'Go on,' he grunted.

'I looked at the boat – sailing one it is – must have cost a bit too. About three o'clock he came up to the car, put the hood down and drove off. I followed him, keeping well back, but he didn't go far; turned up the Calvario and into Avenida Huerto Belon. There he stopped and went into one of those villas – she was there.' Seeing Royce's questioning look, he added, 'The bird he was with at the hotel. She's German, I think, because I pulled up and walked by – they were talking in the garden and she has a strong accent.'

'That would account for the German plates,' said Royce. 'So it's her car and probably her villa: that halfwit couldn't afford a fancy place like that.'

Royce lit a cigar and went over to the edge of the pool, looking at his reflection in the water. 'I think we must go and take a look around the – what do you call the boat?'

'*L'Anticipation*,' answered Tony.

Fifteen minutes later, Royce's Mercedes coupé pulled up in the car park on the highway side of Puerto Banus. The two of them walked along the quayside where the yachts of the rich and famous were berthed.

'Just add up the value of all this lot,' said Tony, but he had said it often before and Royce was not interested. He was interested in the ten-metre motor yacht in white paint with French registration and *L'Anticipation* on the transom. The French registration puzzled him a little, but it wasn't important. You could register a boat wherever you pleased and maybe Charlie had bought this in the South of France.

Royce stood in the aft deck making an issue of lighting a cigar in the late evening light. What he was in fact doing was shielding Tony, who, using a pair of bolt cutters, neatly removed the padlock which secured the main cabin. A few seconds later they were both looking around the cabin, switching on the light to let any passer-by think that all was normal and the crew were on board.

Neither Royce nor Tony had any idea what they were looking for. All they wanted was to get some idea of what, if anything, the owner planned to do to earn an honest – or, more likely, dishonest – crust. Royce studied the partially finished inner skin carpentry of the aft cabin.

'So 'e's 'avin' a little woodwork done, is 'e?' he muttered to himself. ' 'Ave a look at this, Tony boy. He's leaving a nice gap between skins – nice place to put something you want to 'ide, I shouldn't wonder.'

On the opposite side of the cabin Tony moved a picture and fiddled with some wood panelling. It sprang open and revealed a small locker about 20 centimetres square. Inside were some papers, bank statements from Banco Atlantico and two passports. Royce picked up the passports.

' 'Ere we are. "Charles Singer. Occupation: Freelance Writer" '. Royce chuckled. 'Sounds respectable, don't it? This one is 'Enry Southon.'

Royce's beady eyes took in a small brown book on the fruit bowl.

'Address book – could be useful,' he muttered. 'OK, let's go.'

As they crossed the car park they didn't notice the BMW with German plates which had driven hurriedly onto the waterfront in response to a telephone call from a waiter at a bar overlooking *L'Anticipation*'s berth. Henry jumped on board and saw the broken lock, which had been replaced in the hasp. In a way he was glad. At least they weren't here any more. Henry wasn't a coward but he didn't relish the prospect of meeting Royce and one or two of his cronies face-to-face in the cabin. If only half the stories of Royce were only slightly true, then that was enough. But what did Royce want? He had a horrible feeling in the pit of his stomach that he would soon find out...

* * *

The young boat boy looked worried when he arrived at the boat next morning. His English was limited and he started to speak.

'I know,' Henry interjected. 'The lock – we had intruders – bad people – did not take anything – no worry.'

'The lad looked relieved. He didn't know quite what Mr Southon was doing with his boat and he didn't much care; all he knew was that he was paid 1,200 pesetas per hour in cash at the end of every day and he was more than happy with that arrangement. Pedro was keen to do a good job of work for the English gentleman who paid him regularly.

By two o'clock the sun was unbearably hot and Henry suggested to Pedro that they break for a beer at the Shark Club, a small bar adjacent to the jetty. Pedro ran his hand over his forehead and smiled. 'Good idea,' he said, and put away his tools.

The Shark Club was half full and they enjoyed the ice-cold beer on the terrace. Then Pedro's eyes looked up against the sun – a bull of a man with gold chains stood behind his employer.

'Well, if it isn't Charlie! Some old friends you can never get away from. But I believe it's Henry now – Henry Southon, by all accounts, or so they tell me round here.'

Pedro saw Henry Southon's face distort. Then it gained composure.

'Just run along, Pedro. Be seeing you tomorrow, there's a good lad. Tomorrow.'

Royce leaned his huge frame into a chair and called the waiter. ' 'Ow about two nice brandies – just the way old friends should celebrate,' he commented.

Henry started to speak but Royce addressed himself to the waiter and placed the order. As Henry sat motionless, Royce went on.

'I've talked to my old friend Tony – a real pro is Tony – and we are a bit worried about you, Charlie. Real worried. A bit puzzled, you might say. What would a nice man like you be doing spending time round 'ere for months on end with a bird much older than 'imself and a boat all put up to carry what it shouldn't? Don't make sense, I said to Tony. Then Tony an' me – with your interest at 'eart of course – we goes to look over for ourselves and what does we find? A real tidy 'ideaway place in one cabin and an 'ideaway place for papers in the other. So, as I always says, a man is judged by the company 'e keeps, so we judges you an' looks through your address book, Charlie. Then we finds not names but initials in most places. That's strange, Tony says, an' I agrees. It's strange, but when someone's about what 'e shouldn't be then 'e 'as things to 'ide. Then there's a passport in the name of Charlie Singer and another... 'Enry Southon an' we takes 'em away for photocopying. But bein' gents we must 'and 'em back. Now, you an' me is going to be partners. What would you say as a Guards officer, Charlie? – we got to play cricket. 'Owever, I got the bat at the moment, Charlie, an' what's more I got you by the balls.' Royce chuckled at his own joke. 'An' your nice German lady – she don't know much about you, I'll be sure. We could give 'er a clue, of course, by sending 'er your passport photocopy, but, like I says, it wouldn't be cricket. So, Charlie, I'm getting old now an' not into adventure games – just a quiet consultancy or so. You think it over, come up with some ideas for old Royce an' I swear you wouldn't find a better sleeping partner in the 'ole of your bleedin' life. Old Royce is a good partner, but' Royce pushed his cigar onto the tablecloth, burning the fabric – ' 'e makes a fuckin' 'orrible enemy.'

Royce rose, and the little man who looked like an Italian waiter and had been sipping whisky at the next table joined him as he walked towards the car park. Henry went to the gents and was violently sick.

* * *

The old man heard the car horn in the distance and wondered why his daughter was making such a noise – and flashing the lights as well. The Toyota Landcruiser was half a mile away, shimmering in the heat of the Argentinian pampas.

'There must be something up,' he muttered to his head rancher. 'She shouldn't drive so fast on these rough roads, no good for any vehicle.'

The car came to a halt with a cloud of dust and Erika threw her arms around her father.

'Papa, it is all over. Alfonso – look, his letter is here – has his release from the army. I thought he would never do it. The army was his life. Oh, he had those crazy ideas about protecting his country ever since the fighting with the British over the Malvinas – I thought his country meant more to him than I do. But now he says that he misses me so much he wants to be home and not in the military. We will have him back soon. Papa, isn't that wonderful!'

The old man put his arm around his daughter's shoulder and held her to him. Words were not necessary. He knew how worried she had been over her husband's conscription into the Argentine armed forces – it had all seemed such a trauma over nothing, some stupid little islands which most Argentinians neither knew nor cared about. It was worse when he signed on as a regular officer. All because of a principle. The old man had seen enough of principles – people laying down their lives for a cause. It had all been linked to a driving ambition when he was young but he was past that now. He let her loose and looked at her tearful eyes. Somehow he always regarded her as if she was still a little girl, yet she was 38 this coming August. She hadn't changed since she was a five-year-old, on her pony riding over with his lunch to wherever he was on the cattle ranch, maybe seven kiolometres or so from the hacienda. It was a long time ago but like most elderly people he liked to reminisce about the better times – and her childhood had been a very good time.

'Come on, let's go back to the house. I'll cook you the biggest steak you've ever seen and we'll talk about what we'll do when that hero husband of yours returns. You'll have to talk him out of going back to the town and testing people's eyes. He's had a taste of the outside life now. He ought to come and help his old father-in-law.'

The old man took over the wheel of the Toyota and they bumped across the rough track towards the highway, which was marginally less rough. The six workers thought it was a good idea to cut the day short as well. Mrs Fernandez had taken her father home for the day to celebrate. Mr Fernandez was coming home and they liked to have him around. Soon the men were drinking black tea and smoking cigarettes.

* * *

L'Anticipation rose and fell on the waves as she cleared the harbour wall at Puerto Banus. There was a red glow over the sea as the sun gradually sank below the horizon. She carried no lights and moved silently across the choppy water. Charlie Singer could hear the slap of the water against the boards clearer than he had ever done, for on this particular voyage the ten-metre boat had no engine running – her only form of locomotion was a small fishing vessel some 20 metres ahead. A long rope hawser joined the two vessels.

Charlie could hardly bear to look back. He couldn't believe it had been that easy and he had managed to slip away from his mooring unnoticed. A light flashing behind made him jump – another boat in pursuit? But it was only a car turning round at the end of the quay with its lights turned on. Any worry about how soon Royce would discover his sudden departure was suppressed; he had to keep his thoughts on the job in hand: to get the boat to Ceuta before dawn. 'Christ, what a bloody foul-up,' he muttered to himself, and his mind wandered over the events of the last few days – ever since he had run into Royce at Los Monteros. If it hadn't been for Royce all would have gone well. Three months of careful planning – ever since that snivelling Ian had come round to the house with his hysterical story of dying – and his get-rich-quick scheme. It was a good idea and came just at the right time, just when money was low and his ideas of drug trafficking had been thwarted. There was little future in playing games with the Mafia and the two sinister characters who had taken him into a back room at his favourite golf club had made it clear that an extra pair of hands in that business would lead to a very nasty accident. Charlie had accepted that advice – he had little option. Then two days later, just when he was thinking of moving along to new pastures, in came Ian to see his mother-in-law with his Treasure Island story. Fate had been kind to him then but now it had turned against him; that was certain.

His thoughts were interrupted by a call from the towing boat. Young Pedro was calling him with cupped hands. He strained to hear and caught the word '*gasolina*'. The tugboat turned to starboard – they must be putting in for fuel. The departure had been hurried. Pedro had really gone into action with 20,000 pesetas pressed in his hand, and within 30 minutes had engaged the services of a fishing vessel by promising the owner 100,000 pesetas for the night's work. There hadn't been time for the details like refuelling.

Ten minutes later the fishing vessel, with *L'Anticipation* on tow, came alongside the quay at Estepona, and the elderly fisherman made his way to a small garage-like structure on the seafront. Charlie hoped he would be quick.

Pedro came on board. 'We make good time. Carlos fine seaman but trouble with gasoline. He go fetch his brother who has plenty store gasoline.'

Charlie smiled for the first time. 'Great – *bueno*.'

He didn't feel like talking, he was still trying to formulate plans. It was one thing getting to Ceuta but the boat was still far from being fit for a longer trip. There was plenty of work to be done and also he wanted these recesses in the panelling done so professionally that, when he eventually located the stuff that would make him rich for life, he could get it away from the country and to his ready-made market.

He found himself thinking about Ian, and how he disliked him and his disapproving attitude. Still, it had been a good plan, even if Ian hadn't had the perception and drive to carry it out. It was odd, though, if he had disappeared, as Ann had told him on the phone. One thing was certain, however, he thought with an inner smugness – that twit might dig up the whole bloody desert but he wouldn't find anything. Only one person had the real answer to the lost goods, and that stupid Ella had presented it on a plate. It had been hard work getting her confidence but he had done so. The agreeable part was that she was living in such a superb place. He had been taken aback at first when he had heard from Grunner and Grieb in Hamburg that she was in Marbella. He smiled smugly when he thought of the way he had tracked her down and arranged for her to be at a dinner party so he could meet her. She had been younger than he imagined – and stupider, he thought.

Pedro stood up, and the old fisherman passed two large drums of oil into the fishing boat ahead. The two of them filled the tank through a huge funnel. Ten minutes later Charlie was relieved to feel the boat move forward and the tow rope pull her towards the open sea where the wind was freshening.

6

Lorna dressed Sam in his winter coat ready for the visit to the doctor. The boy had hardly slept all night, ensuring that his mother had lost sleep as well. His stomach-ache seemed real enough but in the back of her mind Lorna believed that it was psychosomatic, for all the family had certainly felt the strain of the past few weeks.

Dr Solomon was an old family friend and had quickly agreed to see Sam if Lorna brought him round straight away before his normal surgery started. It was raining and taxis had disappeared off the streets of London as they always seem to do when the weather deteriorates. Adrian volunteered to drive them there, and they nudged through two miles of rush hour traffic to Dr Solomon's Kensington surgery.

The surgery door was open and a white-aproned fresh-faced assistant showed them into the inner sanctum, where grey-haired Dr Solomon greeted them in his usual kindly way. The family had been to Dr Solomon for three years now and they liked his methodical approach and gentle manner. Dr Solomon exuded confidence and his unhurried attitude to life coupled with his keen listening made him a favourite with many patients. Lorna was such a patient.

He gave Sam a thorough examination. 'Looks a bit run down,' he commented, 'but there's nothing very wrong with him. Just a bug. I'll prescribe some antibiotics.' He sat down at his desk.

Lorna felt the time was ripe to explain the recent turn of

events. 'Of course, you wouldn't know this, doctor,' she said quietly, so that Sam wouldn't hear. 'But we've all been through a terrible strain recently with Ian's disappearance – he just vanished and we are all worried and puzzled. There isn't a logical explanation for it.'

Dr Solomon handed her the prescription and adjusted his glasses. Not known for sharp reactions he nevertheless commented quickly, 'Could be related to his health, you know. People do strange things under strain.'

Lorna's brows knitted tightly, 'What on earth do you mean?'

Dr Solomon turned to Sam. 'Look young man, we have some new trains in the toy cupboard and we want some help in putting them together. Why not see what you can do?'

In answer to the buzzer, a young nurse came in and Dr Solomon asked her to show Sam the trains. As the door closed, the doctor turned to Lorna.

'Mrs Lacey, I fear there is something Ian hasn't told you. I asked him to discuss the matter with you and he said he would'

Lorna sat frozen, her hands grasped her knees and then the side of her chair. 'Please tell me,' she whispered.

'Your husband is very ill indeed. I may as well come straight to the point – he has cancer of the liver.'

Lorna felt that her feet were miles from her body. The room seemed to distort as she tried to speak. Her world had changed in a few brief moments.

'It's true, I'm afraid – I wish I could say otherwise,' the doctor went on. 'He came to me a few weeks ago and I sent him to hospital for tests. When the results came through I telephoned him and he came here. He took the news quite well, I thought, as if he had suspected something serious. He was worried about you and Sam. How would he break it to you and how would you manage financially? We doctors face this kind of thing more often than you may think and I gave him the only advice I could – to go away for a few days and think it all out. He asked me how long he had left and I told him between three to six months, although this is largely guesswork and it could be longer.'

Dr Solomon looked up the entry in his appointments diary and told Lorna the date of Ian's last visit. It was two days before he vanished.

Lorna was going to ask him if he could throw any light on Ian's disappearance but her throat had become parched and she found it difficult to speak. Sam was making his presence felt in the adjoining room so she rose on to unsteady feet and walked through to him. Dr Solomon followed, and she took his hand.

'Thank you for everything,' she croaked, and led Sam into the hallway and down the steps of the Regency building. There was no sign of the car so they walked 50 metres in the steady drizzle and stood under the canopy of a newsagent's shop until she saw the red Ford and Adrian.

It was Adrian's 'What's the news?' that broke her. She sobbed and hung on to his arm. Adrian pulled the car into a side street and drove into a 'Residents Only' area.

'Good grief!' he exclaimed. 'What's wrong with the lad?'

'It isn't Sam. He just has some tiny bug and we have a prescription for that. Dad, drive home and let's talk there.'

Sam piped up. 'What's wrong, Mummy?' Why are you crying?' And then he too burst into a flood of tears.

The journey seemed to go on for ever and when they arrived at the house someone had parked partially across the garage doors, so Adrian had some difficulty in getting the car in. Lorna took Sam upstairs and put him to bed with a colouring book and pastels – to hell with all the mess which would undoubtedly result.

When she came down again she threw herself into her father's arms. After a few moments she sat down and told him what Dr Solomon had said.

Adrian got up and sat on the settee beside her, putting his arm around his daughter's shoulder. She wasn't an emotional girl but all this on top of the mysterious disappearance had proved too much and tears ran down her face.

'Do you think it's possible he decided to kill himself?' she asked.

Adrian thought for a minute before replying. 'I don't believe that at all – he just wasn't that kind of person – but maybe he took the doctor's advice and went away somewhere to sort it all out, then on his trip he had an accident or...' His voice faded away. 'Listen,' he suddenly exclaimed, 'did he ever go to Plymouth?'

'Not that I can recall – not in recent years, anyway. Why on earth do you ask?'

Adrian took his wallet from his breast pocket and extracted a small piece of paper. 'When I was driving around I needed some coins for a meter and searched the glove box. I found this – a parking ticket dated the day before he had vanished, marked 'City of Plymouth'.'

But Lorna's mind was exhausted and the tears welling up in her eyes told Adrian that this was a subject to pursue on another occasion.

Adrian turned over again in bed. He doubted whether he would sleep at all that night. From time to time he thought he heard a sound from across the corridor and he wondered if it was Lorna crying. The shock of the news from the surgery had upset him greatly and he had no doubt of the continuing effect it would have on her.

However, tragic though it was, it seemed to eliminate another woman as the reason for Ian's disappearance. But the whole thing was bizarre. He drifted into a short sleep but then awoke. The clock downstairs struck two. Adrian found himself puzzling over the parking ticket he had found in the glove box. Lorna had been unable to think of a reason why her husband should drive to Plymouth. Why *would* someone who had been told some dreadful, indeed fatal news drive 250 miles or so to the West Country the next day? It didn't make sense – unless he went to tell someone to get it off his mind. Or to get a second opinion – but surely that would have been set up through Dr Solomon. And all this seemed totally unrelated to the book which Lorna was convinced had started the chain of events.

Again, Adrian's mind went to Plymouth. He had been there many times and knew from first-hand experience how long it took to drive there. Something very important must have cropped up for Ian to drive immediately, in a shocked state of mind, all that way. He must have stayed the night somewhere in the West Country. Then next day he drove back to London and vanished. There was just no sense in it.

Adrian got up to make himself a cup of tea. Whilst the kettle boiled he scratched down some notes on a pad, trying to get some chronological order and some observations in the margin. When he wrote 'My visit to company' he surprised himself with how little he had found out. Mr Fairson had neatly dismissed the subject, convinced another woman was involved, but surely he should have been more concerned? After all, Ian had worked there for several years and had had a good management position.

The kettle boiled and Adrian made himself tea. The fire was still glowing in the lounge and Adrian sat in front of it, staring at the dying embers. That girl he had met near Harrods – Betty – the one with whom Ian had had an association, had seemed very ill at ease and so had Davies on the telephone. Imagination could run away with you at such times, but with the exception of the secretary who had given him Betty's number, no one else had been very forthcoming. But that didn't necessarily mean anything.

Adrian awoke as Lorna pulled the curtains; he must have fallen asleep. A quick look at Lorna's face told him what he had suspected. She had had a poor night and was exhausted. True to form, she still brought him tea.

Over breakfast Adrian decided to take Sam out for the day and give Lorna a break. She would have to come to grips with the news she had learned the previous day, and perhaps time on her own would help. Sam greeted the news of an outing with youthful enthusiasm and, as it was a dry, clear day, Adrian suggested London Zoo. Adrian hadn't been there for more years than he cared to think. It would make a change – a chance also to stand back from the subject which dominated and clouded his mind.

Lorna sat up in bed with the noise of Sam downstairs. It was four thirty in the afternoon; she must have fallen asleep as she lay on the bed with fretful thoughts whirling inconsistently in her head.

Sam had had a wonderful day with his grandfather and had thoroughly explored the zoo, particularly the reptile house. He was armed with a wide range of postcards and showed his mother what he had seen and where he had been.

After tea Sam went to his room to play and Adrian took Lorna's hand in his as she sat near the fire.

'Look, love, all this is getting us down and we are losing perspective. I know it's starting to rain and we have had a few nasty shocks, but let's go out to dinner – give us a break. Can you get a babysitter for Sam?'

Lorna nodded. 'I'd love to. I'm dreading tonight – I know I won't sleep. I can get a sitter from just down the road. She's the daughter of a friend and Sam adores her. Where shall we go?'

Dinner at Dean Street's Quo Vadis was as enjoyable as ever. The lack of background music and the widely spaced tables meant that they could talk – but not about the subject in the forefront of their minds. Strange how the mind, in times of stress, has a convenient habit of shutting out major items and letting trivia come forward as a balm. They talked about Sam, about a holiday they had had in Spain as a family many years before in a pneumatic tent which leaked air during the night and had to be pumped up every two hours to avoid collapse. The evening was enjoyable despite the strain and concluded with some fine Stilton and a couple of glasses of vintage port.

'Good grief, it's gone eleven!' Lorna exclaimed 'I promised Sara we'd be back by eleven thirty because she has an early start tomorrow.'

Adrian called for the bill and presented his Diner's Card.

A few minutes later they were being helped into their raincoats and followed another couple out into what had become a wet, windy night. The other couple had their car parked outside and Adrian was relieved to see that no one else was waiting for a taxi. He glanced up the street for an available cab. Suddenly he grabbed Lorna's arm as the parked car moved forward.

'That couple in the car – I know her, that's Betty, Ian's ex-secretary. I told you, she's now working in Harrods.'

The car had moved off but not before Adrian had spotted the dealer's sticker in the rear window – 'Pentagon Garage, Plymouth'.

A taxi with its light on appeared and Adrian flagged it down. As the car turned into Soho Square Adrian took Lorna's hand.

'Look, it may be a coincidence – a wild long shot – but that car we just saw with Betty is new and was supplied in Plymouth. There may, just may, be a connection.'

Lorna looked puzzled and Adrian went on quickly to explain. 'The ticket in Ian's car, in the glove box, was from Plymouth. Anyway, tomorrow I'm going to follow that lead – maybe talk to the secretary at Phoenix Marketing. Let's face it, we have not exactly made great progress so any slightly possible lead is worth following.' He wondered how much Lorna knew about the affair and decided she had probably turned a blind eye.

As the taxi crossed Piccadilly Circus Lorna looked at her father. 'We try to put it all out of our minds for an evening but we don't succeed for long, do we, Dad?'

Halfway through the breakfast of bacon and eggs there was a sharp tap as the flap of the letterbox closed and three or four letters dropped onto the kitchen mat. Sam jumped down but Lorna lifted him back and walked over to the door to pick them up. She thumbed through and put two on the mantelpiece behind the clock. Adrian's eyes followed her.

'It's none of my business I know, but that little collection behind that model – is that Ian's mail?'

Lorna nodded. 'You see, I do believe he will come back.'

Adrian looked down. 'That's very possible, but I just wonder whether there may be something in his mail which might cast some light on the matter we have in hand. I know,' he added hastily, 'how strongly you both feel about the privacy of one another's mail, but surely we are dealing with very exceptional circumstances.'

Lorna was reluctant to act against all the codes she and Ian had adhered to – but her father was right. She passed the mail to him and he started reading through what had accumulated over the last few weeks. Most of it was direct mail, but there was a bank statement. He studied it carefully; it revealed nothing significant. There was also a stiff and final notice from his employers stating that in view of his lack of attendance his contract of employment was terminated. Adrian turned to Ian's Diners Club statement.

'Lorna,' he said softly, 'this account has just arrived. It seems Ian drew petrol at Exeter bypass service station on the day before he disappeared, and the following day he did something most extraordinary. He purchased an air ticket. Would he be doing that on business?'

'No, I'm sure not,' Lorna replied, her face full of troubled curiosity.

'Come to think of it,' Adrian recalled, 'that was a Saturday, and, in any event, the company would have mentioned it. No, there's a strange twist here which we must unravel. I'll call Diners Club and ask if they can tell me the branch of Pickfords that ... No, better still, I have a friend at Pickfords who can help. Ian must be on the computer and it shouldn't be too hard a job to discover where he bought the ticket, and the destination.'

Adrian went to the hall telephone and called Philip Ware, who was a member of his club. He explained in some detail what he wanted, and described the mysteries around Ian's disappearance.

'I'll do what I can, Adrian,' came the reply. 'I'll give you a call later today.'

Adrian thanked him and rang off. Lorna joined him in the hall.

'Sam's asking too many questions now,' she commented. 'We'll have to be careful how much we say in front of him. I gather your contact will be able to help.'

Adrian nodded. 'He's a nice guy, Philip. I don't know him that well but we often meet by accident in the club bar and have a drink or two. I don't know his exact position in the company but I imagine he is pretty senior and should be able to get some quick answers. However, I'm not prepared to sit around all day doing nothing. If you let me have a cup of coffee I'll slip round to Ian's company and see if I can nail Fairson's secretary. She put me onto Ian's secretary in the first place and maybe she can throw more light on the scene. In any event, it can't hurt.'

Adrian's journey to Phoenix Marketing was slow, the taxi fighting heavy traffic while the driver assured him, 'Gets worse every week,' and went on to explain how he would solve the problem – but Adrian was thinking.

On his arrival, he took the lift to the fifth floor and was relieved to find Fairson's secretary at the reception desk. She recognised him immediately and, asked him who he would like to see.

'Actually – you,' Adrian answered. 'I'm still trying to fit pieces together and I wonder if you could answer a few questions. Can you explain why Ian – Mr Lacey – should suddenly and without any warning shoot off to Plymouth?'

Lucy, as she introduced herself, shook her head. 'No idea – the company has no connection there that I know of.'

Adrian pressed her further. Did she have any idea, no matter how fanciful, why Mr Lacey should vanish?

'No,' she answered.

The door to the side of the hall opened and a short dapper man with a shock of curly hair crossed to her desk. 'I'm expecting a visitor. A Mr Doaver,' he butted in. 'Tell him I'll be back in a few moments – I've a personal matter to attend to.'

Adrian stopped. The voice, and indeed the face, were familiar. Yes, he had seen the profile before – getting into the car with Betty outside Quo Vadis only last night. The man disappeared into the lift and Adrian eagerly addressed himself to Lucy.

'Who was that?' he enquired.

'That's Mr Davies our Technical Director,' she replied.

So that was the voice connection; it was Davies who had been so abrupt on the telephone and so convinced that Ian had disappeared with another woman. But why should he be dining with Ian's secretary of a year ago?

'Tell me about Mr Davies.'

Lucy looked a little uneasy. 'He's been here all the time I've been here – over three years. He's in the office every Monday, Tuesday and Wednesday and has an office and a secretary. He's always very nice, I must say, and I think he is,' she faltered, 'highly regarded in the company.'

'What about Thursday and Friday?' Adrian asked.

Lucy looked a little perplexed. 'I'm not sure – I'm just the relief receptionist and secretary to Mr Fairson, you know. But I have heard he only works part-time for us and part-time for another company. Sometimes he doesn't come in for a week or so – he's away with the other company.'

'Do you know which company?' Adrian asked.

'No,' she replied, 'but the girl who does his typing should know.'

'Find out as much about the company as you can – who they are, what they make and where they are,' Adrian urged, 'then please call me at this number.' He wrote Lorna's number down on her pad.

Adrian left, hailed a cab and returned to Blenheim Gardens. As he walked in Lorna greeted him.

'Your girlfriend's been on the line. Says she's just spoken to her friend. The company is Dekta Instruments of Plymouth and they manufacture detection equipment. He works there every Thursday and Friday regularly but sometimes takes on longer assignments. Fill me in will you – what's it all about?'

Adrian told her the result of his visit.

'That might explain the Plymouth garage sticker on the car window,' Arian mused, 'but I would like to look into it more – there's something here that is not quite right. I'll go to Harrods and meet up with Betty under the pretext of shopping. I may learn something new.'

The telephone rang and Lorna answered. 'Yes, he's here. I'll put him on the line.'

Adrian picked up the telephone. 'Yes, I understand – the ticket was London to Tunis with a connecting flight to Djerba. I see – that's kind of you. You've spoken to the airline – yes, odd. Really kind of you. Thank you.'

He put the receiver down thoughtfully. 'Our friend at the travel agency. Ian booked a ticket to Tunisia but he didn't use the return, he changed it. It seems that from Tunisia he flew via Paris to Geneva. It gets more interesting – and confusing.'

The taxi pulled up at Harrods' door and the friendly attendant opened the door and touched the peak of his hat. In a period of change Harrods still kept its sense of style, Adrian thought to himself as he paid off the cab. Entering the store, he wondered if he would find Betty. He knew she only worked part-time and that she was involved in make-up. He could, of course, have called her to set up an appointment but he had a feeling she knew more about this whole business than she had declared and he wanted to catch her off her guard.

The store was packed and Adrian marvelled at the amount of money passing over the counter on such luxuries as cosmetics – and there's supposed to be a recession, he mused.

There was no sign of Betty and Adrian eventually approached a young sales assistant and asked for a small bottle of Ma Griffe, Lorna's favourite perfume.

As she wrapped it up he asked, 'I was looking for a friend of mine, a Miss Betty...' he stumbled. 'I can't remember her surname. She doesn't happen to be about, does she?'

'No, I'm afraid not,' the girl replied. 'If you mean Betty Silvester, she has left the company – she was part-time, you know, and she found something else when she was on holiday. A pity really, because I used to enjoy her company. Still, if she has found a better job, good luck to her – she was here last week just finishing off before the new job started.'

'I thought I saw her the other day getting into a car,' Adrian led her on.

'Oh, possibly,' she chattered on, oblivious of other people waiting for attention. 'She had a small Fiat – bought it recently, although why anyone bothers with a car in London I can't think.'

'By the way,' Adrian put in quickly, knowing that he couldn't distract her any longer, 'did she enjoy her holiday? She did tell me where she was going but I forget.'

'Sure she had a great time – apparently that's what caused her to leave here. When she was in Tunisia – not sure where – but she came across a job and decided to pack it in here.'

Adrian picked up his change and thanked her. Leaving the store, he hailed a taxi and sat in contemplation as the cab weaved its way through London. Could that be the simple and straightforward explanation – that Ian had picked up with his former girlfriend and gone off to Tunisia? Would that be the action of a man who had been told he had only a few months to live – to walk out on his entire family? And how did Davies fit into all this? Why hadn't she revealed that she still saw Davies rather than hide it away? She had once worked for him, he remembered. If Ian had decided he would rather die alone than subject his family to the strain of seeing him gradually deteriorate, wouldn't it have been better to leave a note, even if it wasn't the complete truth? However, there was a slotting together of all the pieces in the kaleidoscope. There was another connection; suddenly it hit him – the book was on the North African campaign. This couldn't be a coincidence. Something Ian had read had caused him to go to Tunisia. But why had Betty gone, obviously after he had. To join up with him? And why had he gone so quickly and without leaving a note? The pieces were fitting but the picture was far from complete.

'There's a point you have overlooked,' Lorna commented when Adrian finished his summing up of the overall situation and was pouring them both another gin and tonic. 'If she bought a car recently, why should she buy it in Plymouth rather than London? Davies might go down there from time to time, but even if she goes down there with him, surely she would buy a new car in London.'

'Unless she saw a bargain and snapped it up. If only we had the number. It was foolish of me not to take it down. Of course, it may have been Davies's car they were using.'

'But you do have the dealer's name. Surely they could confirm if they supplied her with a car – and in any event, Father, does it really matter if it's her car or Davies's – how does that help in the search for Ian?'

Adrian's face creased with some understanding. The car is probably part of what is euphemistically known as a 'package' – a way to reduce Davies's tax commitments. Instead of an appropriate salary he had probably asked for a car from the Plymouth company. His curiosity in this company was aroused, but how to find out more without placing himself in a position where he wouldn't justifiably be told to mind his own business? If he telephoned them, perhaps he could ask for a catalogue or some information.

The telephone was answered after a few rings and Adrian thought the woman sounded helpful.

'I wonder if you can help me?' he enquired. 'I'm trying to contact a Mr Davies – he's an old friend and I believe he works for your company. Have you any idea when he will be in the office or where I can contact him now?'

'Mr Davies has been away on holiday for the past two weeks and as he is working only part-time he will not be returning for another two – I believe he has gone abroad and will not be back for some time. I'm sorry I don't have a number where he can be contacted. Can I help you at all?'

'I'm interested in smoke-detection equipment,' replied Adrian, his mind racing to keep the conversation going, 'and I remember Mr Davies saying that he was engaged in detection equipment and I wondered if he could help.'

'That's not really our line, but I'll put you through to one of our sales staff and see if he can help you.'

After a short time the telephone on the other end was picked up by an adenoidal-voiced man who announced himself as 'West'. He understood that Mr Franklin had wanted to speak to Mr Davies about smoke detectors.

'Yes,' Adrian replied, 'I met him about two years ago on a plane and he gave me his card. Now I'm looking for smoke-detection equipment and it occurred to me he might be able to advise or even supply.'

The person at the other end of the telephone hesitated. 'Are you sure it was two years ago? Mr Davies has only been here three months.'

Adrian swallowed. 'Come to think of it, it wasn't all that long ago – I meet so many people, you know.' It was not convincing and he knew it, but the subject was harmless enough so the salesman wasn't on his guard.

'I should try Chubb,' he said. 'There's bound to be an office or agent near you. They have a division dealing with smoke detection – frankly, it's not our field at all.'

'As a matter of interest,' Adrian asked quietly, 'What does your company make?'

'Actually, we don't manufacture as such. We import components, mainly from the Far East and then adapt them for specific functions all over Europe. We have detection equipment for locating pipes underground, for water and for metal. We don't touch security systems – like burglar alarms, airport security scanning, fire alarms etc.'

'When you see Mr Davies, do give him my regards,' Adrian remarked. 'My name is Franklin, but he probably won't remember me.'

'Probably won't even remember me.' joked West. 'After a holiday in North Africa he'll probably forget to come down to Devon.'

Adrian's mind raced. 'I know North Africa well – what part did he visit?' The reply caused him to pause. He pulled himself up sharply – he must ask about the car.

'Probably too relaxed to even contemplate the four-hour drive to Plymouth,' he ventured, thinking it sounded hollow.

'He doesn't drive – finds it tiring, he says. He usually comes down by train or plane. That's part of his agreement, I understand. Still, we need his talent. He's an amazing technician – it's a pity he isn't here now.'

Adrian thanked Mr West, and put down the receiver. 'So Tunisia again,' he murmured, and Lorna raised her eyebrows questioningly. Adrian sipped his gin and tonic. 'I'm going down to Plymouth – can I take your car in the morning?'

Lorna nodded. 'For Christ's sake take it easy,' she said. 'I've a nasty feeling you are on to something rather unpleasant, to say the least.'

The clock struck ten and they both decided to retire early so Adrian could leave early for the 250-mile drive.

7

Steve Smyley, the other member of the unholy trinity who had dined at Los Monteros, let himself into his apartment on the seafront at Marbella. He had every reason to feel pleased with himself. He had made the hour-and-a-half car trip down from Gibraltar to visit the duty-free shops of that remnant of the British empire. His ambitions, however, rose higher than getting goods at a lower price by avoiding tax; his achievement was not paying for them at all. Now, as he put his newly acquired contraband in his wall safe, the owner of a duty-free watch shop in Gibraltar was trying to puzzle out what had happened to six Rolex watches, each valued at between £3,000 and £5,000, whilst the local police were going through the shop for fingerprints.

From his wall safe Steve withdrew four packages, each containing 150,000 pesetas – a fee to Mr Royce Rollason for arranging for the shopkeeper to be away, supplying full details of the safe from the installation company and arranging for an employee of the security firm to ensure that the alarm in the shop had a technical fault.

He drove over to Royce's villa and, after a few words, handed over the packages to his consultant. Royce opened the packages and, after counting them, remarked gruffly. ' 'Ow much is that in real money?'

'About three thousand nicker,' came the reply.

Royce pulled back a wall tile, exposing a small metal flap

and dropped the four packages in there. He saw the reaction on Steve's face.

'Never, ever get ideas, my boy – not on my property. You might be the smartest con on the coast, but touch my manor and I'll 'ave your balls for cocktail olives with my evening vodka.'

Steve smiled. 'You know me, Roycie – I know my place.'

Even with his record of violence, for which he had spent two long stints in Parkhurst, Steve wouldn't tangle with Royce Rollason.

'Want to know how it went?' he asked.

'Nope,' replied Royce. 'S'long as you pays me my money and you make sure there's no line on me, I don't give a shit. Now I've got a little job for you.'

Steve sat up like an alert kestrel. Indeed, with his wide eyes and sharp nose, he resembled a bird.

Royce poured himself a drink and, without asking what he wanted, poured one for Steve and another for Tony, whom he called in from the kitchen.

'Tell 'er to stay out,' he said, and Tony returned to the kitchen to tell the Filipina girl that she should not come into the room while they were talking.

All three sat around the glass-topped table and Royce briefed his henchmen.

'That Charlie – 'e's up to something and I want to know what,' he started. He went over the unlikely association with the German woman, his boat in Puerto Banus harbour for some time, the panels in the boat. 'And,' he went on, ''e owes a lot of money to the boat repair people – that's why they stopped work and 'e took on this Pedro geezer. 'E's after money, quick, and it's always been big money, I give 'im that. Not that 'e's been that successful. I wanna know what 'e's doing – and you are gonna find out.'

Twenty minutes later, when Ella Grieb answered a ring to her door, she was catapulted down the corridor by a man with a bird-like face whilst a short dark man with a toothbrush moustache closed the door quietly.

Ella could hardly breathe. The hand on her throat was pushing her against the wall and the picture behind her seemed to be forcing itself through her skull.

As the hand slightly released she croaked, 'What do you want?'

'Where's Charlie?' asked Bird Face. As he saw the question cross her face he spoke louder. 'Charlie or whatever you call him – your smoothie boyfriend – where is he?'

Ella felt sick with fear. This was like a dreadful scene she had read about – it couldn't be real. 'Can I sit – just let me sit,' she whispered.

Bird Face pulled her away from the wall and pushed her into an armchair. She sat down so rapidly that the chair moved backwards on its castors on the polished tile floor and the back of the chair hit the sideboard.

'Well, where is he – where's Charlie?'

'He's gone – he went away – yesterday morning – I've no idea.'

Steve put his fist to her face but Tony stepped forward smartly. 'Why don't you let her talk, you clown. With all your brute force and bloody ignorance you won't find out a thing. You don't have to believe her, but let her talk.'

Ella's throat was like sandpaper and she asked for a glass of water. Tony went into the kitchen and came back with the water. Ella gulped it and broke into a fit of coughing. When she recovered, she told them, 'What I am going to tell you is true – absolutely true.'

* * *

'That's all I know, I swear it – I've told you everything.' Ella was shaking with fear. What would happen to her now?

The two men pulled at their cigarettes and gazed at her. Both thought the same – the story was too convincing to be made up by a terrified woman on the spur of the moment.

Steve picked up a sheet of paper on the writing desk by the picture window. 'You been writing to him?' he asked.

'No – it's to my son,' she replied.

'Is he around – is he in on all this?' grunted Tony.

'No,' she sighed, 'he works in Hamburg. He's a jeweller and he hasn't been down here for over a year and he's never met Henry.'

'Let's call him Charlie, shall we?' and Tony placed the photocopy of the passport in front of her. 'Charlie Singer, and, as they say in the Sunday papers, he has a history – five years for fraud and one or two for little misdemeanours as well, I believe.'

'All right then, Charlie,' said Ella. 'But Franz, my son, doesn't even know of anyone living here. His father, my husband, died nearly two years ago and I've not wanted him to know of anyone else in my life unless – well, unless it was permanent.'

'I'm going to call up Royce,' said Tony. 'I want to know what the hell we do now. Mind if I use your phone?' he said mockingly.

Ella didn't reply. she had a new deep worry – Bird Face was still holding her letter to Franz, and although she couldn't remember the wording, it made reference to the matter which had triggered off this whole saga. A look of relief swept over her as she remembered that she had written in German. Neither of these two yobbos could read German, surely – probably illiterate in their native English.

Tony stood by the writing desk with the telephone receiver to his ear. 'Christ's sake answer, Royce. Hullo? Christ, go and fetch him – in the bleeding pool is he? Well, tell him to hurry. It's urgent.' His eyes turned on the letter and he picked it up. 'What did you say that place was called – you know, the island?'

Ella faltered. 'Er – the island?'

'Yes, the bloody island off Africa or something – what's its bloody name?'

'Djerba,' Ella answered. 'D-J-E-R-B-A.'

'You said your son wasn't in it – but this place Dee-gerba – that's got something to do with him, hasn't it?' One look at her face told him he was right. 'Now,' he said, 'there's a piece of paper and there's a pen. You sit right here – 'old on, Royce – yes, 'old on – you sit right there and put all that in English.

If you try any tricks – and my friend Royce speaks German – then I promise you no one will want to look at your face again. Get me?'

'What's going on?' Royce's voice was irritated. 'What the 'ell you talking about, me speaking German, you stupid bugger?'

Tony turned his attention to the telephone. 'Now get an earful of this,' he started. The telephone call lasted 15 minutes.

'So Charlie's turned treasure 'unter,' Royce finally said. ' 'Ow he found this bird we don't know and it don't much matter. Now read me what she's written down.'

'Why don't you come around here and see for yourself?' said Tony. But Royce's 'Not bleedin' likely!' eliminated any idea of that. Of course, it flashed through his mind, Royce dealt with trouble with a long, sterilised pole these days.

Tony grabbed the sheet of paper on which Ella had written a translation and read it slowly into the telephone.

' "Dear Franz. This is such a difficult letter to write – please sit down and read it carefully. I thought about telephoning you to discuss my difficult situation, but I thought I would get lost for words. Better, I thought, to lay it down in writing. Since Father died – it seems in many ways longer than two years – I have become immensely lonely, particularly as I live in an area which isn't even my homeland. I met a number of certainly nice people but a woman on her own is always a . . . " '

Tony looked up at Ella. 'What's the blank for?'

'I don't know the English word. It is someone who is the only single person in a party and so stands out as a loner.'

Tony passed this on to Royce.

'Wallflower,' Royce told him.

Tony read on.

' "Anyway, about two months ago I met a charming Englishman, just a little younger than me – he said he had private means and is a writer. He spent most of his time doing up a yacht he has, moored at Puerto Banus – you know, where we took you and Isabel to dinner. Henry and I met at a dinner party given by the Hutchisons. To cut a long story short, we went places together and had dinner and lunch out frequently. The more I knew him the more I liked him. He had had an interesting life – serving in the Coldstream Guards in England – it's one of the top regiments. After a while, Henry came to stay here and I wouldn't have agreed to that if I didn't think we had the basis of a lasting relationship. I was very happy and I thought your father would have liked that. I hope you don't think badly of me.

' "Now, this is what worries me. One evening we went out to dinner at Los Monteros – you remember that place? Henry commented on the Fatima brooch your father gave me and I told him all about Djerba – stupid of me but I did. Well, all went well until the end of the meal, when a most revolting-looking man, a real thug who looked totally out of place in a super hotel..." '

Royce said something indistinguishable into the telephone.

' "... came across to our table and called Henry 'Charlie'. He said something about 'keeping clean' and then went out. Henry was petrified – I'd never seen him look like that. When I asked who the man was, he just said he was someone he'd known a long time ago. Driving back that evening he hardly spoke and when we arrived home I saw him look out behind the curtains as if he was frightened of being followed. Then next day we were talking about the subject of your father's action in the Western Desert, and very foolishly I was persuaded to show him the notebooks. He was very interested and asked a lot of questions, but I was still upset by the meeting with that dreadful man and puzzled by him being called Charlie something – I think it was Singer. Because I was worried I didn't tell him about your Fatima File – just as well as it turns out.

' "So worried was I that I called Uncle Jimmy – he's now retired from the army and spends his time doing useful things. I asked him about Henry Southon. He did some checking and called back to say that there had been such an officer but he was killed in South Africa in a motor accident some time back. I was really worried but I never mentioned it to Henry.

' "Then this morning I went shopping..." '
And here the letter ended.

Tony looked up at Ella. 'What went wrong here?'

Ella's fear was slowly turning to anger at the thought that her letter was the public knowledge of yobbos. 'I didn't have time to finish writing – you grabbed the letter from me. That's what happened.'

'Well, tell me, bloody tell me what 'appened,' he said, 'and speak in the telephone so my boss can hear.'

Ella took the receiver. 'Henry was missing when I came back from the market yesterday morning. I didn't think much of it – I had taken the car so I imagined he had gone for a walk or something. He usually waits for me to come back with the car and then he uses it to go to Puerto Banus. Anyway, at midday I decided he had become tired of waiting for the car and had taken a taxi to the boat – although it was strange he hadn't left a note. Last evening there was still no sign so I drove down to Puerto Banus – down to his mooring. His boat, the *L'Anticipation* – had gone. Anyway, I came back here and waited until two in the morning before I went to bed. There seemed no point in calling the police. They would say he had probably just gone fishing. I'm sure he hadn't because he said he wouldn't put to sea until all the work was done. This morning I got up at seven. I'd hardly slept at all, and I went to see if he had taken any of his belongings. He had taken a few things, pullovers etc. but it's difficult to check.

'I went shopping, but before I did so I went to Banco Atlantico to cash a cheque as the Hypermarket doesn't accept cheques. To my surprise the manager asked me if I was expecting funds. I didn't know what he meant at first but then he told me that 250,000 pesetas were withdrawn the previous day on an Al Portador cheque. I had made it out ready to give to the man who installed the new pool filtration, stupid of me – Al Portador or bearer cheques are common in Spain. The clerk had asked Henry, for that is who presented the cheque, how I was and he had told them I was ill with flu.'

The strain took over and Ella burst into floods of tears.
Royce said something and Tony turned to Ella.

'What's that about the Fatima file?'

'It's Franz's notes on the Tunisian adventures. He called it after an Arab religious figure – a form of reference.'

Tony conveyed the message to Royce and then listened hard whilst the big man spoke. He turned to Steve.

'Royce says I have to go down to Puerto Banus to see if the boat and Charlie are still there. You have to stay here and make sure she doesn't run off. Keep a close eye on her.' Tony put down the receiver and Steve sat down to wait for a telephone call from Hamburg which Royce had said would come later.

* * *

The Wessingstrasse isn't the most salubrious district of Hamburg. Dingy, paint-starved houses line up in dark streets which back off Number 3 dock. It isn't far to walk to the Eros Centre in the Reeperbahn, which is just as well as it is in the flesh trade of that notorious street that many of the inhabitants of Wessingstrasse earn their living directly or indirectly.

Karl Frohlich was no exception to the rule. His squalid house belied the fact that he had amassed a considerable fortune, mainly by supplying young boys to tired business executives whose taste deviated from that which society judges normal. When the telephone rang he imagined that this was just another enquiry and he was surprised to hear the voice of Royce Rollason. He felt a cold chill at the back of his neck, for he well remembered what had happened to a young Dutch seaman he had introduced to Royce. The crazy fool had tried to double-cross Royce. Van Smit's wristwatch had been handed in by a man walking his dog on Luneburg Heide, but the police had investigated in vain. Five years later, Van Smit was still listed as a missing person.

Karl asked Royce how he liked life in retirement in the sun but Royce cut him short. He was in no mood for pleasantries and he thought Karl a dirty little rat for living off his particular trade. Royce knew, however, that he liked the occasional bit of excitement and also owed him a favour. Had it not been for Royce's personal intervention with a certain hotel manager with a keenness to wipe out immorality in his hotel, Karl would even now, after three years, be languishing behind bars.

He listened carefully to what Royce had to say and noted down the Malaga telephone number he was given. Then he put on his coat and went out. It wasn't raining, but a raincoat can conceal bulky items and Karl had good reason to keep a long bar device out of sight as he hailed a taxi to take him to the fashionable district of the city, stopping on the way to pick up three more passengers.

Wilhem Lorke yawned and turned over his copy of the Hamburg evening paper. He had planned to go out for the evening with a couple of friends, but the other nightwatchman had gone down with flu so he had to take over the desk. He had been night porter at 144 Liebigstrasse for six years now – not a bad job for a retired bus driver but a bit boring. He had got to know the people in the flats over the years – rich people, but in the main they were agreeable, particularly over Christmas, when he reckoned that a minimum of a thousand marks would come his way.

He put down his paper as three young men in jeans walked past him and bade him good evening. He called to them as they walked over to the lift; as they ignored him, he walked briskly towards them.

'Excuse me, you should come to reception and I'll call up whoever you want to see. Who are you visiting.' he enquired.

'It's none of your business but I'll tell you just the same. It's Mr Welker and we're friends of his – just good lovely friends of lovely Mr Welker,' said one sarcastically.

Wilhem walked back to his desk and the three stood before him, in line and close together.

As Wilhem called Mr Welker's third-floor flat, a bull-necked man wearing a fawn raincoat opened the main door and took advantage of the cover afforded by the three youths to make his way to the lift. He pressed the button for the eighth floor.

There was no reply from Mr Welker's flat. The boys left and walked home. An easy assignment for 50 marks each.

As he walked down the corridor of the eighth floor, Frohlich took a careful look at the flat doors. They were of standard construction. As they did not have a peephole, he would not have to use the small piece of plastic he carried to distort the image. But there would, almost certainly, be a door security chain. He stopped at 87 and removed the long bolt cutters from under his coat.

He rang the bell and the television inside was turned down. A voice asked who it was and he called, 'Herr Grieb, you should see to your car. Your lights have been left on in the garage.'

There was the sound of a bolt being drawn and the door opened 12 centimetres – the extent of the security chain.

The chain snapped like a piece of cotton and the banged door threw Franz Grieb backwards. In a second he received an excruciatingly painful blow in the groin from the bolt cutters, and as he doubled up, a heavy fist hit him on the back of the neck. The world swirled about him and when he recovered his senses he was bound to a chair and blindfolded. A guttural voice was demanding the file – the Fatima file. Wiry and strong though he was, Franz Grieb was in no condition to put up a fight.

'I don't know what you're talking about,' he replied, and immediately a fist punched him and blood trickled down his face. Frohlich looked at him – good job he had hit him hard early on. Royce hadn't told him what a fine physique his intended victim had. If they had met on even terms Karl Frohlich would have had a very hard time indeed.

Royce had neglected to tell Frohlich something else – that Grieb was a jeweller by profession, and jewellers are usually protected by security systems, not only at their business premises but also at home, where they keep unusual pieces they have collected, as well as work that they bring home for detailed attention. Franz Grieb was no exception. Thinking quickly, he told Frohlich that he thought the file might be in the safe, he wasn't sure.

'Key,' grunted Frohlich, and Grieb indicated a chain in his pocket and told him it was the middle-sized brass-coloured one. What he didn't say was that unless the alarm system on top of the picture above was turned off first, there could be interesting consequences.

On the ground floor Wilhem Lorke jumped as the buzzer went off and he quickly dialled the emergency police service – a call which was immediately relayed to a station less than a kilometre away.

It took less than five minutes for four uniformed officers, equipped with Wilhem's pass key, to be at the door of 87. This time it was Karl Frohlich's turn to have the disadvantage of surprise, and when he was led away with his hands cuffed together, Franz Grieb sat down to make a statement to one of the officers.

Some 40 minutes later, as he was finishing his report and the officer was clarifying a few details, the telephone rang and Officer Kohl took it. It was his sergeant at police headquarters. Officer Kohl took a few notes and, holding the telephone away from his ear, he read out a number which had been found on the prisoner.

Franz Grieb went white. 'Yes, I do know it – it's my mother.'

The bureaucracies of countries may seem to the outsider to be loosely linked, if linked at all, with or without the European Community.

The reality is different and probably the best example of close international co-operation is the police.

Within an hour the Hamburg police had called Madrid with a full report. Madrid alerted Malaga, and in turn Malaga relayed the message to the small station in Marbella.

The Spanish love of noise was subdued in this case and any casual observer would hardly have noticed the six armed police who took up position around the Villa Lava in the Calle Clipper just off the Avenida Huerta Belon. Silently they moved into the neat garden and listened at the open window. One officer moved to the door. The lock proved to be a FAC

– a strong security device consisting mainly of a tensile steel bolt operated by a double lock. The officer whispered to one of his minions, who came forward with a Pucho. This handy little tool is operated like an anti-tank bazooka from the shoulder. Instead of firing a projectile, however, it gives the kick of 30 tormented mules, taking the door off at its hinge end rather than the lock side.

The door flew open with a noise of a thunderbolt and five armed police were through the door within three seconds.

Steve squealed in fear – he never did trust police, but police from another country, and with guns, made the little man sick with fright. He would tell – yes, he would go quietly.

Twenty minutes later his small apartment was turned over to reveal 15 Rolex watches, two million pesetas in rolls, a diamond pendant and earrings which had been reported missing several months before, and other items which shops in the Marbella area were interested in recovering.

At the police headquarters, aided by an interpreter, he told all – all except one thing: the involvement with Royce. A few years in a Spanish jail was a threat enough to make him sweat with fear – but one day he would come out, and the thought of having to face a vengeful Royce made other punishment pale into insignificance. About Royce he would say nothing – the anti-Royce Rollason club was very tiny indeed and its membership was shrinking.

* * *

As Adrian refuelled at the Exeter bypass filling station, he reflected that Ian had called here for the same purpose. He wondered how Ian must have felt, knowing that he was living on borrowed time.

He drove on, deep in thought. It is amazing how on long journeys, without the interruption of passengers, the mind flicks from subject to subject, he thought. He found himself going over the events following his return from Rome. Rome – it seemed a decade since he walked down the Via Veneto to buy the blouson jacket he now wore. Rome had been the big escape from reality. Then he thought of Ann ... When he told her he was going away for a long break she had commented acidly that he wouldn't escape, because he had to take himself with him wherever he went. At the time he had seen this as a cutting comment, but looking back he felt that, like most women, she had to defend her actions – actions over which she was unsure. To hit out at him somehow strengthened her belief in what she was doing in starting a new life with another man. Adrian never understood women and was readily prepared to admit the fact. He suddenly wondered whether Lorna had told her mother what had happened. Maybe Ann could throw some light – Ian had maybe even contacted her. Ian and Ann had always had a very good relationship, and he might, once he had been told the facts about his health, have called her. Adrian reflected that Lorna had never spoken much about her mother since his return, perhaps to save his feelings. He made a mental note to talk to Ann when he returned to London.

As he turned off the A38 to drive into Plymouth, the Fiat distributor stood out on the roadside and Adrian gave a sigh of relief that he wouldn't have to search the city to find it. He parked, and walked through the showrooms, carefully studying a Fiat. A young man with an impish look and jet-black hair asked him if he could help, and Adrian asked a number of questions about the car: what extras were included in the price, likely consumption figures and how soon delivery would be.

'It depends on the colour,' the young man replied.

Adrian saw his chance. 'I'm not sure,' he replied, 'but I know my wife likes the colour of the car you supplied to a Miss Silvester. I've not seen the car myself, but I remember my wife saying she thought it was most attractive.'

The young man replied that he hadn't actually sold that car and didn't know who had, but could soon look up the details in the records. They walked together into the office, and the salesman flicked through the card index.

'Yes, here it is,' he said. 'The car which was bought by Mrs E. Silvester of Mary Tavy. It was Rialto Red.'

He put the card down on the table and offered Adrian a cigarette. Adrian declined. As the salesman lit up, Adrian read the card on the desk: Mrs E. Silvester, Moor View Cottage, Mary Tavy. Cheque number..., Lloyds, Epping, Mr R. Davies.

He collected the promotional literature, thanked the young man profusely and said he would discuss the matter with his wife. The young man saw him out – his expression clearly showing his uncertainty as to whether this was a really keen punter or what the motor trade knows as a 'tyre kicker'.

Adrian Franklin strolled across the Hoe at Plymouth and wondered what truth there was in the story of Drake insisting on finishing his game of bowls before setting sail against the Armada. How long ago was that? 1588 or 1586 – somewhere around there anyway. It was probably just another historical distortion; what he probably said was, 'Christ, stick those bowls in with the canon balls. We need all the ammunition we can lay our fucking hands on.' Adrian smiled as the thought went through his mind. History and reality – a big divide.

He sat on a bench and looked out to sea. The journey hadn't really revealed much so far. So Mrs Silvester – Mrs, not Miss, he mused – had bought a red Fiat in Plymouth, but so bloody what? What was interesting was that she had a house in Mary Tavy, wherever that was. It sounded local somehow, and he might as well go and look. Also, what about going to the detector company and speaking with the nasal Mr West? That might be a bit too obvious, might create suspicion. Anyway, he could drive by and talk to the receptionist. He knew Mr Davies was away, so he would pretend to be a rep and ask to speak to him.

8

'Then it's a deal – we'll drink to it,' shouted the old man. 'Juanito, bring up some more *Caña* – we are going to need it!'

Alfonso was happy – he had hoped that his elderly father-in-law would come up with such an offer and in fact, he had asked Erika about it. Maybe she had surreptitiously put it into his head; she had a way of guiding her father in his decisions.

He looked back over the past years. Testing people's eyes in the Rosario Clinic had never held much appeal; in fact, he had found it downright dull. His conscription into the army during the Malvinas conflict had been a welcome relief, although being taken prisoner by the British and fighting off the bitter cold hadn't been much fun. Still, when hostilities ceased he felt a career as an army officer would be a good way to earn a reasonable living with some travel and good company. Erika hadn't seen it that way and found life in married quarters didn't offer the rural freedom she loved so much. She went back to her father and they had a fortnightly reunion either at the military base 200 kilometres away, or at the ranch. Alfonso was the first to admit it wasn't satisfactory. Now the old man wanted to take a back seat, and he could be with Erika, even if the children were far away. Paco was at the University of Madrid and came back every summer to Argentina. Maria at 17 was a year younger and a student nurse in Buenos Aires. They were developing their own lives, their own careers, and one day Paco would qualify as a doctor and Maria would become a career nurse or have a family.

The old man filled Alfonso's glass. 'You'll be much happier here – nothing like an open-air life. No commuting to the town every day, wasting so much time and petrol on the roads, eh!'

Alfonso laughed in agreement. Yes, he was happy. It was a good deal all round. The old man was well into his eighties now and couldn't go on running the ranch for ever. He relied heavily on his chief rancher and chargehand but they weren't members of the family and could be an idle bunch if they weren't managed. Managing the ranch wasn't too unfamiliar to Alfonso; after all, he had been helping out for the last five years on his weekends at home, and especially when Erika and her father had taken Paco into Buenos Aires during his summer vacation. He had enjoyed being left in command. Now he realised that what was a temporary break was going to be full-time employment. He had a strong feeling he was going to like it.

The sun slipped out of the sky and turned the pampas a dull red, as if the hacienda was on fire. He lit a cigarette and walked across the large terrace to the open double doors. A large dose of laughing from inside told him that Erika and her father were pleased at the new arrangement. He drained his glass and joined them.

Rounding up a few thousand head of cattle is no job for an amateur, especially when they are in a huge plain with no protective corral for the herdsmen. The object of the exercise, which every movie portrays as simple, is in fact a highly skilled operation which if left in the hands of actors would soon lead to a high rise in the Hollywood mortality rate. A stampede of cattle can be lethal, as Alfonso Fernandez knew well.

It took a couple of hours before Alfonso and his three ranchers had penned the cattle according to size, and he felt he needed a beer badly. Within an hour three trucks would be arriving from Rosario to load the beasts for their last journey. He couldn't help feeling attached to the animals and regretted that their free lives should end in this way. Perhaps this is where his father-in-law had the edge on him. He could detach himself from sentiment.

The Toyota appeared in the distance, a solitary vehicle in a wide expanse of flat grassland bisected by an earth track, the wheels throwing up clouds of dust behind it, the result of four weeks without a drop of rain.

The three Argentine ranchers touched their hats in the respect especially reserved for the *jefe's* wife. They liked Señora Fernandez and they appreciated that in the back of the jeep would be a couple of cases of beer with a sack of salt and ice on top.

It took Alfonso only a few seconds to realise something was wrong – he knew his wife so well that he often said he could read her thoughts. As the men unloaded the beer and the bread rolls, Erika drew him aside.

'Big Jake brought the mail this morning.'

Alfonso nodded apprehensively. This was the way the mail came, by a co-operative trucker who came past the hacienda every week. He collected the mail for the Fernandez family from the post office at El Cigarelle and received a few large beers in return.

'Go on – what's up?' he urged her.

'It's Paco. You remember he bought a motor bike to go from his room to the university? Apparently a car went through a red light in the city and...' her voice faltered. 'Anyway, he's in Madrid General Hospital – had a good deal of surgery.' She passed the letter to Alfonso, who read it silently.

'Thank God he's alive.'

He looked up to see a cloud of dust on the savannah. The trucks were arriving.

* * *

'Of course I can manage – I've run this bloody place for years.' The old man couldn't help but chuckle despite the tense atmosphere. 'You two must go where you should be – in Madrid with the boy. We can afford it, it's been a good year.

There's no one like family when you're ill – he's a long way from home, and I know he'll improve rapidly if you are about.'

Erika and Alfonso nodded in unison. They didn't like to point out to the veteran that he was older now and that he might find the physical strain of controlling the ranch, together with running the house, just a trifle more than he remembered. He wanted them to go, they badly wanted to be with Paco, and Paco would want them to be there.

Two days later the blue and white fuselage of the Aerolinas Argentinas 747 jet lifted off the runway at Buenos Aires airport and pointed its nose to a cloudless sky en route to Europe.

* * *

The factory was not in Plymouth itself but in a middle-sized industrial estate at Plympton, about three miles out. Adrian found it a more impressive building than he had anticipated. On arrival he asked to speak to Mr Davies. The petite ash-blonde receptionist told him what he already knew – that Mr Davies was away and wouldn't be back for some time.

'Come to think of it,' Adrian stepped in, 'he did tell me last time we met a few weeks ago that he was going on holiday – to Tunisia, I believe.'

'I really don't know, except that it was all rather sudden, him going off like that. Still, as he's part-time I suppose he can take his holidays when he wants. I wish I could.'

'Your day will come,' commented Adrian, thinking as he said it that the remark was somewhat hollow, but he wanted time to play along. 'Anyway, I suppose the company will want him back soon, with all the research he's doing for you.'

'Oh, I don't know. I think his latest project is nearly finished – my boyfriend's got one, you know.'

'One what?' he enquired.

'A metal detector. Mr Davies was working on a new model, sells for ever such a lot – nearly four hundred pounds. I got one through the company for Derek, for two hundred and eighty. Mind you, he paid – I haven't got that sort of money hanging around. We make all kinds of items and some go for thousands of pounds – the kind professionals use.'

Adrian asked her if she had a brochure and, after vanishing into a side room, she came out with a glossy piece of promotional literature. Thanking her profusely and getting directions for Mary Tavy, he returned to the car and drove back on the motorway, skirting Plymouth and making for the Tavistock road.

Mary Tavy is a small village on the A386, nestling in the lee of Dartmoor, which almost pushes its feet into the village itself. Apart from a post office, a shop, a coach garage and a filling station, there is little else to Mary Tavy, which acquired its strange name from St Mary's Church on the river Tavy.

After enquiring at the post office, Adrian found that Moor View Cottage was almost facing him, so he walked round, making himself as inconspicuous as possible. The cottage seemed unoccupied but he didn't want to be caught out by knocking on the door and being confronted by Betty, who would immediately recognise him. He was pondering his next move when the answer was presented to him. An elderly lady, dressed in pale brown and with a hat resembling a beehive, made her way slowly down the road edging the bottom of the garden. Her slow speed was partly due to age and partly because her brown and white mongrel seemed possessed of an extremely weak bladder. Adrian bade her good afternoon and, like many lonely people, she seized this opportunity to have a chat.

' 'Tis rainin' up at Princetown, they say. 'Tis funny round 'ere – one place 'tis fine like now; few miles away 'tis pourin' down. 'Tis the moor what does it – the clouds 'ave to rise up over the moor, they say.'

'Well, you certainly live in a lovely area. I'm a stranger round here myself, but I'd love to get to know it better. Maybe there's a cottage I could rent in the summer?'

'There's lots of 'em, but they gets booked up early. Lots of London folks buys 'em up for weekend 'omes an' lets 'em out. Makes life difficult for locals...'

Adrian turned to Moor View Cottage. 'This is a lovely little place with apparently no one living there. Is that for rent?'

The old lady chuckled. 'Well, you might say so. Belongs to old Mr Parker but 'e baint usin' it – 'e's a guest of 'er Majesty for the present.'

Adrian missed the point. 'I'm sorry – Her Majesty?'

'Yass. You know – up at Princetown, the 'otel where you don't 'ave to pay the bill. Mind you,' she went on, ' 'is daughter an 'er friend, nice gentleman 'e is, met 'im in the post office, they come down sometimes.'

At Adrian's question, she replied that they had been at the cottage for two nights and they came in a red car. Adrian had very little doubt that the 'nice gentleman' was Mr Davies.

Now he wanted time to think. He bade the old lady goodbye and turned the car towards the moor.

Adrian revelled at the beauty of the scenery as the car climbed the long hill out of Tavistock and towards the upland plateau of Dartmoor. He had heard it described in the travel books as 'Britain's last wilderness', but he had no idea how beautiful it was. He slowed to allow some wild ponies to cross the road, and marvelled at the uncomplicated lives that animals live. 'They have a lot to teach us,' he murmured to himself.

At Rundlestone the road, which had been a long, slow climb for many miles, dropped down a little and Adrian saw the grey, forbidding walls of Dartmoor prison to the right of the road. What a desolate spot in such a lovely setting, he thought. Incarceration in the middle of an expanse of freedom. He drove on, passing Two Bridges, until he spotted a sign to a hotel, with a long, tree-lined drive approach. That will do fine for tonight, he thought.

Adrian found that there were only seven guests that night as the season was reaching its end and, after bathing and changing, he came down to the bar. The barman, who turned out to own the place with his wife, informed him that they had a function that evening – the Prison Officers' Club were having a retirement party for one of their members.

The dining room was small and the eight prison officers (Adrian puzzled over the difference between warden and officer; probably, he assumed, they were the same – but 'officer' sounded more modern) seemed to be enjoying themselves and certainly liked the wine. The other six diners were residents, two elderly couples and one couple obviously on honeymoon.

After dinner, coffee and liqueurs were served in the lounge and Adrian found himself drawn into conversation with the prison officers' party. He had never met a prison officer in his life and was curious to know what kind of man took up this severe calling. To his surprise they were a friendly and extrovert bunch and he soon joined in a lively conversation about fishing – a subject on which he possessed no knowledge at all. It was, nevertheless, interesting to hear about it and he asked questions about fishing rights and seasons, which the prison officers were pleased to answer.

At an appropriate moment Adrian asked one officer, called Arthur McNally, about the prison – how on earth was it built there, when and why? Arthur was delighted to share his knowledge that the prison was built to house prisoners of war during the Napoleonic Wars. It closed in 1815 with the end of the war, but opened up again in 1850 for criminals – when Australia refused to take any more convicts deported from Britain. Not only had it survived, in 1985 it had been expanded and now housed over 700 inmates.

'But it's not top security, you know,' explained Arthur. 'They use the more modern places for that.'

Adrian felt that the time had come, helped along by a glass of vintage port, to put a specific point, even if he had to lie.

'My friend in London has an uncle who is one of your – er – customers,' he remarked casually. 'Name of Parker.'

'Nosey Parker,' commented Arthur. 'A right villain he is – a real con artist. I don't know how long he's in for but he's a real old lag. One of the best fences in the business, they say. Comes in and out, does old Nosey.' Then, as if realising that he had talked too much, he added hastily, 'Well, I'm not really supposed to ... Have another port.'

Adrian gladly accepted, and the conversation turned to snooker. A little later he went to bed. His room was large, with a double four-poster bed. He lay awake, with the moon shining in the window. Strange, he hadn't slept in a four-poster since he was on honeymoon with Ann, some 28 years or so ago. The honeymoon couple at dinner – they probably had a four-poster tonight, he thought. They had life before them, for better or for worse. How he regretted the way life had turned out for him. But you cannot live life in the past and wallow in regret – in any event, he had something important to tackle.

It was so quiet, so restful on the moor, he quickly fell asleep.

Adrian switched the car lights on just as he passed Heathrow. It had been a long drive and, although he had enjoyed the ten miles across the open road of Dartmoor, the rest had been motorway. He wished he had had more time to enjoy the trip and go by the more interesting minor roads.

At Blenheim Gardens he pulled into the residents' parking area and let himself into the house. The greeting from Sam was as if he had been away a year rather than a couple of days. Although he badly wanted to exchange information with Lorna, he accepted that would have to wait until Sam went to bed. Adrian asked Sam how he felt after his upset tummy of a few nights ago.

'I'm better now,' he answered proudly. 'The doctor came to see me. Have you brought me a present again?'

Lorna scolded him for being impolite and sat him down at his supper.

Twenty minutes later, Lorna announced that Sam was in bed and eager for a story. Adrian decided to tell his story of Dartmoor, of the wild ponies and how country folk put out cream for the pixies. He was busily sorting out the next stage of the story when he saw that Sam was asleep so, leaving the room quietly, he went downstairs to join Lorna. A large gin awaited him in his favourite glass and he helped himself to tonic.

Adrian recounted the story of his trip to Devon, the discovery at the garage that Betty had a house at Mary Tavy, the visit to the factory, and laid the metal detector brochure on the coffee table.

'Seems our friend Davies is almost through with this project,' he observed. He went on to describe his visit to the cottage and his talk with the prison officer at the hotel. 'Apparently Daddy Parker was a long-time bad boy and his daughter goes to visit him – his role in the twilight life of crime is that of a fence.'

A long silence followed and Adrian went over to the sideboard and poured himself another gin and tonic. 'Like another?' he asked Lorna.

She shook her head. 'No, I think the time's come for really clear thought,' she remarked. 'I've news for you.'

Adrian sat down. 'Shoot,' he said, lighting a cigarette.

Lorna leaned forward. 'Sam told you that Dr Solomon came to see him – well, that was the way it appeared. Actually, the doctor came to see me. Not that I'm ill,' she added quickly, 'but he has been thinking a lot about Ian's disappearance. When we went to see him in his surgery, he was taken aback that Ian hadn't told me about his illness, and I looked so stunned that he thought it would be unkind to say more. He wanted me to have time to absorb the deadly news, so he comforted me and left it at that. However, there was something he held back and he's been brooding on it. He telephoned and said he would like to come and give Sam a check over. I told him it wasn't necessary, but he said he was passing by.'

Adrian's face was full of anticipation. 'Yes – go on.'

'Well, it appears that a few hours after Ian heard the news, he rang Dr Solomon. He told him that he was desperately worried about my future and Sam's. Three months ago we had cashed in our life insurance to buy new furniture and generally pay off a few outstanding debts. We had planned to take out a new policy later this year and use Ian's pay rise to pay the premiums. However, at that time, and at the present for that matter, there is no insurance on Ian's life. He said he knew that either a medical examination would be necessary for a new policy, or he would have to give an undertaking that there was nothing wrong with him as far as he knew and he hadn't seen a doctor for some time. Either way it amounted to the same: any insurance would be invalid. However, he asked Dr Solomon to...' Lorna hesitated, '... give him a clean bill of health for insurance purposes. He pointed out that if he hadn't complained of pain it was most unlikely that a routine medical examination would show up liver cancer – anyway, that was his view.'

Lorna paused and changed her mind about the drink. Adrian poured her a double.

'Dr Solomon refused – he had to. He explained to me that he would be putting his whole career in jeopardy if he, as he put it "cooked the books". Ian apparently got rather excited – I imagine a bit abusive – but Solomon – he's rightly named, that one – was wise enough to realise that Ian was under severe strain and suggested he give himself a few days' holiday to straighten things out. Ian said he didn't want to add to debts by living it up in the...' Lorna's voice faltered, '... time left to him.'

The grandfather clock struck nine, creating a necessary break. When it stopped, Adrian looked straight at Lorna.

'Well, my love, another piece of the jigsaw emerges – all that we have to do is assemble the pieces and fit them together.'

'You mean motive,' said Lorna.

'Precisely,' he answered. 'Ian obviously had a lot of big debts about and was worried sick about how you would manage alone. Can you tell me what mortgage you have?'

Lorna told him and he gave a low whistle. 'Well, we do have a definite motive. Apparently Ian's first move was to ask Davies for money, but even if he had received an advance on sales it wouldn't have been enough to change the overall scenario. I thought Davies was lying on the phone; I disliked his superior attitude that he knew all the answers – but he may well have been telling the truth. Ian may have wanted money to finance a real "get-rich-quick" scheme. I have a feeling that Ian found the answer in the book which you saw he was reading so avidly. Tomorrow I'm going to be at the library all day and I'm going to study each page intently. There must be something I've missed.'

Adrian walked into the kitchen and came back with an ice tray. He plopped two large ice cubes into Lorna's glass and the same into his own. He swirled the ice around and around the glass.

'Lorna, I haven't spoken about this before – but, well since I came back from Rome we've never talked about your mother, and I thought about that in the car. I appreciate that you know how I feel – how terribly upset I still am – but I presume you are in touch with her and her – her friend. Have you spoken to her about Ian? Maybe he contacted her. They were always on good terms, weren't they?'

'Yes, very,' Lorna replied. 'They were close. When Ian had been away for a couple of days I rang Mum. Sam was at playgroup, and I drove over there and we had a coffee. She was as amazed as I was, indeed am. We talked about it all afternoon, but I think she had the opinion he was chasing some girl or other but didn't like to say it. She was full of ideas, she really tried hard to cast some light on the mystery. One of the suggestions she made was that a work colleague he plays snooker with every week – Pat Henderson – might have an idea, the sort of casual remark which might be made over a beer or two and a few frames of snooker. He always got on well with Pat, who is something to do with accounts. I was pretty upset talking about it and Mum suggested I call Pat from the study where her...' Lorna hesitated.

'Boyfriend,' interjected Adrian.

'OK, boyfriend, usually works when he's at home – he's a kind of journalist. Anyway, I made the call and Pat was ever so sympathetic, but apart from saying that Ian had complained about being unwell and saying the usual nonsense about winning the pools, he couldn't cast much light on the subject. He recalled they had discussed a lot of business, about budget cuts, when they last met. But Dad,' she added quietly, 'there was something odd – maybe I am losing my sense of proportion with all this – but there was something rather strange in that study. As I say, it's so small and it probably means nothing, but Ian always smokes Camel cigarettes – has done for years. The desk in the study was incredibly untidy, papers all over the place, but that's the way journalists work (I should know, I was once a secretary to one). Well, as I was speaking on the phone I saw a packet of Camel, nearly empty, just sticking out of some papers. It meant nothing then and means nothing now, but Ian hadn't been to the house for two months, possibly more. Surely they wouldn't still be there after so long if he had left them behind?'

'Of course,' Adrian put in, 'this journalist chap – whatever his name – could smoke them too. Did you see him there?'

'No, he was away on an assignment – anyway, it came up in conversation how he hates people smoking. Mum said she had stopped because of it.'

'Do you disbelieve your mother?' Adrian asked incredulously.

'Of course not,' she replied with alacrity. 'But it's just odd – it's not an everyday brand, is it?' Adrian shook his head. 'But if Mum says he wasn't there, he wasn't there. Anyway, she told me at the time Ian went off she was away for a couple of days on her book-illustrating work.'

'But he could have gone over without making a call first – that's his style – just dropped in. Did he have a key?'

'Yes,' Lorna replied. 'Well, he could have dropped in and killed time,' she swallowed at the significance of the word, 'and waited around.'

'True,' said Adrian, 'but I know Ian and he liked his privacy and respected other people's – he wouldn't go into someone's private study uninvited, whatever strain he was under. However, it's possible someone invited him in, the user of the study – your mother's friend – whatever is his name?'

'Henry – Henry Southon,' answered Lorna.

* * *

As soon as the library was open, on the stroke of ten, Adrian entered. He was the first customer and he made his way immediately to the History section with the subheading

'Military History'. To his dismay the book was missing and he mentally kicked himself. He should have retained it and paid the resulting fines, or renewed it.

The chubby-faced girl with the winged glasses was the epitome of a librarian. Adrian couldn't think of her in any other job. She checked her records – yes, the book was out on loan.

Adrian thought for a minute. 'Refresh my memory – who is the publisher?' he asked.

The librarian went back to her records and checked through. 'Youngman and Pearson.'

Adrian thanked her and went to the telephone directory. Sure enough, there it was: Youngman and Pearson, 17 Floral Street, WC1 – a short taxi ride from where he now was.

The offices of Youngman and Pearson were on the third floor of a modern block, close to Covent Garden. Adrian wondered how he could go about an errand of simply buying a book and at the same time speak to someone senior – particularly as he really hadn't formulated any questions.

He was fortunate. After describing what he wanted, the receptionist rang through for Mr Peter Bennett, a bright, immaculately dressed man in his early thirties. This was a small publishing company and it soon became apparent that Mr Bennett knew just about everything that was going on. This particular book, he explained, was being revised at the present moment and would soon be reissued. Adrian asked him the reason, and Mr Bennett took great pains to explain. He obviously loved books and anyone interested in them had his full attention.

'This book is one of three by Major General Peter Collingson. They sold well – war books do, as many retired people with time on their hands to read, like to relive the dramatic years of their lives, quite apart from youngsters who like to read factual action rather than fiction. We published the first of the books five years ago. The subject was about Market Garden in the battle for Arnhem, where the author commanded a squadron with General Horrocks, 30 Corps. It went well and we were pleased to follow it up shortly afterwards with a second book, on Operation Overlord – the D-Day landings.

'The following year came the third book, which we had had in manuscript form for some time. The subject was the Western Desert, but at the time of the action the author was only a young subaltern – probably early twenties or even late teens – so it was written very much from first-hand impression rather than any overall view. All his books were like that really, the various actions seen through the eyes of a young officer rather than an exact military history – not that any history is exact. The author really recounted his personal experience and impressions. We think that is what gave the books charm – you know, helping the reader to live the experience or to consider how his life was different in the same circumstances. It's better than strategy issued from the top.

'Anyway,' continued Mr Bennett, offering Adrian a cigarette and lighting one himself, 'we did get a certain amount of – not exactly criticism, but corrective comment. Collingson, even as a young officer, could have checked his facts better when he wrote a long time later. By the time he had reached senior rank he could have studied military records and checked his personal recollections and notes with published facts and by talking to colleagues.'

'Can you give an example?' Adrian interjected.

'Well,' continued Bennett, 'in the battle of Arnhem he was very muddled about divisions of the US Army and confused the dropping zones of certain units – even the names of senior officers. I can't be more precise than that because I am relying on what I myself recall when we set about revising the edition in the early part of last year. We were corrected by quite a number of letters – helpful letters – from informed people. Collingson himself had no objection to getting in advisers to get the facts right. I'm not suggesting it was full of errors, because it wasn't – I'm just saying that a few basic facts needed straightening out.'

Both of the first books had been corrected and were selling well, he explained. The third was just about to be republished but they had hit a bit of a snag. That particular book had been written with an adviser – a retired German colonel called Sneider, to get both sides of the picture. He had set about working on the manuscript correction when he fell ill and had to pass the whole exercise over to a friend. The author lived in Switzerland, and he and the newly appointed German checker didn't hit it off and there had been a certain amount of disagreement over facts, but they were hoping to have sight of a revised manuscript soon.

Mr Bennett stopped short, conscious that he had rambled on. Adrian felt a little uncomfortable in the silence which fell. He thanked Mr Bennett for all the help he had given, and asked for a copy of the current edition. Then he made his purchase and left.

So there was going to be a revised edition, he reflected in the taxi. How would that vary from the original, he wondered. But first to go over the original, step by step.

Mr Bennett greeted Adrian Franklin politely, yet his face showed the question he was longing to ask: 'Why this constant interest in a book – especially its background?' He was forming the impression that Franklin was using the background material for a novel of his own – if so, why not be open about it and then arrangements could be made.

Adrian had decided, to make a free explanation to Peter Bennett, and now he painstakingly went through the whole story of Ian Lacey's disappearance.

'And how can I help you?' Peter Bennett asked, when Adrian had finished.

'It isn't what was contained in the book that was important,' he explained. 'That's what has led me up the garden path up to now. I believe it was something which was left out. The margin notes in the copy which Ian had, and God knows where that is now, were corrections. As in the Arnhem book, the author and his adviser were correcting points which they had discovered by investigation or, more likely, from letters sent by interested readers. The numbers in the margin puzzled me but I now firmly believe that these referred to lengthy letters. Obviously they couldn't put the whole letter of comment in the margin but they could put the letter reference. So my question is, were the letters numbered for reference?'

Peter Bennett left the room, asking Adrian to help himself to coffee. He returned with three files and opened up the first. He thumbed through quickly with just an occasional murmur.

'You are right,' he confirmed. 'All the letters are numbered. It seems sure that when a correction from a letter was planned, the letter number was placed in the original book margin. Look – here, for example, in *Normandy Landings* there is a marginal note against the statement "The Omaha beach proved more difficult, mainly because of the fact that Bradley had arranged for the landing craft to discharge some 12 miles offshore in heavy seas. The decision was a strange one and in speaking with the commanding officer afterwards I learned that a mistake had been made in assessing the distance. It is certain that Bradley had been misinformed."'

'Now look over here in the file,' said Bennett, 'and check this against letter 4 – the number in the margin note. It says: 'Dear Sir, I have just been reading *Normandy Landings* by Major General Collingson. I was an officer in the battalion to which the writer refers. I do not believe that Bradley had been misinformed. What I do say was that the poor weather conditions, particularly visibility, must have led to a misassessment of the distance. The defensive fire was extremely strong and engineers had not been able to clear the beach of mines. The inference in the book..."

'So,' said Peter Bennett, 'there's your answer. The margin notes by the author or his adviser do most certainly refer to letters. Not all letters have been acted upon. The checker took photocopies of the letters he wanted, and then related them to the existing text.

'The problem with the Western Desert book is that we do not have the book with the notes and numbers – for your vanishing Mr Lacey had the copy which had been put out for correcting, although how he got it I can't make out at the moment. All we have are the letters and the numbers.'

'Is there any possibility I could borrow that file?' asked Adrian Franklin sharply.

Peter Bennett's face creased. 'I really couldn't let a company file just leave the office with someone not connected with the company,' he replied. 'I could, however, put it to Mr Youngman, our Managing Director, and maybe he would agree.'

'I'd be pleased if you would do that,' Adrian told him, and Peter Bennett left the room wishing he hadn't gone so far in this whole exercise – he had plenty of matters he wished his superior to approve and he felt that by getting this inconsequential matter cleared he would use up some of his approval points.

Mr Youngman, in his late sixties, wearing a full beard but with a head as bald as the proverbial coot, hadn't reached his position by being a yes man. He heard the young executive's story and then sat back in his reclining desk chair with a loud creak.

'Are you sure this is genuine?' he asked, his beard standing in the air as he leaned fully back.

'I'm convinced of it,' the young man replied.

'Very well, then. Let him read the letters here. I don't want letters from readers addressed to this company to go running outside loose – no telling where such matters end. Also I want a personal assurance that he will not contact any writer of those letters without my personal approval, and I want that assurance in writing.'

Adrian was only too pleased to write a note straightaway confirming his agreement to the proviso. Peter Bennett showed him into a spare office, gave him the file and said he would arrange for more coffee to be sent in later. Adrian lit a cigarette, took a sip at his cold coffee and started to read.

This was going to be time-consuming, he thought, wishing he had sight of the original book with its numbers. That would save him reading through so much material unrelated to Ian's disappearance. He put the thought out of his mind – after all, he had made more progress in the past two days than he had done for several weeks.

He read on. It seemed as if most correspondents wanted to prove how observant and smart they were rather than submit a genuine correction. No doubt it would make a good pub story: 'How I put the publisher right about a war report', instead of 'How I won the war', Adrian thought sarcastically. War bores – in more than one way he was glad he hadn't served. National Service was sufficient...

Adrian read on through the afternoon. The clock in the next office struck and he looked at his watch to check – surely it couldn't be four o'clock? But it was.

It was just turned 4.25 when he found the reference he sought. It was letter 24 and getting to the bottom of the file.

> Dear Sirs,
>
> Much as I enjoyed the book *The North African Campaign* by General Collingson I must confess I am surprised at a big omission. His previous books have been rich in atmosphere, somewhat loose in actual reporting detail but always covering the subject broadly.
>
> I knew him well. When he was a captain I served in his troop, indeed I was his Sherman driver during the advance across North Africa – from Alamein to Tunis.

Adrian stopped and noted in the margin that someone had pencilled 'Panzer' against 'Sherman'. He read on.

> Your author never mentions Parker, his batman who served him for such a long time, indeed saved his life at Alamein. Without Parker, no author – no book. Yet the author never gives him a mention. Odd!
>
> Odd, too, his coverage of the events around Zarzis. Although he describes the finding of a lone German officer called Grubb or something similar surrendering in the desert, he doesn't mention the subsequent interview (Collingson spoke fluent German) with this officer and other officers taken prisoner that day. Apparently the officer had been placed under house arrest for stealing military documents. Odd place to find a spy, I thought!
>
> Next day we went to the island of Djerba and Collingson tells in graphic detail of the German attack on the synagogue a few days before, followed by the mass killing of the Jews in

the village of Houm Souk. It upset Colly (as we called him behind his back) enormously – more than he makes out in the book. What he misses out is that one old man had been away from the village at the time of the arrests and so lived to tell the tale. Colly spent some time with him and then ordered us up to a valley area to flail with the tank rotors. When we unearthed an old trunk, Colly took it to a derelict house and afterwards he informed us that it contained military documents stolen by Grubb. Papers which he said were so valuable they could change the course of the war.

Colly and Parker set off by Military Police jeep that evening to take the trunk to Intelligence and then on to the airstrip for despatch to Blighty.

All of this came to no avail – the aircraft crashed on take-off, Parker told me sometime later when we broke off at the Mareth line. He was very upset about it.

Very strange that your author never mentions all this. If the papers were so interesting and read by Colly, surely Intelligence would have extracted something before they were sent on. If so, what? Yet it never gets a mention.

I hope we shall have more books from the general. I never saw him after the war but I followed his career when he hit the heights.

His books help me to relive the past. Not always a bad thing!

Yours truly,
A.J. Phillips

Adrian took a deep breath. Parker – yes, Parker, if that was the Parker he had unearthed in Devon... Owner of a country cottage in Mary Tavy and now languishing in Dartmoor Prison.

Adrian screwed up his eyes as his thoughts ran on. If it was the same Parker, he was the father of Betty, one-time girlfriend of Ian and now the associate of Davies. Of course, she would stay at the cottage when she visited her father. Davies would go to his work at the Plymouth factory. It all made sense – to a degree anyway. But everything was based on the assumption that the Parker in the letter was the same Parker in the prison; after all, it wasn't an unusual name.

'I wonder – I just wonder,' Adrian said out loud.
'Wonder what, Mr Franklin?'
Adrian turned around quickly to see Mr Bennett.
'Oh – nothing. It is all so interesting, yet still in pieces. Do you think I could possibly have another cup of coffee?'
Adrian started to read the letter again.

Whilst Lorna bathed Sam, Adrian sorted out his notes on the table and kept an eye on the coffee percolator. Although he had not been able to take the letters from the publishers' office or make photocopies, he had nevertheless made copious notes and these acted as *aides memoires* to form an overall scene. Adrian sucked his pen and stared at the fire – the pieces were coming together, albeit slowly, and he felt like a man who had undertaken his first jigsaw, except this one had 2,000 pieces rather than the modest 500 for the novice.

Any chance of quiet thinking was dashed by Sam, who was due to go to bed and wanted a story. It made a break for his racing mind, which had been working overtime since he had left the publishers' office. Adrian enjoyed reading to the boy and answering the questions which he often asked during the story – simple questions, simple thoughts. How uncluttered and unconditioned a child's mind was – there was so much to learn from that perspective. The clock struck seven. Adrian kissed Sam goodnight and sat down again at the dining room table.

Working on the supposition that the Parker in the letter was the Parker in Dartmoor – Betty's father – then Ian could have learned the story from Parker or Betty – an old soldier's tale. Hardly exciting – finding military documents some 40-odd years before. But supposing the German 'military documents' were in fact valuables and Parker had known or suspected the truth – then that would make a story for anyone to tell years later. 'How I nearly became rich' – that would be a story indeed, especially for a man who had led a life of unsuccessful crime. Phillips had said in the letter that Parker was upset. No wonder! Strange, too, that the surviving Jew from the massacre should guide Collingson to where the papers were hidden so that the tank could flail. Why, how should he know or care? The raid on the synagogue had been reported in the book, but did synagogues hold valuable goods? Probably not, indeed almost certainly they would not.

A.J. Phillips: a chance letter from an interested and involved party had been a real breakthrough. Adrian remembered he had given a firm promise to the publishers that he would not contact any of the writers of the letters and he intended to keep his word. But what about people mentioned in the letter – like Parker? The only way he could get some lead on Parker would be from the prison officer – Arthur McNally, he remembered – he had met at the hotel on Dartmoor. But if he phoned, McNally might suspect something. Prison officers weren't supposed to be free with information about their inmates and, after all, their acquaintanceship was only of an hour's duration. Reluctantly he came to the conclusion that he would have to go down to Dartmoor again in order to talk to Arthur when he was relaxed; he might just learn something. He found the number, and got through. Yes, Arthur was free Thursday night and would be delighted to have a game of snooker at the prison officers' club.

Adrian's break of 36 pleased him. He was on top form and the long drive coupled with the tense feeling he had over the approach for information had in no way spoilt the game. Arthur played a good game so eventually the result hung on the black ball, after Arthur had sunk the blue and pink in succession. After a poor shot Arthur left the black sitting on the pocket and Adrian pocketed it. There was only time for one game as a number of prison officers were waiting to play. Adrian and Arthur adjourned to the bar. Adrian had rehearsed a story of wanting to buy property in the area and seeing one at Mary Tavy which he knew belonged to Parker. He suddenly decided to come clean with Arthur and tell him the whole story; he liked the man and a good rapport existed between them. His problem on how to broach the subject was answered when Arthur proudly announced that he had become a grandfather in the past few days. Adrian talked about his grandson, and a few gin and tonics later the story of Sam's father's disappearance emerged. Adrian was good at putting a story across without boring his listener and today he excelled. Arthur listened intently, looking up sharply when Parker's name was mentioned. Adrian closed the story and Arthur rose, picking up the two glasses. As he walked over to the bar Adrian's eyes followed him. He wondered whether he had given offence for by now Arthur knew the real reason for his visit.

Arthur returned to the table and placed the glasses and tonic water before them.

'I'll be straight with you, Adrian,' he said softly. 'I'm not being a messenger boy between you and an old con. I'll find out whether he served in North Africa and what he was doing there – that's all.'

Adrian breathed a sigh of relief. That was all he could hope for.

An hour later and somewhat inebriated Adrian left his car in the car park in favour of a taxi to Prince Hall Hotel.

In the privacy of his room Adrian switched off the centre light and with only the bedside light to illuminate the room he let his mind run over the events of the last few days. Something was missing – a piece of that jigsaw had somehow gone astray so he couldn't fit it into the picture.

Strange how the mind runs on when sleep takes over the tired body. Adrian woke with a start. Of course, Ian hadn't seen the letter, hadn't been to the publishers' office – all he had seen was the margin notes in the book. So what had made him think he was onto a financial life-raft for his family? Hardly a note in the margin. Adrian mentally kicked himself for assuming that because he had seen Phillip's letter, Ian had too. At least now he knew what he sought for the next move – what had spurred Ian into action. Unless – yes, something was odd.

Adrian looked out of the large Georgian windows. The moon playing with passing clouds sent wide shafts of light over the moorland; not a house was in sight. The river Dart stumbled through boulders 300 metres away. He went back to bed and picked up the book he had placed on his side table. A book – it had all started with a book. He wondered if... He picked up the telephone.

Lorna sounded half asleep. 'Dad, for Heaven's sake, what's up? It's gone midnight.'

'I know – sorry to disturb you so late but I'm lying in bed thinking. Lorna, you remember when Ian bought the shelf of books at the house sale. What did he do with them when he arrived home?'

'Put them in the bookcase, the one in the alcove of the dining room.'

'Yes, but when did he start reading them? Think carefully.'

'No need to think about it,' Lorna replied. 'He got absorbed in that book that same evening – I know for sure because I was going away the next day for the trip up north to my friend. I remember him saying that he would have plenty of time to read them. That was the evening he said he had discovered something which could change our lives.' Lorna faltered as she said 'lives'. 'Of course that was a few days before he knew his life...'

'I know, my love,' Adrian said soothingly. 'But a few things strike me as odd, very odd indeed – one thing to buy the books but to start reading immediately and then to select the very book which gave the key information is another. Then if I remember rightly the bit about the synagogue on the island comes well on – yet he went to it straightaway, within a hour or two of getting there. Now, doesn't that strike you as a very strange coincidence?'

Lorna now sounded very awake. 'I think the answer is waving at us. I remember one book had pieces of paper sticking out of it – which one I don't know, but I'll bet one thing. Ian noticed that book because it did have those papers. They were probably photocopies of key letters sent in to correct the narrative, stuck in the relevant page. Ian would look at that part of the book as a result of reading one of the letters. Then suddenly realise–'

Adrian broke in. 'That he was reading a version of something he had heard from Betty and Parker. It was a chance in a million that those stories linked up.'

There was a long silence then Lorna said, 'But why did only one book of the series have papers?'

'Because that was the one being checked and corrected prior to reprint. The others had already been checked out and corrected, and no doubt the person responsible had the new revised editions, the fruit of his work This one was under review, the one he was working on. But why should he dispose of it?' Adrian questioned. 'Unless he was one of the team the publishers spoke of – the one who died.'

'And that certainly accounts for Ian's curious statement about contacting the owner of the book,' Lorna said.

Adrian wrinkled his face. 'And that we have done – and it got us nowhere. Still, tomorrow I'll get confirmation that the Parker in the letter is the Parker in the jug some three miles away. I think I know the answer.'

After Adrian said goodnight he lay in bed but his mind was racing too fast for sleep.

Dinner at the hotel the next evening was as good as usual and Adrian and Arthur enjoyed their food before returning to the elegant lounge, where Adrian ordered two vintage ports. There were only ten guests in the small hotel that evening and the others had decided to walk after dinner or go to bed. They had the lounge to themselves and soon Arthur told Adrian all he had discovered from a casual chat with the old con, Nosey – Frederick John Parker. He had served in the North African campaign and at one time had been batman to General Collingson. Arthur asked him whether that was the General Collingson who had written books on World War II and Parker confirmed that it was. Arthur said that he had read somewhere that Collingson had been involved in a controversy over some valuable goods but Parker had closed up then.

Arthur poured himself a large brandy while Adrian worked it out that whilst Parker claimed to have served the general – an ego boost – it was certainly when the officer was at a junior stage of his career.

'That's all I can tell you, Adrian old son – except one thing. Parker hated Collingson's guts, kept on saying that he should be in the nick rather than him.'

Adrian swirled his brandy around the balloon glass. 'And when will our friend Nosey be loose in the big outside world?'

The answer made his heart sink.

'Another two years.'

As he sped along the M4 Adrian's thoughts raced over the conversation of the night before. The omission in the book was a key factor in Ian's disappearance. It was only a stroke of luck to have discovered Nosey Parker. Parker probably knew the truth of the missing story of the 'documents' which had been so important in the Western Desert. His daughter, who visited him regularly, did she know the truth? Had Parker told her, and was that why she had gone to Tunisia on holiday? How did Davies fit in? Of course, Davies had worked with Ian. There was a line, however dotted and indirect, between Ian and Parker. Ian's colleague's girlfriend – his own former girlfriend – was Parker's daughter. At long last he had established a connection.

Ian had been examining the book with its margin notes and numbers. If he had had access to the letter he would have seen the reference to Parker and the story of the missing case. Ian, however, hadn't been to the publisher, he was certain of that, so that didn't advance that theory. Another point was that Ian was under no bond not to contact A.J. Phillips, the writer of the letter, if he had, by chance, seen the letter. It was all still a considerable mystery although he was pleased that he had at least established some connections – the first part of the jigsaw was put together and the rest would surely start to fall into place. One thing was certain: Major General Collingson was obviously someone to contact, but Adrian's gut feeling here was to tread with caution.

Adrian swerved violently as a high truck passed him. Somehow he must have wandered close to the centre lane during his deliberations. Perhaps the motorway wasn't the place for deep thought. Adrian decided to have some coffee at Membury service station before continuing to London.

9

Franz Grieb declined the copy of the *International Herald Tribune* which the Lufthansa stewardess offered him. The flight from Hamburg would shortly be landing at Düsseldorf, and then, after a short stop, would take off again for Malaga. He wished there wasn't this delay in Düsseldorf – the delay over the last few days with the committal proceedings of his assailant had been bad enough, for he wanted desperately to be with his mother after her ordeal. He had called her frequently but, despite her assurances, he knew she would like to have him with her.

All this trouble seemed to revolve around his father's activity in North Africa some 40-odd years before – it seemed crazy. Was any fortune worth all this sacrifice of human safety – the sheer loss of peace of mind? One thing was sure. Whoever was after this trove of hidden valuables was convinced it was actually there – just as his father had been. Franz had found himself doubting. He always had found his father's obsession for discovering the trove a little puzzling – almost as if he wanted to prove a point, satisfy a curiosity, rather than benefit financially. In any event they would have a near impossible task to get it out of the country – and it would have to be done illegally. Was it worth it?

The aircraft touched the tarmac at Düsseldorf airport and gently nosed its way to a pier. Franz glanced through a school exercise book called 'Fatima File' – this was obviously an important part in the whole affair and he was going to keep it close by him until some future plan was made. He was tired of the whole exercise; it had brought nothing but trouble.

The flight took off again and Franz picked up *Bordbuch*, the in-flight magazine of Lufthansa. He opened the map section and studied the route from Düsseldorf to Malaga – just short of two hours more. Turning the page, he studied a small island off the Tunisian coast – small in geographic size, enormous in problems. How many times had they spent holidays on the island, partly to swim and sunbathe, partly to enjoy the local atmosphere and partly to dig and rake. No question about it, he had enjoyed those days.

Food was served; Franz enjoyed two small bottles of red wine and, as the flight was lightly loaded, reclined his seat.

He awoke as they were approaching Malaga and 20 minutes later the Boeing 737 was disgorging its passengers. Once through Customs, he took his mother in his arms and held her. She burst into tears; the strain of the past few days had been too much.

* * *

'So that's how he found you.' Franz sighed, pouring himself another coffee after dinner. His mother looked puzzled. The recounting of both stories had taken a long time and both were getting tired.

'Let me explain,' Franz went on. 'About a month ago I had a telephone call from England – a man calling himself Paul Chapman, or something similar to that, said he would like to speak to Father. I told him of Father's death and he went on about how sorry he was as he had known him in business. I asked if I could help as I was involved in the business now, and he went off that point, saying that he had met Father several times, partly on business but mainly socially. He asked how you were and I told him you were fine and living in Spain – in fact this smooth talker had me fooled completely. He went on about how good that must be for you and how he would like to write to you to pay his respects and express condolences over father's death. I gave him your address – there seemed no harm in it.

'What apparently happened is that Paul Chapman, alias Henry – whatever he calls himself – turns up in Marbella, gets to meet your friends, not difficult in a relatively small expatriot community, and then gets to know you. He then,' Franz faltered. 'Gets emotionally involved with you and works slowly to get information on Djerba. It was imprudent of you to lend him the notebooks but no more so than my indiscretion in giving him your address.

'It now appears that his plans were thwarted by the unexpected arrival on the scene of three skeletons out of the cupboard of his unsavoury past – these people wanted to get in on the act. One of them is now sweating it out in a Spanish jail. Then there is the other one who was here, and the police are now seeking him. Then finally the boss man they called for instructions and who obviously sent the local German henchman to knock me about and obtain what they saw as the vital file. I don't believe for one moment that any of them were in league with Henry – Charles – whatever they call him.

'One thing still puzzles me,' Franz went on. 'How did Henry find out where I lived, or even my existence in the first place? He called me, knew where to find me – knew about Father. He obviously had some line on the Djerba affair – how, just how did he get it?'

Ella turned to her son. 'Look, Franz, whatever comes out of all this, let's leave that stuff where it belongs – under the desert sand. It's caused us enough trouble already. Don't let's pursue it, let's get on with living peaceful lives. After all, it didn't belong to your father in the first place and there seems to be a jinx on it. I read a book in English recently called *Armorel of Lyonesse*. In it the family came by riches when a ship was wrecked and they illegally retained the goods. From that moment they experienced great unhappiness. I feel that about Djerba. All that stuff may be valuable in a material sense but otherwise it's bad news.'

Franz agreed. 'OK, but I think we should do everything possible to help the police in apprehending our charming friend, who, after all, has relieved you of a considerable sum of money. Are they making progress?'

Ella shook her head.

Franz and Ella strolled leisurely along the Paseo Maritimo at Marbella. The steps went down to the marina and they decided that a midday drink wouldn't be a bad idea. Each knew that the other was desperately trying to put recent events out of mind – and with little success.

Franz leaned over the table and took his mother's hands in his. 'We cannot fool ourselves, my love. We want no more traumas but the fact is that this is an unfinished symphony. Your friend somehow knew more about this treasure hoard than you and I know – and just how he found it and what it is must be the key to the whole thing. You told me that Henry came here from England, and it was from England that he called me, or so he said. It could well be that he stumbled across the vital link in England that sent him on the trail to me. It would now seem that he had a certain degree of information but needed more, and that's why he came down here.'

His mother wasn't listening. She was looking towards the harbour, and her face had gone white.

'What's the matter?' Franz enquired anxiously.

'That sports car, the open Mercedes, the man getting into it – that's him!'

Franz looked up just as the brown car pulled out from the parking place, driven by a giant of a man with a bull neck encompassed by a gold chain.

'That's the man we saw at Los Monteros, the boss of the two thugs who broke in – they telephoned him from my house. I remember what they called him – and Henry called him. His name's Royce.'

Franz was out of his chair like a shot and reached the roadside just in time to see the car turn the corner onto the Paseo Maritimo. However, he could now identify the car and could soon track down the driver.

They sat together for half an hour, until the frowning proprietor indicated that two drinks for an hour's occupation of a table wasn't exactly profitable. As they walked back, Franz came to the conclusion Henry had some new information and Royce and his henchmen had somehow caught onto it. All this clearly exceeded what Franz's father had recorded some years ago – yet he had been at the forefront of the original incident. Some new factor must have emerged and this, when fed into the overall equation, had put them well ahead.

That evening Franz told his mother that he planned to drive around the coast – he wanted to be alone in order to think. Ella knew her son liked to enjoy his own company from time to time. He had always been like that as a boy. Her agreement would not have been so forthcoming, however, had she known of his real intentions. Franz was now resolved to discover the whereabouts of Royce, knowing a distinctive car like that would soon show up.

For the next three hours Franz combed the streets of Marbella and its surroundings. It had always seemed a small town to him but its honeycomb of streets caused him to drive a considerable distance at a snail's pace. The town was celebrating its patron Saint Bernarbe that week and the streets were crowded with people making their way to a fairground on the northern perimeter. The noise from the fairground was augmented by street fireworks. At around nine o'clock, as it started to get dark, he saw the car parked in a narrow street to the west of the town. There was no question about it: a dark brown Mercedes with a black roof and Spanish plates in front of an opulent villa with a wide balcony overlooking a small swimming pool. He circled the block and came slowly by to take another look. As he did so, the giant figure of Royce appeared and threw his massive weight into the driver's seat. Franz accelerated away to the end of the street and waited. Within seconds the Mercedes passed him and turned into the main road. Franz followed him, leaving about 200 metres between the two cars. Along the Ricardo Sorriano the sports car turned left and stopped outside the Bliss Club. Franz passed it as Royce handed a note to the doorman, and then the big man entered the club. This was Franz's chance. With Royce seeking entertainment for the evening and his two henchmen involved with the Spanish police, it was possible that the house was unoccupied. Certainly it was worth a try.

Five minutes later Franz pulled up in the Calle Vittoria – and walked the 300 or so metres towards Royce's villa. 'Villa Lamorna', stated a pale blue and yellow tile on the gate pillar. There were no dogs in evidence and Franz let himself quietly into the garden. It was odd that the gate was unlocked. He walked quietly into the garden at the side of the house. There was a light burning upstairs and the sound of a TV programme indicated that someone was present. As he watched, a young girl passed the window and disappeared. The television was turned up high; it was showing a Spanish programme. Franz concluded that the girl was a Spanish domestic who was taking an easy evening while the master was out.

The appearance of the heavy front door meant there was no direct access but Franz was astonished to see the *reja* bars were missing from the windows. Had he known Royce's aversion to bars he would have known why – but to him it seemed the golden opportunity for entry as the only security seemed to be flimsy flick locks which could soon be opened with a penknife. Within a few minutes Franz was lowering himself onto the floor of the villa. If there was a burglar alarm, he decided, it must be either a pad placed under the expensive rug which covered most of the study floor, or a ray system. He could eliminate the first by staying on the tile surround and the second he would have to leave to chance. A massive Catalan-style desk at the side of the window caught his eye. That would be the first area for investigation, he resolved, for it was information he sought, not property.

The desk was open and untidily scattered with papers. Franz rummaged through them. A foolscap pad of notes, a few old bullfight tickets and nightclub details. There was nothing of any significance. Then a small notebook caught his eye – it appeared to be a list of addresses and telephone numbers and was in a different handwriting to the rest of the debris. Franz put it in his pocket. The drawers of the desk revealed nothing of any consequence so Franz moved slowly and silently to the sideboard and then to a small cupboard near the door.

Franz sighed. He hadn't known what to expect but he had hoped to discover something which would throw a light on the whole affair. Finally, he moved gingerly towards the table in the centre of the floor and pulled open the drawer. A Smith & Wesson revolver of .45 calibre lay on its side, fully loaded. He placed it back in the drawer when he heard a door bang upstairs, and made his way rapidly to the window. As he did so a shrill scream from the burglar alarm in the hallway broke the silence and he dived through the open window and ran towards the gate. As he ran, a man's voice rang out in Spanish. He tore flat out down the street, threw himself behind the steering wheel and accelerated away with tyres screeching. The fireworks for the feast of St Barnabe drowned the shots.

Back at his mother's villa, Franz deduced that Royce's caretaker had been entertaining himself with the maid upstairs. Franz wondered how Royce would react when he heard of his employees' negligence. He had only seen Royce, but if his character was anything like his appearance then he reckoned that the staff would be in for a tough time.

'You are a fool – a complete fool. As if we haven't had enough trouble so far,' Ella scolded her son as if he was 11 years of age. Franz took it all in his stride, realising that his mother had been through a stressful time and she had his interest and safety very much at heart.

Coffee and rolls were cleared away by the Spanish maid who came in for two hours every morning and, as the day was obviously going to be hot, Franz and his mother poured another orange juice and took the drinks out onto the terrace which overlooked the town with the sea beyond. Franz placed the book on the table and turned it towards his mother.

'I awoke during the night and looked through this time and time again. It means nothing to me. It's just a list of telephone numbers and addresses, but it's marked.' He stopped talking as he saw his mother's face go taut.

'It's his!' she shouted. 'It's Henry's writing.' She picked it up and looked at it. 'There's the telephone number of the chandler in Puerto Banus, the Los Monteros Hotel...' She studied it more closely. 'Why on earth should Royce want this, and, what's more to the point, how did he get it? I've never seen it here, so maybe Henry kept it on the boat. Is Royce working with Henry? I doubt it; Henry was only too pleased to keep away from him. Maybe Royce stole it from the boat. Maybe Royce knows where Henry is.'

Franz moved across to Ella's side of the table and they looked through the book.

'Where was he living just prior to coming here?' Franz asked his mother.

'He was living in North London – staying with friends whose name I don't know, and he never called them from here as far as I know.'

Franz sucked a pencil and furrowed his brow as he thought.

'Mother, your number is in blue-black ballpoint and so is mine. There are only a few written that way; some are in blue ballpoint, some in felt-tip, but most are in ordinary old-fashioned ink. It would appear that he lost his fountain pen and then used various throwaway replacements. There are eight numbers in blue-black ballpoint – yours, mine, G.S. Boatyard here, Antonio's restaurant in Marbella, the Puerto Banus harbourmaster, the Los Monteros Hotel, a Pedro Lopez in Marbella – whoever that is – and a number in London, just named "AF". Apparently these are recent numbers. Maybe the Pedro and the AF of London are connected with this affair.'

Ella's face puckered with thought. 'That London number is familiar. I remember it now because there are so many twos in it – Henry had a poor memory for figures and he had that number written on a copy of the *Daily Telegraph* one day. We were going to the beach and he wanted to make a telephone call on a business matter. He took the paper with him, then left it in the telephone cabin. I like reading British papers, so he went back to collect it, but when he returned the corner with the number had been torn off. I thought nothing of it at the time, but now everything is in a different perspective and it does look decidedly odd.'

Franz looked at the number again. 'It's a London number and Henry was in London before he came here. There are other London numbers, but this one seems to be a contact, business or otherwise, that he has maintained from here. The only way to find out is to call and ask to speak to Henry. It would be interesting to find the reaction.'

Ella nodded. 'We seem to be embroiled in this matter somehow. I just wish we could let it all drop. What can we gain?'

Franz looked out to sea for some time before answering. 'What you say is true, Mother, but something here ties up with father's obsession about the stuff hidden in Tunisia. It was that which triggered off our friend Henry. He went to a lot of trouble to trace you through me – then to spend time building a relationship with you until you told him about father's secret. A confidence trickster like him takes slow yet deliberate steps and, no doubt, is fed information – he is no amateur. That number in London may help us to discover something that will help us trace Henry. and I'll be honest with you, I am curious – very curious indeed – to discover what actually happened all those years ago.'

His mother nodded. 'Yes. Call AF.'

Franz dialled the number. After a long time the telephone was answered.

'Ann Franklin speaking.'

10

At Blenheim Gardens Lorna had just made tea and Adrian sat down at the table, tired after his long drive. Sam had brought a friend home and their interest in tea was curtailed by their wish to go back to play in Sam's bedroom. As soon as Lorna and Adrian were alone, Adrian started to talk, but Lorna interrupted him.

'Father, whatever your news, I must tell you mine. I had a telephone call from Mother – she had a call from a Mr Grieb living in Marbella. It seems that Henry had been there and then disappeared. Mother said she had no idea where he was, she thought he was on a journalist assignment. Mother became somewhat intrigued by the call because it seems she is a little uneasy about Henry. She asked this man Grieb why he was so keen to speak to Henry and he said it was about an assignment in Tunisia. I had told Mother about Ian's tickets to Tunisia so she realised that it could have some connection with Ian. She played along and asked for Mr Grieb's telephone number, saying that if she found out anything she would call him. He seemed pleased about this – apparently Mother liked the sound of him. Anyway, here is the telephone number.'

Adrian pushed tea aside and reached out to the sideboard. His favourite glass was deftly filled with a gin and tonic and he was so preoccupied that he forgot the ice.

'So another piece presents itself for fitting into the puzzle.

Now hear what I have discovered about ex-Lance Corporal Parker.'

Lorna listened intently whilst Adrian unfolded the story of his snooker game at the prison officers' club and the subsequent dinner.

She sighed when Adrian said that Parker still had two years of his sentence to run. 'If only we could talk to him.'

'I don't think that would get us far,' Adrian responded. 'Whatever he knows, he is capitalising on through his daughter, and they don't want us in on the act. No, our best plan is through people who are on our side. We have the jigsaw and it is coming together slowly. The only thing is, I believe other people have pieces in their pockets, and until we recover those pieces we will never get a complete picture. Now this fellow Grieb – and I've heard that name somewhere before recently – might...' His voice trailed off. 'I want to go over some points, just leave me a while.'

Adrian sat in the lounge flicking through his notes for nearly two hours before joining Lorna in the kitchen. 'I'm no further on but I've got used to that by now. However, I'll call Grieb.'

* * *

The Iberia plane touched down at Malaga airport 40 minutes late and taxied towards the airport building. Adrian looked at the scatter of buildings and pondered what Grieb would be like. The telephone call had been short but to the point. Grieb was obviously surprised to hear from Adrian Franklin, but had readily told him that a man calling himself Henry Southon had befriended his mother and then gone off with a considerable sum of money. He himself had been attacked in his flat in Hamburg for no apparent motive and his mother had been attacked in Marbella. He had reason to believe that Henry, although probably not behind the attempted mayhem, might know something about it.

Adrian collected his bag and moved through Customs. The herd of car rental touts distracted him, then the young German stepped forward from the back.

'Mr Franklin, I'm Franz Grieb. Welcome to Malaga and the Costa del Sol on most days – today being an exception.'

Franz had a car waiting and soon they were on the hazardous highway for the 50-kilometre drive from the airport to Marbella. Grieb was right, Adrian thought. This dull grey day wasn't what he had expected from a place with such a name.

Adrian hadn't visited Andalucia before and the journey was spent in discussing the weather, the property prices in the area and the fast-developing new highway to relieve the vast amount of traffic which plunges in and out of spreading urban developments along the coast from Malaga as far as Gibraltar. They also talked about the future of Gibraltar, avoiding the one subject which was the cause of the meeting.

In Marbella, a much larger town than Adrian had imagined, Franz turned off right and drove into a development of luxury villas. At Villa Lava, Ella Grieb was waiting and, after introductions and pleasantries, the three sat on the terrace with a pot of coffee. The sun occasionally broke through the large cumulus clouds which scuttled across the sky.

Franz Grieb broke the silence which had suddenly developed.

'Mr Franklin – or may I call you Adrian? We Germans aren't so formal nowadays as we used to be. Perhaps the best way to start is to ask you why you take the time, and trouble and considerable expense to visit us in Marbella. After all, the problem of attack and losing money is really ours. What is your interest in this matter?'

Adrian looked at the two Griebs, their faces studying him intently.

'Which is a way of saying that I serve first,' he laughed. 'OK, that's fine. I'm interested because my son-in-law disappeared several weeks ago and I set out to find him.'

If it had been possible to increase the Griebs' attention this remark would undoubtedly have done so.

The sun had broken through and the terrace was blazing hot when Adrian finished his story. On the aircraft he had written some guideline notes on the back of an envelope in order that he should not miss out any point and that everything should be in chronological order. He replaced the envelope in the blazer which hung over the back of his chair.

'And that's my story.'

Franz Grieb mopped his forehead with his handkerchief. 'My God – this is most interesting. Can I get you a drink, Adrian?'

Adrian said he would love a gin and tonic with a whole load of ice and, as Franz disappeared into the lounge, Ella looked pensive.

'What I don't understand, Adrian, is that you are no further on with Ian's disappearance. You have established that he had a problem with his illness but the connection between the prisoner and the writer of the book – it's interesting but doesn't move you forward in locating your son-in-law.'

Adrian nodded. 'It's a matter of fitting the jigsaw pieces together – and I believe you have, unwittingly, some of the pieces.'

'And I believe we may – just may,' replied Franz, as he placed the three tall glasses of ice and gin on the table and passed Adrian a bottle of Schweppes' tonic. 'The main connecting factor is the Western Desert campaign – my father was in it.'

'Of course,' breathed Adrian. 'That's where I heard the name Grieb – I'm sure he was mentioned somewhere.'

'In not too complementary a fashion, I suspect,' Franz replied. 'Father wasn't at all interested in soldiering. Found it a bore and a waste of life – he often used to refer to the campaign in North Africa as "two bald men squabbling over a comb".'

Adrian was brimming with curiosity to hear Franz's side of the story. The young German poured himself another drink and started.

Just over an hour later, Franz drew his narrative to a close. For several seconds no one spoke and then Adrian broke the silence.

'It seems the key to this whole drama is the tin trunk which was buried by someone in the desert all those years ago. It seems likely that the box of documents found by Collingson's tank was in fact the trunk of valuables. Your father spent some time trying to find them but they had already gone – probably recovered by Collingson. Something in the book by Collingson triggered Ian into action – which is strange because according to our letter written by A. J. Phillips there was no mention of the discovery in the book. This in itself seems odd – Collingson is hiding the facts here and for good reason. Ian found out something from the margin notes – or rather the letters relating to the margin notes – which put him on the track to make a quick fortune to support his wife and family after his impending death. The pieces are fitting together again but there are still a lot which don't fit – like Henry. He probably got wind of any easy win when Ian visited my wife – soon to be my ex-wife – at her home and met Henry. Ian may have told him something, realising he would need help. Ian needed financing on the operation and he had gone in vain to Davies.

Ella stepped in abruptly. 'One thing which bewilders me is Henry's obsession over preparing the boat. If the scene of this action is the desert, why does he require a yacht? Useful to smuggle goods out of Tunisia but there must be simpler ways than that of doing it.'

'I think we're going round in circles,' Adrian sighed. 'Maybe the best plan is to sleep on it, and I'd really like to take you out to dinner if you can recommend somewhere – not far, because I guess you are as tired as I am.'

Franz went to the telephone and booked a table at Antonio's in the centre of Marbella, and 30 minutes later they walked together through the estate of luxury villas and settled down to a fine seafood meal.

* * *

The little Spaniard reeled from the blow to the face and fell to the ground.

'Get up, you miserable erk,' growled Royce Rollason. 'I leave you to guard this fucking house and what do you do – go bonking my maid upstairs whilst some miserable little bleeder goes over my desk.'

The Spaniard screamed as Royce kicked him in the groin.
'Get up, you slug, and tell me what you know.'

With the pain, Salvadore lost command of his limited English and broke into a stream of Spanish which ended in another scream as Royce kicked him in the chest. The Filipina maid was curled up on the couch whimpering and Royce grabbed her and pulled her to her feet by her collar.

'You want the same?' He looked her straight in the eyes. 'You'll bleeding well get it if I don't learn something.'

The maid sobbed out the little she knew. They had been together in the bedroom and had heard nothing until the alarm went off and they heard the crash of glass and the shot by Salvadore. She had seen nothing.

Royce dragged her across the room and dropped her on the ground.

'It's that worm Charlie what done it. And I know what 'e took too – 'e was after 'is address list. I 'ad it 'ere.'

Royce Rollason shook with anger as he poured himself a large brandy. He sat his huge frame on a stool and looked over the scene.

'What's the importance of a bleedin' book?' he murmured. 'Taking this chance just for a book. I'll find 'im if it's the last thing I do, so help me.'

Grabbing the telephone, Royce called a local number and said, 'Royce 'ere. I want to see you at the villa quick.'

Eduardo Fuertes knew better that to argue with Royce. He had, in any case, heard that Royce had lost two of his best men to the Spanish police and hoped that some lucrative work was coming his way. It took him only seven minutes to drive to the villa. He glanced at a small man gripping his stomach in a corner and an Oriental girl sobbing in a chair. With Rollason you were surprised at nothing.

It didn't take Royce long to brief Eduardo on his assignment. He wanted Charlie alias Henry and he wanted him brought in without delay. The best contact, Royce told him, was the boat boy who worked for Charlie in Puerto Banus. Within 20 minutes Eduardo, knowing as much as Royce wanted him to know, was back in his Fiat and heading towards the luxury port. Eduardo had an insatiable thirst and the bars of Puerto Banus presented him with no problem. At his fourth call, gulping his Scotch and water noisily, he gleaned the information he sought from the Spanish barman. Pedro's mother and father had a small apartment in the back street of the port over the small café where they worked. Eduardo walked briskly around and ran up the steps at the back of the café, which led directly to the apartment. Pedro's father answered the knock on the door and Eduardo asked to speak to his friend Pedro as he had a message for him.

'He's away at the moment,' the café assistant answered. 'You've just missed him on the telephone. He called the café with a message not to worry about him – he's with his boss at Ceuta.'

As Eduardo drove back to Royce Rollason's villa he reflected that this was the easiest money he had earned for some time.

Royce peeled off 20 thousand-peseta notes, his heavy eyebrows knitting. So Charlie had continued his journey on – and was now in Ceuta. That being so, he couldn't possibly have been the raider on his villa. If Charlie wasn't the intruder, then who was?

'What do you mean, a little geezer with red 'air?' Royce shouted.

Salvadore found it difficult to speak, with the thought of another beating like yesterday's uppermost in his mind and with a wide range of bruises to remind him.

'He was small, thin like, with a sweater up to the neck like this and he had red hair. He was young, about twenty-seven, maybe younger. I saw him and he jumped over the fence because I switched the lights on. He had to scramble up the fence so he was before my eyes for five, maybe more, seconds. He was about one metre 70 like me, no – bigger, and his hair was bright coloured. I had the gun, loaded, on the table of my room, like you told me. I shot at him, but...'

Royce gesticulated for the little Spaniard to leave. So it definitely wasn't Charlie. But who else would want to rifle through his desk and why? No normal thief, for he would have taken the Georgian candlesticks which Royce had acquired during a tour of a stately home in England some years before. There was only one way to find out and that was to contact Charlie, but this was one job he would have to do personally. He had overwhelming conviction that Charlie was on to something good, and Royce Rollason wanted part of the action.

Royce eased his giant frame out of the plunge pool in his garden. He wasn't a good swimmer, so a small plunge pool was all he needed to keep cool. Today was going to be a scorcher, no doubt about it. He tottered across the grass to the small wooden building which he used as a changing room and cursed as he stood on a sharp stone. One of the reasons he employed that nonentity Salvadore was to cut the grass and keep it clear of stones. He picked up the sharp object and threw it over the wall to the road beyond. As he turned back, something caught his eye: a five peseta piece. He picked it up and noticed another. He recovered that too, muttering about that bloody little Salvadore. His sharp eyes stood still. This wasn't another Spanish coin, it was a German mark. Royce's face set in question. The coins had been only one or two paces from the gate, just where the intruder had made his rapid exit. Royce stood staring at the coin – there was only one recent connection with Germany, and that was the exercise he had set Frohlich on. The fact that he hadn't heard from Frohlich concerned him. Maybe Frohlich had found out too much and had entered the operation by himself. Doubtful – Frohlich was dim-witted and cowardly; he knew what would happen to him if he interfered with one of Royce Rollason's operations. No, more likely that Grieb boy from Hamburg, the one Frohlich had done over, had come down to Marbella to meet up with his mother. Royce threw the coin into the plunge pool. Too much was going wrong. Whatever Charlie was after was getting too hot; he was losing too many supporters and he didn't know why. It would be risky to go after Charlie himself. Life was comfortable now in Marbella and he didn't want to spoil it – a few more years behind bars would finish him and he shook at the thought they might be Spanish bars. No, he would have to get someone else involved. He had no one immediately in mind, and even if he had, what would he direct them to do? His face creased into what might pass as a smile. He had an idea...

Angie wanted to keep the job. Indeed, she needed it badly. Working for Royce Rollason wasn't that difficult. From time to time she was required to sleep with him, but it paid well. The alternative was to be unemployed in an area where jobs weren't that easy to obtain. In a short time she would be forced back to the Philippines with civil war in the offing, no job and five sisters and two brothers all trying to earn enough money to eat. Putting it bluntly, that meant working in the sordid massage parlours in Manila, but with AIDS and the decline in tourism since the political storms following the Marcos regime, she doubted whether that was even a possibility, especially since the American forces had pulled out. It was better for her to fit into Mr Rollason's plans.

The taxi parked in a side road opposite the Grieb villa. Royce had decided not to use the high-profile Mercedes coupé in case Grieb recognised it. The young German seemed to know too much about him. Through binoculars Royce studied the sun balcony where a cleaning woman was dusting the rails. She picked up a can and watered the flowers. A tall grey-haired man in his fifties appeared and lit a cigarette. Royce frowned – he didn't know who he was and he certainly didn't fit into the scene as Royce knew it. The taxi driver muttered about his next appointment then promptly forgot about it when a 5,000-peseta note appeared over his shoulder in a fat ringed hand. Royce stiffened suddenly.

'That's 'im – look at 'im.'

He passed the binoculars to Angie, who carefully studied the little ginger-haired figure who had appeared on the balcony with a cigarette in his hand. She nodded and Royce told the driver to take them home.

Franz Grieb had left Hamburg unprepared for the heat of the Costa del Sol. A short-sleeved shirt or two, a pair of lightweight slacks and some light shoes would certainly make life more pleasurable, and as he planned to stay with his mother for several days it seemed a good idea to make some purchases at a smart-looking clothing shop whose window he had studied. He walked down to the Avenida Ricardo, leaving his mother talking to Adrian at the villa. The two of them seemed to be getting on well and Franz wanted a break from the subject which they had discussed continuously over the last two days. He took several shirts from the rack and held them in turn against his chest. He was a clothes-conscious man and was prepared to pay a good amount for something if it was right for him. A pretty Filipina girl thumbing through the blouses smiled at him.

'Do you think it suits me?' he asked her.

She looked questioningly and pulled a light green and brown one out of the rack. 'With your hair, I think this is better. Maybe they have it in your size – why don't you ask?'

Fifteen minutes later Franz presented his Diners card and picked up the package of new clothing. He and Angie left to have coffee and cakes in a coffee bar just off the Avenida Ricardo.

At just after midnight Angie kissed Franz goodnight and thanked him for the lovely dinner. She promised to meet him the following evening and let herself into Villa Lamorna, where Royce Rollason was sitting up, whisky glass in hand, waiting for her.

Half an hour later Royce finished the glass and refilled it.

'So that's what that 'erk Charlie is after,' he breathed. 'Sees 'imself as a treasure 'unter after all that bleeding stuff that...' His voice trailed off.

He told Angie to go to bed in her own room and walked out into the garden. He had never been to Tunisia and wasn't quite sure exactly where it was. He would soon find out, for he had more than a small conviction that that was where he would be going, ahead of Charlie. Franz had been loose-tongued after a number of drinks with a pretty girl. Although he had abbreviated the story, he had mentioned several names and Angie had remembered some. Royce scratched down as many as he could recall, together with a note. He grimaced as he wrote 'Dartmoor Prison' and had good reason to do so. No one called Nosey Parker had been there in his day. He studied the list carefully.

This Collingson geezer, he must know something, he thought. He wrote the book. Must have left something out on purpose.

It was three thirty before Royce switched off the light beside his bed. Under the extinguished light was a list of questions he wanted Angie to ask Franz carefully the next day. Whatever happened, he mustn't be put on his guard.

The background music was real, a fact which appealed to Franz Grieb as he took in the scene. The Marbella Club was a good choice and he was thoroughly enjoying the company of his latest girlfriend. Angie was an agreeable and interesting companion who had shown a lot of interest in his recent saga – indeed had come up with some possible solutions to the various questions which preoccupied him.

Franz had booked one of the luxury beachside apartments for the night and, after a short dance together, the pair strolled leisurely across the garden to the mini-villa.

As Angie fell into his arms she had a strong wish that she hadn't allowed herself to get caught up with this sordid business. She liked the young German and his boyish ways but business was business and she needed the bonus which Royce Rollason had promised her. The notes in her handbag, scribbled hastily in the ladies toilet during a break in the evening, would interest him – she didn't know why and didn't care. Interfering in her employer's business affairs could lead to uncomfortable repercussions, that she did know.

* * *

Ceuta, once a Roman colony of some importance, is one of Spain's twin enclaves on the Moroccan Mediterranean coast.

Although a touchy point between Spain and Morocco, the simple fact is that Spain exercised sovereignty over Melilla and neighbouring Ceuta long before modern Morocco came into being. It was in Melilla that the first shots of the Spanish Civil War were fired, and after the death of Franco, the city fathers of this soft underbelly of Spain hinted that they were opposed to the radical changes being introduced by Madrid. Madrid's reaction was to leave the twin cities well alone. Few Spaniards knew of their existence and fewer still were interested.

It was to this outpost of Spain that *L'Anticipation* arrived on an early Sunday morning – still under tow and creating little interest from the local people and officials. A Moroccan harbourmaster took details of the port of departure and likely stay in Ceuta. He lightened up when Charlie Singer, alias Henry Southon, told him of his intention to have repairs done, and said he would arrange for his brother, by all accounts the best engineer in Morocco, to call. Charlie refrained from correcting him about which country he was in.

Hassan was around within two hours and to Charlie's relief he spoke perfect English. He could start immediately and he made no reference to being paid in advance – which was just as well. Hassan set to work without delay and Southon quickly realised that his brother's boast was not an idle one.

Three days later, with great progress being made, Charlie put a proposition to Hassan – a chance to make a considerable amount of money in a very short time. Hassan agreed when he heard that no drugs were involved; he had lost too many friends who had been caught red-handed in that overstaffed industry. He promised Charlie that he would get *L'Anticipation* ready for sea within the week if he worked flat out. That was music to Charlie's ears. He was confident that Royce would never think of Ceuta – and it would give him a week to prepare for action on the rock he could just see – the British colony of Gibraltar.

* * *

The cubicle or 'heads', which was the shower room and toilet in an area not much more than a metre square, was cramped for one person. Charles Singer cursed that he couldn't stand bolt upright as he shaved. Why boats of a reasonable size had to be designed for midgets puzzled him and he promised himself that when he became wealthy he would indulge in a vessel with more adequate accommodation. He smiled in the shaving mirror. Wealth might not be that far away if he could get the work on the boat completed and if the weather, which looked uncertain, held. A morning breeze had stiffened and even now the vessel rocked suddenly. He hoped that he would get the kind of weather one would expect from the south Mediterranean coastline, although the Med, because of its occasional shallow water, could become surprisingly rough for an inland sea.

Charlie dried his face and opened the toilet door. At once he was grabbed by devastating nausea followed by a dryness of the throat which prevented him from speaking. His mind spun. He now knew why the vessel had rocked – it had received the bulky frame of someone he had hoped never to see again. That squalid mass now sat in a low chair, his fat legs crossed, and something in his hand below his right thigh looked suspiciously threatening.

Like a startled rabbit Charlie made for the door to Royce Rollason's left, but as he reached it a searing pain across the back of his legs sent him sprawling and then, gasping for air, he was picked up by his hair and dropped into a chair.

The pain in his legs was excruciating. Through his hazed vision he saw what had caused it. Royce was standing over him with an iron bar like a shortened cricket stump.

'Now start talking,' Royce growled.

'What – what about?' Charlie whispered, and then screamed as the iron stump cracked down on his right foot.

'You know bloody well, you bloody little Tenner. You know. Always was on the bleeding make and now you're a fucking treasure 'unter. I'm not blaming you for that – in fact I want to come in on it with you for part of the action, as they say. Now, Charlie you little worm, are you talking or not?' And Royce brought the bar down on the table with a sharp crack.

'OK, you win. I'll tell you, Royce, I'll tell you all that happened.'

'Tell me one lie and the only Singer you'll be is a soprano in the choir,' Royce snapped.

Forty minutes later, Royce lit a cigar and threw the match at Charlie.

'So, that's why you shacked up with that German bird. Let's be sure I get it right – put me straight if I 'aven't and I'll make you only one promise if you've lied to me, Charlie boy. I'll 'ave to throw this bar into the sea 'cos it will be too bent and too messy for further use.'

Charlie nodded his head. 'I wouldn't lie to you Royce – I'm not that crazy and I think we could make a deal between us, really I do.'

'Right, that's it then. I'll sum it all up.' Royce sneered as he spoke. 'When you were pissing around in England working on some fancy fencing racket – bloody fine chance you'd 'ave at that, I tell you – you met up with this Ann woman who 'ad broken up with 'er old man. She was comfortably off and that suited you. Then just as you was wondering what to do to earn a 'onest living,' Royce grinned, 'up jumps her son-in-law with a fine old tale of buying a book on the North African campaign during World War Two and finding notes correcting the original book. He had called someone called Phillips who had been mentioned in the notes, and then this Ian knew someone – his ex-secretary – who had been working on the subject with her new boss. Sounds a bit complicated. Anyway, you talk the matter over with him and look over the notes in the sneaky way you've always operated. Then you decide as this Ian isn't much longer for this world to let 'im go off in an 'urry to Tunisia to see what he can find while you stay behind and search out what you can in background material. Then you would join him later in the digging in Tunisia. This Ian – what did you say his name was?'

'Lacey,' supplied Charlie.

'Yes, with Ian Lacey out the way, you start ferreting around and calls this jeweller in 'Amburg – who I might add 'as been a pain in the arse to me. Anyway, 'e puts you onto his mum, this German bird in Marbella, and who should pop up in Marbella that chat 'er up at a party but yours truly. Nice work. She tells you all about what 'appened in Djerba, 'ow her old man and 'er son 'av been diggin' there for years and not come up with anything. So then off you go to someone else you've met in your searching around.

'Lacey had called Phillips and asked about the campaign, saying he was writing a book. When he mentioned Collingson – who wrote this bleeding book – Phillips asked which Collingson he meant...' Royce trailed off. 'You tell me again.'

Charlie took up the story.

'Lacey found there were two Collingsons. Knowing what he did from the notes in the book and Phillips's letter, he was soon convinced that the tin box contained not papers but precious material from the house adjoining the synagogue. When he discovered that the aircraft carrying the trunk, along with wounded troops, and piloted by General Collingson's brother, had crashed, he wanted to find out more. Phillips told him that he didn't know more but that the Imperial War Graves Commission would know full details. That was a Saturday and Lacey wanted to get moving. We agreed that he would go down to Tunisia, locate the spot where the material had been buried, the nearest airfield, and get as much information as he could. Lacey spoke French fluently and would get as much information as he could from local people. French is quite widely used in Tunisia,' he explained, seeing Royce's questioning look. 'Lacey had an expert on metal detection come down with equipment.

'I went to the Imperial War Graves Commission on the Monday and asked about Wing Commander Collingson – then I discovered that Lacey was barking up the wrong tree, and so was the Grieb family in Hamburg and in Marbella.'

'Both in Marbella now, I can tell you,' snorted Royce.

Charlie looked puzzled but continued. 'The aircraft hadn't crashed on take-off from Djerba, it had taken the long route avoiding occupied territory and had overflown Tunisia and Algeria to fly over the west coast of Spain and up across the Bay of Biscay. What had happened was that it crashed on take-off after a stop to pick up passengers at Gibraltar.'

'And that,' interrupted Royce, 'is over there – that bloody plane hit the water on take-off from Gibraltar, just a few bleeding miles out there with enough to keep us 'appy for life. Charlie, I'll tell you one thing – you're bloody lucky to 'ave Roycie on your side.'

Royce cursed as he banged his head on the lamp of the cabin roof. 'Not much of a place for comfort, this, 'Ow the 'ell I'm going to sleep 'ere I don't know. Look at that little bed – what you call it, bunk? I would go out over the side of that and fall on the floor, I'm sure of that. Made for midgets, these places.'

'It's not too bad when you get used to it,' Charlie replied. 'If it gets rough at sea I'll put a strap round you like a car seat belt – you'll be OK.'

'Rough – not bleeding likely. I 'ate boats. I went through 'ell getting 'ere to find you, Charlie Singer, and I'm not suffering no more. Why did you go so far as this place? I suppose to get away from me.'

He didn't need an answer to know he was right.

Charlie was in no condition to be amused. He continued bandaging his calves, hoping that the pain would soon ease. He wondered what had become of Hassan and mentioned to Royce that the boy was late.

'Met 'im last night in a bar – bumped into 'im on purpose so to speak. Gave 'im the day off and said you 'ad agreed. 'E was 'appy enough with the cash I gave 'im to enjoy 'imself – gives us time to talk things over.'

Royce lit a cigar and crawled out of the tiny cabin. In the cockpit he felt less claustrophobic and we wanted to be alone to think things out. No doubt about it that Charlie was smarter than he had given him credit for. That move to go to the Imperial War Graves Commission had been smart. He had a pretty good idea where the stuff lay, but 'pretty good' wasn't good enough. Surely some attempt must have been made to raise the aircraft and it must have failed. That was why it had been declared officially a grave at sea – he had read something about that in the papers about the *Titanic*. It must be lying in some fairly deep water. They would have to locate it and then dive to it. This wasn't work for amateurs. Then there was the fencing of the goods when the box was raised. No good walking around with a load of gold hoping someone would buy. Charlie must have planned this. He called into the cabin and Charlie stumbled out, his legs still paramount in his mind. Royce outlined his thoughts and Charlie listened, rubbing his legs from time to time. Then he spoke.

'Lacey had the answer. That's one of the reasons he got excited over the book. He was working with a man who was some technical expert, worked part-time for the company Lacey worked for and part-time for another in Plymouth – Dekta Equipment – which produce metal detectors. Lacey went to see his associate – man named Davies – and said he would cut him in on the action. Davies went down to Plymouth with Lacey, and Lacey brought back some pricey equipment – how he afforded it I don't know. Maybe he did a deal with Davies. When Lacey left for Tunisia the next day he had some problem over getting the machine to work but he couldn't contact Davies to discuss it. I agreed to see Davies, sort out the tuning problem and then come on to meet up with him. We believed, both of us, that the site of the action would be Tunisia. So did Davies. In fact as far as I know the only person who knows that Gibraltar is concerned is me, and that's the only problem now – the depth of the water for the tuning. Another way in which Lacey helped is in the fencing. He had had a short affair with his secretary – she had confided in Lacey that her father was doing time in Dartmoor.'

Royce grunted. 'Poor sod. What's 'is name?'

'Parker,' Charlie went on, and Royce didn't react; this information tied up with what Angie had told him. 'So Ian Lacey had the means to detect the box and the means to fence the goods because Parker has a reputation of being a king fence. His problem was he couldn't wait for Parker to complete his porridge but his daughter said she could get a lead from her father when she visited him. You know, even if someone's listening it's –'

'I know all right,' Royce said feelingly.

'So,' Charlie went on, 'Lacey had the lot – except for one thing. He was working on Tunisia, the wrong place. The Griebs hadn't even got a lead. They were working on the Tunisia line also – but they were working on the assumption that the goods were buried in their original place, under the desert sand. In fact, the son kept a file on the exact areas they had searched. When I was living with Ella she told me she was convinced it had never been uncovered. But Lacey had shown me this letter from Phillips which was in the book, saying about the unearthing of the tin, so I know the Griebs were wrong.'

'Why did you come down and live with this Grieb bird?' Royce interjected.

'Because I had a nasty shock when I heard she was living in Marbella – too close to Gib. I thought maybe the family had caught on to the fact that the aircraft had come down off Gib and that's why they moved here – to be close to the scene. For all I knew, they might have made the recovery and had the stuff in the house. Anyway, I soon found out that the stuff was still where it went down.'

''Ow did you get on to the Griebs?' Royce asked.

'Across the letter from Phillips someone had scribbled the name "Grieb" and some exclamation marks – obviously put in by whoever read the letter because it was a different hand, and in pencil too. Then Ian found it again in the margin of the book, which was full of German language notes, against where they found the German officer holding up his handkerchief to surrender. Then there was another reference, I forget exactly where, but in the margin someone had written *Grieb gest*-something. Anyway, Ian looked it up – means jewels. That's what got old Ian's pants hot – he felt he was on to something big. As all the margin notes were written in German, and Grieb is a German name, that started me thinking. I've been in publishing for four years or so with a company which publishes trade directories. I know the trade directory publishers in Germany – they are based in Munich – so I called on a friend of mine there and asked him if Grieb meant anything to him. It didn't. He went through the directory until he came across Grunner and Grieb, jewellers in Hamburg with the address and telephone number. When I called them I asked for Mr Grieb – I was going to ask him if he was in North Africa during the war and that I would like to fly over to discuss his participation for inclusion in a book. The voice which said he was Mr Grieb threw me a little – such a young voice. Then when I asked for Mr Grieb senior I was told he had died. I gave the young man a story about being a friend of his father's and pushed along that line. Then when I asked about his mother, chancy one that, he came up with the news she was living in Spain and gave me her address – 'cos I said I wanted to write to her. Worried me at the time, though as I've said. Was she on to the Gibraltar angle?'

'You're smarter than I've given you credit for, Charlie, smarter by bloody 'arf. You really thought this through and now you're sensible enough to take me on as a partner – one of the smartest moves you've ever made, I'll tell you. You got rid of Ian by sendin' 'im on a chaser, an' don't try that on me, Tenner, 'cos you'd be sorry. Just one question. You've set up all this nicely but you 'aven't got a diver to go down for the stuff, and even if you get it who's going to fence it for you?'

'I have a diver coming down from England – an old friend with a great record who I went to see before I came down. He's in on a cut of the action. As for the fence, I'm not needing one – I have a ready customer.'

'And who's that?' Royce said through closed teeth as he lit a cigar.

'The original owners – the Jewish family.'

Royce's match went out and his cigar dropped. 'Fucking 'ell!' was all he could manage.

'Lacey went down to Tunisia in advance – I've told you that already,' Charlie went on, after Royce had managed to light his cigar. 'He was expecting me to come down in a few days and I was using that time to see the War Graves people and to locate Grieb.'

'I know – you've just told me that,' muttered Royce.

'So – I played for time, knowing that he would telephone and ask what was going on. I had a problem. I didn't want him to speak to his mother-in-law, whose home I had been living in, so after three days or so I had to stand around the house ready to answer the phone. He had given me a note to give to his mother-in-law and I burned that. The phone was in the room I used as a study, so I spent a lot of time in there – and I tried to arrange for Ann to go out as much as possible so she wouldn't spend time at home. Sure enough, one afternoon Lacey comes on – he had had a bad time getting through and the line wasn't good. He had found a small hotel there and asked me when I was coming down. I told him there were a few problems with the equipment but I would be down in a few days. I asked him what progress he had made and he told me that he hadn't got too far – no one he spoke to had any knowledge of an aircraft coming down in the sea during the war. He told me that he had divers arranged – at Agim there are sponge divers who go down incredible depths with no equipment, just stones for weight, and come up with sponges. He felt sure he could use them. Then he had found out the name of the synagogue which had been raided. He had talked to the members of the Jewish community there and they were only too pleased to talk about the attack and the family who lived in the villa. The family was called Carlucci and what remained of the family had left and were now living in Italy – in Genoa. Before coming down here I flew to Genoa, looked them up in the telephone book and went to see them. They were children at the time and had lost most of the family, not just in the raid itself but apparently a few days later they were rounded up again; all except the kids, and an elderly man who had been hidden in the town. The German officer, who spoke Italian to them – they found that upsetting – wanted to know what had happened to the jewellery from the synagogue and the villa. They didn't know and he didn't believe them. Apparently they were mostly all shot.

'The children were then around six or seven but they

remembered the incident well. Who wouldn't? They were looked after by the elderly man, and after the war they returned to Italy. They've been more than successful, I can tell you – in fact they are well off indeed. They lent me the boat, which they had in France.'

'That accounts for the French registration.' observed Royce.

'Right, but they're not all that liberal with their cash. It was a rather old and troublesome tub – hence the long stay in Puerto Banus which held me up a lot, although I used the time getting info from Ella.'

'And meeting up with me – which wasn't a bad thing,' Royce smiled.

'Anyway, the Italian family are prepared to buy back the stuff their family lost all those years ago.'

'Did they give you any idea of what they would pay?' Royce asked.

'They offered half a million – and they didn't mean lire.'

Royce whistled. 'We'd better start looking fast, Charlie. I might even get over my seasickness. Who knows?'

11

Adrian thought over the two misfits carefully. How did Ian know the content of the letters? And why did Henry spend his time on the boat? He got up and sat at the dressing room table, opening the school exercise book of notes he had made since the beginning of his quest. He decided to go through from the beginning in case he had missed something. So much had happened that his mind had become blurred. Now in the early morning his thoughts were clear. Suddenly, on the first page, he stopped. His ballpoint pen hung over a brief note. *Why was Ian anxious to contact the owner of the book – no mention of the author?* he had written. A thought swirled through his mind, something the publisher had said. He flipped through the pages until he came to a heading 'Youngman and Pearson (Publishers)'. *YP (Mr Bennett) stated that inaccuracies in the books had led them to appoint informed people to read for fact – illness of one had led to appointment of another in case of Western Desert.*

He walked across to the window and looked out across the sea where the first glow of dawn was making itself felt. Anyone checking the facts might well see the margin notes and would also have access to the publisher's records and files – might even have photocopies. The book had come into Ian's possession at a sale following the death of the owner. He flicked through his notes again. The widow of the owner, whom he had visited with Lorna was a Mrs Girdler. There was another note. *Mrs Girdler showed little interest in books belonging to her late husband – military man.* He resolved that on his return to England Mrs Girdler would be at the head of his visiting list.

Adrian felt uncomfortable about Ella's suggestion that Franz should go back to England with him and contact A.J. Phillips. He had, after all, given his personal promise to the publishers that he would not contact the writers of the letters, and Franz would be acting under his direct instruction and information. Still, to progress the search further he had to dispense with semantics. From the conversation they had had and the notes they had put together, the common factor was Tunisia – especially the island of Djerba. If that visit was to be undertaken he wanted to go with Franz. After all, he had not the faintest idea of how to start looking for – and examining – what he sought.

His deliberations were broken by the telephone ringing and he heard Franz answer in the lounge. It was for Adrian. Lorna's voice came on the line. She was well and everything was fine back at home. She was delighted to hear her father would be back in a few days. Franz Grieb would stay at the Lansdowne Club.

* * *

As Heathrow was close to Mrs Girdler's house in Windsor, Adrian called her from the airport to see if he could see her that afternoon. The call was unanswered so he decided to go to Windsor for the afternoon and try again later. All he hoped was that she hadn't gone away for a holiday.

In the taxi to Windsor Adrian remembered his talk with Mrs Girdler. So much had happened since he called on her and she had welcomed him into her home. Yet Mrs Girdler had been unable to throw any light on the annotations in German in the margin; indeed she had been insistent that her late husband would never deface a book.

A strong wind was blowing as Adrian made his way into Caleys department store and then strolled down Peascod Street. At a telephone box he called Mrs Girdler. This time he was in luck. Yes, she remembered Mr Franklin and she would be happy if he would pop around straight away. She would put tea on and her husband would be interested to meet Mr Franklin. He would soon be back.

Adrian started to walk the ten-minute journey to the house. He stopped. *Her husband would be back.* But her husband, the military gentleman, she had called him, was dead. She had sold the house – that's why his books were in the sale. Adrian's brow furrowed as he strolled purposefully along the pavement. Soon that would be explained, he told himself.

Mrs Girdler greeted him with enthusiasm and led him through to the lounge where they had had their first meeting so many weeks ago. Her hair was tied in the same tight bun as when they had last met and she wore exactly the same clothes. Indeed, Adrian thought, it could have been a direct continuation of the first encounter.

A tall, grey-haired man was standing at the window as they entered the lounge and Mrs Girdler introduced her husband. They exchanged pleasantries as Mr Girdler asked about the weather in Spain; Englishmen always talk about the weather and Mr Girdler was obviously English.

'I understand you have talked to my wife before, Mr Franklin – any progress with the search for your son?'

'Son-in-law, actually,' corrected Adrian. 'No – the straight answer is that we haven't located him but there has been a course of events which have left me with a jigsaw puzzle, some pieces fitting and some in the box. The reason, or one of the reasons, for coming here today is that the North African campaign seems to play a role in young Ian's disappearance. As I told your wife before, it all started with his strong interest, almost obsession, with your books – the one on the Western Desert particularly.'

'Not my books, actually,' Mr Girdler put in. 'The books which your son-in-law purchased at the sale at the last house belonged to my wife's former husband, who died a short while back.'

Adrian hesitated. 'I'm sorry, I didn't realise that.'

'Of course you couldn't know,' Mrs Girdler assured him.

'When my husband died our close friend Guy, whose wife passed away some years ago, was a great comfort, and as time passed it seemed a good idea to set up home together, so we married early this year, sold both our houses and a lot of contents and moved here, where, I'm happy to say, we are very much at home.'

'So your first husband,' Adrian found himself thinking out loud, 'his name wasn't . . .'

'No – he was a Gunter Sneider.'

'And he was in the army?'

'Yes – the German Army. He served all his working life in the army and was very keen on military history. That's why he had those books.'

Sneider – Adrian's thoughts raced as Mrs Girdler poured tea. Sneider – that was the name of the commanding officer who had placed Otto Grieb under arrest, according to Franz and Ella. That explained the German notes.

'Mr Franklin, your tea.'

Adrian took the tea. The publisher had mentioned Sneider in connection with the book – somehow. Adrian couldn't get it straight and wasn't helped by Mrs Girdler's continuous chatter. Then suddenly, in a flash, he had it – of course, Colonel Sneider was one of the people who was going to check and if necessary correct the original text of the book. The name hadn't meant a thing when it was first mentioned in the publisher's office and he had attached no importance to it. Now a few more pieces fell into place. Mrs Girdler's former husband was a key figure in the drama in Tunisia all those years before, and because of his knowledge of the campaign from the German side, he had been selected to check facts in the narrative.

'May I ask you a few questions, Mrs Girdler? Who asked Colonel Sneider to check over the narrative?'

'You surprise me, Mr Franklin. I didn't say that he had been asked to check the narrative and I certainly didn't give you his rank.' Mrs Girdler looked worried, as if she felt Adrian wasn't playing straight with her.

Adrian squirmed mentally – yes, he was stringing her

along. The long silence which fell only added to the uncomfortable atmosphere. Adrian wished he could disappear for a few moments so he could take stock of the situation. But it wasn't possible and two curious faces were studying him intently. On his way to England with Franz he had resolved not to divulge the full story to anyone, and Franz had agreed that the same would apply to his talk with Phillips. Now, however, he was faced with a situation where the Girdlers were very much on guard, and unless he made some explanation no more information would be forthcoming.

Adrian took a long sip at his tea.

'Just before Ian's disappearance, as you know, he was making a very careful study of one of the books he obtained from you. For some reason or other just after that he went to the West of England and then on to Tunisia. I was so convinced that that book was critical to his disappearance that I went to the publishers and talked with them. They told me that Colonel Sneider had been involved in correcting the revised edition of General Collingson's book. I didn't know this meant that there was any connection, Mrs Girdler, between you and Colonel Sneider – indeed, when you referred to your husband as a military man I assumed his name was Girdler and that he had been in the British Army. I made wrong assumptions.'

He took a deep breath and, looking at the Girdlers facing him, he knew that the explanation had been accepted and he inwardly congratulated himself that he hadn't told the story in such a way as would lead to the disclosure of events in Plymouth, Marbella and Hamburg, for that matter. He had told enough to satisfy their curiosity and dissolve their reserve.

'Yes, Gunter did do some correcting work,' volunteered Mrs Girdler. 'He knew Mr Youngman through the Rotary Club and was asked to do it – Mr Youngman knew he had served in North Africa. Gunter did quite a lot until he fell ill.'

Adrian had had time to think. 'When I asked you about the notes in German in the margin, you said he would not have written them.'

'That's correct, he would not. Firstly he would have written in English; after all, he had lived here for thirty-odd years and thought in English. Also, I believe I told you it was out of character for him to deface a book. No, the most likely explanation is that Robert wrote them – the friend of Gunter's who helped him when he became ill.'

'Robert?' queried Adrian, and Mrs Girdler, now in full swing, was pleased to pick the conversation again.

'Robert Whiteman was an old friend of Gunter. He was one of his officers, as adjutant then a company commander, I think – during the war. They have always stayed in touch even though Robert worked in Latin America for many years. He lives locally and Gunter asked him to help to refresh his memory and also to give more relevant information on one book – on Arnhem, I believe. Robert was on General Model's staff and knew more about the Arnhem incident. Gunter was in reserve in General von Rundstedt's headquarters. I knew General von Rundstedt and I remember I said to Roberto that it was a pity he never met him – such a fine gentleman.'

Adrian chipped in. 'You called him Roberto then...'

'Yes, his mother was Italian and Roberto was his real name. Sometimes we called him Roberto through habit – we had known him for so many years and old habits die hard.'

'So is Robert, or Roberto, continuing the corrections now?'

'Oh yes, I believe so – I haven't seen much of him recently but he came to our wedding.' She gave her husband's hand an affectionate squeeze. 'I asked him how things were going, and he said he felt a closeness to Gunter in continuing his work – one of those nice things one says at weddings when you are searching for something to say. Probably felt a little uneasy about me remarrying. He was close to Gunter. He told me he had been to see General Collingson about the book he was checking. The general was very ill, and I understand he died very recently.'

Adrian found himself searching for the next question and wishing he had made a list before making the visit.

'I wonder if I put some names to you, would you tell me if they mean anything to you?' he asked.

Mrs Girdler smiled. 'Of course – anything I can do to help, especially as it concerns someone who has...' She hesitated, and Adrian added, 'disappeared.'

'I was actually going to say, "lost his memory".'

Adrian shook his head. 'That's an explanation, but I don't think a very probable one – I don't know why I say that but I really don't believe that Ian lost his memory. Anyway, on the subject of memory, let me ask you, does Otto Grieb mean anything to you?'

Mrs Girdler shook her head. 'No – but I've heard it before somewhere – no, I cannot recall.'

'Or Betty Silvester?'

Mrs Girdler indicated a negative.

'Or Davies – or Southon – or Rollason?'

'I'm sorry – these names mean nothing at all to me. I don't seem to be much help, do I?'

'What about Parker?'

Mrs Girdler again shook her head but Mr Girdler leant forward.

'Yes, that means something to me, but then it's not an unusual name. I was at Roberto's home in Cookham with Gunter. As I explained to you, I knew Gunter for years, indeed both Gunter and Alice were good friends of mine when they were married. One day I drove over to Cookham Dean with Gunter to deliver some papers to Robert – work on the narrative, I believe – and over coffee they talked about having to make a visit to ask Parker. From what I gathered, Parker was somewhat inaccessible. There was a girl there – worked for Robert, I imagine – who said that would be a good idea, and it was agreed that she would go and see him. I really didn't pay much attention as it was nothing to do with me and I was sitting by the fire having coffee. In fact, the only reason I was there was to be Gunter's chauffeur because he wasn't too well by then.'

Adrian tried to think. So Robert had possibly written the notes. Robert or Roberto was an old friend of Sneider's and had served in the Middle East theatre and knew or knew of Parker. But if the Parker they spoke about was the Parker in

Dartmoor – and that was a possibility but no more – then ... Adrian stopped. As far as he knew, only one girl would have reasonable access to Nosey Parker – his daughter.

'Can you describe this girl?' Adrian asked.

'Oh yes. She was damned good-looking – small – very slight, around early twenties. Robert called her Betty. I remember because it was the name of my first wife.'

Mrs Girdler returned with a fresh pot of tea and some cakes and Adrian thanked her.

'You have both been most helpful over this whole affair,' he said nervously 'There must be other information which could lead to Ian but I don't know the questions to ask – you have surprised me in so many ways. Maybe I could call you if new things crop up. Meanwhile, could you let me have the address and telephone number of Robert – I feel I should meet him.'

Mrs Girdler went to the writing desk at the far side of the room and wrote. As she handed it to Adrian and he thanked her, a thought occurred.

'May I ask you to keep our conversation today just between ourselves – please don't mention it to Mr Robert Whiteman, for example.'

Again, the worried look came to Mrs Girdler's face. 'How will you explain the fact that you have his name and address?' she asked.

'I'll tell a white lie and say the publishers told me.'

Wishing them goodbye and thanking them for their hospitality, Adrian left. As he walked slowly back to the railway station he looked at the piece of paper. Cookham Dean wasn't that far away. At the railway station he got into a cab and gave the driver the address.

'Don't stop there, just drive slowly by, very slowly,' Adrian instructed.

As the car passed the entrance to the elegant house Adrian drew his breath. Parked in the short driveway was a red Fiat. He couldn't read the sign in the rear window but he would put a substantial bet on the fact that the car had been supplied by Pentagon Garage of Plymouth to Mrs Betty Silvester of Mary Tavy, one-time girlfriend of Ian Lacey and current companion of one Davies.

* * *

The 18-year-old wobbled unsteadily on his stick as he made his way down the hospital steps. Erika held her son's arm and chided him for being too ambitious in his first hour outside. The taxi was waiting with its engine running.

At the Hotel Emperatriz Alfonso waited for his son. At breakfast they had decided that only Erika would go to collect Paco. Madrid taxis are generally rather small and Paco would probably need a lot of room to spread out his leg.

In the bar of the old-fashioned three-star hotel with its view of the entrance foyer, Alfonso ran his mind over the past ten days. It had been quite a shock to see Paco with his leg in plaster and a gash across his forehead which 15 stitches had done their best to hold together. There was no question about it, his grandfather had been right about making the trip to Spain, for they had observed a remarkable improvement in the boy. Eighteen-year-olds have great resilience, but inactivity was an anathema to a sport-loving student and the games of chess with his parents had helped to pass the time over the past week.

Now Paco was going to join them for a few days at the hotel. Alfonso thought over the suggestion which his father-in-law had sprung on them on the telephone only the previous evening – that they should have a short holiday in London to round off their European trip. Neither he nor Erika had ever been to England. It would be an interesting experience. They had considered it some years before but the confrontation between Britain and the Argentine over the Malvinas had put paid to that. Erika had a couple of cousins in England and it would be fun to look them up. Yes, he would talk Erika into the idea of a holiday; after all, the ranch was in good hands and running smoothly.

* * *

After he had parted from Adrian, Franz drove the Hertz Ford

carefully out of the Heathrow airport concourse and onto the motorway. His telephone call with A.J. Phillips had had an immediate effect. Mr Phillips was leaving for the USA that evening and if Mr Grieb wanted to talk to him about the letter there was no time like the present.

As he cruised gently down the M4, he felt uneasy. His mother was still in Marbella and the architect of the recent attack on her was still at large. Angie had been a loving companion for a few days but he didn't want one more innocent person brought into this violent affair and he wished he hadn't told her as much as he had. Another thought which kept passing through his mind was the business in Hamburg. Gerd Blücher was a good manager; he had been valuable to the business whilst Franz's father was alive but he was getting elderly and tended to be old-fashioned. He tended to buy stock which was too traditional and therefore slow-moving.

A fast coach overtaking him caused the car to rock in its wake and he decided he had better concentrate on the job in hand and arrive at his destination without mishap.

Cirencester, despite its unimposing approach, was all that he had come to expect of a typical English town and Franz regretted that his last two visits to England had been restricted to London. It was in an environment like this that he felt most at home. He found a parking spot close to a café and after enjoying his coffee he asked the waitress for directions to Darington House.

When Franz swung the Ford into the driveway of Darington House he wasn't surprised the waitress knew it. Its long driveway of beeches soon opened onto spacious lawns where an elderly gardener was busily raking. The house was imposing, built of the local stone he had observed throughout the town. Franz wasn't up on English architecture but he guessed it was late seventeenth century.

The door was opened by a fat, cheerful housekeeper in an apron, who showed him through the house to the lounge where Mr Phillips sat. Franz was mildly surprised. Mr A.J. Phillips was in a wheelchair. He was in his seventies, a slim man with grey hair and an extremely ruddy complexion; a combination of fresh air and whisky, Franz thought. His guess was quickly confirmed by the offer of a drink, which he declined as he would be driving.

Mr Phillips made the sound of usual pleasantries about Grieb's trip and how was the weather in Malaga.

'Played golf at Nueva Andulacia many times,' he commented, 'when my wife was alive that was – marvellous course and great climate.'

The conversation lagged and Mr Phillips gave Franz his opening.

'What can I do for you, my boy?'

Franz explained that he was doing some military history research, concentrating especially on the Western Desert campaign. This was for a German publisher and he had been doing a great deal of reading of British accounts of the war. He understood that Mr Phillips had corrected publishers about certain errors or omissions – he deliberately used the plural to avoid using the name of Youngman and Pearson. Mr Phillips listened intently to the young German and then sat back in his wheelchair.

'I'll tell you my story as well as I can remember it,' he said deliberately. 'Mind you, I was on the opposite side to your – your...' He hesitated, 'Well, let's say we were enemies and not beat about the bush. You would have won if you hadn't had all those bloody Italians on your side. I've a lot of respect for the German soldier, especially your Field Marshal Rommel. Even Auchinleck had to issue orders that the legends about him had to be discouraged. That's how much effect he had on our side.'

Anthony John Phillips had joined the army at the outbreak of war and was posted to Catterick, where he became wedded to tanks. After basic training he went to Salisbury, and then in 1942, when Montgomery was appointed Commander in Chief Middle East Land Forces, Phillips found himself in the famous Eighth Army in Egypt, preparing for the big push in October at El Alamein. After Alamein there was a sustained push across the desert until a terrific rainstorm flooded the land. 'End of first week in November, if I recall, your Rommel was back then and giving us a hard time. That rain let him pull back forces to Tunisia – and we were pushing on hard to that objective. We had heard that the Americans had landed at Casablanca and at Algiers. Big plan was to meet up with them.'

All went according to plan until they approached the Mareth line. They knew that Rommel had retreated to form a strong defensive position around Mareth and had diverted some of his forces to attack the American forces, which were coming in a pincer movement following the landings at Casablanca.

The approach to Mareth met with little resistance and they took a number of Italian prisoners. Mareth was taken by the New Zealand division, which went around the hills and attacked Rommel's defences from the rear.

'I think the defences might have held if Rommel had remained in command,' Mr Phillips opined, 'but apparently he was recalled to Germany because of his health. Anyway, we broke through the Mareth defences and then it was a clear run to Tunis – we met up on the way with the Americans who had landed in Morocco and made them very cross. They wanted to do the job single-handed.'

Tony Phillips wheeled over to the sideboard and took his pipe from the rack. His puff of smoke seemed to be the epilogue of his narrative, and Franz felt that now he would have to ask questions. But he didn't want to put his subject too much on his guard.

'There was someone called Collingson. I believe you mentioned him in a letter to one publisher.'

Phillips looked up sharply. 'Do you mean Captain or Wing Commander?'

Franz was thrown for a second and then murmured, 'There was something to do with a trunk of papers.'

'Oh yes, rum affair that was. Both Collingsons were involved. I knew Peter Collingson well – Captain Collingson he was. Went on to be a general. He was my squadron commander as a young officer – same tank as a matter of fact, for much of the advance anyway. We were out in that stinking Libyan desert and knew we were approaching problems. We had mopped up a lot of Wops – Italians I mean,' he added hastily, seeing Franz's raised eyebrows.

'We suddenly came across a German captain on his own in the desert, waving a flag. He certainly seemed pissed off with fighting and was more than willing to be taken prisoner. Collingson took him on board and they talked German together; I believe the captain had studied it at university. Anyway, I had a natter with him during our refuel stop and he was saying he had fallen foul of the German authorities and had been charged with stealing a box of valuables – which he said he had not.'

'Do you recall his name?' Franz asked.

Phillips nodded. 'It sounded like Grubb. He was handed over to the local cooler and that was the end of his little war – one less bloody Kraut to fight!'

A.J. Phillips bit his lip as he remembered Franz's nationality. He need not have worried. Franz Grieb's mind was elsewhere. 'It's a small world' always sounded trite but the stark reality was that the man telling his story had actually been involved in taking his father prisoner all those years before. It was just too incredible. But Phillips was now in full swing and continuing the story.

'We had to clear some mines around the approach to the airfield on some island called Djerba. We went out there with flail tanks – chains which revolve on a drum and explode mines ahead of the tanks. Jerry had laid some beauties just on the approach, as we had been told. Then Captain Collingson ordered us to clear a hill overlooking the causeway. It was a waste of time – no mines at all – but one tank did throw up a tin trunk. We thought it was some kind of booby trap but Collingson examined it and said it was documentation. We took it in our tank and Collingson spent some time going over it – apparently the papers were confidential German documents. Young Parker, Collingson's batman, took them into Divisional HQ for examination. We were told they were a valuable find and Parker was quite excited about it. He told me later that it was tragic that they should have been lost. That's what happened, of course.'

Grieb didn't understand the 'of course' so he made a questioning noise.

'All the stuff was loaded onto an aircraft, a Liberator, for taking back to the UK along with some wounded men. Apparently, according to Parker, the aircraft crashed into the sea on take-off – everyone on board and everything was lost. That's war – we got used to that sort of thing.'

'You mentioned two Collingsons – the one we have just talked about and another.'

'Yes – Wing Commander. I don't recall his first name but he was Peter Collingson's elder brother. They were pretty close. He was flying sorties out of North Africa at the time, hitting enemy targets around Sfax and Sousse, I guess. Anyway, he was the pilot of the aircraft which went down with the box on board. One brother found it, one brother lost it – irony of life, I suppose.' Phillips straightened his shoulders and wheeled across to the open fire.

'It's such a fascinating story. I wonder why Collingson didn't include it in his book?' Franz questioned.

Phillips smiled. 'Not only that but he never made any reference to old Fred Parker, his batman. Fred was with Collingson right through North Africa, saved his life once, pulled him clear of a sniper's bullet, yet Colly never made a mention – not a bloody word. Always struck me that Collingson was up to something – I don't know what. Maybe he didn't mention the box affair because of his brother's death. He was really cut up over that, I can tell you.

'Never mentioned the Jews, either. Whole lot of them shot by the – well, anyway, they had all been executed at Djerba. Terrible scene it was when we moved in. That upset Colly. Only one had escaped and he had two kids with him. Upset them that the officer who was in charge was Italian, or spoke Italian.'

The housekeeper came in with a tray of tea. As she left Franz asked, 'What about Parker – whatever became of him?'

'No idea. Just vanished after the war. We stayed in the same tank up to Tunis then after a while we were regrouped for landing in Sicily. I saw him once or twice – we met up in Rome the following summer – but then, you know how it goes, life moves on. May be dead, as far as I know. Bit of a sharp dealer was Parker, but a nice guy.'

'And the German, the officer wandering in the desert – whatever became of him?'

'Good God, heaven knows. Went in the can with the others. Funny, come to mention it, Parky talked about him when we met in Rome, said he was into a deal with Collingson then – but, Christ Almighty, that's a long time ago and my memory plays tricks. He's probably one of those rich industrialists in Germany now, like most Nazis.'

'He wasn't necessarily a Nazi, was he,' corrected Franz.

'Well, he looked like one. Tough-looking bugger, tallish, red hair like you – bit taller than you.'

Franz finished his tea. There seemed little else to say. He thanked Mr Phillips for his time and wished him well on his visit to the United States.

'It's a pleasure to help, Mr Grieb, a real pleasure, and I hope you have some material which you can use in your book. The last interview I gave seemed to produce nothing. He said he would come back to me in a few days but never did. He was a flaky kind of case, I thought – sounded like his head was in the clouds.'

'What interview?' asked Franz.

'Oh, someone called me on the phone a couple of months or so ago and asked me a lot of questions on the same subject as yourself. He was putting an article together on the Western Desert campaign. I remember his name – same name as my gardener – Lacey, John or Ian Lacey. As I say, sounded a strange cove. Said he would come and see me – never did.'

Franz returned to the Cirencester café. The last thing he wanted was tea but he wanted to think without the distraction of driving. The notes he had made were sparse and seemed to have trailed off when he reached the point of his father's capture. That really was amazing – he had been talking to his father's captor, or one of his captors. His mind focused, however, on the final part of the conversation on the doorstep. So Adrian's son-in-law had phoned Phillips – strange he hadn't visited him – and Ian's enquiries were on the same line. So he must have seen the letter, as they suspected. How else could he have discovered the existence of Mr Phillips?

Another odd thing struck Franz. The British Army was almost as class-conscious as the German Army, yet in the 1940s it appeared that there was a close relationship between Collingson, a career officer who would one day make general officer rank, and his batman.

As Franz looked at his bill, he saw under the heading *Queen Ann Teashop* the words *Proprietor A. J. Phillips* in small print. He asked the waitress if that was the Mr Phillips of Darington House.

'Yes indeed,' she replied. 'He owns a lot around here – seems to turn everything to profit. That's why people call him Mr Goldfinger.'

It took Franz a little over two hours to reach London. Carrington Street car park, which Adrian had suggested to him, was close to the Lansdowne Club, and shortly after seven he was signing the register. It appeared that member Mr Adrian Franklin had not yet arrived so Franz settled into his room and decided to call his mother.

Ella's voice came over on the line. It was incredible that he had been with her only early on that same day. So much had happened. Yes, she was fine. She asked how had things gone in England. Franz realised that he couldn't condense it all into a telephone call so he limited himself to a few facts.

'Extraordinary thing to tell you, Mother. That man Phillips, he was one of the British soldiers who took Father prisoner – a million-to-one chance of meeting him, but there's so much more to tell you when we meet.'

'I've had a strange experience too, Franz,' Ella exclaimed. 'I was fetching a few things at the hypermarket today – you know, the one on the way to Puerto Banus – when I saw that ghastly Royce fellow. He was sitting in his Mercedes coupé. I kept well away and went to my car. Then a girl came out – a young Oriental-looking girl with a load of groceries. She got into the car and they drove off.'

Franz's mouth went dry. 'A young Oriental girl? Oh no, it couldn't be.'

As Ella tried to describe her, Franz found his head spinning. Just how much had he told her?

When he put the receiver down he walked in a daze to the elegant baroque lounge. He had often been accused by his father of being gullible but never to such a stupid degree as this.

Franz was relieved to see Adrian come in. Most of the members had adjourned to the bar, but they agreed it would be better if they stayed in the lounge where they could have privacy.

Franz recounted his experience first and Adrian interrupted only once, to ask what career Phillips had followed during his working life. Franz had to confess that he didn't know. He finished up by saying that Ian had telephoned Phillips. Adrian sat upright.

'When was that?' he asked.

'Phillips said perhaps a couple of months ago,' Franz replied.

Now it was Adrian's turn to recount the events of his day and Franz broke in excitedly when Adrian revealed that Mrs Girdler had been married to Colonel Sneider.

'Good God, that is just incredible. I've been with my father's captor, or rather one of them, today and you've been with the widow of father's commanding officer! Father disliked Sneider – typical Herrenvolk German officer who worshipped the Third Reich, he used to say – and felt he hadn't been treated fairly over the Djerba incident. Sneider had been too quick to accuse and condemn at a stroke, but Father felt he had been put up to it by the adjutant, who was the real troublemaker. But I interrupt you. Please go on.'

Adrian related how Mr Girdler had reacted to the name

Parker. Franz listened intently, and his eyes flashed when Adrian mentioned the presence of the red Fiat in the drive of the house at Cookham Dean.

'That really does tie up. First we had the connection with the Silvester girl plus Davies and Parker – you picked that up in the West Country – now we have a tie-up with Sneider's assistant or replacement. The pieces really are beginning to fit.'

'So the relationship between Davies and our new-found character Robert or Roberto Whiteman is a new question.'

'Did you say Roberto?' Franz asked.

'That's right,' Adrian replied. 'Mrs Girdler mentioned that they sometimes call him Roberto, which used to be his name. He had an Italian mother but I suppose he anglicised it to Robert.'

Franz's face had gone white.

'Give me time to think this over. I don't want to make a mistake.' Franz sat staring at the ornate ceiling for several minutes. 'Yes, I remember now. When Father was telling me the story of the Djerba incident, he went on about the adjutant. Nasty little bastard, he used to call him – nickname of undertaker – and he was called Roberto. I remember because it's a bloody odd name for a German. Father told me that he was half Italian and probably had a chip on his shoulder about it. Although the Italians were on our side during the war they were regarded as a liability. Father always reckoned that if Rommel hadn't been handicapped by Italians and there hadn't been an Italian commander-in-chief at the later stages of the Libyan campaign, the Allied forces would have been defeated. Yes,' he went on after a pause, 'that adjutant was Roberto, but I cannot for the life of me remember his surname. Sons don't listen too attentively to their fathers reminiscing. It could be in Father's notes – in the Fatima file.'

'The Fatima file?' queried Adrian.

'Yes, we made notes on holiday about the areas we had covered and Father wrote a few memories in there – it listed the ground which we covered without finding anything.

Trying to find by elimination. But you must remember I mentioned the Fatima file, that thug who roughed me up in Hamburg was after it. I have it right here.' Franz opened his brief case and took out a worn file. He sat reading and thumbing through. 'Weissman, father's adjustant Weissman.'

'Let's go and have a drink,' Adrian suggested.

'Just a minute. There's just one thing I haven't told you.' Franz told Adrian of his telephone call to his mother and the sighting of the 'Oriental girl'.

'I've a nasty feeling – a very nasty feeling – that this girl is the Filipina I've been knocking around with in the past few days, and if so I've been with Rollason's associate.'

'Christ. I need that drink,' Adrian groaned.

12

The 'In and Out' is affectionately so called by its members because of its prominent double gates indicating to members and visitors which they should use. In correct parlance it is the Army and Navy Club and its members are officers and ex-officers of the armed forces.

The club was only five minutes' walk from Berkeley Square, and Jimmy Slattery, delighted to have a call from his old friend's son, told Franz that he would have no difficulty finding it. He would be delighted to entertain him to lunch there and would meet him in the foyer at twelve thirty. Franz, unsure of the protocol of such a bastion of British upper society as a gentleman's club, refrained from asking if Adrian could join them – so whilst Franz walked towards the In and Out, Adrian settled down to write notes and to attempt to achieve some semblance of order in the many facts they had assembled.

Jimmy Slattery grasped Franz warmly by the hand. 'Delighted, my dear boy. What a splendid surprise – absolutely splendid. Just been trying to work out when we last met up. Best forgotten, eh? Time flies so quickly. Remind me of your father, you do – grown more like him, and that's a compliment, my boy. Come and have a snifter.'

In the elegant yet subdued bar, Colonel Slattery ordered drinks and they took them to a side table.

'Heard from your mother few weeks ago – asked me to check up on some chap, forgotten his name, chap who died in South Africa. Can't think what it was all about and she didn't appear to want to tell me. Women are like that, always want to be secretive – never did understand them and that's a strength, Franz my boy. You're always at a disadvantage if you think you understand – you let your guard down. Mind you, your mother's a fine lady, fine lady. You're lucky to have her as your mother.'

Jimmy Slattery with two double whiskies on board in the course of ten minutes, was in great form and clearly wanted to do all the talking. It took two more double whiskies before he led Franz to the dining room, where the two Dover soles, ordered in the bar, awaited them. Slattery enjoyed his food and concentrated on the task in hand.

'Never have 'em off the bone – spoils the fun,' he remarked, and apologised to Franz about the choice of wine. 'Should have had German wine, my boy, in honour of my German visitor, but frankly I'm a French wine man myself and this Pouilly Fumé is right up my alley – just the job.'

The sole consumed, Slattery called for two large brandies and then fixed his military eyes on Franz.

'You've told me all about your mother and about your business but you haven't told me much about yourself. What brings you to London and is there anything an old buffer like me can do to help a young feller?'

'Actually, yes.' Franz decided that now was the moment to strike but he didn't want to say too much. All the background about Ian Lacey's disappearance, the hidden valuables, the attacks, seemed superfluous. 'The fact is,' he continued, leaning forward, 'I have been reading my father's notes about his war experiences. I would like to talk to a few people who served with him – to get to know him better, so to speak. I wish now I had learned more of his past.'

'Well, as you know, I was on the other side. Funny world, we were enemies in the war yet we became good friends in the fifties – some feller wrote a poem about it. Don't know who, though.'

'You may be able to put me in touch with people in the German Army who knew him – people in his regiment. I know you were in Germany after the war – the BAOR, wasn't it? And you must have met up with regular German officers. For example, I wonder if you know of the adjutant of Father's – Major or Captain Weissman?'

Slattery shook his head.

'Or Sneider, Colonel Sneider?'

Slattery pursed his lips and sipped his brandy, 'No, my boy, can't help, I'm afraid. Rum chance, mind, if I did know 'em. But I don't know either of those two officers.'

Jim Slattery furrowed his forehead. He obviously found it strange that this young man should suddenly choose to dig up his father's past and his father's previous associates. The loud 'Huh' seemed to sum up his opinion that this was a strange young man – but people were strange and seemed to be getting stranger.

'Tell you what,' Slattery volunteered. 'Might be people in the club who knew the chaps on the other side – old Braithwaite, retired brigadier he is – used to be one of those infantry chaps before he got drawn into Military Intelligence – he might know – he was in BAOR. I'll see if he's in the lounge. Often comes in, second home, this place – got a wife who runs committees and things, house full of women in hats.' The moment was ripe for another double brandy and Jimmy Slattery swirled it around his balloon glass with fervour. 'Yes, Bunny's our man. Let's go and see.'

The cards had fallen well for Franz that day, for within a few minutes he was introduced to Brigadier Francis Braithwaite. With his mutton chop whiskers and florid complexion he looked as if he should be in hunting pink ready to ride to hounds; indeed he sat as if he was astride a horse. Slattery asked him about a horse which had been lame. He then asked the question Franz wanted.

'Young Franz here – good chap, as I said. I knew his father for years – and his mother too. Fact is I introduced them, so if I hadn't been about, this young man wouldn't be around now!' He laughed at his own joke. 'Anyway, young Franz here's trying to find out about his father's associates in the last shemozzle – chap called Sneider, and another fellow called Weissman – Captain or Major.'

'Know that Weissman's first name?' he asked, turning to Franz.

'Roberto,' Franz replied. 'Sneider was called Gunter.'

Jim Slattery turned to Brigadier Braithwaite. If he had had a florid complexion before, he had now turned deep purple and his grey military moustache seemed to horizontally contract and expand.

'My God Almighty!' he exclaimed. 'Never mind this Sneider fellow, but I wish I could lay my hands on that Roberto Weissman. Christ I do – make me a hero in retirement. By Christ, get me a knighthood I wouldn't wonder.'

Franz couldn't contain his curiosity. 'Why?'

'Why? I'll tell you why, young man. It's people like Weissman who – who – who besmirched your nation – that's the only word I can put to it. That Weissman was the officer commanding B-Unit at Dachau in the last few months before it was liberated. We've all had a good lunch so I won't go into details, but Weissman is one of the most wanted war criminals alive, if he is alive, today. The Wiesenthal Institute has been trying to trace him for years – took up the search after the British Army intelligence stopped actually hunting him. Bloody difficult job. Unlike the rest of 'em, he was rarely photographed. I'll tell you one thing. Whoever gets hold of Weissman is well on the path to Martin Bormann. I forget the details without checking up some notes, but they knew one another before the war – maybe at school or something – and if I remember rightly, intelligence established that they flew the coop together just before the surrender. The *Bozenflucht* they called it, the buggering off of the top brass in the Nazi party. Remember Bormann, the Brown Shadow, supposed to cast a shadow darker than the Führer? He had outstanding power, only Bormann could sign orders "By order of the Führer".'

The old officer took a long swig of his malt whisky.

'By God, I wish I did know. Steward, I'll have another of those – just top everything up, will you, there's a good chap.'

Brigadier Braithwaite had finished his speech and had nothing more to say. He puffed into his whisky and hoped Franz would enjoy his visit to London.

Twenty minutes later Franz said farewell to Jimmy Slattery and thanked him for a splendid lunch. Slattery hailed a cab and waved Franz goodbye.

'Rum cove,' he said to the driver, 'but smart young man – pity he's a German.'

When Franz arrived back at the Lansdowne Club he went straight to the lounge and ordered tea. He sat in the green old-fashioned armchair and stared penetratingly at the carpet. What he had learned had shaken him badly and he was acutely embarrassed. Like most young Germans he was very much aware of what had happened in his fatherland in the thirties and early forties. Somehow modern German youth had inherited the taint, war had been waged from primordial time and the world accepted man's inherent drive to fight and to covet, often using religion as a justification. That was one thing and few people indeed could claim that their forefathers had not shared some guilt. The genocide of Hitler's 'Final Solution' was an opprobrium on Germany which would be a stubborn one to erase and generations would need to come and go before it was fully ascribed to history. His father had talked of it and had commented that he had little idea about the concentration camps. He had personally witnessed the Kristalnacht, when the windows of Jewish property in Germany had been smashed by youngsters impelled by their indoctrination or by sheer herd instinct. His father had said that the only way to escape persecution, arrest or maybe worse, was to cast the proverbial blind eye. Even now sitting in the heart of London in a traditional British club Franz felt deeply shocked and emotionally wounded by the reopening of doors he chose to leave closed.

He walked down the stairs and stood on the balcony, looking at the swimmers in the Olympic-size pool. There was nothing he could really do until Adrian returned. A little later he ran into Adrian in the hallway.

'Let's find a quiet corner.' Franz could not wait to expose what he had discovered. 'What I've stumbled across is really...' He stumbled for a word. 'Well, just sit down and listen.'

Adrian's face was strained and white as Franz recounted the conversation after lunch at the 'In and Out'. He interrupted when Bormann's name came up.

'Christ Almighty – so – so if he's alive, the most wanted war criminal not brought before the Nuremberg courts, we have a line on him. There's always been talk of him being still alive – must be an old man now – but as Hitler's right-hand man, possible successor, he would be a monumental find. But I still don't relate all this to Ian.'

'There was a Genoa entry in Ian's Diners Club account,' Adrian said, 'It fits with Weissman being half Italian, but that's a very loose thread indeed. I've put that on ice for a time. However, I did pick up another link which may be...'

He stopped speaking as Franz leaned over and grabbed his forearm.

'I've just thought of something,' Franz said. 'You remember when I called you to tell you about Phillips's story yesterday of the execution of the Jews? Phillips said the survivors were distressed because the officer spoke Italian. That struck me then as odd, but now it occurs to me they were upset because they were Italian Jews. The Italian persecution of Jews was pretty minimal, and such as there was they wouldn't have heard about. These survivors were particularly distressed because they believed a fellow countryman had assassinated their family and friends. We all know the Italians are close-knit. I'll ring Phillips to see if he can confirm the nationality of the family in Djerba. Maybe he even knows their name.'

'Hold on a moment. Maybe there are other questions to put to Phillips.'

Adrian told Franz of the call on the girl at the Plymouth factory and her reference to the metal detector.

'If Davies was working on metal detection devices, there is a connection with the valuables which we are so involved in... Of course this could be a red herring. But Ian went to Plymouth, where Davies had his testing station on the project. Maybe Ian bought one – maybe Davies did come to an agreement with him. I don't know if the receptionist would remember Ian if he did go there; it was some time ago and there must be a lot of visitors. But it could be that a photograph would jolt her memory.'

Franz nodded his head. 'Whatever we are following is leading us, slowly and surely, somewhere that we are not going to like. There are sinister facets of this case which go far beyond a hoard of valuables in North Africa. But I agree with you, you should see this girl and I'd like to go with you to Devon. What interests me is where Ian stopped, for example. He must have paid cash because there is no entry on his credit card for accommodation or food, just for petrol. Where did he stay and with whom? There's only one way to find out. I'll call Mother to make sure she is OK. Then if all seems happy in Marbella we'll head for the West Country.'

'Let's go tomorrow but let's tap Phillips first,' Adrian suggested.

* * *

The Cirencester number was answered by a woman's voice and Franz asked to speak to Mr Phillips. He cursed inwardly when he heard that Mr Phillips had gone to the United States and would be away several weeks. Franz established that he was the visitor of the day before, and the housekeeper supplied the telephone number in Florida where Mr Phillips could be reached. Franz thanked her and a few hours later he was explaining to Mr Phillips the reason for his call.

'Oh yes, I remember everything very clearly – very clearly indeed,' Mr Phillips responded. 'It was a most distressing scene, I can tell you. I remember Colly, Captain Collingson, saying that they were Italian; he was a bit of a linguist and liked everyone to know it. Most of the family had been wiped out and just an old man and a couple of kids were around. Collingson took some time talking with the old man – getting some rapport, I suppose. Arab community was pretty upset too. The Germans had been careful not to disturb them more than necessary. In fact the Germans gave them much less hassle than the British; that's why they were pretty supportive of the Wehrmacht. But an execution in the town – even of Jews – really cut them up.'

Franz asked a question and Phillips answered, 'Oh, Christ no – I don't know who the family was or whatever became of them. They were very influential in the town, I believe. Collingson might remember if you can get hold of him – shouldn't be too difficult, he was a bigwig in the army later on.'

Franz thanked him and expressed a hope that they would meet again. As he started to place the receiver back on its cradle, a voice bawled, 'Hold on – just a moment! Just had a thought.' Phillips was pleased he had caught the German before the call was cut off.

'Another person who might help you. Collingson was bumbling around talking to the Jews in Italian, as I said, but he really didn't grasp the language. We had a sergeant in the squadron who had been brought up in Italy as a child. Believe his father was working there on something. Anyway, this fellow spoke Italian fluently. He wasn't in our troop but part of our squadron so Collingson sent for him to sort out something he couldn't make sense of. I remember his name because it was so unusual – Sergeant Waterman. It was a bit of a joke having a Waterman in the bloody desert with no water for bloody miles! Bernard Waterman, that was his name. Parkie hated his guts – we talked about old Parker the other day, didn't we? When I met up with Parker in Rome later on he was carrying on about Waterman being promoted to warrant officer because of his languages – Waterman had been transferred to the military governor staff in Rome because he could talk to the local people in their own lingo. Where you'd find Waterman now I'm damned if I know, but he was a smart guy, I'll give him that, and he would probably remember the family's name and all about them. Why do you ask about all this?'

'It's a gap in the narrative I'm writing – I just want to get all the facts straight even if they do reflect badly on my country. I feel this family could contribute quite a lot. Do you have any idea how I could trace Waterman?'

Phillips thought for a few moments. 'No idea – like all of us, we went our way after the war was over. No, Collingson would be easier to trace. All I can tell you is Waterman was a Geordie, North Country anyway, had a strong Geordie accent.'

Franz thanked Phillips again for all his help and rang off. He repeated what he had discovered to Adrian, who was sitting on the bed in Franz's room.

'I suppose there's a chance – just a chance – that Waterman is still in Tyneside. We'll have to go through the telephone directories covering Northumberland – Tyne and Wear they call it now – and see if we can find him.'

The two men left the Lansdowne and walked across Berkeley Square, following the hall porter's accurate description on where the local library could be found. They split the directories between them and were searching out all the Watermans, hoping that the ex-warrant officer hadn't opted to be ex-directory. They compared notes; between them they had 27 Watermans, but none with 'B' or 'Bernard'. There was no short cut, Adrian decided; all would have to be called. They retired to the Lansdowne Club to start the tedious task.

Luck was on their side, and on the seventh call, when Adrian asked if he could speak to Mr Bernard Waterman, a puzzled, quavering voice responded. 'You mean my brother, but he doesn't live here – he's in London.'

Adrian quickly asked for his number, and the man quickly obliged. Adrian thanked him for his help and left an elderly Tyneside schoolteacher gazing at the telephone wondering why anyone should think that Bernard, whom he had not seen for nearly four years, would live at that address.

When he dialled it he was pleased to get a reply. He explained that he was putting together a history of the desert war and would like to have the first-hand views of someone who had been in on the action.

'I was only a warrant officer, you know,' Waterman interjected. 'Perhaps you should talk to some top brass.'

'Not at all,' Adrian replied, 'I want some down-to-earth examples of life as it was with the troops, some good anecdotes, some private views.'

The vibes told Adrian that the ex-sergeant major was delighted at the prospect of reliving his war years, and within a few minutes he suggested that Adrian came around to his home in Hounslow. Adrian accepted with enthusiasm and quickly glanced at his watch, which showed just after eight.

'Would it be too late this evening?' he asked, and Waterman assured him that he would be more than welcome.

'All I was going to do is soak up the bloody telly and that's a pack of rubbish – just come on out and have a drink.'

Adrian decided on two points. First, not to suggest that Franz came. Some elderly people – especially old soldiers – were still not at ease with Germans. Secondly, he decided to take a taxi rather than pick the car up from Lorna's.

The taxi wound its way through the evening traffic and across the flyover towards the M4. After 20 minutes it turned into a long street with renovated Victorian villas and the driver, after reconsidering the address Adrian had given him, pulled up outside number 27.

Mr Bernard Waterman answered the door as soon as Adrian rang and warmly welcomed him. 'What a delightful surprise to meet you.' Adrian felt like a long-lost friend who has suddenly reappeared after a 20-year absence. 'Sit down and let me tell the wife you're here – she so much wants to meet you.'

The sergeant major disappeared into the back and ushered back a mouse of a woman who twittered something about the traffic out of London and Adrian agreed it was bad. That seemed the end of her contribution and she vanished into the area from whence she had come.

'You'll have a glass or two, I'm sure,' said Mr Waterman. As his host attended to his bar duties Adrian summed him up – about 75, stocky and medium height, probably a retired bank manager.

'Now what can I do for you?' Bernard Waterman asked.

'How does it come about that you have homed in on a run-of-the-mill old warrior like me? I hope you're not looking for a hero – bloody interpreter in Intelligence was all I was for a great deal of it.'

'That's an area I particularly – indeed specifically – want to touch on.' Adrian grabbed the opportunity with alacrity. 'I believe you acted as interpreter when an Italian family – Italian Jews – were executed in Houm Souk, on the island of Djerba. I was researching the story and I spoke to a Mr Phillips, A. J. Phillips, who said you would be able to help me. Do you recall Mr Phillips?'

Waterman furrowed his brow. 'No, I don't remember him at all. No, sorry – but as far as the Djerba incident is concerned, too bloody right I remember it. Who could ever forget it? Seemed like the Germans from the mainland made a raid on the synagogue and the houses around and then were counter-attacked by the Jews. People on the island thought the war would pass 'em by but wasn't to be. Anyway, a couple of days or so later another party of German soldiers arrived under a major and asked questions about stolen material and who had shot the earlier party. No one seemed to know what the hell he was talking about – he talked Italian to them and spoke it fluently. Then they lined them up and shot them. An old man and two kids were coming back from somewhere and they were the only ones to escape. They saw, or rather heard, all the talking and shouting going on and then the gunshots. When they came out of hiding later the murdering bastards had all gone. All Raoul and Rebecca saw when they went into the square were the bodies of their parents, brothers and sisters. Frankly, I don't think they have ever got over it – in fact, Rebecca spent some time in a mental home years afterwards and I always thought it was the imprint on her mind of that terrible day. Made a hell of an impact on me, I can tell you. All those bodies heaped up in a barn and the Arabs arguing about burying them – problems about religion, I guess.'

Adrian leaned across the coffee table. 'You said Raoul and Rebecca – you know the names?'

'Of course I know them!' Waterman replied. 'Known them for years. I thought you knew that when you spoke about it. The old man took care of them and then took them back to Genoa after the war – he couldn't bear to stay on Djerba. He was their grandfather and was very well off, even though the Germans had raided his property and taken some very valuable stuff. I read about the family in a magazine – trade thing about men's fashion. I recognised the name. Back in Italy he bought a house and raised the kids as if they were his own. When he died back in the early sixties he left them comfortably off. I met up with the family just before the old man passed on. My wife and I were in north Italy; as I speak the language it's always been our sun land, Italy. We were in Genoa one day and we decided to see if we could find the Carluccis. Wasn't difficult – they were in the telephone book so we called and then dropped in, just as you've done this evening. We had a great evening and even talked about the bad times when we first met. Now, let me refill your glass.'

Whilst Bernard Waterman went to the kitchen to get ice Adrian's mind raced over what had happened. He had wanted a lucky break all along and this was more than he could have expected.

'So – we had a good evening, as I said,' Waterman continued as he came into the room. 'Young Raoul was about, let me see, around twenty-seven then and Rebecca was twenty-four or twenty-five. We agreed to see more of one another.

'Shortly after that I heard from them that Raoul was getting married – nice Jewish girl she was, refugee from Germany. Over the years I've seen a lot of them. He comes over to England – he's in the fashion business, good quality clothing. Done well, got a big manufacturing business in Genoa. I work for them on a part-time basis. She came from a wealthy family too – managed to get their money into Switzerland before the confiscations really got under way. Most of her family managed to get away, too. Now they are well off and have a couple of kids of their own – grown up and in the business.'

'I would very much like to meet Mr Carlucci sometime,' put in Adrian.

'Well, you could be in luck,' came the unexpected reply, 'Raoul is coming to London tomorrow – he's usually over four or five times a year. It's my birthday tomorrow and Raoul called me up the other evening and asked me to dinner. Asked my wife as well, but she's really not one for dining out. I can't invite you in on his dinner party, of course, but I'm picking him up at Heathrow and driving him to Claridges. Why don't you meet me at the airport midday tomorrow and we can all drive together to the hotel? I'm sure Raoul would be pleased to give you an hour to put you in the picture.'

Mrs Waterman came into the room with a tray of coffee and biscuits and sat on the settee opposite. The conversation switched to matters not related to the reason for Adrian's visit but this didn't bother him. He felt he had taken a major stride in his investigation and that tomorrow would be another time of real development.

* * *

The freshly pressed orange juice stand is a better place to meet than most at Heathrow's Terminal Two. It has telephones nearby if you need to make a call, there is a liberal supply of juice and a news-stand in front should your wait be extended. The Airport Information Desk is also facing you. Bernard Waterman had suggested the rendezvous and Adrian had arrived by tube some 30 minutes early. The selection of such a site impressed him; the former sergeant-major was obviously a well-organised man.

Adrian's mind ran over the conversation he had had with Lorna over a late breakfast, after Sam had been taken to play school by a neighbour. Lorna had confessed that she had given up hope of ever seeing Ian again. Adrian had masked his growing pessimism and told her that he was sure it would all work out eventually. He refrained from saying that any reunion would be on borrowed time anyway. There was no kind way he knew of expressing that inescapable truth.

Shortly before breakfast he had called Franz at the

Lansdowne Club and told him of the previous evening's conversation with Waterman. Franz agreed that the trip to the West Country would have to wait – a chance to talk to the Carlucci family was too good to miss. Franz had sounded hesitant on the telephone, perhaps, Adrian realised, because he was about to meet a member of the family that his father had robbed, albeit on orders, all those years before. His father's actions, even in wartime conditions and carried out reluctantly, sat uneasily on the shoulders of low-key, peace-loving Franz.

'That makes us both on time!'

Adrian started in surprise to find Bernard Waterman beside him.

'Flight's punctual, I see, so they should be through in a moment. Raoul's secretary called early on – they are both coming.'

Passengers from the Alitalia flight from Milan started coming through the arrival area within five minutes and Waterman's face lit up in recognition as an immaculately dressed couple carrying duty-free bags came over and greeted him in the back-slapping manner so frowned on by the reserved English. Adrian wondered why it was that extremely wealthy people of any nationality never seemed to be able to resist the temptation of getting a couple of pounds off a bottle of whisky or a carton of cigarettes.

Waterman turned to Adrian and apologised profusely. 'We're such old friends we get carried away – allow me to introduce Signor and Signora Carlucci. Mr Adrian Franklin, who is a recent friend – tell you more about it later.'

The quartet walked over the connecting bridge to the multi-storey car park, where a two-year-old blue Rolls Royce awaited them. Adrian's eyes must have betrayed his private thoughts that such a car didn't relate to a retired executive living in a comfortable yet modest house in middle-class suburbia.

Waterman laughed. 'Not mine, Adrian my boy. I'm its groom. Belongs to our charming visitors here. I just keep it fed and stabled when they are not in England – Raoul uses it to visit the various clients around the country.'

Raoul Carlucci decided that Waterman and he should sit in the front, and Adrian slipped into the soft leather of the rear seat with Mrs Carlucci. The silent car slid into the underpass which leads from the world's busiest international airport and Carlucci and Waterman started an earnest conversation over business. Adrian was a little surprised for he had had no previous indication of anything but a casual business arrangement between them. Gerda Carlucci, who spoke perfect English with a pronounced German accent, asked Adrian about his relationship with Mr Waterman, and Adrian skirted around the matter by saying that Waterman was helping him with a book. He didn't want to play his cards too soon and he wanted an uninterrupted audience with the principally involved character – Mr Carlucci himself.

As the car sped silently along the M4 towards the capital Adrian took stock of Raoul Carlucci. About 55, with an air of great affluence. Not tall, he carried an air of great charisma, which, with immaculate clothing, made him the kind of person who stood out in a crowd. From the back seat the most prominent feature about him was a symmetrical area of baldness on the crown of his head, which otherwise was covered with a luxuriant shock of greying hair – very handy for the retention of a skullcap, thought Adrian.

At the stroke of noon the doors were opened by the hatted doorman and the elegant soft leather suitcases were spirited away into the exclusive foyer of Claridges.

Whilst the Carluccis went up to reception, Adrian and Bernard Waterman moved to the bar.

'Call me Bernard,' suggested the affable old soldier, and the two settled down to a drink, awaiting the reappearance of the Italians.

* * *

Whilst Adrian and Bernard enjoyed their drinks in the heart of London's Mayfair, Charlie and Royce were aboard the *L'Anticipation* tossing in the slight swell off the coast of Gibraltar. The impressive lion-head rock, six and a half square miles over which Britain and Spain had quarrelled and negotiated for so many years, towered in the distance, yet it stood only 430 metres above the sea.

It was not the Rock which was the most important feature in Charlie's mind but the narrow isthmus which joined it to the mainland of Spain – a flat pancake of land which held the airport, now one of the important points of entry for tourists visiting the Costa del Sol. As Pedro lacked the necessary passport for Spanish nationals to visit the British colony, Charlie went round the bars himself to ask about crashed aircraft in the war years. He found to his surprise that he was readily accepted and the Gibraltarians, known affectionately as Rock Scorpions and nearly all of Italian, Spanish and Portuguese descent, were only too happy to impart knowledge. Charlie went to talk to the older inhabitants of the Rock, who might well have had first-hand experience of the ditching of a British aircraft near the airfield. He particularly wanted to establish whether it had made its departure to the east, towards the main Mediterranean, or westwards towards the Atlantic, which lay 35 miles away.

It was in a small bar off Casemate Square that he struck lucky. An elderly man with a face like a walnut and a voice which crackled like poor reception on a cheap radio told Charlie to 'speak to old Felipe – Felipe Sanchez – the oldest guide – he knows everything worth talking about'.

He found out that Sanchez operated on the tourist buses in the square and 20 minutes later located the old guide just as he was checking off work for the day and pacifying an elderly American tourist who thought Britain should give Gibraltar back to Spain. Patiently the guide explained that as it was a Crown Colony, constitutionally Britain couldn't give it back, the British could only hand over to the Rock's inhabitants, who would then have the alternative of holding or losing it. A referendum had shown that Gibraltarians steadfastly wanted to be independent of Spain.

When Charlie spoke to him, the old guide looked him up and down quizzically.

'No, I wasn't on your trip but I do want information for research I'm doing,' Charlie explained quickly.

He watched the old man's face relax as he accepted the 1,000-peseta note.

'Yes, I remember it all so well. There were two crashes here in the war. One received a great deal of publicity – that was in the summer of forty-three and it killed the Polish Prime Minister in exile, Sikorski, and his family. People still talk of that because there was a rumour that the British created it. Sikorski was being an embarrassment to the allied forces because of his bitter criticism of the Russians.

'The earlier one was rather put in the shade. That was at the end of forty-two and that is the one you are talking about. There was engine failure on take-off. The plane had come in from North Africa – Tunisia, I believe – and was refuelling and picking up passengers here.'

'You seem a mine of useful information,' Charlie commented, and the elderly Gibraltarian raised his head.

'It's a job to keep people informed – they ask a lot of questions. Sometimes we get people who were based here during the war, so you have to know the war history as well as the history of the Rock going back to Roman times – and beyond.'

'Would you have any idea where the plane came down?' Charlie asked, trying to seem reasonably casual.

'Somewhere out to the east – over there.' The old man pointed across the expanse of shimmering sea. 'But I can find out more if you want – I could put an hour or two in on it this evening,' he said with a strong suggestion in his voice.

Charlie didn't miss the hint and passed the veteran guide another 1,000-peseta note.

It was nearly eleven that evening when Charlie and Royce finished dinner in a very English restaurant off Main Street. They walked down to the small bar where Charlie had agreed to meet Felipe Sanchez. On the way Charlie stopped to look in the window of a jeweller's shop. Royce walked on; back in his villa at Marbella lay his share of cash from goods which rightfully belonged to the shopkeeper but had been spirited away, with Royce's know-how and Steve's sleight of hand. Royce, like many old-timers, was a superstitious man and believed in never revisiting the scene of a crime.

Sanchez had found it necessary to consume an inordinate amount of alcohol in order to get the information from his friends and he lurched alarmingly on the bar stool as he passed it on to Charlie. The aircraft was a Liberator transport, a converted four-engined, long-distance bomber and had plunged into the water within a minute of take-off to the east. There was one survivor.

Several people have been here over the years, asking about it. People are funny, aren't they? One old Irishman – he was here for a few weeks – booked our senior guide to help him. Wasted his time. He packed up and went home.

As Royce and Charlie walked back to the *L'Anticipation* they were of the opinion that the next day's tourists might have a somewhat incoherent account of the Rock from a very hung-over guide.

13

The question took Adrian by surprise so he asked the dapper Italian to repeat it.

'I said, are you a member of a synthesis or playing to an oversubscribed maker?'

Waterman leaned forward and whispered in the Italian's ear.

'I'm sorry, my English sometimes lets me down. I meant "syndicate".'

Adrian looked puzzled. 'I understand what you mean but not why you ask it – could you explain please?'

Carlucci leaned forward and put his hands together with fingertips touching. 'Mr Franklin, several weeks ago, months indeed, I had a visit from an Englishman, a Mr Southon. He told me that he and his associate were working on a project which had established the whereabouts of a considerable amount of my family possessions. He knew a great deal about certain incidents in my life – incidents, I would add, of which my good friend Mr Waterman here is well aware. This Mr Southon needed money to finance the project and asked for quite a considerable sum. I'm not in the habit of passing money to strangers so I declined. I offered him a small advance and the use of a yacht which I have had in France for some time and which my son learned to sail on some years back. It's up for sale but it needs work doing on it. Southon said he would do a lot of it himself, and he certainly knew what he was talking about as far as boats are concerned. I gave him the necessary papers to collect *L'Anticipation* and an advance for some of the work. I told him that when it had reached a certain standard I would put up some more. We then talked about the lost valuables of my family and I offered him a good reward if they were returned to me or to the Jewish community. He accepted my offer. I never heard from him again, although it was part of the deal that he kept in touch regularly.

'Then another, younger man turned up on the doorstep – completely unexpected. By this time I was having serious second thoughts about my offer to Southon. After all, he was a complete stranger to me, and Gerda here said she didn't trust him and that I had been foolish – maybe I had. When this other Englishman turned up, about a week after Southon left, he told me a similar tale. He came to my office and was a very pleasant young fellow. I expressed surprise that after many years I should suddenly be questioned twice about the same subject within a week or so. This young man was surprised too. He confirmed that he and Southon were working together, but he was obviously worried when I told him I had lent Southon the boat and that Southon had said he was going to Marbella. That had struck me as strange too – why should he go to Spain when we were talking about stuff hidden in Tunisia? When I asked him, Southon had said that Spain was important – that the goods weren't in Tunisia any more. Anyway, to get back to the story – I told the second man that when he met up with Southon to ask him to call me; ten days had gone by and I hadn't heard a word. This Lacey chap was obviously deeply –'

'What did you say his name was?' Adrian chipped in.

'Lacey. I'm good at remembering names, important when you're in selling like me – not a very usual name either – anyway, he was worried about the whole exercise, and I was too busy to go into the whole exercise all over again so he left to find Southon. Now, stranger and stranger. You raise the same matter. That's why I asked whether you are working solo or in a...' He waved his hand as he sought the word.

Adrian wasn't listening. This was the first time that Ian's

name had come up in all the weeks of investigation. This could, just could, be the breakthrough he had sought.

'Mr Carlucci, I feel an explanation is called for – and an apology to you, Bernard. I've not been completely frank with you,' Adrian croaked hoarsely.

He wished he had told them everything from the start and recalled that he had felt the same just a few days before when he was with the Girdlers. They had shut up like clams when they became suspicious and the last thing he wanted was for the Carluccis to do the same. Mrs Carlucci was looking at him with flashing dark eyes; was there a touch of hostility? he wondered.

'I want to tell you my story,' Adrian began, ' a story of a son-in-law who disappeared and for whom I have been searching in vain. I have only come across one person who has seen him and that, sir, is you.'

He had an instantly interested audience...

It wasn't because he was uninterested that he looked at his watch; far from it. The time was turned two and Mr Carlucci put the tips of the fingers of both hands together as he broke into Adrian's revelations.

'Mr Franklin, I am very interested in what you say – extremely interested – and I appreciate your frankness. My situation is that I have an appointment in Hampstead at three o'clock and I cannot delay it – indeed it is one of my main reasons for coming to London. I have an idea. Tonight I have a private dinner party upstairs. I should be delighted if you and your wife would join us. If you come along early I will tell you our side of the story after you have finished relating your experience of this strange case.'

Adrian's mind raced. He was inclined to suggest bringing Franz as he had no wife to bring but he felt that a German at this particular dinner would be as welcome as a pork sausage in a synagogue. A thought sprang to his mind. 'I would love to come – my wife and I are separated, I'm sorry to say. May I bring my daughter?'

Mr Carlucci was delighted. A glance at Mrs Carlucci was

enough to show that she had accepted him and the little group broke up with plenty on their minds.

Adrian took the five-minute walk down Davies Street and across Berkeley Square to the Lansdowne Club to meet Franz. He had been a little surprised by Waterman's reaction to the true story – perhaps the old soldier was annoyed at being deceived. After all, he had set up the meeting with the Carluccis on the pretext of research for a book. Adrian regretted not being open with him from the start, but on the other hand all these people were strangers and in a situation which he felt was sinister, dangerous perhaps, then a covert approach seemed prudent.

At the end of the street Adrian glanced up – Davies Street. That was another unsolved mystery. Who was Davies and how did he fit into the picture?

It is a strange fact of life that when suddenly confronted with a number of situations, the human mind has a knack of rearranging them in an order for consideration not at all in keeping with their importance. Adrian found that it was difficult to think about Ian's first appearance on the scene. That was a number of weeks ago, and Adrian felt uneasy about telling Lorna what he had found out. First of all, he decided, he would explain the situation to Franz, and that would help him to develop a line of approach to Lorna.

When he arrived at the Lansdowne Club Adrian found a note from Franz to say that he would be back at three thirty as he had gone to Foyle's to get a book. Adrian was glad. It gave him a chance to collect his thoughts and he settled down in the round room, where, some 200 years before, the first constitution of the United States of America had been drafted. A room for quiet reflection and mediation, thought Adrian, as he read the plaque on the wall.

What concerned Adrian deeply was that even now he hadn't revealed all to the Carluccis. How could he possibly say that his partner in this wide-flying search was a German whose father had been involved in the ransacking of that family's house in Tunisia? Furthermore, that young man's interest in the whole affair was to continue his father's quest for the valuables to which he was far from legally entitled. The fact that Franz was German was enough to stop the flow of information. The ancillary facts were guaranteed to cause the immediate severance of any further relationship. Overall, Adrian reflected, enough had been said.

Adrian sat back in the comfortable club chair. Something Ian had found out in Djerba had led him to the Jewish family now settled in Genoa. But Southon obviously knew of the Carluccis – he had visited them a week earlier. And had he suggested to Ian that he call on them? Apparently not, because Raoul had been sure that Ian was astonished when he heard that Southon had been there before him. If the packet of Camel cigarettes found by Lorna was anything to go by, Ian and Southon had met up at Ann's house – he shuddered to think of his ex-wife being intimately associated with this character. It had all the makings of Southon pulling a double-cross on Ian. But what had happened to Ian after he left Genoa and why had Southon gone to Marbella? To pick Ella's brains? Perhaps, but he could have done that and moved on. Then there was the mysterious gold-chained thug, Rollason, who had sent his sidekicks to forcibly extract information from Ella. With the information gained, another man had attacked Franz in Hamburg – obviously set up by Rollason to get more information. But what exactly was the information he hoped to get – an exact location of the valuables? And how did Rollason tie up with Henry Southon? Ella had said that Southon was scared out of his wits when he met Rollason in the hotel. Did the two tie up at all?

From what Franz had learned at the In and Out Club, it seemed that the mysterious Weissman was a major war criminal. Davies was involved somehow – and the girl, Betty Silvester. Was it a casual affair – young girls in their twenties had had affairs with sugar daddies before now – or was there something else to it? After all, Betty's father was a person of some reputation.

Adrian was startled. Franz was standing looking at him.

'I thought you were asleep – you were in the clouds.'

Adrian pulled himself together. 'Sit down, Franz. I've a lot to tell you. At last, at long last, I have met someone who has seen Ian.'

As Adrian sat in the back of the taxi on his way to Blenheim Gardens and Lorna, he couldn't feel any resentment with Franz for wanting to move on. The developments of the last few days had hardly moved him towards his personal goal of unearthing the treasure which his father had sought so earnestly. He would go down to the West Country with Adrian in the next day or two but after that he would fly to Hamburg to check on the business and then take a quick trip down to the Costa del Sol to make sure his mother was safe – and remained safe. Adrian appreciated that – he liked Ella enormously and he worried about her being on her own with a pack of hoodlums in the neighbourhood who had caused her enough trouble.

He paid off the taxi and used his own key to let himself into number 37 Blenheim Gardens. Lorna and Sam were delighted to see him and Adrian drew Lorna aside.

'Fix a baby-sitter for tonight – we're going to a dinner party which might prove most interesting.'

Lorna looked blank. Adrian gave her a warm smile. 'At last we have someone who has seen Ian. Sit down and I'll tell you all about it.'

* * *

Raoul Carlucci lit a cigarette and studied Lorna and Adrian carefully.

'I've told my story a few times over the years but what happened so long ago is of little interest to many young people – I think people would prefer to let bygones be bygones. However, they didn't live through it as we did. They were bad days and we are only here tonight because of sheer luck and some help from really good people – I remember Bernard here and the way he comforted us back in 1942. I don't suppose I would tell you my story except that I am apparently – and with surprise – the last person to see your husband...' He faltered.

'I think Lorna is coming to terms with the fact that Ian may have died,' Adrian added gently.

Raoul Carlucci rose from his chair and walked over to the fireplace of the elegant Claridges suite. A small figure, he was nevertheless imposing. Difficult to imagine him in strained circumstances. 'I'll tell you my story right from the beginning so that I miss nothing. Our other guests will be here in an hour so there's time to tell it in full – I only hope that something emerges which will be beneficial to us all and have some bearing on the disappearance of Mr Lacey.'

The origins of the Carlucci business were in the early twenties when Abraham Carlucci started in the olive oil trade in Sienna. After three years they bought additional land for a vineyard and started to produce Chianti. In 1922, when Italy occupied Libya, Abraham saw a great future in a country where land was cheap and labour plentiful and low-paid, so at the age of 40 and assisted by his son Luigi he bought a large villa outside Tripoli. Within five years they were in possession of 1000 hectares of olive trees and were also growing dates. Luigi, Raoul's father was becoming more and more involved in the management of the estates. In mid-1933, shortly after Adolf Hitler became Germany's Chancellor, he met his future wife during a business trip to Berlin. She came from a wealthy Jewish family. In 1935 with the persecution gathering momentum, they married in Berlin and then immediately set up home in Libya. A business trip to Albania and the acquisition of a large olive oil-processing factory in that country led to Luigi being on close terms with King Zog. After the overthrow of the Albanian royal family, Zog and his wife stayed for two months in the Carlucci holiday villa in Antibes.

In 1937 war clouds were gathering across Europe and Italian troops were moved into Libya. Raoul was born in the July, and shortly afterwards Luigi was offered a large amount of money for the Libyan estates. The wealthy family moved intact to Tunisia, to a villa on the island of Djerba. The villa was large enough for them to live under one roof – so characteristic of both Jewish and Italian families. A daughter was born the following year.

The fighting in Libya and Tripoli in 1942 did not affect the family – if there was to be bitter warfare it would be over the Suez Canal and they were thankful that would be some 1,500 miles away. When news reached them in October 1942 of the Afrika Korps' defeat at El Alamein and of the retreat of the Wehrmacht across the North African deserts, the family were convinced that a surrender was imminent. The villa was positioned close to a large synagogue which served the substantial local Jewish community and the family spent a considerable amount of money on refurbishing the place of worship, thus ensuring their eventual burial in the much coveted three-metre perimeter of the building.

The family were surprised and pleased to hear radio reports of an American landing in Morocco. Now it was just a matter of time before North Africa was free, and perhaps this was the long-awaited turning point of the war.

Late in 1942 an Arab driver who worked on the Carlucci estates returned from Sfax with some disturbing news. At Mareth the Germans were digging in for a major stand against the Allied advance. The German soldiers, under direct instructions from Rommel, treated the local people well and the Arab community was strongly in favour of a victory for the Third Reich. The driver told of tank blockades, gun positions being built and a determination among the German troops to hold back the advancing enemy – now that they were out of Libya.

Raoul paused to fill glasses and explained, 'Whilst the Germans were in Libya they were technically on Italian soil so Rommel had to report to the Italian High Command. In Tunisia he was relieved of what he saw as that tiresome burden and the troops had obviously seized on this upswing with verve – such was the leadership and magnetism of Field Marshal Erwin Rommel. I'm afraid the Italians had no stomach for the war.'

It was at the end of the year that a scout car with the cross insignia came across the causeway which linked Djerba to the mainland. It toured the island, spending some time at the airstrip and then stopped briefly outside the Carlucci villa. It left, and that apparently was an end to the matter for although there was considerable movement on the mainland no troops crossed the causeway. The Carlucci family assumed that the war was fading out on the mainland – and in any event what would anyone want of a Jewish community on a small island?

One day, in the early morning, a worker in the olive groves ran to the house to report that he had seen a small truck cross the causeway and turn left on the track which led to the synagogue. Armed troops were aboard, he reported. The family alerted the worshippers in the synagogue, who opted to continue their devotions. The family and as many workers as they could muster in the short time available ran down the hillside to a small depression in the sandy hill. To their horror they saw a squad of troops under a young officer enter the synagogue and the abandoned villa and come out a few minutes later with the occupants of the synagogue as prisoners. The rabbi remonstrated with the troops for their conduct and was struck on the face. Other troops were taking goods from the synagogue and the villa. A large tin trunk which the Carluccis had used on a Mediterranean cruise several years before was carried over and loaded into the back of the truck, which was driven off.

Luigi Carlucci decided on an immediate counter-attack and sent two men back to the villa to get hunting rifles and ammunition which were locked onto the wall by chain. In the meanwhile the men, leaving the women and children behind, ran across the sand towards a crossroads. Until the arms arrived they wanted to delay the truck. As the truck appeared they backed a camel cart across the road, and the trick worked. The truck skidded on the loose sand and hit the cart of watermelons.

Luigi reckoned that the tin trunk had been used to carry ammunition for the rifles and also the four or five sports revolvers which were kept in the house. Using the ditch at the side of the road, they made their way to the empty cab. The driver and the officer were in the open road shouting at the camel driver and examining the damage. The troops and their prisoners were packed in the back. It was comparatively simple to collect the box and carry it down the steep dune. It didn't contain the armaments. Instead, they were distressed to find a wide selection of the family jewellery and some cups belonging to the synagogue. A considerable fortune had been collected in a few moments, including a solid gold statue which had been presented to the family by King Zog.

'You understand,' Raoul went on, 'we were just little kids hiding in the sand thinking it was fun – we learned all about it from our grandfather in the years ahead. Of course we had no idea of the value then.'

The two men who had been sent to the house returned to the group with the hunting rifles, and whilst the German troops sorted out the accident Luigi arranged a counter-attack. They noted with surprise the officer and a private walking away from the group and scanning the area with binoculars. As they walked across the desert waste Luigi and his partisan group made their attack, using rifle butts as much as possible to keep down the noise. Within a few moments the German soldiers who had jumped down from the truck had been annihilated and the Jews had released their friends. It was then a matter of making a fast escape.

For the next few days the Jewish community hid in the capital of the island, Houm Souk, staying with the local community who were willing to hide them.

A few days later Raoul and his sister were taken by their grandfather for a long walk around the harbour and to the fish market. As they started back towards the town they saw three German army lorries at the end of the market square. The old man pulled the two children into a house overlooking the square, and whilst the children sat on the floor their grandfather listened at a partly opened window. To his surprise the officer, in the uniform of a German major, spoke Italian to the group lined up in front of him. They were later to hear that the group contained their parents. There was much shouting and then silence. Ten minutes passed and then there was a sudden sound of rifle fire.

'Even after all these years,' Raoul continued, 'I feel sick, bitter, about what I saw when Grandfather let us leave the house. Twenty-seven of my people, my mother, father and uncles and school friends lay in the square – dead. The only survivor was a young man who was a cousin. He was badly wounded with spinal injuries and he died after a month. We looked after him as well as we could and learned certain things from him. He was angered and distressed, as Grandfather was, that an Italian had been in charge of the execution squad, although he was probably a German who spoke Italian. We were too young to understand that but in later years that upset and puzzled us. That was our meeting with the notorious butcher Weissman. Ibrim had heard his *Stabsfeldwebel* address him by name. Grandfather told us that the German troops wanted retribution for the death of their troops who had been attacked a week before. Weissman told them they could be spared if they would reveal the location of the treasure. Whether it was panic, call it what you will, the family didn't understand what he was talking about – he was very excited and shouting.

'The high pitch of his voice was something I shall never forget – like an insane scream. Later on I met other Jewish people who experienced Weissman in Dachau and they say the same. He was totally out of control – completely insane.

'The Germans had left rapidly because the British and New Zealand forces were advancing, and the dead were put in a barn. The Arabs spent all evening digging graves but Grandfather would not let us go near.

'The next day was as much of a reversal as anyone could expect. A tank appeared on the horizon, followed by three more. Everyone scattered until it was clear that they were British. Grandfather Carlucci then brought us two young children to the officer in charge – Captain Collingson he turned out to be. The officer was keen to interview Grandfather but no one spoke English and none of the British troops spoke Italian, except the captain, but his Italian was very poor. The captain radioed the mainland and shortly afterwards a translator appeared.'

Raoul Carlucci paused in his story and turned to Bernard Waterman. 'You take up the story.'

Waterman cleared his throat. 'What I saw was dreadful – imprinted on my mind to this day. The bodies of the executed Jews were lying in a barn, covered with cloths, and two small children were hanging onto an old gentleman who turned out to be their grandfather. Collingson, with me acting as interpreter, wanted to know what had happened, where the German force had gone, why the executions had taken place. When they mentioned the tin box, Collingson became extremely interested – by now the old man had had time to think and realised the Germans had not just sought retribution for the death of their comrades but were very keen to find out where the goods taken from the villa and the synagogue were hidden. Raoul and I have discussed this a million times. Anyway, Collingson took a lot of notes and then dismissed me. I spent a few moments with the remains of the family and tried to comfort them. The old man told me that the Italian-speaking officer was called Weissman – he had been addressed by name. It upset the old man to think he was Italian, or partly Italian – although the Carluccis were Jewish he regarded Italy as his true home as he had lived most of his life there. He said that after the war he would go back to Genoa, where he had lived as a child and where he had friends – or so he hoped.

'As we talked, Captain Collingson came over and asked me why I was still about – he was pretty tense I remember. I left, drove over the causeway and joined my unit. I didn't see the family again until the mid-sixties when my wife and I were in Northern Italy on holiday and we decided to trace them. They were in the Genoa telephone book so we met up easily and have stayed friends ever since.'

Raoul took up the story. 'We saw out the war years – the three of us – living in Houm Souk. It was a lonely, strange life. The family and my wife's family had considerable financial reserves in Switzerland, and after we returned to Italy in 1946 Grandfather set up in clothing manufacturing. We joined him in the business a few years later, in the early fifties, and the operation grew until it became of quite a respectable size; indeed today we are the fourth largest manufacturer of quality menswear in Italy and we export all over Europe and the USA. We were delighted to see Bernard Waterman again when he dropped in on us and he has become a close friend. When he returned we took him into the company as a representative for the London area and he's been very successful. We often talked of what happened in Djerba. We learned more of Weissman. When his name came up once, talking to some Jewish friends of mine in London, it emerged that he had been commander of B-Unit in Dachau and some dreadful – unspeakable – things had been done by him. He wasn't just a killer, he was a sadist who enjoyed doing what he did. One group of young men were tied up naked and Weissman moved slowly from one to another and shot them through the stomach. I heard this from a very good friend who was a survivor. At one time we tried to trace Weissman and went to the Wiesenthal Institute but we didn't get far. The story of Djerba passed into history until one day this year in Genoa I was visited by a man called Henry Southon. He told me that he had direct knowledge of where my family possessions were buried. Of course in the post-war years we had tried to find them with Grandfather, but he was old, and two men whom my father had sent out the evening after the day when they were hidden temporarily never returned, according to Grandfather. But Southon's story was convincing – he knew Collingson's name, he knew the units in the forces involved. Of course, he could have looked them up in military records, but that wasn't the way it came across. I agreed to buy back anything he found, and after a certain discussion about finance – and I certainly wasn't going to put up much money to someone I didn't know – I offered him the yacht which we kept for my son to sail on the Med. It wasn't in good order but Southon said he would do it up. I was curious to know why he wanted a boat and he became very – I think the English word is "cagey" – he said that the family valuables were in the sea. He wouldn't tell me more. I didn't hear from him for a few days then he called me from San Feliu de

Guixols in Spain. He said he was having mechanical trouble with the boat but I declined to advance more money. Then I didn't hear from him for a week or so.

'One day another Englishman – a younger man – turned up at my office.' Raoul turned to Lorna. 'You may not like what I tell you but I must recount it as it happened. He told me that he had knowledge of the family valuables and wanted to work with me. I cut him short and asked him if he was in partnership with Mr Southon. He was clearly shaken and even more shaken when I said that I had loaned Southon a boat and that he was in Spain. He kept muttering and he looked ill as well as acutely surprised. I was extremely busy and I already had regrets at getting involved with Southon. Frankly, I distrusted Mr Lacey – maybe because of his association with Southon. He said he had just come from Djerba and asked me if I knew anything about an aircraft coming down in the sea. I said I didn't, and he then said something which rather surprised me. He said, "I suppose Collingson would know".'

Adrian interrupted gently. 'Did he say he was in touch with Collingson?'

Raoul shook his head. 'I don't recall he did, but as I said, he was not very coherent and I was busy. I'm afraid I didn't give him much time and he left.'

Lorna turned to Raoul from the window where she had been standing, looking over the roofs of London. 'Did he mention us – his family – at all?' Lorna asked.

Raoul furrowed his brow. 'He said he needed money quickly – I'm sorry, Mrs Lacey, but I hear that story so often that I must harden to it – and he said he would be back in England soon as the family would be back. I was quite glad to hear that because he appeared to have the character of a persistent person and I – well, frankly, I wanted nothing to do with him.'

The door bell rang. The first of Raoul Carlucci's guests had arrived for dinner.

'My dear, what a delightful surprise!' Dr Solomon took Lorna's hand between his two hands and kissed her on the cheek. 'I had no idea you were a friend of Raoul's.'

'Dr Solomon – I never knew you were coming – that you...' She turned to Adrian. 'You know my father, of course.'

'Of course, of course – back from Italy. Is that how you know Raoul?'

'Well, no – actually – it's really in connection with Ian and the matter of his disappearance.'

The doctor shuffled uncomfortably. There was a very awkward pause and Raoul Carlucci sensed it. 'Ikki – what will you have now, the usual single malt or have you taken the advice you give your patients eh? – no smoke, no drink and we'll discuss the sex side later?' The doctor excused himself and moved over to the sideboard, where Raoul poured him a large malt.

'How come you know Mrs Lacey and her father?' he asked Raoul.

Raoul Carlucci lit a cigar. 'You'll never believe this, Ikki, but I expect you know that Ian Lacey disappeared suddenly. Well, by a whole string of circumstance they found Bernard and he put them on to me. It seems like I was the last person to see Lacey alive. Apparently he was tearing up the desert in North Africa after my family treasure – the stuff I once told you about – and he came to see me in Genoa to get my involvement. Then no one seems to have seen him again.' Raoul stopped. 'Ikki, are you OK?' The old doctor was decidedly white and slumped into a chair, spilling his precious Glenmorangie.

14

The old guide burst into laughter. 'Fine chance you have, fine chance!'

Royce glanced at him coldly; he didn't like being taken lightly. He had Charlie working on the sounding equipment on board *L'Anticipation* – no need for two of them to spend time talking to the guide. Time was slipping by and he had invested quite a considerable sum of money on the project by now. He wanted results.

'What you talking about?' he growled.

The old guide slid off his bar stool and beckoned. 'Come and see.' Five minutes later the Fiat Panda was winding its way towards Europa Point, about a mile from the town.

The car pulled up on a lay-by and Sanchez pointed a finger down towards the sea. The sight of hundreds of abandoned scrap cars meant nothing to Rolls and then suddenly he realised.

When Spain closed its border to Gibraltar in the mid-sixties the already strained facilities for disposing of rubbish in the tiny colony, with its ultra-dense population, reached breaking point, and the authorities decided to dispose of the incombustible material into the sea. Close to Europa Point was built a crushing plant and a disposal system to tip the expended consumer durables of the affluent society – cars, washing machines, refrigerators and much more – to a watery grave.

Royce stared at the sea. 'Bloody 'ell – all that sodding metal at the bottom!'

The old guide wiped his face with a large handkerchief. ''Bout as much chance of finding anything down there as a...'

'That bloody Charlie...' Royce's voice creaked.

'See what I mean, there's –' the old guide went on.

'Shut your bloody face and take me back. I'll show you where – and quick!'

As soon as the cabin door opened, Charlie's heart missed a beat. The expression on the bull face of Royce Rollason could not be misinterpreted. The giant frame advanced menacingly across the floor and Charlie stepped back, only to realise that he was against the cabin wall.

Royce exploded with rage. 'You and your bloody metal detection – thousands of tons, thousands of tons of metal crap down the bottom of that sea – all the junk of years all down there with your precious aircraft. You and your planning – I s'pose it never occurred to you to take a trip down and look over the place? All the money I've put up for you to go on this bloody treasure 'unt and you've never even looked over the pitch – I tell you, you've always been a noovo, a fucking amateur, that's what you are and always 'ave bin. Stuck my neck out on this one and lost a lot of cash.' Royce swung a blow to Charlie's head and the younger man fell to his knees.

'I don't know what you mean, Royce. Tell me what you're talking about.'

Royce picked Charlie up by the lapels and shook him in anger. ''Ow the 'ell do you detect metal when the 'ole fucking place is a scrapyard, tell me that?' He threw Charlie against the wall and walked out of the cabin into the aft cockpit. He must have time to think – all this time and money wasted just because the basic research hadn't been done. He had always worked with professionals and, in later years, through professionals. The job on the duty-free shop in Gibraltar had been a classic, which he himself had masterminded from the bent employee of the security company, arranged for the shop owner to be invited out for dinner, the calculation of the police patrol schedule and the choice of the man to carry out the job itself. Royce hadn't ever touched the merchandise or even seen it – he had been the brain behind the deal and had cashed in well on the result. All because of half a day of careful planning in Gibraltar. He shook with anger, this little sod hadn't even been to the area where the plane went down, he wiped his forehead with a white handkerchief and stared out to sea. One thing for sure, he wouldn't give up this whole exercise easily – that metal detector expert Charlie talked about, Davies, he must be able to help. His mind ran to a story he had read in the English papers not long ago about the Loch Ness Monster, how an image intensifier could show a scan on the shape of objects on the lake bottom. Maybe that could work here; after all, Charlie had led the man to believe that Tunisia was the area for search and maybe, if it was explained that they were looking off Gibraltar with deep water and a mountain of garbage... Royce stood up and gazed at the Rock. The first thing would be to get Charlie back to talk to the expert. 'No, by Christ, not bloody Charlie again!' he said out loud. 'I'll go myself.' He lit a small cigar and pushed open the cabin door.

Royce froze. He wasn't easily scared but the scene before him stopped him in his tracks. Charlie was in a sitting position on the floor with his back against the cooker. His eyes were glazed and a trickle of blood had run from the left corner of his mouth across his chin and onto his blue shirt. Royce crossed the tiny cabin and shook the figure on the floor. The head slumped forward and Royce felt the pulse. He didn't need medical knowledge to acquire the truth. 'Christ Almighty, I've bleeding well killed him – bloody Charlie's gone and landed me right in the shit this time. 'E's bloody well gone and let me kill 'im, the rotten bastard.'

* * *

Royce Rollason fastened his seat belt. As the jet left the ground Royce looked down from the starboard side window. Down there, under a swelling sea the body of one

Charles Singer, or whatever name he might have used, lay for no one to observe or bother about. Royce smiled with self-satisfaction at the way only three days before he had operated the dinghy, under engine power, out into the open sea at night. Then, with the body strapped with strong nylon cord to a one and half metre steel girder that a builder had left on a site close to the harbour, he had committed the body of Charlie Singer to the deep. The chances of anyone ever missing Charlie, let alone doing a deep-sea search for him, were remote to say the least. The boat boy had been told that Mr Southon had had to return to England suddenly on business and had been more than happy to return to his home 40 miles away on the Costa del Sol with a handsome pay-off. Yes, Royce thought to himself, you've got matters under control now, Royce my son, no camp followers of doubtful ability – just yourself. He smiled and when the stewardess came past, ordered a double Scotch. From now on, he promised himself, this was going to be well organised. He tapped the notebook in his pocket – yes, a well run exercise.

Flying had never been an enjoyable experience in the life of Royce Rollason and he was glad when the aircraft arrived at Gatwick and he was on terra firma. He cleared Customs with a clear conscience and took the train to London Victoria. The English countryside looked so green and he thought back to the time he had left Her Majesty's hospitality in the Scrubs and a few days later had left, via Luxembourg to pick up deposited funds, for Spain. As a man of private means he had then been able to take out residential status in Spain which was comparatively easy at the time. He had resolved never to return to England for there was no extradition treaty between the two countries which even when repealed would not be retroactive – this was an important consideration when there was still a large unsolved crime of a raid on a Midland warehouse where Royce had played a substantial role. The British police, he reflected, had a nasty habit of being tenacious over a long period of time and several of his friends had experienced early morning calls from the law when they thought their activity had been committed to police archives. No, Royce thought, he wasn't pleased at being back in England but the loss of his two lieutenants and the complexity of the situation meant that he had to deal with the situation – and deal with it diplomatically and discreetly. No one knew he was coming. He had decided not to call Davies for Davies would ask for his number and Royce gave his telephone number to very few people indeed. If he had given his number to that pimp Frohlich the Spanish police would have visited him and not that German woman's house to pick up Steve and – 'Frohlich must have written the number down.' Rolls shook his head. 'Surrounded by bloody amateurs – Christ Almighty, is there no professionalism left?' he mumbled to himself.

At Victoria Royce took a taxi to the May Fair Hotel and half an hour after checking in he walked through Berkeley Square towards Oxford Street to purchase clothes for his mission. At the top of Berkeley Square he paused to cross the road and then his pulse leapt. On the opposite side a young red-haired man was also waiting for a lull in the traffic. Royce recognised him instantly – the young German he had put Angie on to in Marbella. Royce drew away and pretended to read some notes from his pocket book. The young man crossed the road and walked down the side of the square. Royce moved to a vantage point in the park which lies within the square and watched the young German enter a large building at the bottom of the square. Crossing the road, he noticed the only sign on the building was the number, nine, and as the building spread across the corner into Curzon Street the windows on the ground floor were bricked in. Royce scratched his head – he couldn't make sense of it. What was the son of that Grieb woman, Charlie Singer's ex-girlfriend, doing in London when he had been so very recently in Marbella?

Royce went about his mission of buying a respectable blazer, dark glasses and grey trousers but his mind was on other matters. Had Charlie told him everything, or was there something he did not know? One thing was certain: he wouldn't get any more information from Charlie Singer. Still, it was a puzzle that German being there – and Royce Rollason could do without teasers.

* * *

The theatre audience emptied into Shaftsbury Avenue and Erika took Alfonso's arm as they strolled leisurely towards Piccadilly Circus. They watched the lights in fascination and then consulted a tourist map. 'It's not far to Buckingham Palace. Let's wander down towards it and then get a taxi,' Erika suggested.

'It's a lovely city – it's a shame your father has never seen it – probably never will. OK let's walk,' Alfonso agreed.

Just off Pall Mall they paused and asked the way from a lone pedestrian. 'Your English gets better every moment,' commented Erika, as Alfonso thanked the elderly gentleman for his help.

'Don't forget I was a prisoner of the British during the Malvinas trouble – or the Falklands War as they called it,' Alfonso laughed. 'But going back to your father, shouldn't you call him when we are back at the hotel – the telephone will be cheaper at night and it must be early evening back in Argentina. I'm not sure of the actual time difference but it must be a reasonable hour.'

Erika nodded. 'I'll do that.'

The couple arrived at the Palace and looked at the floodlit building in wonderment. A taxi arrived with its light shining and Alfonso waved it down and asked the driver to take them to the Penta Hotel.

Fifteen minutes later in their room on the tenth floor of the Penta, Erika spoke to her father on a crackling line. Alfonso read a magazine and tried to follow the conversation. All was not well, apparently, but he couldn't find out exactly what the problem was. 'I'll discuss it with Alfonso,' Erika shouted down the line to her father. 'I said I'll discuss it. We'll probably come back, OK? Give me his number – the number yes!' She scribbled on a pad bedside the telephone and after a prolonged goodbye returned the receiver to its cradle.

'What's all that about Erika?'

'Father is finding it all too much. One of the ranchers got involved in a fight and the foreman fired him – he turned up at the house and was unpleasant to Father. Then one of his friends decided to quit in protest so Perez came to Father and said he was two short now on his team and could Father hire some extra help. He's old, Alfonso. It's tough on a man in his eighties. I think we'll have to go home and cut short our visit to England.'

Alfonso went to the window and looked over the lights of London. 'Look, darling, why don't you stay on and meet your family here in London as planned – I'll fly back to Argentina and sort out our ranch problems. After all, they are your family, not really mine and you won't have to hurry. I can take over from your father.'

Erika joined him at the window. 'I'll sleep on it.'

Over breakfast a decision was made. Alfonso would fly back to Argentina, Erika would stay on to see the Tate and National galleries and then look up relatives. The travel agent in the foyer was very helpful. The reservation was made and after a day of shopping Alfonso kissed Erika goodbye and took a taxi to Heathrow.

Erika went to her room and decided to set up her agenda for the next few days. She rang the London number that her father had given her.

* * *

It is all so green, she murmured to herself. Erika's eyes were fixed on the countryside. The long lush green fields, the stately oaks and beeches in full leaf. All so very different from the arid pampas of Argentina or even the outskirts of Madrid where she had taken her son only last week. The other passengers of the railway coach seemed oblivious to the beauty of the land – her thoughts ran to something she had read in English somewhere, 'England's green and pleasant land'. It was that, and she was pleased that her telephone call had resulted in her getting this trip to the West Country.

At the time she had regretted having to make the four-hour journey but her cousin had been insistent: 'I cannot get back for a few days, I'm in the office now, but I should so much like to see you – please come and join me, it's a scenic and interesting journey and I have a cottage and a car down here.' It had all sounded very inviting when she had called him on the advice of the housekeeper at his London home. She wondered what Roland was like. He had sounded pleasant enough on the telephone, and he was the son of her mother's sister.

Her thoughts were interrupted as the train ran so close to the sea that she could see the bathers and the people sitting in deckchairs. The sea fascinated her; in all her 38 years she had only seen it from the air. Then it had seemed awesome – the vastness of it all. Now, seeing it as the playground of adults and children alike, it had a friendly air. She suddenly felt so lonely – the sea separated her from her husband and her father, and from her convalescing son. Was she right in letting Alfonso go home alone? She justified her action to herself; after all, her father wasn't ill, just finding the work more of a strain than he expected – he was well into his eighties and the ranch needed a younger man to run it. Although her father had a military background he found the tough, hard-drinking ranchos too much to handle.

As the train pulled into Plymouth station Erika looked out of the window for the man who would be carrying a copy of a pink newspaper. As she descended onto the platform she saw him and he recognised her from her description.

'And you are cousin Erika.' He took her hand. 'Welcome to England's West Country – where when you cannot see the hills it is raining, and when you can see them it is about to rain!' Erika laughed and restrained herself from kissing him. Englishmen don't as a rule, she had been told.

He took her bag and ten minutes later they were heading towards Tavistock.

'I'm working a short day today,' Roland announced at breakfast. 'They pay by the day on this consultancy job but I can slip off to write up my report here in the cottage and then go back tomorrow to finish off the week's work. I'll drive you around the moor this afternoon. Dartmoor is so lovely – they call it one of the last wildernesses of Europe.'

Erika was glad. She didn't particularly want to spend all day alone in a small village, and it would be fun to be driven around. In the meanwhile there was the village of Mary Tavy to explore and maybe she would walk along the country lanes which ran off the main road.

At three o'clock Roland returned and the two cousins drove over Dartmoor. They had a cream tea at Dartmeet and then looked round the tiny village of Widecombe. At Buckland-in-the-Moor Roland stopped the car and pointed to the clock on the tower of the church. 'Can you read what it says?' he asked her. Erika tried but her English wasn't up to deciphering the ornate letters. She shook her head.

'The numbers have been replaced by letters by someone who wanted to create a memorial. It reads *My Dear Mother*,' Roland said.

Erika's face lit up. 'Of course, I see it now – my poor English, I'm sorry.' Roland drove on and Erika suddenly asked him, 'Do you remember my mother?'

Roland screwed his face. 'Only slightly. I was a small child at the time – your parents came to the Far East, to Thailand when we were there about 1946. They didn't stay long and we stayed on for several years before my parents came back to Europe. Opportunities presented themselves to my father, and when the mess created by the war was all cleared up Father thought that Europe was the place to be. Your parents chose Latin America and so the two sisters split – I don't think they ever met again. My mother died in England some twenty years ago and I think your mother died shortly afterwards.' Erika nodded. 'It's all so long ago – we live in a different world now,' he added.

Erika smiled. 'That's what Father often says.'

When they arrived back at Mary Tavy, Roland announced that he wanted to walk down the lane and see the man who did the garden. 'Then we'll go out to dinner at a nice little place I know – a real country pub.'

As Erika was getting out of the bath there was a sharp knock on the front door. Sweeping back her wet hair and donning a dressing gown, she opened the door. A young girl in her twenties stood there. Her mouth fell open and then, muttering something about 'Mr Davies, Roland – I'm sorry to have disturbed you', she hurriedly left.

Ten minutes later Roland returned and they took the car to the restaurant.

* * *

As the powerful rented BMW ate up the miles on the way to Plymouth, Royce contemplated the unexpected arrival of the young German in London. He was on to something, but just how had he pieced Royce into the picture? That was the problem. Frohlich had well and truly screwed up getting information in Hamburg, and after his arrest the young man had come down to his mother in Marbella. Frohlich must have talked. Frohlich didn't have answers; but he did have the telephone number. 'That's it!' Rolls said out loud. 'The little bugger gave 'em the number 'e was supposed to call.'

So the German had contacted his mother and then come down to meet up with her. Somehow they had found Royce's connection with the attack and he had broken into Royce's house – not difficult with that bloody Salvadore on guard. The young man was well on his way to getting hold of a fortune, but if he told everything to Angie he still didn't have any idea about Gibraltar. That was the key to it all; the only person besides himself who knew about Gibraltar was conveniently lying on the bed of the Mediterranean in company with 50 kilos of iron girder. All he had to do was to get the information from Davies about deep-water scanning in an area where there was a considerable amount of metal dumped. He wished he could remember what he had heard about image scanning – something to do with the *Titanic*. Royce grunted. He hated doing everything for himself – it meant too much exposure, and the last thing he wanted was any slight interrogation. His eyes dropped to the speedometer, which registered 90 – better cut back to 70 – an over-zealous police patrol wouldn't help; he, Royce Rollason, had long hoped that his future personal encounters with the police would be limited to someone in a helmet directing traffic and nothing closer. His mind went back to – his mind struggled for the name – Grieb, that was it. What the bloody hell was he doing in London? Royce chilled. If Grieb had recognised him perhaps he would refer the matter to the police – it might surface Royce was wanted in Marbella. But if that was the case, why hadn't he gone straight to the Spanish police? The whole thing didn't make sense. Royce pulled into the Exeter motorway service station for fuel and a snack.

Royce frowned in dismay. It was three o'clock. ' 'Ow can 'e be finished for the day?;

The receptionist at Dekta Instruments shrugged her shoulders. 'I don't know – he just left half an hour ago and said he would be working at his cottage on notes and would be in tomorrow morning.'

'Where does 'e live then?'

The young girl shook her head. 'He has a cottage down here, I know that, and he brings a young lady down with him sometimes – but I don't know where it is. I know it's not on the telephone, though, because one of our directors asked for his number one day and we couldn't find it. When I asked him next day for his number at the cottage he said he wasn't on the telephone.'

Royce sat down in the brown plastic-covered armchair which served for visitors. It was so irritating to drive down to Plymouth – he had missed Davies at Phoenix Marketing in London – and then have to kill so much time. He had hoped to talk to Davies, get his co-operation and advice, perhaps obtain the necessary equipment and then drive back to London, where he had retained his room at the May Fair.

'If I made it worth your while could you ask around?' Royce said, with his wallet in his hand.

The receptionist shook her head. 'I wouldn't know where

to ask. I couldn't ask the boss, even if I had the nerve, because he's out all afternoon. Mr Davies would be angry if you went to his home, I'm sure of that – but as I tell you, I don't know where he lives.'

Royce thanked her for her efforts and said he would return in the morning. Half an hour later he checked in at the Plymouth Holiday Inn.

Roland Davies tapped his pen impatiently on his desk. He was irritated that the flighty young receptionist had fixed an appointment with someone he didn't know; he wanted to get on the road to London before four so that he could be home for dinner. He couldn't understand what had happened to Betty. Mrs Summers, the housekeeper, had told him that she had packed and left; perhaps she had decided to come down to Plymouth and might arrive any time now – but that in itself was odd. He wanted to leave and take Erika with him to meet Betty and they could all go out to dinner in London.

Now this vast man in a blue blazer and flashy tie had arranged to see him at the start of the day.

'Mr Rollason, what can I do to help you? I'm afraid I have a packed day and must leave for London.'

Royce cleared his throat. 'I'm working with Ian Lacey and a friend of his – Charlie, er Henry –' He stopped.

Davies's mouth fell open and he quickly composed himself. 'Lacey used to work in a company for which I do engineering consultancy in London. Suppose you tell me what this is all about.'

Royce had rehearsed his next move but now he sat facing the man who could answer his problem he felt uncomfortable. One thing he was resolved not to disclose was the actual location of his coveted fortune.

'I believe you are an expert on detectors and were advising my friends about locating some valuable material hidden in North Africa.' He stopped as if waiting for confirmation but Davies wasn't to be drawn.

'I'm not an expert on detectors,' he replied. 'I am an engineer who dabbles in inventing. I work freelance with marketing companies who import equipment, mainly Japanese, and who need technical advice and assistance but have no need for a full-time technical director. As for the second part – you tell me.'

Royce shuffled uneasily in his chair. His subject was a slippery customer and wasn't giving anything away. He made the next move in the pitting of wits. 'Well, my friends told me you were helping them and now they need more help – so they asked me to come and see you.'

'And why didn't they come themselves?'

Royce swallowed. 'Well, they are very busy indeed at the moment. They think they are onto something but they have a problem.'

'And you – or they – think I have the answer?'

Royce wished he wouldn't interrupt. 'Yes – the problem is that they have discovered that the goods in question are not under sand but in water – in the sea and at some depth.' Davies stirred but Royce continued. 'Not only is it in deep water but it is surrounded by a mountain of scrap – old cars, ovens and, well, they wondered about imaging.' Royce's voice faded as his normal blustery confidence dried up. Imaging was a word he had read in an article on underwater surveying – and he was more than a little uncertain of the meaning.

'Tell me, what exactly is your profession, Mr Rollason?'

'I'm retired now. I used to be in finance in London.'

'Mr Rollason – Royce Rollason, I believe – friend and confident of the underworld – well-known fence and conman.'

Royce's mouth dried and his accent dropped. ' 'Ow you know that – it's a bloody lie!'

Davies returned to his desk and doodled on a sheet of white paper in front of him. 'Mr Rollason, you can deny all you like and I shall bid you farewell. Whether you like it or not, you enjoy a certain degree of notoriety and a certain inmate of an institution on the moor not fifteen miles from here told me about you – calls you one of the best fences he had ever met, last heard of living on the Costa Brava, I believe.'

'Costa de Sol,' corrected Royce.

'I'm sorry – the fashionable Costa del Sol, and now hard at work in Tunisia.'

The door opened and a pale-faced girl placed a tray of coffee on the desk. Davies murmured his thanks.

'The only way you are going to get anywhere with me is to tell me everything and then...' He stopped as the telephone rang and picked up the receiver. The call obviously surprised him and his forehead furrowed. He listened intently and then spoke in a language Royce couldn't understand. It wasn't Spanish – German maybe. He became even more uncomfortable. After a long discussion Davies put down the telephone.

'Mr Rollason, I must return to London. My father is elderly and he has had a shock. Something has upset him badly and I must be with him. I will go to see him this afternoon and I suggest you go there this evening. I want you to meet people who are interested in what you have to offer and could help you – but I warn you to tell the truth. My friends don't suffer fools lightly and are more than contemptuous of liars.'

Royce got up and Davies escorted him to the door and into the foyer. 'There's just one thing I would like to know, Mr Rollason. Where are your friends working on their deep-water assignment?'

Royce looked Davies in the eyes. 'I told you – Tunisia. I was with 'em a few days ago.'

Davies scribbled on a piece of paper. 'This is the address – but come prepared to tell the truth.'

A cool breeze was blowing as Royce walked across the car park. He was glad of it as his shirt was wet and clinging to his massive frame. It was unlike him to feel afraid, but he judged that he had lost a battle of wits which only an hour ago he had been confident of winning.

15

Adrian and Lorna strolled leisurely down Davies Street and into Berkeley Square. Somewhere a clock was striking eleven and they had had a considerable amount to drink with their generous hosts. They had liked the two Carluccis and had thoroughly enjoyed the evening. A quiet walk would give them time to talk, to compare notes. Adrian broke the silence. 'It certainly seems that Ian was onto something when he saw Carlucci – and it's interesting that he spoke of visiting Collingson. That is obviously an area which we have to look into.'

'I'm also interested in Dr Solomon,' Lorna added. 'He had a shock when Raoul spoke of Ian's search – he got over the shock all right but did you notice how he kept away from us for the rest of the evening? I can't help thinking he knows more than he has told us. That day he called on me at home and told me of the insurance deal which Ian wanted to set up – I felt then that there was something that he wanted to tell me but changed his mind and decided not to say. It's odd that he should turn up like that.'

'Not really,' Adrian replied. 'They are part of the Jewish community and stick together. It's surprising who knows who in life – it is just that one doesn't ask.'

As they walked past the Lansdowne Club at the bottom of the square, Adrian hesitated. 'Maybe Franz is still up. Come in and meet him. You've spoken often enough on the phone.'

Adrian turned out to be correct and they found Franz sitting in the lounge reading a book. He was delighted to meet Lorna and the two exchanged the usual pleasantries. Turning to Adrian he said, 'Now I do have news for you – we have a visitor in town, none other than our old heavy-handed friend Mr Rollason. I almost bumped into him crossing the road at the top of Berkeley Square. He doesn't think I recognised him, I'm sure. Be that as it may, the key question is, what the hell is he doing here? His search has put him on the trail, but who is he here to see and why?'

Adrian suggested that they sat down. 'I want you to listen to our interesting dinner party – not just what was said but who was there – and although it's late I have a feeling we are going to have some interesting discussion. Perhaps tomorrow we will go west to the factory in Plymouth just to see if anyone recognises Ian's photograph,'

Lorna looked at her watch. 'My God, I didn't realise – I must call the babysitter and tell her we are on the way. She'll be getting worried. You chaps finish off your drinks.'

It was three minutes later that Lorna returned. She looked puzzled.

'You've had a telephone call, Adrian. It was Betty Silvester and she says it's urgent, very urgent. Asks you to go to her place, or rather a friend's place, in Fulham Road. The babysitter said she was very upset you were not at home – and asked for you to go there immediately you got back. I suppose you had better do it. The cab can drop me at home and take you on. Here's the address.'

* * *

The taxi pulled off the Fulham Road and into a small cul-de-sac. Number 47 was close to the end, a large Victorian villa with an array of door bells and an entry phone. Adrian paid off the driver and pushed 'Flat 5'. He didn't have long to wait; the door opened and the girl he had last spoken to in a coffee shop near Harrods stood in the dim hall. She held out her hand.

'Mr Franklin, it is so good – so kind of you to come.'

Adrian recalled that on their last meeting she had called him by his first name, but that was only one difference in the girl he had met previously. Betty Silvester had been crying, was untidy and was very obviously pregnant. She opened a side door and showed Adrian into a small bedsitter where another girl, slightly younger and with long red hair, sat reading a book. They were introduced and Vanessa went to make coffee. Adrian realised that with the Carluccis' hospitality he had had more to drink than he should have done and made a stumbled apology. Betty smiled and Adrian saw a resemblance to the young vivacious girl he had known briefly just two months ago.

There was a long silence. 'What can I do to help?' Adrian asked, hoping that did not sound trite.

'Vanessa suggested that I call you. Things have turned out so badly that I didn't know which way to turn. I suppose I ought to tell you straight away that my father is what is known as a habitual criminal – ever since Mother met him he's been promising to go straight but then another job would come along. The last one, the one to make us rich, he always said, and he would be off again. Two years ago Mother couldn't stand it any longer and she left him and got a job abroad.'

'I know about your father,' Adrian said softly, and then promptly wished he hadn't, for Betty raised her eyes.

'How could you know?'

'Look, Betty,' Adrian said comfortingly, 'suppose you start from the beginning and tell me all. Davies is involved, isn't he? And I know all about the house in Devon, but I would rather hear it all from you. You must have called me to tell me everything. Why you chose me I'm not sure.'

'Because of Ian.' She was close to tears.

'OK – let's have the story.'

The conversation was interrupted by the arrival of coffee. Vanessa poured three mugs and Adrian could not help but observe the irony that his mug was inscribed 'Keep Smiling'. Vanessa said she was going to watch television in the kitchen and left.

Betty Silvester had joined Phoenix Marketing shortly after

her marriage to a City foreign exchange broker had collapsed. Her husband had moved most of their money overseas and into offshore funds so the likelihood of her getting any financial support was small. She liked the job as secretary to Ian Lacey and became very involved with the company's activities. Apart from disliking Mr Fenton, the Managing Director, she had been very happy. She had grown very fond of Ian and eventually they had an affair. He was obviously very committed to his wife and child so it was a strange relationship, more physical than anything, and both realised that no long-term commitment could develop; indeed, in the cool light of day, neither wanted it. Ian had a happy marriage and Betty was too close to the breakdown of her marriage to want to start another permanent relationship – she needed freedom. She had told Ian about her father's past in an unguarded moment. In fact, Ian had met her father and the two had got on well.

After a while both agreed that the affair should stop and to ease matters it was arranged that Betty should change jobs and work for the Technical Director, Mr Davies, and Ian would find a new secretary.

On Betty's birthday, 23 October, Davies invited her to lunch at one of his favourite restaurants, Quo Vadis, and the conversation somehow turned to nicknames. She told Davies that her father called her 'Monty', and when he asked why she told him that her father had fought under General Montgomery at the Battle of El Alamein on 23 October 1942. Davies mentioned that his father's neighbour had also been in the North African campaign and was at that moment researching the subject.

Shortly after that the two started seeing more of one another, and although Davies was old enough to be her father an affair had developed. The two of them went down to her father's peaceful cottage near Tavistock in Devon. It fitted in well because Davies had a consultancy for two or three days every week in Plymouth – sometimes she took a few days' holiday from her part-time job at Harrods and went down with him but more often he went down by air and she travelled down by train on Friday evening. On one weekend he bought her a new car – a red Fiat.

'Where did Davies live in London?' Adrian asked.

'He has a house in Hampstead but there's a weekend cottage in Cookham Dean,' she replied. 'He lived in Cookham with his father. He and his wife are separated. She's a solicitor with a practice in the Midlands and they rarely meet. There are no children.'

One weekend when she was alone in her flat – Davies was at Sandown Park races with some friends and Betty didn't care for racing – she had a telephone call from Ian Lacey. She was surprised to hear from him.

She had told Adrian this at their previous meeting, but he let her continue. After all, she might remember something fresh.

He sounded agitated and after a while he asked for Davies's telephone number at home. 'Roland is very sensitive about his number,' Betty explained, 'so I asked what it was all about. He said he had discovered something important, a chance of a lifetime, and it could make him rich quickly. He had been looking so ill recently that I asked him more but he was very sharp, bit my head off, so to speak.' Reluctantly she gave him Roland Davies's number but told Ian that he wouldn't be in until the early evening.

Later that day Davies told Betty his father, who had been an MP, was keenly interested in history, especially military history. He and a friend were rewriting a manuscript on the North African campaign and wanted to get some first-hand experiences, so he suggested their fathers should have a talk.

The two men met at the Cookham house and got on extremely well, and then Davies introduced his neighbour who was also involved in the rewrite.

'Father used to go up to Cookham often. The three of them chatted and then had some drinks, a little too many,' Betty recalled. 'Dad would say that he had come up in the world, a barrow boy and former batman drinking with a former senior MP and also with an Italian aristocrat, even if he was on the wrong side of the war.'

Adrian couldn't contain the question he had been longing to ask. 'This neighbour, this Italian aristocrat, uses the name Whiteman, Robert Whiteman?'

Betty looked Adrian squarely in the face. 'Yes. Funny name for an Italian. But he was only part Italian, he said. I expect he changed it, but how did you know?'

'I'll tell you sometime but I'd rather listen to you now. So you knew Whiteman?'

'Yes, I did. Very military gentleman he was, old and with very fixed views. Oh the three of them used to meet a lot – and argue a lot – but they had fun. I think they spent more time drinking than they did doing the book. Mr Whiteman lived next door and they shared a drive. He used to pop across the garden and home after the sessions. It was a bit of fun for them, and Roland and I used to join them sometimes.

'Matters changed suddenly,' Betty went on, 'because very early one morning my father was arrested. It was something he had done several years before. One of his so-called friends was picked up, and in order to get a lighter sentence turned what I believe they call Queen's Evidence. Father, because of his past record, didn't get bail and when the case came up at the Old Bailey he got three years – he's in Dartmoor now.'

Her eyes told her sorrow and Adrian said softly, 'I know.'

Betty looked at him quizzically. 'How could you know that?'

'Please keep talking,' Adrian urged. 'I'll tell you my story later.'

'Mr Davies and Mr Whiteman went on working on the book. I think they took it more seriously when Dad wasn't there, and sometimes Roland used to get involved. The book was being reprinted and some of the points were being corrected. Most of the work had been done by a Colonel Sneider, who came over once but he was very ill. He was a German, a typical German, and he wanted the book correct in every detail. It irritated him he couldn't continue due to his health. The author was in Switzerland. His name was General Collingson and sometimes they used to call him. He was ill as well and never came over but the work continued.

Then Colonel Sneider died and Roland's father and Mr Whiteman went on with the work. It became a bit of an obsession with them.

'Shortly after Ian disappeared, Roland suggested we went down to Tunisia for a holiday. It was very sudden, and when we arrived in Tunisia he said he would be working for a few days. I found this odd and asked him what he was doing. He was very vague and said it was to do with the book that he was helping his father with. It was all so out of character, Mr Franklin, because as far as I knew they weren't being paid and Roland isn't the kind of man to work for nothing. Anyway, one day the strangest thing happened. Roland went off early in the morning and I hung around the pool. An elderly gentleman was carrying a tray of drinks and dropped a glass near me. He and his wife cleared up the broken glass and I helped. We just fell into conversation. They had a hire car and were going to drive around the island in the afternoon. They invited me and we went over to the ferry at Ajim where the sponge divers work. It's a local tourist attraction. We were on the quayside and looking over the boats harboured there when I saw Roland.' Betty leant forward and put her hand on Adrian's. 'Mr Franklin, he wasn't alone – he was with Ian, Ian Lacey, and they were obviously arguing.'

Adrian's mouth dried. 'Are you sure – absolutely sure?'

'Yes. And that evening when he came back I asked him how the day had gone and if he had had an interesting time. He said nothing about seeing Ian, nothing at all. A few days later we went back to England and nothing more has been said. I was worried about what was going on, particularly as you had told me about Ian's disappearance. I thought about calling you but decided against it; I didn't want any trouble and if Ian was about he would certainly go home. If I said I had seen him in Tunisia a lot of awkward questions would be – well – unasked, if you see what I mean.'

Adrian broke in. 'Where was this place Ajim – whereabouts in Tunisia?'

'In Djerba, an island off the south coast,' Betty answered.

'And what happened when you returned to England?'

'One evening I heard Roland's father say to Roland that he was going to telephone Collingson. I imagined that it was to enquire how he was as about a week earlier they had talked about his health and Roland had commented that he probably wasn't long for this world. Although I had never met the gentleman, I knew he was old and frail. Sometimes when they had called to check the manuscript they had been told he was in bed.

'It was that evening when I came into the library end of the L-shaped room to get a book. I didn't know Mr Davies was on the telephone. When I entered he was obviously listening. Suddenly Mr Davies spoke very angrily, almost shouting into the instrument, "There was no crash at Djerba, Roland's been down and checked it over." Then he got even angrier and called him a "double-crossing bastard – you know bloody well where." There was a long silence and I imagine he was listening again. Then I heard Roland calling so I slipped quietly out. What struck me as odd was that the name Djerba had come up. That was why we had gone there, to investigate a crash, yet Roland had said nothing to me about it. The second odd thing is that you don't usually talk to a very ill man so aggressively. Since that time I've been worried, desperately worried, about Ian. I was very fond of him, you know, and if he hadn't been so involved with his family we would be together now.' Betty broke off and sat looking at the carpet, which had seen better days.

'Did Roland and his father discuss this telephone conversation?' Adrian asked.

Betty shook her head. 'Not in front of me... The only time that General Collingson's name came up was several days later, when Mr Davies opened the mail at breakfast – must have been Saturday as we were there for the weekend. The letter said that General Collingson had died. Both Roland and his father were disturbed, not upset. Roland said something like, "That's torn it – now we'll never know."'

'There's one point I'm not clear on – come to think of it, two,' Adrian said. 'First, why did you go down to Dartmoor to ask your father questions about his war experiences, and second, why did you suddenly tell me all this now?'

'I went down because they asked me – to get Dad to give them the name of someone who could fence some stolen goods, valuable antiques. I became even more worried then; just how much of this connected with Ian, our trip to Tunisia and indeed me? I don't want to follow in Dad's footsteps. I was amazed that Roland was involved in anything like this. He assured me he wasn't – it was information for a friend of his father.'

'And did you get the name of the friend?' Adrian asked gently.

'No but he's a doctor in London – they refer to him as "The Doc". There was another one. I forget his name, he lived in Spain.'

Adrian took a sharp breath and lay back in his chair. Could this be the reason the honourable doctor had been put off his dinner only a few hours before?

'And the second point – why contact me now?'

Betty's face hardened. 'Roland had the keys to Dad's cottage. He went down this week to work at the Plymouth firm where he does consultancy work and said that as he was busy I should stay at home. He was busy all right, but not with work – he took a girl with him. I found out because I needed to contact him. I couldn't find the key to the utility room at Hampstead. I called Sara, a friend who lives in Mary Tavy, and asked her to go round with a message – we don't have a telephone in the cottage. She called me back and told me. I am so upset, so bloody angry, that my loyalty to that creep has gone out the window. Imagine taking a floosie to my cottage! I packed my things and then I drove over to the cottage at Cookham Dean to pick up some things I had left there. I let myself in with my key went to the room we use and threw everything in a bag. Mr Davies senior is a bit deaf and didn't hear me. I didn't want to disturb him because he had visitors – there were several cars outside. When I came down the stairs they were talking in the lounge, the L-shaped room I told you about. I thought I had better say goodbye; after all, it wasn't the old man's fault that his son had been a real shit. I put my head around the corner and had a dreadful fright – you can never imagine what I saw.' Betty's eyes displayed horror.

Adrian took her hands in his. 'Tell me.'

'They were all in uniform, Mr Franklin, military uniform. They were all old men, and one, I think it was the old man from the next house, was standing up talking. He had a swastika on his arm and a picture was behind him on the wall – a picture of Adolf Hitler. He stopped talking when he saw me and someone shouted. I just ran from the room and down to my car. Two old men ran after me and shouted but I drove off as fast as I could.'

Betty stopped and Adrian continued to hold her hands. 'Betty, my love, does anyone know where you are now, anyone?'

Betty thought. 'No one but Vanessa, unless I mentioned it to Sara, but Roland knows I'm friendly with Vanessa and her number is in the front of the telephone directory at the house – the page for numbers you use regularly.'

Adrian thought quickly. 'Get packed, put your stuff together as fast as you can. We're going to my home. Don't tell Vanessa anything – just that you're going to friends. Let's get you well away, then we'll think over the next move.'

Lorna awoke suddenly as she heard the front door. It was a quarter past five and she realised she had been in the armchair for several hours. Adrian's muffled voice was in the hallway. He must have someone with him, she thought. She opened the lounge door and saw a slightly built girl in her early twenties, with Adrian carrying a suitcase behind. Adrian ushered the young girl into the lounge and closed the door.

'This is Betty Silvester, Lorna, and I think it is best if she stays here. When you hear her story I think that you will agree.'

Adrian quickly outlined what had happened, a useful exercise in its own right, he thought, as it helped him to clarify things in his own mind.

Lorna sat upright in her chair when Ian's name was mentioned. 'That's the second time in twenty-four hours that someone has said they've seen him; first Mr Carlucci and now you, Betty.'

'And the interesting thing is, if I have my details right, that these sightings took place within two or three days of one another. After his meeting with Davies in Tunisia he must have gone to Genoa to meet with Carlucci. Anyway, let Betty tell you what happened next.'

Betty shook her head so Adrian continued. When he reached the Cookham military party, Lorna interrupted. 'Ian must have stumbled across something – God knows what. Are you going to tell the police?'

Adrian frowned. 'Tell them what? A group of senile gentlemen like dressing up in uniform? They have enough problems with people's kinky habits. God knows how many old ladies ring the local cop shop daily and say they have a man opposite who appears in maid's uniform and lipstick. No, at present all we would do is drive them to ground and the police would put the matter down to a bunch of degenerates engaged in private theatricals being reported by someone with puritanical views.'

He yawned. 'Let's snatch some sleep. We need it,' he said. 'I'll show you your room, Betty, and tomorrow we'll start thinking again. I'll call Franz and get him over to breakfast. I want to get Dr Solomon around to have him give you a check over. You've had a shock and that's not good news in your condition – yes, I've noticed. Is it Davies?' Adrian asked gently.

Betty nodded.

'Maybe I'll get the good doctor to stay awhile – I've a strong feeling he can contribute when you tell your story. I forgot to tell you, by the way, that you have a young man in your room tonight – he has a habit of waking early and making a noise. Perhaps you would try to explain to Sam that you are a friend of Mum's and stayed the night.'

Betty's face broke into a smile. 'I wish I had come to you sooner, Mr Franklin. I feel so much better – and I'll sleep, my God how I'll sleep.'

As Adrian went to his room, the thought struck him that without thinking he had brought Ian's ex-mistress into the house of Ian's wife – or widow. It was a strange thing for a father to do. But circumstances were strange and getting stranger.

Adrian had hardly replaced the receiver after calling Franz when the telephone rang. He was surprised to hear Raoul Carlucci.

'Sorry to call you so early but I'm leaving for Birmingham at midday and I have rather a tight schedule. I enjoyed meeting you – and your charming daughter – and I'm sorry we cannot help more in the search for her husband. Bad business that. I've been thinking over what we discussed and I feel that man Southon isn't up to any good – I haven't heard a word from him for weeks. Italy's an hour ahead so I called up an old friend of mine, the Chief of Police in Genoa, and asked him to put a search out for a stolen boat, because I do regard it as stolen. I'll let you know what happens.'

Adrian listened distractedly as his mind raced. There was a question he wanted to ask but his tired brain couldn't focus on it. Carlucci was making signs as if to ring off so Adrian asked him to hold on – then suddenly it occurred to him.

'Raoul, answer me a question, will you? How long have you known Dr Solomon?'

Raoul Carlucci laughed. 'Old Solly? Oh years, years and years. He's a well-trusted family friend. He came over to England from Israel in the mid-fifties as a young doctor. I met him through Bernard – you know, Waterman – some twenty years ago. Bernard and I had met up after years, as I told you last night, and I was staying in London. One day Bernard and I had lunch and towards the evening I felt ill – probably a bad oyster. I needed a doctor and Bernard ran me round to Solly. But why do you ask?'

'He had a nasty shock last night when Ian's name came up – and his disappearance was discussed.'

'That's true, but Solly is a funny old stick, lives alone, never married and gets obsessed with his interests. He's involved with all sorts of activities. He's a specialist in antiques and fine arts, sails a small boat, writes medical articles for women's magazines and all that kind of thing. Then he puts in a lot of work for the Simon Wiesenthal Institute in detecting war criminals and I've given him little bits of information there. No, he's a strange man but he's an honest one and good company – I like him.'

Adrian wanted to answer but his mind and mouth were temporarily out of gear. He wanted time to think – just to think. He thanked Raoul and rang off.

Breakfast would be late so Lorna had time to slip out and buy some kippers. She knew Adrian liked them and hoped that Franz and Betty would too. Franz arrived shortly after nine fifteen and Adrian introduced him to Betty.

The kippers were evenly divided; Franz's face was a mask of horror. The young German was accustomed to his rolls and coffee and no more. Betty politely declined as she was feeling rather unwell.

Breakfast was eaten and cleared away, then between them Adrian and Betty related the events of the previous night to Franz. The young German studied the tabletop with embarrassment as the incident of the uniformed group under the picture of Adolf Hitler was related.

'And was Weissman in the group?' he asked Betty.

'I only recognised Roland's father, no one else, and I don't know anyone called Weissman.' Betty looked puzzled.

Adrian cut in. 'But you know someone called Robert Whiteman, don't you?'

Betty's face paled. 'Oh, my God, of course – that was the one who was speaking, the one standing up and shouting – I remember now. Mr Davies and Mr Whiteman were friends – well, they were working on the book together because of Mr Sneider's illness. But how does he tie up with Mr Wise –' She hesitated.

'Weissman,' Franz said softly. 'Robert Weissman, and if the brigadier I met in the In and Out Club is correct, we are talking of a wanted war criminal and close confidant, probably relative, of Martin Bormann.'

Betty look puzzled.

'One of the principal Nazis who should have been tried at Nuremberg and would certainly have been hanged – he was Hitler's right-hand man, a Nazi party chief, who vanished a few days before the end of the war,' Adrian explained.

The group sat in silence and after what seemed an age Lorna spoke.

'All this is intriguing, but where does Ian fit in?'

Adrian shook his head. 'I haven't the slightest idea.'

Dr Solomon shook the rain off his hat and entered the house. Adrian had told him that a young lady staying with them was suffering from shock. The family didn't usually call him out unless it was serious but Adrian had seemed disinclined to say more on the telephone – except to say she was pregnant.

Adrian showed Dr Solomon to Betty's bedroom. When he came downstairs Lorna was in the hall, just returned from taking Sam to playgroup.

'The doctor's here,' he said.

Lorna nodded. 'I saw his car outside.'

Fifteen minutes later Dr Solomon and Betty came down the stairs. Adrian offered coffee, and the old man accepted and sat down.

'I think the best plan is to come straight to the point,' Adrian began. 'Oh, I'm sorry, I didn't introduce Mr Franz Grieb. Franz, this is Dr Isaac Solomon.'

The two shook hands and Adrian leant forward.

'I asked you to see Betty Silvester this morning because in her pregnant state she has been subjected to a great shock. After leaving the dinner party at Raoul's last night I had a message from Betty, a message saying she wanted to see me urgently. I believe you are involved in the detection of Nazi war criminals who escaped the net?'

The old man's eyes shone. 'Yes – trying to redress the wrongs of my past. I have worked with several independent institutions and organisations which either act independently or refer to the Israeli Secret Service.'

Adrian turned to Betty. 'You had better tell the story in your own words.'

* * *

There was a long silence when Betty stopped speaking, and all eyes were turned to the doctor to see his reaction. Whatever his feelings or his surprise, he showed nothing. His face was ashen and fixed, his eyes looked straight ahead as if an item of outstanding interest was on the facing wall. Lorna broke the silence by suggesting fresh coffee and there was a murmur of assent. On her return there was still silence and the elderly Jew was writing notes on a pocket pad. The atmosphere was tense and the sound of coffee being distributed seemed to restore a real-life world. Franz was slumped in a chair in a desolate way and Lorna realised what he must be feeling. She felt sorry for the young German.

To everyone's surprise it was Franz who stirred the action. He rose from his low armchair and walked to the fireplace. 'It seems that we have discovered my country's dirty linen in the cupboard. Just how it relates to the disappearance of Ian I don't know, possibly none of us knows. I have no sympathy, no time at all for such people, but the question is what do we do about it and what does all this achieve?'

Dr Solomon looked up at the young man. 'This is more far-reaching than you can possibly imagine, Franz. What we have unearthed in the cupboard, as you put it so well, has very great consequences indeed. Before I explain things to you I should like to make a telephone call so that this information is passed to the right quarter. Do you agree with this?'

There were various sounds from the room but Adrian asked the question in everyone's mind. 'Will any action these people take endanger Ian – assuming that he is alive?'

The old man shook his wavy white hair. 'Let me assure you that if he is alive, and I must say I fear he is not, there will be no danger.'

Adrian showed the doctor to the tiny study with a telephone on the desk.

* * *

'I would rather stand and talk,' said the doctor on his return. 'What I tell you must be completely correct, and I think clearer standing up; it must be old age.' He smiled for the first time since he had entered the house and Lorna caught his eye. She liked the old man even if he had not been completely straight with her.

'I suppose the story really starts in the immediate pre-war years, 1936 and 1937. Hitler had become Chancellor in 1933 at Hindenburg's instigation. In the following year he declared himself Führer and had all members of the armed forces take an oath of personal allegiance to him. He declared that German supremacy without force was not possible – a fact ignored and scarcely reported. From a very early stage Hitler was preparing for war and in order to achieve complete control over countries he planned to invade he enlisted influential sympathisers to his cause in those countries. Mussert was the Nazi leader in Holland and he had a number of powerful men under him. There was Claussen in Denmark, Szalassy in Hungary, Sima in Rumania – all Hitler's men. In Norway Quisling became the willing planted man and in France there was quite a wide selection when Vichy France was proclaimed – a France which ran itself according to German requirements but without active German presence, particularly for the first part of the war. In Austria Hitler had a zealous supporter in the form of Seyss-Inquart and indeed Austria was annexed because Seyss-Inquart invited the German forces in. I say this again, invited the German forces in, not dissimilar to Afghanistan inviting the Russian forces in more recent times.' He turned to Betty and Franz. 'I mention that to you youngsters because it is before your time, and history does repeat itself.

'In Britain the Führer had an additional challenge. It would be one of the last, perhaps the last, European country to come under the domination of the Third Reich and by that time German troops available for the occupation of conquered countries would be thin on the ground. He believed that Italy and Spain would come in with him and their troops would be available for occupation duties – but he couldn't rely on it and, as history was to show, his doubts were justified. Italy came in late and very half-heartedly. Spain had had enough with her civil war.

'Be that as it may, in 1937 a number of prominent people in Britain made visits to Germany ostensibly to create a bond between the two countries. Both countries had a common fear, the rise of Bolshevism. The British were convinced, wrongly, that the General Strike in the twenties was Soviet-influenced, and the Germans under Hitler's influence blamed not only the Treaty of Versailles for Germany's economic and inflationary chaos in the early thirties, but also the Russian Revolution.

'I said "ostensibly to create a bond" – but what was really happening was that Hitler was creating an elite management body to govern Britain when his Operation Sealion, as the invasion of this country was code-named, was successful. These were very influential, very powerful people indeed and included a publisher, several prominent Members of Parliament, a writer-broadcaster, a peer and several chairmen of large corporations. When Rudolf Hess made his dramatic visit to Scotland in 1941 and was captured, there was much speculation about why he was flying over Britain in the first place. The truth was that he was Hitler's appointee to coordinate the activities of such Nazi devotees and he was here to brief them of their role in the coming invasion. You may wonder why Hess was never released. Quite a few people were relieved, to say the least, that he never was, for he knew the identity of the people involved. I personally believe that the powers that be ensured that Hess was kept well away from where he could make a statement implicating certain pillars of society. Even though he became insane, he went to great lengths at Nuremberg to show he was not. He could have caused chaos if his statements had appeared in print.

'After the war, Nazi war criminals were tried at Nuremberg

and hanged. Some committed suicide, but many, and I really mean many, escaped and scattered over the world, where they set up new lives, most of them with considerable wealth. A clandestine escape organisation called *Die Spinne* had been set up when Germany's collapse seemed certain – even though the Führer himself refused to believe that his Reich could tumble. *Die Spinne* set up an involved flight of party chiefs – they called it the *Bonzenflucht*. Nazis and SS chiefs would scatter across the world. A major centre was set up in Walchensee and a vast amount of money from the Reichsbank in Berlin was brought to the neighbouring villages and hidden in mines, in lakes and even in a remote forester's hut. The purpose was simple – the creation of a Fourth Reich based in Bavaria.

'Even at the closing stages of the war Nazi party chiefs believed that they could do a deal with Churchill and create a power to keep the Russians at bay. They knew that ever since the Russian Revolution the British had lived in dread of Bolshevik influence and infiltration. A common enemy would bring Germany and Britain together. Colossal funds were hoarded for that purpose.

'And what became of British Nazi supporters? We know what happened to the Continental ones; many were killed by their own people. The British ones just evaporated because no one knew for sure who they were, although there were strong suspicions. Many no doubt retired to positions of influence and power after the war and lived with their frustrated secret ambitions of power for the rest of their lives. Of course there were suspicions, strong suspicions. But nothing could be proved, and perhaps the British Government didn't want to expose such people – it would be embarrassing, to put it mildly, if enquiries revealed that several of its own members, perhaps even of Cabinet rank, were exposed. No, the war was won and the focus was on bringing to justice those who had committed atrocities, who had betrayed their fellow countrymen, rather than those who had harboured aspirations to serve the Third Reich as puppet governors.

'The identity of these people was, of course, known not

only to Hess but to certain members of the hierarchy in the Nazi party in Germany. However strong the security, some people just have to know. There is no doubt that after the war, maybe many years after, certain wanted war criminals living in Britain made contact with their former British supporters and enlisted further assistance. Not all had access to funds deposited in Switzerland. Perhaps some of those approached wanted to close the book and considered the cause lost, in which case blackmail would be applied. The actual contact would not be the German himself, he had too much to lose – he would work through an intermediary. On the other hand, there were those of influence and affluence who still believed in the Nazi cause, still idolised a man who brought Germany from chaos in 1933 to a condition six years later where she could declare war virtually on the world. Hitler's pre-war achievements, which were colossal and astonishing, are often forgotten by students of history who regard his wartime activities as inept and brutal. But there was, after the war, an active Nazi party which believed that Germany would reunite and that Aryan supremacy, taught by the Führer, would again come to the fore. The enemy – Bolshevism – would be defeated by the Fourth Reich. Britain and France would eventually recognise the true threat to world peace and form part of that Reich.'

The old man paused as if to think of the next thing he should say and Franz took the opportunity to make a point.

'Is the Jewish community committed to exposing such people? Is that your function, doctor?'

'Oh dear no, certainly not. The Jewish community has enough on its hands, enough commitments, usually strained by lack of cash. Yes, there are many rich Jews all over the world and many are prepared to contribute handsomely for the benefit of Israel. No, the Jews never forget the Holocaust and few of them indeed did not lose relatives or close friends. Many lost their whole families and I number in that group. The suffering was immense and the years have not dulled our memories. You can call it justice, revenge or what you will but many of us were determined to locate and deal with those who escaped the net. In recent years the authorities waned considerably in their search, partly because of the Genocide Act, partly because many wanted men had died naturally and partly because it was all history. But not to us. That is why we discovered Eichmann in 1960 and more recently Barbie, who committed such fearful atrocities in Lyons. The Jews – like elephants, I suppose – never forget. No, we are not interested in aspiring Nazi leaders of a conquered Britain. If the British want they can find them, but, as I've explained, I think the government even today would choose to escape the embarrassment. No, the Jewish community wants to lay its hands on the mass murderers of our people.'

The old man crossed the room and poured himself some coffee. As he drank his eyes looked at the assembled audience over the rim of the cup. That he had an attentive audience was in no doubt.

'The old men you saw at Cookham – they may be harmless old fools playing games, they may not. They could be wanted or they could lead us to the beasts we really want to lay hands on. We shall see.

'You may wonder, as I wondered at first, why Davies should be interested in the – for want of a better expression I call it the treasure trove in North Africa. He is somehow connected with the party but is much too young as you describe him to me, to have been involved in the war. No, that treasure was stolen from the Jews, from the Carlucci family, and the remnants of the Third Reich believe it is rightfully theirs. Money is getting short, leading members have died, their supporters in certain countries have died or vanished. It takes money to keep a party going, especially an illegal one. I have no doubt that bribes are paid. Recruitment of new members, not just in Germany, is necessary. Remember these people believe – believe down to their toes – in the emergence of a new Reich under a new leader.

'A minute ago I mentioned bribes. But there are those who cannot be bribed, who discover something like, say, rape or murder and who are so incensed and disgusted by what they discover that they are determined to reveal all, whatever the cost. These are men or women of whom we should all be proud, but regrettably they pay too high a price. When you deal with men who hold life cheap, the price is your own life. That is what I fear, Lorna – that Ian stumbled across something else when he sought the valuables. He did not find assets which would ensure your financial security. He found out something which disgusted him, and when he didn't succumb to bribes he was killed. I hate to say this but it is very much on my mind. However, I must say that I have not a shred of evidence. Maybe my young friends associated with the Mossad or what you would call our Israeli Secret Service will discover something. We shall see. All I regret was that it was through me that Ian went on this chase – just one more regret to add to my list, I suppose.'

The doctor stopped talking and sat down.

'I think we have done all we can now – let's leave it to the doctor's helpers,' Adrian suggested. 'Certainly Betty must stay here until all this is sorted out. The question I ask myself is what the group at Cookham plan to do. It could be that they think Betty will do nothing, and just pretend it didn't happen. I doubt it. I think they will associate her disappearance with what she discovered at the house rather than her finding out about Davies occupying her house in the West Country with a girlfriend. But I do believe one thing – we should do nothing and say nothing.'

Betty and Lorna left the room, asking who would like tea or coffee. When the door closed there was an eerie silence as everyone present absorbed the stories, mentally assessing the implications. The elderly doctor was obviously in a state of considerable agitation and Adrian watched him carefully.

'Dr Solomon, I saw your reaction last night. You were shaken when the subject of the missing goods was brought up, surprised when you found out that we knew the Carluccis.' The doctor nodded. 'I want to put it to you that you know considerably more about this whole affair than you have disclosed up to now. You knew about Ian's discovery of the book and the fact that he was going off, didn't you?'

The old man's voice was no more than a whisper as he answered, 'Yes.'

When Betty and Lorna came back into the room with the tea trolley Adrian asked the doctor to go on with his story. 'Tell us about Ian,' he added softly.

The elderly Jew wrung his hands. 'I had no idea how complicated things would become – no idea at all. Ian came to me with that crazy insurance idea – swindle I suppose you could call it. I had to turn him down. I couldn't get involved in anything like that. He was desperate to get some money, went on and on about his wife and son being left without money. He wanted me to tell him how long he had and I hesitated about that – people vary quite a lot with that kind of cancer. He had been to see a specialist at my instigation and I asked him if he would like another opinion. He didn't. He left in a bad state, I can tell you, and I was worried about him. To my surprise he was back in the surgery next morning. He told me that he had a lucky opportunity to make some money fast; he wanted me to confirm that he would be fit enough to travel to Tunisia and do a certain amount of digging. At first I thought he was suffering from a mental derangement – it's not unknown for someone to react irrationally and uncontrollably when given dramatically bad news. He could see what I was thinking so he told me that he had been to a house book sale and had bought a collection of books on World War II. They had been marked in the margin and the markings were either corrections or references to letters. A photocopy of a letter had marked a page. He had gone out to discover the owners of the books, had some problem finding them – it turned out that they belonged to a German officer who was correcting them when he died. He told me the story of the raid on the synagogue back in '42 and then it suddenly struck me – I had heard the story before. What he was telling me was the story I had heard from Raoul Carlucci and his rescuer and now friend Bernard Waterman. I had met Carlucci through Waterman a number of years ago – he came to me via Bernard and is now not just a patient but a friend. In fact, he's been a great help in my little hobby of trying to trace war criminals.'

'Tell us about that,' Adrian prompted.

Solomon unbuttoned his cuff and rolled back his right sleeve to reveal a tattooed number, '49176'. His eyes fixed on Adrian as he spoke. 'That's why I've used my time in this way – to bring the filth of the earth to justice. That was my number in Dachau.'

The old man's eyes turned to Franz, who was looking at the carpet. 'Come on, my boy, it was years before your time. I have many German friends and I don't hold anything against them – every nation has scum. As I said, I realised that Ian was talking about the Carlucci family treasure. He had letters indicating exactly where it was and he claimed to know someone called Parker, who was the writer's driver/batman.'

'My father,' broke in Betty.

Solomon hesitated then continued. 'It seemed that he stood a sporting chance to recover the goods – and even if he didn't it would provide something to occupy his mind. He was obsessed with the idea – said he had everything lined up, knew a man who was an expert in underground metal detection and that he was confident he could sell the goods if he found them. I think I surprised him when I told him that I would help him – I was thinking of Raoul but I decided to say nothing to Raoul, not to raise faint hope. As Ian went on about having spare time and his family being away with friends I thought he should go ahead and try it. It could lead to no harm and a sick man – a dying man – in a fine climate for a week or so could only gain a sense of purpose and would benefit from some sun. I advised him to have a shot at it but suggested that he took someone with him who was fit and strong. The next thing I heard was that he had disappeared.'

'Why didn't you mention this to Lorna when she brought Sam to your surgery?' Adrian asked.

The elderly doctor looked down at the carpet and shook his head. 'It's difficult to tell you – almost impossible for you to understand, but there are things in my past better forgotten. It's a different and new world now.'

Dr Solomon put his hands through his shock of white hair and paused to think.

'In the late thirties, when I was a young doctor in Munich, the Jews were being rounded up and sent away – don't forget the concentration camps existed since 1933 but the world, although aware, chose to ignore them. The Nazis in Munich, indeed everywhere, required all Jews to have a medical examination before they were sent by train to a camp. It was bizarre; they were going to die anyway. I think they did it to create the illusion that they were going to work camps; it eased public opinion. Anyway, I was chosen to examine thousands of potential candidates for the camps, to give them a medical examination and to decide if they should go. In fact I was ordered to approve about ninety-nine per cent of anyone I saw. Then I myself went to a camp, to Dachau. I suppose being a doctor gave me some status and I was appointed an orderly. One day I was sent for by the camp commandant; he had syphilis and wanted to conceal the fact from his superiors. I had no drugs to treat him but I told him what I required and he obtained them. When he was cured he told me that I would be given a special status, as senior orderly. What did that mean? I'll tell you. It meant a licence to live, in exchange for certain duties. I was to be responsible for organising the parties to go to the gas chambers, stripping them of personal belongings and shepherding them to the place where they would die. The Germans obviously wanted to keep out – the smell and diseases were offensive. I want you to know how ashamed I am that I earned my right to live in this way. I wouldn't want my friends in the Jewish community to know about it now. I did it to live but...' The old man's face was fixed to the floor and his voice had a cracked tone to it. 'Then there were the medical experiments...'

'I still don't understand why you didn't tell Lorna about Ian – I seem to have missed the point,' Adrian persisted.

'I know,' the doctor broke in. 'I must explain now. A few days after Ian's disappearance I had an anonymous telephone call, a voice I didn't recognise at all. He started off by saying he would like to give me a history lesson and he recounted accurately what I had done at Dachau. He called me a "Kapo" – I suppose I was. Then he told me that if I said anything about Lacey and his mission, anything at all, then the past would be made public. You realise what this would do to my practice, my career. I asked the caller about Ian and said that he was ill but the caller hung up on me.'

There was a long silence and then Dr Solomon went on. 'When Mrs Lacey first came to see me I was amazed that she did not know of her husband's illness. I needed time to think. I wanted to tell her something, but if I told her of his assignment I dreaded the consequences. I went to see her on a pretext of looking at Sam but told her of his intention of raising money and of the insurance matter. He did want to raise money desperately, that is true, and when I refused the insurance idea he went on to the idea of searching in North Africa for the valuables. I was puzzled about one thing, though – how did the anonymous caller know that Lacey had been to see me?'

'Perhaps Ian told him, or told someone who passed on the information,' Lorna added.

The doctor nodded. 'Well, yes. Anyway, you know everything now, and all I can ask is that you keep what I have told you to yourselves – not to protect my name and career. Simply because I feel we are all in danger and I mean that sincerely. Lie low, do nothing and say nothing.'

16

As Roland Davies drove towards London on the M4 he kept up a polite conversation with his passenger but his thoughts were elsewhere. He badly wanted to talk to Erika but he could not. Just how much did she know he asked himself a dozen times, and then concluded that she probably, almost certainly, knew nothing.

Erika was happy enough as the countryside passed by. She had been a little surprised by the speedy departure from the little cottage but maybe Roland was impatient to be back in London. He certainly seemed worried about something and had muttered things about a call from his father. In two days' time she would be on the plane back to Argentina but there was still time enough to see a play and visit another art gallery in London. On one side she wished she could stay longer but she missed her home, her husband and her father. A rest from the frail old man had been welcome but she kept thinking of him and wondering how he was managing, even though Alfonso was home by now.

'We'll be approaching London soon, Erika. I suggest we call and see Father. He'd love to see his niece and there are one or two other people I'd like you to meet. It's not far off the motorway and we can then drive up to London and I'll drop you at your hotel.'

'Will I be meeting your friend Betty?'

Roland winced. He had not intended to mention Betty but it had come out over dinner the previous evening. 'It's strange, but Father says she has gone off somewhere – he's old and he may have got it all wrong. I cannot for the life of me imagine where she's gone but I'm sure there is a simple explanation.'

The car slowed to take the turn-off for Maidenhead. Erika was glad to have a change from the motorway driving, which was so monotonous whichever country was being crossed. Again the green fields in real English countryside took over for the three-mile stretch from Maidenhead to Cookham.

The car turned into a short driveway with two houses at the end. Roland became tense. She could feel it and wondered why he should be so apprehensive about seeing his father.

The elderly gentleman stood on the steps of the house and with the aid of a stick made his way to the car. 'My dear, I'm so glad to see you. Rosa's daughter, little Erika – I've ...' He cut short his words and turned to Roland.

The two went into the house and Erika took in the surroundings of the tastefully furnished hall, small but exquisite and fanatically tidy. They ushered Erika into the lounge and to her surprise took their leave and left. She was amazed to find herself alone and felt just a little uncomfortable. They obviously wanted to talk privately. Then it occurred to her there was possibly some problem with Betty. Roland had said last night that she was considerably younger and then had closed up on the subject as if he was talking too much. Then in the car he had said she had gone off, whatever that meant. The sudden departure from Mary Tavy and the tense atmosphere in the car suggested that something upsetting had happened. Erika stood at the window and admired the flowers in the evening sunlight – so different to the flowers at home. It was a typical English garden. The garden ran into the plot of the adjacent house and an elderly gentleman with a shock of white hair was walking across the lawn towards her. The bell rang and the guest was admitted. Erika hoped that someone would pay some attention to her soon. She was getting excessively bored and wanted to return to her hotel. There were theatre tickets to arrange for her last night in London.

The door opened and Roland came into the room.

'I'm sorry. Come and join us in the dining room. My father wants to talk with you and he has some friends who are most interested to meet you and hear about Argentina.'

* * *

As the BMW cruised towards London Royce Rollason mentally chastised himself. He had underestimated Davies and he had lost on points. He was puzzled how the man could know so much about him and surprised at Davies's confident attitude, his enigmatic gaze, as if he knew more than he would disclose. Royce had gone to the meeting resolved to keep the Gibraltar location strictly to himself but now, cruising along the M4 towards London, he felt that pressure would be exerted on him. What kind of pressure he wasn't sure. Perhaps going to Davies's father's house in Berkshire on the way back would be taking an unnecessary risk – 'and for what purpose?' he muttered to himself. The problem was that he didn't know how to contact anyone else with knowledge of underwater detection. There must be other people and Davies himself had said that he wasn't an expert. Rollason reflected that the whole exercise had already cost him more than he had bargained for – and with no return in sight he felt out of his depth. He had a ready buyer when he had his hands on the goods – Charlie Singer had told him the name of the Italian family and where they lived – he, and only he, knew the location of the wreck; but it was the detection procedure which baffled him.

Royce needed time to think. He certainly didn't want to step into a trap in the house in Cookham. He decided the most cautious step would be to take a look at the house from the outside and then make a decision.

It was just turned eight thirty when the big car turned off the motorway and nosed its way through Maidenhead and along the minor road to Cookham. In the village he asked the way and was directed to Cookham Dean – outside the village centre and at the top of a hill. He quickly found it from the directions and was relieved to see that a large thick wood lay on the other side of the road. He drove past slowly and parked the car 500 metres past the house in a small lay-by. Like many overweight men he was surprisingly nimble on his feet, and locking the car he moved silently into the wood. He didn't want to get too close – just close enough to see who might be there. Two cars were in the shared driveway. The lights were on in what he took to be the lounge and an elderly man passed the window. The hall light went on and then a small frosted glass window was illuminated; the toilet presumably.

Royce froze. The sound of voices. Not from the house but in front of him. He crouched down and his keen eyes scanned the bushes. There was a slight movement and another voice, too far away and too subdued to hear what was said. Royce knew that this is what he had feared – a trap. Once inside the house the old man and Davies would try to coax information from him, but if co-operation was not forthcoming they could try more persuasive methods. Why did a respectable engineer require strong-arm men? Royce dismissed the thought; it didn't make sense.

Softly he moved back along the path towards the car. As he looked over his shoulder he froze again and crouched. The front door of the house was open and an attractive middle-aged woman stood in the pool of light with Davies. An elderly man kissed her and then went back into the house. The woman went to the car and Davies returned to the house and helped out another old man. A few moments of talking and the car started up. Royce looked to his right as he heard movement; two men were sprinting towards a small car parked at the edge of the woods some 20 or 30 metres away. As Davies's car drove down the driveway the old man called out. Royce was surprised – it was not English.

The car reached the roadway, stopped and turned left towards Cookham village. As it reached the end of the wood and disappeared down the hill, the dark blue car in the woods started up and slid out of its hiding place in unobtrusive pursuit. Royce stared ahead. The soft voices started again – so there were more than two in the observing party. Creeping well down, Royce reached his car and started the engine. He turned in the opposite direction, towards Marlow, and realised that despite the cool evening his massive body was sweating profusely. As he approached Marlow he spotted a well-lit hotel on the river bank. He badly wanted a drink and parked the BMW in the large car park. The bar was inviting. He sat on a tall stool, studying himself in the mirror behind the bar. All this was proving too much for someone who had retired from crime. It was strange that Davies's car should be followed. Perhaps they were police. Who was the woman with Davies and why did the old man shout out just a few words in another language? Royce hadn't seen much of her face but her build was... He knocked back the whisky quickly. 'Fucking 'ell – it might be that Grieb woman – 'er son's 'ere in England, after all,' he muttered. The barman turned at the muffled sound. 'I'll have another – a double – with nothing it it, just neat.' He stared at the mirror again. No, this was no scene of action for an old man with a record; it could have very nasty consequences. Back to Marbella and look for a new deal. He downed the whisky quickly and made for the door. The sooner he was back in the hotel in London, the better.

The big engine sprang into life and Royce Rollason's hand went to the gear. Suddenly he was gasping for air. He struggled painfully as the rope around his neck pulled him back into the headrest and the world reeled around him; the rope was cutting, digging into his thick neck. Suddenly it was released.

'Tell me who you are and what you were doing in those bushes. Start talking now,' a soft, heavily accented voice said from the back seat.

As Royce gulped for air the rope tightened again.

'Now, I said start talking.'

'OK,' he croaked, 'I'll tell you all I know. It's in the bleeding sea off Gibraltar.'

'What the hell are you gabbling about?' The voice was irritated and even more threatening. 'I want to know who you are and what you were doing spying on that house.'

'Christ's sake let that rope loose. I'll tell you every bloody thing – just let it loose. I've 'ad my fill of everything. I'll answer all you want to know. Just give me a break.' Royce's voice creaked and he realised that his ligature was a wire and not a rope.

* * *

Roland Davies's interest in gadgetry was apparent in his own luxury home in Hampstead. As he approached the house the garage doors opened in response to the push of a button on the car facia. He was glad to be back. He had deposited Erika at her hotel; she hadn't asked questions about Betty and why she hadn't been invited to meet her, and she had taken the questioning at his father's home in good heart. Indeed she suspected nothing and would return to Argentina in two days, taking good wishes with her and having enjoyed her stay in England.

The fact that Royce hadn't shown up perplexed him but there might be a simple explanation. He might go to Cookham later, and he had asked his father to give him the Hampstead address. Yes, Royce needed help and he would come to get it – Davies was sure.

He switched on the car security system and went through the service door which joined the garage to the house. From the lounge emerged Mrs Summers, his housekeeper for five years, who normally left at seven o'clock. 'I know I shouldn't be here, Mr Davies,' she greeted him, 'but with the young lady leaving so sudden I thought you would like a meal after a long drive. I thought you would bring the Australian lady, your cousin, back for dinner. She sounded nice on the telephone.'

'Argentinian, Mrs Summers,' Davies corrected. 'No, she's gone back to her hotel. Now tell me what's happened.'

'It was so strange. Miss Betty, she was all in a state because she couldn't find the utility door key. She thought you must have taken it with you. She couldn't get in touch with you at the cottage so she called her friend Sara somewhere down in Devon and asked her to drop in on you. Then the friend called back an hour or so later. It was a long call and Miss Betty got really upset. When she put the telephone down she had tears in her eyes. I went out to the kitchen and the next thing I know she was in the hall with everything packed. "I'm going out, Mrs Summers," she says – and when I asked where she didn't reply but looked so upset. Then a taxi came and off she went. She asked the driver to take her to Fulham.'

Davies's mind was working. 'What time was that?'

'Oh, late afternoon, I'm not sure.'

'So how did she get to Cookham to see my father? It's not an easy place to go from Fulham.'

'I didn't know she had been to Cookham to see Mr Davies senior – she must have used her friend's car.'

'Friend?' Davies asked, puzzled.

'I know she has a friend in Fulham – she came up here about three weeks ago – "Vanessa" Miss Betty called her. She had a little car, I remember it in the driveway. Maybe she went to see her – but I don't know for sure.'

'You haven't, I suppose, any idea of the address or telephone number?'

Mrs Summers shook her head. 'No idea, Mr Davies.'

Davies left the lounge and went to the study. An idea occurred to him and he dialled a Mary Tavy number. He didn't like Sara Cook, he regarded her as a country busybody with time on her hands and little in her head. However, she and Betty were good acquaintances if not good friends and Sara did have a telephone and could take messages. Why on earth Betty didn't have a telephone in her house he didn't know – it irritated him more than a little. Sara Cook answered and immediately she heard his voice he could detect a chill atmosphere.

'Look, Sara, what the hell's gone wrong – what's up? Why has Betty gone? More than that, where has she gone?'

As Davies listened to the tirade which followed – 'taking a girl to Betty's own cottage ... trusted you to be away for a few days ... she would never do that to you, would she?' – he closed his eyes. Eventually there was a gap.

'Sara, for God's sake listen for a moment, will you? That girl, as you put it, was my cousin from Argentina. She came to England from Madrid – actually she's from Argentina but she had been visiting her son in Madrid where he was in hospital.

In London her husband had to return suddenly to Argentina and as she had never been to England before, she decided to look around and she gave me a call. My housekeeper put her in touch with me down in the West Country She wanted to see more of England than just London and I asked her down. There's nothing else to it. You happened to come around for information about keys, saw Erika in the cottage when I was out, I assume, and drew the wrong conclusion completely. Not stopping to check anything, you called Betty, who blew up and collected all her things and shoved off.'

There was a long silence. 'Oh, my God, I've really done it. I'm sorry, Roland – really.'

Davies snorted. 'Well, so you should be. Now let's get things sorted out. Where has she gone?'

'I don't think I have the number but I know she said she would stay for a few days with Vanessa in Fulham.'

'Vanessa – I've heard her mentioned. What's her surname?'

'Pritchard or Pritchett or something like that.'

Davies grunted a gruff farewell, replaced the receiver and opened the telephone directory. No V. Pritchard or V. Pritchett appeared in the Fulham area. He turned to the front page, where Betty logged the various numbers she used regularly. There was the address: 17 Courtenay Crescent.

A few moments later the red Fiat was moving out of Hampstead and heading towards Fulham. Davies glanced at his Rolex – it was just turned eleven and it had started to rain.

It took Davies nearly an hour to reach Fulham. Rather than plot a route through the suburbs of the metropolis he chose to drive into the West End, through Hyde Park and along the Fulham Road. A quick stop to consult his *A-to-Z* and he swung the car into Courtenay Crescent. The car trailing him did not turn in but pulled up on the main road.

Vanessa Pritchard looked surprised and frightened when she came to the door, and he recalled that he had met her very briefly several months before.

'Betty isn't here,' she said, in answer to his question.

'I know she came here yesterday – she told several people. If she isn't here now, where is she?'

'I have no idea. She just left – said she was going to friends.'

'What friends?' Davies shouted.

Vanessa put her hand on the door edge. Things were becoming too hot for her liking. 'I don't know, she just stayed a short while then she put all her stuff in the car and drove off.'

'What car – I had her car!'

'No – his car, I mean...' the girl faltered.

'I know she came here, and if she isn't here, who did she go with? Bloody well tell me!'

'I don't know.'

Davies pushed her roughly into the hallway of the Victorian house. 'What's her game – and what's yours?' he shouted.

'And yours?'

The voice came from the doorway and Davies spun to see a tall dark man with curly black hair standing menacingly. 'I asked you your game.' The stranger spoke with a strange accent. Davies made a quick decision – he wanted out of this. He pushed the stranger aside and ran for his car. Vanessa put her hand to her head in relief and then looked up at the newcomer.

'Thank you so much, I'm really grateful to you. He was getting a bit – well – out of hand.'

The stranger gave a slight grin. 'It's nothing. Now you can help me.'

Vanessa looked at him quizzically.

'It's OK – you can help me with my enquiries. Who was Davies looking for and why? I'm sorry, here's my card. We've been briefed to keep an eye on you. I was following Davies. My colleague will now tail him.'

'Oh, Good God. Come on in. I wish Betty had never involved me in all this.' Vanessa closed the door behind her and took the stranger into her room.

* * *

As Royce walked towards the house it occurred to him that the next day would be his birthday.

'Fifty-six – too fucking old for all this,' he muttered. It was some distance to walk – the hooligan who had roughed him up in the car had driven him to within a quarter of a mile of the place and then told him to walk. He was well aware that he was being watched from the woodland. If only he had stayed in Spain... Why the hell had he got involved in all this? He was a retired man with a lovely villa and a young Filipina to look after him. He had a nice set of wheels to drive around and a willing, if depleted, body of people to work for him and bring him a steady income without exposing him to any risk. No, he could think of many more agreeable ways to spend a birthday, but he didn't have any options; that thug had hurt him badly. He was a tough bastard, no doubt about that, and Royce was sure that he wasn't alone.

He was surprised to see two cars in the driveway of the house. They hadn't been there before. He walked past the two Rovers and rang the bell. It was strange how the house was built; one drive seemed to be shared by the two houses, perhaps because of the restricted number of openings allowed onto a dangerous and narrow road. There was no reply and Royce breathed a sigh of relief. He glanced at his watch; it was just turned eleven – maybe they had gone to bed.

Royce shrugged his shoulders and walked back down the driveway. He had taken only a few paces when the door of the adjacent house opened and an elderly man stood in the dim light. 'Are you looking for me? I'm Roland Davies's father. This is my home – my son was expecting you.'

'My name's Mr Rollason. I'm a – sort of – I know your son.'

'I know. We were expecting you earlier. I'm with my neighbour. Come on in.'

Royce stepped across a dividing flower bed and walked to the door. The old man motioned him in and Royce walked through a small hall and into a brightly lit lounge. To his surprise the room was full of people, two elderly men and five much younger, ranging between 25 and 40 years of age. A young woman was pouring coffee. No introductions were made and for a while no one spoke. Mr Davies senior broke the silence. 'My son tells me that you need assistance in recovering some property which has been lost for many years.'

Royce nodded. ' 's right.'

'This property is of great interest to us, indeed it is rightfully ours. This doesn't mean that we are going to be selfish about it – far from it. We have a ready market for it and we are quite prepared to pay you handsomely.'

Royce grunted and nodded. His mind ran on what his unfriendly back-seat passenger had instructed him to say only half an hour ago.

'I don't know where it is. I'm working for two blokes who know all about it – Mr Southon and Mr Lacey. You'll 'ave to ask them.'

The second elderly man leant forward in his chair with both hands on his walking stick. 'You are a fool to lie to us, Rollason. I thought Roland advised you about that. Tell me the truth.'

Royce noticed he spoke with an accent. 'I 'ave told you. Christ Almighty, what do you think I am?'

'A crook and a liar, but we can change all that. Allow me to introduce Sepp. I won't tell you his family name but if I did you would recognise it. His grandfather was a very great man, a famous man, who achieved much for his country by not suffering liars or fools. In fact, you could say his methods were persuasive but his grandson's are more so. His grandfather would be proud of him.'

The young man sitting on a stool in front of the fireplace stood up and took a revolver from his pocket. Swiftly he raised the butt and brought it down with a resounding crack onto Royce's left kneecap. The big man squealed with pain and he leant forward to hug his knee, which seared with pain. As he did, the revolver descended again, between his shoulder blades. He gasped for air.

'OK. Christ stop. OK, give me a chance. Christ Almighty!' Royce rocked backward and forwards, sick with pain. His hand went to his pocket and he produced a handkerchief. He retched violently.

'Start talking,' the old man ordered, when Royce had recovered from his nausea.

'Look, never mind about the bleeding stuff. I'll tell you something – I've been made to come 'ere, forced against my bleeding will. There is a group of people out there looking at this bloody 'ouse and the one next door through field glasses. They gave me this.' Royce felt in his pocket and produced a cigarette packet. 'Told me to play with it – it's a camera and I'm supposed to take pictures of you lot. Christ, I didn't know there would be an 'ole bloody party 'ere or that you would all be bloody maniacs. Christ you've 'alf killed me!'

Even in his pain Royce was well aware that what he said had created an electric response throughout the room. The packet was snatched by a young man who had been sitting opposite and passed around.

'Where's Betty Silvester? She started all this – where is she?' Davies Senior asked.

'Oh, Christ, I don't know who the 'ell you're talking about,' Royce groaned. 'Look, I'll tell you anything, all I want is to get 'ome.'

The old man leaned forward on his stick. 'You're talking garbage. We don't understand you. Who gave you the camera? Start talking, and tell the truth – quickly.'

Royce spilled out all he knew, stopping from time to time to nurse his knee. When he mentioned Gibraltar the atmosphere became electric. 'You're a hundred per cent sure?' asked Davies Senior.

'Christ Almighty – course I'm sure. Why do you think I'm bloody 'ere,' Royce groaned.

When he had finished talking, the company moved into the next room, leaving Royce with the girl. She passed him a cup of coffee and then moved to the back of his chair. He felt the steel of a revolver against his neck. It needed no words to tell him that any unplanned exit could be rapidly curtailed – not that he could move quickly, he reflected. After ten minutes the two elderly men returned.

'So you know nothing about us – just that our property lies

off Gibraltar and you came to England to get Roland's help in finding it,' said Davies senior.

'That's right, I swear it – I don't know who you are or what the 'ell's going on. I don't know who those buggers are in the wood outside neither. I don't much bloody care – I wish I'd never got involved in all this.'

'Where is Southon?' asked Davies, and Royce groaned. He didn't know how much they knew and the pain in his leg was excruciating. He didn't want to take another chance of violence.

'He sort of 'ad an accident – 'e died. The other one, Lacey, I don't know but 'e kind of vanished.'

'We know about Lacey.' The voice was cool.

'Look, I've told you everything. Now can I go? I'll bugger off back to Spain and forget all about the bloody loot,' Royce croaked convincingly. 'I'm bloody well fifty-six today, so 'elp me. I want to see a few more years yet.'

'You may just do that. Stay here – try to move and you'll find a broken kneecap the least of your damage.'

The five young men had slipped quietly out of the back door. Two moved silently to the edge of the lawn bordering Davies's house. The other three crouched beside the hedge of the neighbour's garden. At the road they stopped and listened. The sound of classical music came across the air from a nearby house. They froze as a car came up the hill, its headlights on full. As the car disappeared down the other side of the hill they moved silently into the wood, stopped and listened. A nightjar screeched. Then came the sound of a car starting its engine a few hundred metres away. Again they waited and listened. Systematically they searched through the small wood. Suddenly one whispered loudly and the others closed to him. A patch of compressed low undergrowth told them all they wanted to know. Someone had been lying there very recently indeed. Perhaps the departing car a few minutes before was related. In any event, no one was in the wood now, of that they were sure.

As the five young men returned to the house they heard raised voices.

'What name did you say?' the old man leant forward menacingly on his stick.

'I said I didn't know what you was up to – and was you tied up with the Grieb woman.'

'What Grieb woman?'

'I told you all about it before – the woman in Marbella and 'er son who came down – Christ I told you all about it!'

'You said a woman who you thought was German, you didn't mention her name.'

'I didn't think it was important – that's 'er name and 'er son 'es called Franz or Fritz or something and 'e's in London – I saw 'im myself. But you were asking about a Betty someone or other.'

'Now I'm interested in this Grieb – it must be the same. Tell me how you got on to her.'

Royce rocked his leg. 'Henry Southon – bloody Charlie – 'e found it out through the notes in the side of the book which said something like "Grieb Jewellers". Then 'e looked it up in a directory, found that Grieb was a jeweller in 'Amburg, so he calls 'im up. Young Grieb gives 'im 'is mother's address 'cos 'e thinks 'e's a friend of old man Grieb, who died. 'E thought she might be on to something with living so close to Gibraltar like, so 'e checks 'er out and looks at 'er notes. She didn't know the plane 'ad come down off Gib – she was sure it was Tunisia. Until now everyone thought it was bloody Tunisia. Well, now you lot know and I want to see the end of it all, I can tell you.'

The conversation was interrupted as the young men entered. Sepp whispered in the old man's ear and he nodded.

The old man rose and beckoned to Mr Davies senior. The two moved into the hallway and called Sepp. Royce was aware that Davies was making a telephone call from the study next door. Royce looked up as the clock struck twelve. He was desperately tired and yet he knew that even if he was in bed the pain of his leg would prevent sleep.

* * *

It was during breakfast that Franz announced his intention

of returning to Hamburg immediately. Adrian wasn't surprised because the young man had been aching to get back to the business and was getting increasingly concerned at leaving it in the hands of an old college friend of his father plus a young girl who came in during the afternoons. Adrian reflected that the young man's concern originally had been for his mother's safety and a degree of curiosity in following up his father's search for what had been lost years before – and what had obsessed his father for some time. Perhaps his dwindling interest had been rekindled by the attack in the Hamburg flat and the thought that someone else was closing in on discovering what his father had sought. But after all, Franz had been drawn into the search for Ian, someone he had never met and, if signs were correct, never would meet. His interest or curiosity only had certain limits and those limits had been met, apart from finding the treasure.

'The only concern I have is for my mother. That thug is still about, in London for some strange reason, but he does live in Marbella and will presently be going back there. The question in my mind is how safe is my mother?' Franz confessed to Adrian.

Adrian buttered more toast and concealed his private thoughts. He would like to see more of Ella. She was an intelligent, attractive woman and he could do with some female company. He had enjoyed her company unselfishly. However, it would seem a bit obvious to say the least if he was to declare his intention of returning to Marbella.

'I'm sure she can look after herself,' he said comfortingly. 'She's on her guard now – but I suggest you get a first-class security system fitted. That Rollason fellow has lost his henchman and it would seem that he doesn't like to do his own dirty work. I've a feeling that whatever they were seeking they have found. I'd relax if I were you.'

After breakfast Franz called Lufthansa and booked a seat on a Hamburg flight leaving that afternoon. He made a quick call to the shop and told them that he would be at work the next morning. The old man sounded relieved.

Franz needed to go back to the Lansdowne to collect his

belongings. He had stayed at Lorna's home the previous night and slept on the large sofa. Somehow he had felt that the stronger the guard on the house the safer it would be for Betty. He had little doubt that the Cookham contingent, however much he hated the thought, would like to locate her. These men would stop at nothing; he had heard that from his father. They could have been behind the disappearance of Ian Lacey. Perhaps Lacey had tried to blackmail them. The thought had come back to him time and time again as he lay restlessly on the sofa.

Franz said his farewell at noon and took a taxi to the Lansdowne Club. Holding the taxi, he settled his bill then reappeared with his luggage and instructed the driver to take him to Heathrow.

As Franz was watching the Hyde Park traffic through the cab window, Lorna called Adrian to the telephone. 'It's Raoul Carlucci from Genoa.' Adrian was mildly surprised but considerably more surprised when he heard Carlucci's news. On his return to Genoa he had been visited by the police about the theft of his boat. An alert had been put out, especially to Spain, where the boat was last heard of. The Puerto Banus harbour authority reported that the boat had departed a few weeks before, leaving unpaid harbour dues, and some trade suppliers were owed substantial sums. This information was followed by even more positive news – the boat was lying deserted off the marina in Gibraltar. The Gibraltar police, acting on information, had boarded *L'Anticipation* and made a routine search. They were particularly interested in cavities in the bulkhead and had suspected drug running. No drugs were found but what the search did reveal were bloodstains on the floor. They had been mopped up but had shown up when the boat was dusted for fingerprints.

'The police report that they are also looking for a thickset, tallish man of around 100 kilos and around sixty years of age,' Raoul went on. 'Apparently he was on the yacht with Southon, and then the two of them disappeared. The vessel has lain there for several days unattended, according to other owners berthed nearby. Does it mean anything to you?

Regarding the bloodstains – we are looking for a missing man, aren't we?'

'If you mean my son-in-law, yes we are,' Adrian agreed. 'Forensic tests should show that up – he must have had blood tests done, and Solomon should be able to help there. As far as the thickset individual is concerned, I know he is in London – Franz saw him in Berkeley Square. I'm sure the police would have no trouble finding him for questioning.'

'I'll tell my police inspector friend here,' Raoul answered. 'They should be able to set something up. I think they believe they are on to more than the theft of my little *L'Anticipation.*'

Adrian made a humming noise. 'And I think they could well be right.'

'As far as the boat is concerned,' Raoul went on, 'I'm sending Bernard down to sort out all the formalities. It's in police hands at the moment. He's time to spare and he can go down there and appoint yacht brokers to sell it – I shall be glad to see the back of it. The situation isn't as easy as it appears; the tax has to be paid and there are a lot of petty formalities – it may even have to be re-registered.'

Adrian was thoughtful as he returned the receiver to its cradle and Lorna, who had been reading the daily paper, looked at him enquiringly. He told her what had happened, omitting any reference to Carlucci's theory about the blood. Lorna looked puzzled. 'But why Gibraltar – he was supposed to be making for Tunisia, wasn't he?'

Adrian stroked his chin. 'Young Grieb's father was a prisoner on Gib – but I can't see any connection there. No, I don't understand it.'

Adrian decided he would have to tell Lorna about Raoul's theory, after all. The British police would be contacted by the Italians, Solomon would be required to give details of blood grouping and Lorna would find out, sooner or later.

'Lorna – there's something that Raoul said. There may or may not be something in it, but I must tell you.'

'It's to do with Ian.' Her eyes narrowed.

'It may have – it may not. Let me tell you.'

17

At Malaga airport the heavy box marked 'Fragile, Technical Equipment' attracted the attention of the *Aduana*. The Customs officers required it to be opened and the strange mass of disjointed arms and complex dials laid on the table. The officer retired to a telephone and Royce felt uneasy. It was bad enough having to come to Malaga rather than fly direct to Gibraltar. The flights were full all day and Davies had been anxious to get away. Why he had offered to start work and why Davies had brought his father puzzled Royce. The pain in his leg was excruciating, and he wished they could have gone straight to Gibraltar. He could have put them in touch with the old guide who knew all that there was to know. He could then have gone home and called his doctor to attend to his leg. Why did they want to keep him? He felt uneasy. There must be a reason. Now, however, he had more problems with the Customs people. But both Davieses seemed strangely relaxed.

Roland Davies explained to the senior officer the purpose of the equipment – the tracing of the seabed and interesting objects on it. This was equipment being brought into Spain for testing and would be taken out within two weeks. The elegant young official listened patiently, his expression betraying that he only partially understood the English. He quickly made a decision. Shrugging his shoulders and raising his hands he walked away. The three men collected their baggage and walked through to the Hertz desk in the main lobby. Ten minutes later Roland Davies was at the wheel of a hire car heading towards the N340 to Gibraltar some two hours away.

As the car edged through the Marbella traffic Royce Rollason looked towards his home. If he could get away he would, but he knew that his leg wouldn't stand his ample weight for long. These people were not playing games. They were clearly involved in their quest and he was convinced that he would not be released easily. With his leg outstretched in the passenger seat of the Ford Granada he could see Davies's father slumped on the back seat. Maybe Davies had brought him to get away from the trouble at the house; no doubt about it, they were worried at the house being under surveillance. What was going on there? Royce wondered. The whole thing was beyond comprehension. Suddenly it occurred to him that his car was in a garage at La Linea. If only he could get to the car, maybe get them to park this hire car in the same garage and then limp off to the toilet. It would give him a chance to get clear and escape this atmosphere, which was becoming increasingly unsavoury. He involuntarily groaned as he remembered he had left his car keys in his abandoned clothing at the May Fair Hotel. No, he reasoned, they must be checking in somewhere at a hotel, and that would be his moment to get away. At least they had no idea of the location of his house on the Costa del Sol – he would get there and lie low for a few days. He was deep in thought as they approached Sotagrande and the traffic ahead started to slow.

* * *

Detective Inspector Forbes came straight to the point. He understood that Mr Franklin had seen a person whom the Gibraltar police wished to interview in connection with a certain enquiry. Making these telephone calls was a bore – dozens of them in one day only to find the informant was mistaken or had changed his mind. This lead had come from Italy and it was all very vague.

Adrian was surprised to get a call so soon. 'I must correct you there, inspector. I didn't see this man Rollason, indeed I couldn't possibly recognise him. The person you need for a description is a young German gentleman, Franz Grieb. He is at this moment at Heathrow – booked on the mid-afternoon Lufthansa flight to Hamburg.'

The inspector thanked him and rang off. Betty came into the room with coffee. Should he have mentioned to the inspector that he had a young girl in the house in need of protection? No – Betty had stumbled on a group of old men dressed in German military uniform and they had shouted at her. On the face of it, it was laughable. Adrian's strong gut feeling was that Betty was in acute danger and he did not know how to handle the situation. He sipped his coffee. Maybe all three of them could get away and go down to Marbella. He would like to see Ella again and there didn't seem to be any connection between Rollason and the German group which could endanger Betty if Rollason returned to Spain. It needed thinking about, carefully. One thing was sure, he couldn't go yet – not until the blood tests had revealed the identity of the victim who had been on the boat now berthed in Gibraltar.

* * *

Above the noise and clatter of London Heathrow, Terminal Two, the announcement was loud and clear.

'Would Mr Franz Grieb, Lufthansa passenger to Hamburg, please come immediately to Airport Information.'

It was then repeated in German.

Franz was the next in line to check in his baggage. He was surprised. He asked the clerk in charge for directions and took the elevator to the first floor, where a huge sign indicated that he was at the Information Desk. To his greater surprise, a young uniformed policeman introduced himself as PC Keen of the airport police and asked Franz to go with him to help the police in their enquiries. Franz asked whether he would miss his flight. 'I'm afraid so, sir, but it is important and we'll take care you get on the late flight. Very sorry about this, sir.' Franz shrugged his shoulders and followed the officer to a small office in the back of the building.

In the small office Franz was surprised yet again when a detective sergeant told him that the Gibraltar police had informed him that a certain person answering to the description of a man they wanted to interview had been seen by Mr Grieb. Franz looked puzzled. The officer went on to mention the yacht *L'Anticipation* berthed in Gibraltar.

'My God, that's Henry Southon, or Charlie Singer – a friend of my mother's – that's the yacht he owned!'

'Not exactly owned, sir. Our information is that it was stolen.'

Franz grimaced. 'I'm not surprised – not surprised at all. He stole from my mother and I think the Spanish police would like to talk with him, but I haven't seen him.'

'I'm talking of a heavy, thickset man, about sixty, who was also on the yacht – our information is that you could possibly have seen him in London, sir.'

Franz thought for a few seconds. 'That sounds like Royce Rollason, the thug who managed to terrify my mother with his yobbos and who had me knocked about in Hamburg. But as far as I know there is no connection between the two. All I know is that I saw Rollason in Berkeley Square the other day.'

'Shall we start at the beginning, sir – just to get the facts straight – and then we may ask you to look at some pictures.' The police officer started to write.

Once the police had, in their phraseology, a 'make', the machinery sprang into action. David Arthur Rollason, aged 56, of heavy build and 5 feet 11 inches tall was the man they wished to interview in connection with a stolen yacht in Gibraltar which had traces of human blood and hair on the floor and which was equipped to conceal. That Rollason had a long history of violence was of great interest to the investigating officers. Seven years ago he had been interviewed in connection with a particularly vicious bank robbery but was released as there had been insufficient evidence to proceed with the case.

The recent sighting of Rollason in Berkeley Square meant that it was possible he was staying in that area. Here the police had a lucky break. One of the first hotels they visited was the May Fair, where one of the receptionists instantly recognised the slightly younger photograph of Rollason. An examination of his room and a talk to the chambermaid revealed that although he had retained the room, he had not slept in the bed for two nights. The breezy young girl at the front desk confirmed that Rollason had hired a car. Avis supplied the car number within a few minutes and then were able to confirm that the vehicle had been handed in to Heathrow depot some four hours previously. In the computerised medley of Heathrow airport it was a simple matter to discover that the man the police wanted to interview had left earlier in the day on an Iberia flight for Malaga.

* * *

Salvador Garcia Cortes of the Guardia Civil answered the radio telephone in his car by the roadside and heard the voice of his superior at Algeciras. The British police had asked for help in connection with a possible murder enquiry relating to a yacht which had recently been berthed at Puerto Banus. The suspect had been on the flight which had arrived two hours before at Malaga. It was possible that he could have a hire car although none of the rental desks could confirm anyone answering to the description. This could be accounted for by the fact that some desks had changed clerks in the past couple of hours.

Officer Garcia finished taking notes. It would make a change from the routine checks which were almost an everyday duty on the N340. Drug smuggling was big business, not just on northbound traffic but in all directions and on all types of roads as peddlers became more devious in the distribution of their goods. Four officers and two sniffer dogs searched cars, one officer was stationed a few hundred metres before the checkpoint to slow down the approaching traffic. Another officer was stationed 300 metres beyond the checkpoint to stop any car which might try to jump the check. This officer was equipped with a dramatic piece of equipment known as a shredder – a chain with spikes inserted, which, when pulled across the road, did precisely what its name indicated to car tyres.

Calling his men together, Officer Garcia briefed them on the new assignment. They were to continue in drug surveillance but at the same time keep a close eye for a well-built Englishman, 1 metre 85, 100 kilos, of dark complexion and with thin hair. Police files in Britain had also discovered that the suspect had a bluebird tattooed on his right hand.

Roland Davies glanced at Royce questioningly.

'It's one of those bloody checks. They're always doing 'em – looking for drugs. They 'ave bloody dogs to sniff the car – nothing to bother about – all in the day's work,' Royce explained. Deep down he hated these checks. Although he was clean on drugs, he felt more than uneasy about any confrontation with the police beyond a parking ticket, and even those he paid promptly to avoid a personal visit. The automatic Granada edged forward as the queue passed through the control.

The young officer peered through the open window and spoke to Roland Davies in Spanish. Davies turned to Royce. 'You speak more of this than I do.'

Royce waved his hand and started. '*Solemente vacaciones, de nada a...*'

The Spaniard stared at the hand. The tattoo – it was several seconds before he resorted to the inevitable Spanish police reaction of blowing his whistle. Royce's reaction was lightning. He threw himself across Davies, opened the car door and pushed him into the road. With a leg searing with pain he rolled into the driving seat and put his foot flat down on the accelerator. No way was Royce Rollason going to be arrested in Spain or anywhere ever again.

The powerful car leapt forward. The back-seat passenger, Davies's father, shouted and grasped his shoulders, but Royce's adrenaline was up and the car was already in excess of 80 kph when the shredder's chain of spikes was pulled across the road. Royce kept his foot down as the car, on its wheel rims, ricocheted off the highway crash barrier and swerved towards the central reservation. He jammed his foot flat onto the brake pedal, and the car swung around 180 degrees in a scream of burning rubber and ran across the central reservation. There was a sickening crash of breaking glass as the big car embedded itself in a truck delivering concrete to a nearby site.

When Salvador Garcia and two assistants opened the door of the car with a crowbar they found an elderly man dead on the back seat and an injured heavily built man in the driving seat. Lying in the road was a strange piece of equipment that Officer Garcia had never seen before. Ordering his men to seal off the road, he ran back to call an ambulance and to interview the ejected driver, who was handcuffed to his patrolman at the control.

* * *

As Adrian stood on the kerbside watching for an unbooked cab he felt more relieved than he had done for some time. Inspector Forbes had told him that the analysis of the blood sample and the comparison with Dr Solomon's notes had confirmed that the victim, whoever he was, could not possibly have been Ian. In a strange way, and he rebuked himself for the transitory thought, he wished it had been Ian, for at least it would have explained the disappearance of his son-in-law. No, he was free now of the terrible task of making the information known to Lorna and he felt more relaxed than he had done for some time.

Adrian spotted the light on the roof of a cab. He hailed it and settled in the back seat. The inspector had asked if he had any idea who else could have been on the yacht. There was only one answer – Henry Southon or whatever his name really was. The ex-lover of his ex-wife. He had given Ann's address to the inspector, who wanted to locate the suspected victim's medical records. The inspector had also asked for Southon's last known address in Spain, and Adrian had given him Ella's address. At the time he had felt uneasy about doing this, and now he suddenly realised why. It wasn't the unease of imparting the information which troubled him it was what it represented. This man Southon had not only been his ex-wife's lover but also an ex-lover of the woman to whom he felt more than a little attracted. The thought went through his mind that if he and Ella married then both his wives would both have slept with the same other man. The thought was not only bizarre but disturbing, particularly as he regarded the man in question as an exceptionally unsavoury character.

As he paid off the cab and walked up the steps his thoughts were on returning to Spain just as soon as he could.

Lorna was in the kitchen with Betty when he let himself into the house.

'There have been two calls for you – Inspector Forbes says he has additional news and would you call him back. Also Bernard Waterman called – he wonders if you have a few days spare to help him with the yacht,' Lorna told him.

* * *

The British Vice Consul listened patiently as Roland Davies told his story. It was hot in the small interview room at Sotagrande police station and he wondered why the Spanish police had to have glass as well as bars. That wasn't the only thing which puzzled him.

As Davies finished speaking the Vice Consul leaned forward. 'I'm trying to help you, Mr Davies, but you're not helping yourself by this nonsense story. I have your passports here, and when they were handed to me I instantly recognised your father. I knew him vaguely when he was the Member of Parliament where I lived – a bright man, always wondered what happened to him. Next I hear is that he is found dead in the back seat of a getaway car being driven by a man with a long criminal record. Not only that but his son has been pushed out of the driving seat by this thug Arthur Rollason. What exactly is the story? This isn't the scene for a former political star and his son who is, I understand, a professional man.'

Davies put his head in his hands. 'I can't tell you anything – I just cannot think straight. It's enough that Father is dead.

The man you want is Rollason and I understand you have him. Leave it at that.'

The Vice Consul left the room. A few minutes later, after discussing the matter with the Guardia Civil, he was suggesting to London that a search of the Davies's houses at Cookham and Hampstead would be a good idea – and there should be no problem in getting a warrant on the grounds of non-cooperation by the detained Roland Davies.

* * *

It took the two police officers a little over ten minutes to open the back door of the house at Cookham. Everything was tidy; no sign of any hasty departure. In the small study a few papers were scattered but there was nothing of any significance. The two men searched through the bedroom and then the en-suite dressing room. 'Must have been a collector of some kind,' muttered the younger of the two as he pointed to a red and white flag with a black swastika on it. 'Probably brought it back from the war – he was pretty old by all accounts.'

His colleague made a few notes in his book and the two left the house as unobtrusively as they had arrived.

Had they looked very carefully at the house next door they would have seen a slightly parted curtain and an elderly grey face behind it. Not that this would have been significant; the attendance of the police always attracted the attention of neighbours hungry for any form of scandal.

The face at the window disappeared as the car moved away. It was even more worried than it had been over the past few days. The observer was rapidly coming to the conclusion that the time had come for action – and that action must be decisive and quick.

* * *

Adrian awoke with a start. Sam was crying and he could hear Lorna comforting him. He got up and went into the kitchen. He had been sleeping fitfully anyway and Sam's nightmare had broken even the thin layer of sleep he had managed to achieve. So much had happened, so much was left unanswered.

Lorna joined him in the kitchen and he made another cup of coffee. They sat at the small table and Adrian decided to come up with the thought he had had the previous evening.

'Lorna, my love, we could do with a break. Let's go down to Marbella and spend some time with Ella. Bernard phoned yesterday and I promised to go down to Gib with him to sort out the business with the boat. Now the police have sorted out the gory task of bloodstains they want to get shot of the thing – and Bernard's brief is to get it cleaned up and sell it. I'd like to go back anyway, and as Raoul Carlucci has offered my fare too, why not?'

Lorna smiled and shook her head. 'My dear unrealistic father, do you realise we are running desperately short of money? And you must be feeling the pinch too. We must concentrate our attention on making money, not on spending it. I've already decided on selling the house, paying off the horrifying mortgage and moving out into the country. And anyway, you've forgotten about Betty. We can't leave her here, in danger.'

Adrian put his arm around his daughter. 'Don't worry about money. Bernard said another thing – he wants to retire from working for Carlucci and go back north to breed dogs or something. He talked about it to Raoul and Raoul told him to approach me to see if I would be interested. It's not big money but it's all I need as it isn't really full-time – just being Carlucci's man on the spot in Britain and doing a service operation for them for big imports. I've told Bernard I would like to do it. Cheap fares to Malaga are plentiful at this time of the year, especially as we are only staying a short time, so we can take Betty with us. Also I have another reason for us all going – especially you.'

Lorna raised her eyes and Adrian looked embarrassed. 'I want you to meet someone rather special.'

* * *

The old man carried his two suitcases to the porch and looked at his lounge for the last time. His home for the past ten years would soon gather dust and decay. There was, sadly, nothing he could do about it. A few treasures were packed and he had arranged to sell his car at a ridiculously low price to a dealer near the airport. He would like to have said his farewells to his neighbour but he was sure that something had happened to his old friend – why else would the police have called?

The old man turned the car and drove slowly down the driveway, stopping to look at the rhododendrons he had planted the previous year. Two young men were engaged in eager conversation on the pavement outside his gate and he gave a short toot on the horn. To his alarm the two men sprinted either side and opened the passenger door and the rear door behind him. He froze at the wheel, his mouth drying instantly. 'What do you want of me?'

The man in the front seat smiled. 'You going away, Herr Weissman?'

The old man's heart jumped. 'You make a mistake – my name is Whiteman.'

The young man kept smiling. 'Your ticket for inspection please, Herr Weissman.'

The old man fumbled in his jacket pocket and produced the Aerolineas Argentinas ticket. The young man read it.

'We've already bought you a ticket, Herr Weissman. We have many people who want to meet you. Unfortunately, many who would like to make your acquaintance again are no longer alive – but then you know that. Just one would like to see you for old times' sake – you remember Dr Solomon? He'll be at the airport to see you off; he has always wanted that pleasure. We'll go with you.'

The old man's mind raced. 'I cannot understand you – I don't know what you mean. Why do you come with me to the airport?'

'Oh no – Herr Weissman, we know exactly who you are. Just to put you right on one thing. We are not just coming with you to the airport – we are travelling with you on the plane.'

The old man shook his head. 'You are coming with me to Buenos Aires?'

The man in the back seat laughed and the old man turned to look at his jet black eyes. 'I'm sorry Herr Weissman, my friend forgot to tell you we have changed your destination. The ticket we have for you is for Tel Aviv. We promise you there is a lovely reception – in recognition for all you have done.'

Roberto Weissman's face sank into his chest and he breathed heavily. 'The car ... you drive.'

On the way to the airport the old man never spoke. As the car parked in the Terminal Three car park Dr Isaac Solomon opened the door and Colonel Roberto Weissman stepped out into the cool breeze. The speech Solomon had prepared somehow dried on his lips. He just watched as the trio crossed the road to the check-in for El Al.

18

'Christ Almighty!' Bernard Waterman exploded as he took in the scene.

The little yacht was in a dreadful state and the two men were dismayed. Neither had seen the yacht before but both expected something larger and certainly tidier. The Gibraltar police had searched the small vessel thoroughly. Carpets had been taken up, a section of carpet had been removed for forensic examination, side panels had been unscrewed and lockers had been emptied and the contents stacked on the floor or on the side benches. Bernard muttered something about the police being obliged to restore everything to its place following a search but Adrian took a more realistic approach.

'By the time you fill in forms and have an inspector down here it will be days before they do anything. Let's just get on with it.'

The two men changed into shorts and set about sorting out the mess. They had allocated a couple of days to set up a sale with a yacht broker and get a clearance from police; obviously it would take longer, but that would allow Ella and Lorna time to get to know one another, Adrian told himself. Betty was still rather shocked over the news from Inspector Forbes. She had no time for Roland Davies and the fact that his father was dead and he was detained in Algeciras didn't cause any obvious distress. But Roland was the father of her unborn baby and women act strangely over these things. No,

Adrian convinced himself, a few days with the women on their own, especially with Sam as a catalyst, would only do good. The two men worked through the afternoon and stopped only to discuss the sale of the vessel over a couple of bottles of beer. Bernard suggested that they should have dinner in the town and ask around for the name of the most reputable sales agent. Neither had been involved in selling a boat before but it seemed straightforward, and the police, whom they had visited on their arrival from Marbella earlier in the day, had raised no objection. The police had made no comment to their questions about Davies and Rollason; perhaps because of the lack of communication and co-operation between Spain and Gibraltar, the information had not filtered through to them.

At seven o'clock the two men were about to leave for a meal out in the town when they heard shouting from the quayside. A wizened old man with a face like a peeled chestnut was standing on the quayside looking at *L'Anticipation*. 'Are you there?' he called again.

Adrian pushed himself into the fo'c's'le and the old man looked surprised. 'Mr Southon – is he there?'

Adrian explained that Mr Southon had rented the boat and that Mr Waterman and he were representatives of the owner. The brown face wrinkled even further.

'He asked me to get some information for him – now I have it and he isn't here.'

Adrian wasn't slow in grasping the lead and suggested that as they would be seeing Mr Southon soon, they could pass the information on to him.

The man wasn't as forthcoming as they had expected. 'The police, they came on the boat the other day, people in the town are talking about it. They were on board for some time – some people talk of trouble.'

Waterman joined them. He had heard the conversation in detail. 'Seems like Mr Southon didn't pay his harbour dues at Puerto Banus and he left a few debts there too. The police put a message through and the local police picked up the lead and searched the boat. Mr Southon seems to have suddenly departed and we are expecting to hear from him. May I ask who you are?'

The chestnut face relaxed and smiled. 'Franco Gomez – I'm the senior guide around here, I work for the tourist board. Mr Southon was making enquiries about someone who came here some years back, an Irish gentleman he was. He had been searching for an aircraft, one under the sea. He looked for a long time and spent a lot of money, I believe. He was interested in old planes and this one had crashed in the war – I remember it but I was only a youngster then. Mr Southon wanted to find it as well. Seems strange to be interested in an old wreck but people are strange – I had one visitor the other day wanted to bottle some water off Gibraltar, collects water from different parts of the world – strange I call it but...'

Bernard Waterman brought him back to the point. 'But what about this Irishman? Why did Southon want to see him and who is he?'

'Mr Southon wanted help to find the place – seems like he ran into problems. All the junk on the sea floor, I guess – or maybe he just didn't have a clue where to look. When we were talking about it I mentioned the Irish gentleman who had been working there for weeks – I told Mr Southon that he hadn't been lucky and had spent time and money on it. Mr Southon suddenly became interested and asked for his name. I couldn't remember, it was some time ago, and he paid me cash for a few days' help. I know he lived towards Ronda. I thought about it and the other day I met an old friend, Ramon, who has been working in Estepona. I asked him if he remembered the Irish gentleman's name. He did. It was Sean Donnelly. Smart-looking gentleman he was. Full of action, and he must have been in his late sixties, maybe older. He has an old farmhouse up in the hills outside Ronda.'

Adrian suddenly realised that the information, interesting as it was, was not being received with much hospitality and he suggested that Gomez might like to come on board for a drink. The old guide smiled and shook his head.

'I've some friends to meet up with in the bar. Any other information you need I can always find it out and...' He hesitated. 'I don't charge like so many people around here, but sometimes I...'

He smiled and Bernard took the lead.

'Mr Gomez, you have been of great help to us. Allow me to buy you and some of your friends a drink.'

The brown creased face broke into a toothpaste-ad smile and the guide folded the ten-pound note. 'Any time, sir. You remember my name, Franco Gomez – everyone knows me around here.'

As the old guide skipped gleefully along the quay Adrian retired to the cabin and sat with a thud on the bottom bunk. 'Bloody hell, I can't think of anything else to say. There is young Franz and his father before him combing the desert for the stuff and all the time it is here. Raoul never considered for one minute that it was anywhere but in the desert or had been gathered up by the German forces in 1942. No one thought it could be in Gibraltar of all places.'

'Except Southon,' Bernard said softly.

'As you say, except Southon and the mysterious Mr Donnelly. That thug Rollason, he also seems to have been on the right track. Not one of us ever considered Gibraltar, yet we were all surprised at Southon coming to Tunisia via Spain – that didn't make sense.'

'It was Gibraltar he set out for from the start,' Bernard put in, 'and now we know why he wanted a boat. He never had any intention of desert combing – he was on the right track from square one.'

'We must call Ella and Lorna about it,' Adrian went on, 'and you know where we are heading tomorrow?'

Bernard smiled. 'I think it's going to be Ronda to visit our friend Donnelly.'

* * *

As the hired Ford eased its way through the mountains on the difficult road between Algeciras and Ronda the two men avoided the topic in the forefront of their minds. Both had been intrigued at the news from Franco Gomez but even more so at the interest which Southon had shown in the Irishman. How did the Irishman Donnelly get to know of the wreck and why had he spent so much time and money on a search which had proved to be fruitless? He knew of the submerged aircraft and obviously knew it had valuable cargo on board and that in itself pointed to him being in the forces in the area during the war.

'I thought Ireland was neutral in the war,' Adrian suddenly exclaimed, and Bernard Waterman turned towards him in surprise.

'Thought you were dozing off, you've been quiet for some time. No, to answer your question, Ireland was neutral but quite a number of Irishmen volunteered for service; in fact, a number of complete Irish regiments saw active service. You've been thinking along the lines I have – to have information he must have been serving in Tunisia where the aircraft was loaded, or in Gib. God knows, but we may find out. It's going to be difficult to explain our part in this venture so perhaps it's better to say nothing about Ian's disappearance; somehow that seems very detached from the whole exercise. Anyway, if you don't mind, I want to concentrate on driving. I'm finding some of these bends and drops just a little alarming.'

It was just after one o'clock when they arrived in Ronda and decided to have a bite of lunch and take a look at the spectacular gorge linked by the eighteenth-century bridge.

'I hate to admit it but I suffer from terrible vertigo – the road here was bad enough,' Bernard confessed.

Adrian smiled. He hadn't found the car journey too easy either. From a distance both stood and admired the incredible piece of engineering. A fellow observer told them that the engineer who built it died in a spectacular fall from the parapet the day the bridge was opened. Tourist magnet tale or not, the visitors certainly were plentiful in Ronda and the restaurant they visited was doing a roaring trade in film and souvenirs as well as food.

The *camarero* who served them some roast chicken was

eager to answer their question. Of course he knew Señor Donnelly – everyone in Ronda knew him. He had been living in Spain for many years and he was married to a Spanish lady.

'He isn't like normal English – he speaks Spanish.'

Adrian smiled and accepted the truism. 'Irish, actually,' he corrected.

The waiter shrugged. 'That explains it.'

Neither Adrian nor Bernard could see why, but it didn't matter.

Following the waiter's careful plan drawn on the back of a paper napkin, they drove across the bridge and out on the road towards St Pedro de Alcantara. After a few kilometres they took the indicated unsurfaced road, which became worse the further they went. The house, of considerable opulence, suddenly appeared as they rounded a hill bank of rock, and a sign indicated that they had found their destination. Finca Tranquila certainly lived up to its name; the views across the *serrania* were dramatic and Adrian switched off the car engine for a few moments so that they could enjoy the silence, punctuated only by the cry of a bird of prey hovering overhead.

The sound of the gate bell brought a frenzied reaction in the form of two Alsatians, and within a minute a tall, elderly man appeared and called them to heel. In answer to Adrian's question he confirmed that he was Donnelly and invited the two men in.

'Why don't we sit on the terrace – it's so lovely here. I want you to look at my garden. I get few visitors so no one admires it.'

The three men sat on the terrace in the strong sunlight and Sean Donnelly asked them what he could do to help. Before they could answer, a young, bright-eyed Spanish woman appeared and Donnelly introduced his wife Pilar. They accepted her offer of a drink and she returned to the house.

Adrian had already resolved to tell only enough of the story to justify the visit; Ian's disappearance, the existence of young Grieb, the theft of the yacht and the police investigation in Gibraltar all seemed irrelevant and even distracting from the purpose of their presence in the lovely old *finca*.

Bernard started. 'A friend of ours, name of Southon, has been involved for some time in searching for a wartime bomber which went down in the sea of Gibraltar late in 1942. He had the help of a local guide who mentioned that you had been engaged on the same venture some years ago but abandoned the search for some reason. We thought that you might have information which, with our information, might lead to locating the wreck.'

Donnelly inhaled deeply on his cigarette and puffed a large smoke ring skywards. 'And why on earth should I, or anyone else, want to locate an old bomber sunk off Gibraltar all those years ago?'

Adrian explained that he believed that valuables taken from the Jewish people of Tunisia were on board, and Donnelly's face darkened visibly. 'Are you suggesting that British forces stole Jewish property?'

Adrian shook his head. 'It was property recovered from German hands which was being sent to England for whatever purpose – I suppose safe keeping. The aircraft had injured men on board and the pilot undertook to carry the goods as freight within the aircraft.'

Donnelly said nothing for a minute, then, 'I suppose you think I set about, how would you put it – treasure hunting – to steal from the dead, so to speak. I am not like that.' His voice had a cold and distinctly hostile ring to it.

Adrian gave a wan smile. 'Mr Donnelly, I'm not suggesting anything of the kind. If valuables, particularly works of art, do lie abandoned on the seabed it would seem good sense to recover them and take steps to return them to their rightful owners. It seems to me that nothing but good would be done and the finder should be substantially recompensed for his action.'

'And what is your interest in all this?' Donnelly asked, and Bernard Waterman cleared his throat. Before he had time to reply, Pilar Donnelly arrived with a tray of beer and profuse apologies for taking such a long time. She and Donnelly spoke Spanish for a minute then she went back to the house.

'I represent the original owner, Mr Donnelly,' Bernard began. 'The family lived in Tunisia during the war and, as Jews, were rounded up by the German forces. Their possessions were confiscated in the way Adrian has described. The family are, of course, very interested in recovery, and would pay a substantial reward, which we can discuss in detail later, to anyone who can help in that recovery.'

'I wish I could be of assistance to you but I cannot, I regret to say.' Donnelly lay back in his chair and looked at the sky. 'I tried to find the plane – spent several months at it. There is too much junk on the seabed – I found nothing. For all I know, the aircraft went down somewhere else. Anyway, I tried and I got nowhere.'

'But surely you had substantial evidence that the aircraft did go down off Gib before getting so heavily involved,' Bernard put in.

'Of course I did,' Donnelly answered with irritation in his voice. 'I listened to a pack of old locals – and I was a fool to listen to them. I had just become interested in metal detection, a kind of new hobby, and I got caught up in local gossip. It cost me a great deal of money – money I can ill afford to lose. The whole thing was a farce and I would rather forget about it, if you don't mind.'

The tall man stood up and walked over to the balcony. He pointed his hand towards the *serrania*. 'Don't waste your time on trivia – there is so much beauty here more worthy of our time. I've lived here for as many years as I can remember and I know. Now, how about another beer and let's stroll around the garden as we drink. The climate here is so wonderful, everything grows. In Andulucia it seems a crime to kill the weeds, they are so beautiful.'

The three men walked leisurely through the large luxuriant garden whilst their host introduced plants as if they were fellow guests. There was no doubt that he wanted a diversion, and although both Adrian and Bernard were disappointed in the result of their visit, they nevertheless enjoyed their stroll.

'Pepe – he's my head gardener and has been with me for years – works full-time and has two boys who come in at weekends. I'm getting past the heavy work but I like to choose plants. I'm an armchair gardener!' Sean Donnelly laughed. 'But it's fun. Let's go into the shed and see what's going on.'

Pepe was busily engaged in potting, and Donnelly explained in rapid Spanish that his guests from England were interested in the garden. The Spanish gardener smiled and showed them a new plant he had found. Donnelly translated and then sharply suggested that they go back to the house.

Once back on the terrace Donnelly suggested another drink, but the others declined. The journey back to Gibraltar would take around two hours and it wasn't the easiest of roads.

'Friendly though your Spanish police seem to be, I guess they are the same as any others about drivers over the alcohol limit,' Bernard remarked. 'But before we go I would appreciate the use of your bathroom.'

Donnelly directed him to a small passageway at the back of the hallway and then took Adrian into a room to show him some photographs he had taken of the spectacular gorge.

'Another hobby – but an interesting and absorbing one. One of my pictures is used for a book on Ronda. I'll show it to you.' He pulled a glossy, expensive book from the bookshelves. 'I love books – I have thousands of them and I feel proud to have a picture in such a book as . . .' His voice tailed away as he followed Adrian's gaze. 'Do you see a book you like?'

Adrian reached up and pulled a book from the shelves. 'It is just that I am interested in the author – Major General Collingson. He wrote a number of books on World War Two, I believe.'

'Indeed he did.' Donnelly's voice was thin and he turned to Bernard Waterman, who had just entered the room. 'I have some. I should have the others, but it isn't that easy getting new books out here – English books, I mean. No, Collingson is someone I should order.'

Adrian flicked over the pages and returned it to the shelf. 'I'll send you one. In fact, I know the publishers so I'll get you the revised editions – a present for your splendid forbearance and hospitality.'

Donnelly smiled and mumbled his thanks. Adrian tapped the spine of the book on the shelf. 'Such a pity people write in books – I imagine that wasn't you as you love your books so much.'

'I don't know what you mean,' Donnelly said guardedly.

Adrian pulled the book out again. 'Take a look – someone has written in it, in German, would you believe.'

Donnelly shook his head. 'It's strange. Maybe I got it second-hand – that's more than likely. There are lots of second-hand bookshops on the coast – I go to them often.'

Bernard walked across and took the book., 'You must read the revised edition when Adrian sends it to you, Wing Commander. You would find it most interesting. I know I did, because I served under Collingson when he was a young officer. He missed out quite a lot of detail and the publishers have managed, with the author's help just before he died, to correct certain things: it's good to have accuracy in a work of historical record. I'm sure you agree. By the way, I will accept that drink you offered me a few minutes ago. And just one point – do the initials MPD mean anything to you?'

There was a silence, a complete silence, for a minute and then from above the terrace a bird of prey's raucous call rang out. Donnelly's face was ashen grey and he was visibly shaking. He poured the contents of a can of beer into a glass and passed it to Waterman.

'You called me Wing Commander, Mr Waterman. I'm afraid I'm not quite with you. I am not an officer of the Royal Air Force or any other air force for that matter – I'm an Irishman living in Spain and with official residence here.'

Bernard picked up the book which Adrian had put on the coffee table and turned to the author's biography. ' "Born in Dublin in 1919 to an English father, professor of surgery at Trinity College, and an Irish mother. The family moved to London when the author was nine. He joined the army at the outbreak of the Second World War and saw service in North Africa and Italy as a commissioned officer. Later he..." But you know the rest, Wing Commander. After all, you were only two years older than your brother. I would take a guess that your adopted name, Donnelly, was your mother's maiden name and you used that after your unscheduled visit to Spain in 1942. It must have been easy to settle here with no questions asked in those times. Quite a few deserters settled here.'

'What do you mean, deserter?' There was bitterness in Donnelly's voice as he spat the words.

'I mean that you conveniently rowed your life-raft towards the Spanish shore – or let's be charitable and say that you were blown this way – and with some precious cargo on board, you decided that a rich retired officer in Spain was better than a poor one in the Royal Air Force with a strong possibility of being killed. I expect the Spanish detained you in one of their camps for the duration of the war – that was the usual form, I believe. MPD by the way was "Missing Presumed Dead". You would, of course know that air force phrase. It fits, don't you think?'

'And what if you are right? There was a free pardon given to deserters some years after the war, so I have nothing to answer for now.' Donnelly walked to the windows, which opened onto terrace, and lit a cigarette.

'I'm not sure about that,' Adrian put in. 'As far as I know, robbery and murder are not included in any pardon, particularly as one of the offences took place very recently indeed.'

'I think you had better go. I find the two of you offensive and abusive and this whole exercise an affront, to put it mildly. I feel you have both abused my hospitality and I would like you to go. All I would advise you, and you came here originally for advice, is not to repeat anything you have said. Spanish law is slow, no doubt about that, but it is thorough and efficient. Slander and libel apply here as well as in Britain.' Donnelly walked across the terrace towards the car.

It was a cold parting and neither Adrian nor Bernard spoke until the car ceased jolting over the unmade road.

Adrian stopped the car and breathed out loudly. 'Now what do you make of that?'

Bernard smiled. 'I thought his face was familiar when we arrived. He really is remarkably like his brother, but then in the small hallway leading to the toilets there is a wall niche.

In it was the figurine which I know used to belong to the Carluccis. King Zog gave it to Raoul's father, or grandfather, I forget which, but Raoul once showed me a picture of it and it really is beautiful. I suppose when he sold off the rest of the stuff he couldn't bear to part with it and decided to keep it as an investment. Of course, there is no telling how much he took – as I understand the story, the stuff weighed several hundredweight and he couldn't possibly have taken it all in a life-raft.'

'But who says it was all in one container? It was originally in a tin trunk but I reckon that could raise questions when it arrived at its destination airport in England even in wartime. It is more likely that the brothers Collingson split the load into several bags and our friend there grabbed two or so when the aircraft hit the drink.'

'Which accounts for him being interested in locating the remainder with his detection devices,' Bernard added. 'But how does the general fit into all this?'

Adrian thought for a moment. 'I believe he knew his brother was alive in Spain, God knows how, and made an arrangement, a kind of low-key blackmail – I'll keep quiet about you as a deserter in Spain providing I get my share of the goodies which are rightfully mine. It's an interesting theory.'

'Why did you mention murder?' Bernard questioned.

'It was a try-on, but I had a reason. You see, my son-in-law Ian has been to the house.'

Bernard shot upright in the car seat as if he had had an electric shock. 'Christ Almighty, how do you know that?'

'Because he always smoked Camel cigarettes – only about ten a day – but he used to buy them in drums vacuum-packed. Said they stayed fresher when not exposed to air. Lot of rubbish, I think. Anyway, when we went to inspect the skills of the Wing Commander's gardener, on the shelf of the tool-shed, probably holding nails or something, was a newish tin with the Camel label. I believe that Ian was there and that he probably gave some cigarettes to the gardener and the chap kept the tin.'

'But you never asked Donnelly, sorry, Collingson, about it.'

Adrian grunted. 'No, I was tempted to. But it wouldn't be difficult to trace the gardener if we ask at the *venta*. Everyone goes to the local in the evenings or during the siesta, I'm sure of that, and he has worked for Donnelly for ten years. The proprietors and customers at the bars will know who he is and where he lives. I suggest we stay the night at the local hotel and do some questioning.'

He started the car and drove towards Ronda.

'There's another thing,' Bernard remarked. 'As you know, I speak Italian – that's how I got involved with Captain Collingson in the first place, back in the desert. Italian isn't all that different to Spanish; if you understand one you can get the gist of the other. I have a number of phrases even if I can't say with any justification that I speak Spanish.'

'Well?' Adrian kept his eyes on the road but his face was puzzled.

'Well, Collingson told the gardener to speak Spanish and cut him short in the shed when the chap started to say something about "the other Englishman who came here" or something like that. Didn't mean anything to me then but Collingson certainly ushered us out in quick time.'

'Interesting – most interesting,' Adrian murmured, and pointed to a sign on the roadside advertising the Reina Victoria Hotel.

The hotel was built at the end of the last century for the British garrison stationed in Gibraltar. Officers who wished to escape the heat of the Rock would retire into the hills for a long weekend and Ronda was a favourite haunt. Although Spanish in style, it has a distinct British atmosphere and Adrian and Bernard were glad that they had stumbled across it. They explained to the desk clerk that they had no luggage as they had expected to be in Ronda for only one day but had been detained on business. The clerk smiled and asked if they would like an overnight pack of toothpaste and toothbrush so on. They accepted gladly and were shown to adjoining single rooms. Old-world hospitality still reigned here.

After two hours the two men met in the bar. The events of

the day seemed to justify a number of gin and tonics.

'So our friend Collingson or Donnelly seems to fill several gaps,' Adrian remarked.

'He does indeed,' Bernard agreed. 'He was devious – so like his brother. But let's pull the whole act together. We have a wing commander who deserted in World War Two, which in itself may be a fairly big deal but doesn't help us in tracing your son-in-law.'

'Except for the fact that he was certainly at the house,' Adrian chipped in. 'That book is the real trump card. I cannot believe there are many copies with annotations in the margin. That was the copy Ian bought at the sale, I'm convinced of it.'

Bernard Waterman grunted. 'Oh – I concede that, but it doesn't get us too far. Let's meet the gardener at the *venta* – that should sure as hell reveal something.'

The bar at the Venta Morenos was full even in the early evening and Bernard and Adrian had hardly touched their long glasses of gin with more than adequate ice, when Bernard nodded to the corner. A group of locals were playing dominoes, and one of the four sitting at the table was instantly recognisable as the man they sought. At that moment the game ended and Pepe collected up some glasses and moved to the bar. Bernard strolled over to him.

'*Bueonos tardes, señor.* So we meet again. "*Quere usted una copa.*"'

The bronzed Spaniard flashed a smile of recognition and to Bernard's surprise replied in English. 'Oh, good evening, sir. I didn't realise you were going to stay and see our lovely Ronda. Do you like it here?'

'I'm sorry, I didn't know – you speak perfect English. But let mc buy you a drink,' Bernard commented.

'Thank you – I will take a *cerveza*. But yes, my father was English. He was with Mr Donnelly in the war, the Second World War, I mean. He used to be Mr Donnelly's gardener many years ago and he married a local Spanish lady. I went to England to school and worked there. I came back to Spain after my father had died and my mother was alone. Of course I had been down here often on holiday. Mr Donnelly asked me if I would like to come back. To come back to Spain was – well, it was living, if you know what I mean. Colour – in the lovely flowers and the people. Look at Ronda now.' The Spaniard beckoned and led Bernard onto the balcony. 'Can you think of a more beautiful place to live? It is paradise. I want to spend the rest of my days here – a good place to live and a good place to die.'

'You've a bit more time to think about that,' Bernard laughed.

'Oh, I don't know,' Pepe replied. 'Who was it, one of your English poets, I think, who said "In the midst of life we are in death."'

Adrian had quietly joined them. 'I think it is in the Prayer Book, something to do with the funeral service,' he chipped in.

'Yes – yes, you're right. I'm not a religious man but I heard it not long ago when we had the accident here. I went to church then – the wording was a little different in Spanish, lacked the same ring of language, but it meant the same and I thought how right it is. Enjoy life – you don't know how much you have, that's my philosophy. Mr...'

'Just call me Bernard,' the Englishman prompted. 'But this funeral you went to, this was a friend of yours?'

'No, I hardly knew him. He came to see Mr Donnelly and I met him as he was looking around the garden. Spanish, but spoke English, about my age, maybe younger. We talked. He came from London, he said, and he wanted to have a big garden. He told me he was ill – didn't have long to live – so he wanted to enjoy beautiful things like gardens. He told me about his wife and son. Oh, he was an interesting man.'

'What was his name?' Adrian's face was alight.

'Diego something, I don't remember his last name. Yes, Diego East – Est... I'll remember in a moment.'

Adrian's face vividly showed his disappointment. 'You say he spoke English. I suppose he learned it in England?'

'Yes – strange that. After the accident Mr Donnelly told me he was Spanish, had spent some time in England and liked to be considered English. He was just wandering across Spain on holiday, Mr Donnelly told me, and had come to Ronda to see the historic buildings and the gorge. Someone had told him about the gardens at Mr Donnelly's villa so he called in. He knew Mr Donnelly spoke English and so I suppose Mr Donnelly, who's lonely and likes someone to talk to in English, asked him to stay a couple of nights. They seemed to argue a lot – I heard them when I was walking on the terrace. Anyway, the man left two days later and went exploring the gorge. Then the day after that Mr Donnelly told me what had happened.'

'And what did happen?' The two English voices spoke in unison.

'He must have slipped when he was climbing around at the top of the gorge – the bit where it isn't fenced. Maybe he was looking for relics or flowers – who knows? Anyway, he was found at the bottom of the gorge – dead. Mr Donnelly was very upset and the Guardia Civil were around asking questions. He didn't have a national identity card and that was puzzling them – all Spaniards have to carry them. Mr Donnelly said he had lost it in the garden here – he had mentioned it to Mr Donnelly – and I was told to keep an eye open for it. There was no identity on the body but someone in the town said that he had been staying here so the police came up. Mr Donnelly was able to identify him and give them his name. He had no relatives, he was just on his own, so he was buried here in Ronda.'

'But I thought you said he had a wife and son.'

'Yes – that's what he told me, Bernard, but apparently he was having a holiday because he had a bad mental problem. That's why he was taking it easy. He had told all this to Mr Donnelly and, being such a kind man, Mr Donnelly took him in for a couple of nights.'

'Took him in – yes you could say that,' Adrian put in softly. He laid his wallet on the table and pulled out a photograph. Pepe's bow crinkled as he looked at it: a man, a woman and a baby, obviously during the christening. 'My God – that's Diego. You know him?'

'Yes, I know him,' Adrian said softly. 'That is or was Ian Lacey, my son-in-law, and I think you should listen to a long story. I promise you that you will find it interesting, certainly distressing. Let's go where we can talk quietly – back at the hotel.'

Pepe stubbed another cigarette butt into an overfull ashtray and stood up. He gazed at the floor and crossed to the long window where magnificent views over the *serrania* were illuminated by the full moon.

'I cannot believe what you have told me – yet in so many ways it makes sense. Father talked about how Mr Donnelly and he were survivors from an aircraft, but I understood that it was at the end of the war and they came here afterwards – Mr Donnelly when the war ended and my father several years later. Now it seems Mr Donnelly made his way by life-raft to the shore after the crash and then stayed here as a deserter – with some of the valuables he managed to get from the plane. That's hard to believe, rather like a fairy story. Then General Collingson – that piece fits. An elderly gentleman used to come down here regularly. Mr Donnelly said he was a cousin. I know he died recently in Switzerland because Mr Donnelly told me; he was very upset when the general died. I never knew his name – one of those people who kept himself to himself. Father just called him "the general" and that's how we knew him. Mr Donnelly always had plenty of money – Father said it had come from investment, but what you are telling me is that Father knew about the desertion. But why did Father come here?'

'It's just a guess,' Adrian put in, 'but maybe your father, with a family at home, mother and father probably, didn't want to do a disappearing act. On the other hand, he saw no reason to blow open the story of the wing commander. After the war he may have made contact with his former colleague – on holiday or something.'

'Of course!' Pepe blew a cloud of smoke into the air.

'Father came down to Gibraltar, working for a marine engineering company, in the early fifties. He was there for around a year. That's probably when he met Mr Donnelly again, either in Ronda or in Gib. It was somewhere in the mid-fifties that he was out of a job so he took up the idea of working for Mr Donnelly. Do you think he knew about the goods Mr Donnelly had taken from the aircraft?'

Adrian shrugged his shoulders and Pepe went on. 'I'm sure Mother never did – convinced in fact. She died two years ago – she would never have wanted to be a party to all this.' Pepe turned from the window. 'You know, when you look at all this it really isn't so bad. I mean, it happened so many years ago. Surely the time has come to close the book on the war.'

'Except that there has been a murder recently,' Bernard said softly.

Pepe looked up sharply. 'You're only guessing – and my guess is that he slipped and fell. It's easy to do on those cliffs.'

'Then why change his name? Why not say he was an Englishman visiting – in fact tell the truth? Donnelly must have had a reason for lying,' Adrian said.

Pepe thought carefully. 'Yes, he must have had a reason. But don't you think, Adrian, and you, Bernard, that the time for guessing is over? Mr Donnelly has been good to me, good to my whole family over the years and I don't like hearing those things about him. I suggest we go to the house and ask him – give him a chance to explain. I think that's the least we can do. There may be a simple explanation to it all.'

Adrian looked at his watch. 'We'll leave it until the morning – it's too late now.'

Pepe nodded. "Mr Donnelly does turn in early. I'll meet you tomorrow. I still believe we can sort all this out.'

In the Finca Tranquila Collingson had retired early, but after an hour he got up and went out of the French window onto the balcony. He and his wife slept in separate rooms, an arrangement they had made several years ago, not because of any flaw in their relationship but simply because he was such a restless sleeper at the best of times. Now especially, this wasn't the best of times.

As he sat on the terrace with the moon lighting up the dramatic mountain range around Ronda his mind ran over the past. All those years ago it had been so easy – the chance of a lifetime to come out of the war alive, unscathed and even a hero, for his name had appeared in the roll of honour at his old school. That had meant a lot to him when he heard about it from an old school friend who, for a financial consideration, had agreed to keep silent. To get out not just alive but with a considerable fortune which, even after parting with half to his brother Peter, still left him more than comfortably off. 'The general'. His face broke into a smile. The war hero turned author who had lived in his retirement on Nazi-seized goods, goods which had been seized back by his brother. No, he hadn't been above living illegally on the spoils of war. And a rich general with the co-operation of a dead wing commander. It was bizarre but it worked. He lit a cigarette and blew smoke rings leisurely into the air.

There had been problems, of course. Pepe's father had turned up years after the war and he had worried that he was after blackmail. He remembered the relief when he discovered that the man hadn't realised the value of the suitcase of goods in the dinghy – all he wanted was a job, and it was good to have an English-speaking person around. His mind wandered back over the search for the remainder of the missing treasure in Gibraltar. Months were spent on it, so many that it had become a bit of an obsession. People were starting to ask questions so the decision to abandon it was the right one. Then, years later, came the change in luck with that infernal Ian Lacey and all his talk of dying and his wife being left poor. Christ, what a snivelling bastard he was, sniffing around the dead general's house and getting wind from the staff of Peter often going to Spain to spend holidays with his brother. That in itself wouldn't have meant anything to Lacey, but it was when that stupid housekeeper Rachel showed him the necklace with the Star of David that Peter had given her just before he died – that was the connecting point, and Lacey had then turned into a real embarrassment. The first real threat after all those years of comfortable living. He grimaced as he thought of it. It had, however, been easier to solve than he would have imagined. It was not difficult to give a push to a sick man on a friendly country walk along the gorge whilst they were discussing what Lacey had called 'terms'. It couldn't really be called murder.– it was merely advancing his death by a month or so. Surely a better way to go than a lingering end, and so much more convenient for all concerned.

Like most weak people, Collingson was good at justifying his actions. He justified his disposal of Ian Lacey, as he had justified his desertion from the armed forces.

Things were getting uncomfortably hot, there was no doubt about that. Those two interfering bastards who had turned up the previous day – one of them Lacey's father-in-law – he could, of course, continue to deny that he was Collingson, and they would be hard put to prove it. He started as he thought of a new aspect. They were tenacious people, no doubt about that. If they returned to England and searched RAF records, in all probability his parents' names would be given, their nationality and his mother's maiden name. He realised how foolish it had been to take her name, but she had meant a great deal to him before she died when he was only a child. Yet that might confirm their suspicions. There had been a parole granted to war deserters, he knew, but the extent of the parole was something of which he was uncertain. Would it extend to officers who had not just deserted but acquired property illegally in the course of their duty? He lay on the bed and lit a cigarette. Then there was the matter of that layabout Lacey. It had been a clean fall but he had insisted to the Guardia Civil that the man was Spanish with a knowledge of English. That had been a smart move at the time, for, if it had been established that he was English, it would not have been difficult to trace passengers who had come from London and not used their return tickets. No, he had been right at the time to declare Lacey a Spanish citizen who had lost his identity card. But now things were different and if the two visitors of the previous day could prove to the police that Lacey was British, then some extremely awkward questions would be asked and the house could be subject to a search. Collingson's eyes fixed on a small menorah in the hallway, of limited value, 400,000 pesetas at the most. That was why he had retained it – most of the valuable stuff had all been melted down years ago and turned into cash to finance his enterprise and comfortable living – this property in Ronda and the stylish yacht in Puerto Banus. Peter's comfortable living as well – it certainly had allowed Peter to relax in Switzerland and write. Maybe the retaining of items of small intrinsic value had been a grave mistake, certainly the necklace which Peter had given his talkative housekeeper had been the lead for Lacey.

Collingson picked up the menorah and played with it in his hand. Sleep was far from his mind and he was deeply concerned about the turn of events. Now, with the past apparently well and truly buried, ghosts had arisen to haunt him. The prospect of a long prison sentence was something he could not face, not when he was so accustomed – conditioned indeed – to luxury and total freedom. Maybe Peter had died at the right moment, spared from disgrace and without a worry in the world.

He strode slowly around the room, deep in thought. At the dresser he paused to open a drawer and place the candelabrum out of sight. He would have to dispose of these minor items or at least find a very secure hiding place – not for the first time they had been buried – or he might take them with him. As he closed the drawer his eye caught a line of files, one in particular: 'Offshore Banking'. Maybe that was it – grab the money he had in Gibraltar and make a break for it, start a new life ... but where? Europe was useless, the EC had proved more than an economic community – co-operation between police forces, he had read in a Spanish newspaper only the other day, surpassed even the co-operation between taxation authorities. No, it would have to be outside Europe, somewhat remote and preferably where he could fade into the background with his fluent Spanish.

He lit another cigarette and strolled through the French windows, across the terrace and down the steps into the garden, pausing only to switch on the lights which illuminated a row of palm trees. That young man who had spent three weeks on a vacation job last summer and had so painstakingly built the fish pond – Paco, a medical student from Argentina – he was a nice lad. He had really liked having him around, and the letter from his hospital bed about his motorcycle accident on the way back to the University of Madrid had upset him. Collingson had been so upset at the news that he had flown up to Madrid to see him in hospital and had met the boy's parents. He liked Erika and Alfonso, too, and they had a very pleasant lunch on the Plaza Major. At the time their invitation to visit them in Argentina had seemed pie in the sky – but why not? He could stay with them for a week or so and then find himself somewhere to live. He opened a file and flicked through the statements. Interest had certainly pushed the balance up and his account in the Bank of Gibraltar stood at close to £150,000 and there was another in ABN bank for £20,000. He could draw that and also the current account money in the Bank of Andalucia, close on £9,000. A total of close on £180,000, most of which he could draw in pounds sterling. And the few valuables left could be sold for a tidy sum – they could be recovered from their 'safe' by simply removing a certain crenated tile on the top of a garden wall. His mind raced. If he was going to disappear completely for the second time in his life he would have to do it quickly – a decision on the spur of the moment as it had been forty odd years ago. Circumstances then had presented themselves quickly. When the bomber hit the water, he had made a decision to vanish. Now the circumstances bore a remarkable similarity. He could contact Pilar later – just as he had contacted Peter after the event.

Collingson prodded the lilies of the fish pond with a piece of garden cane. The builder of the pool, young Paco, his parents and homeland might just be the answer. He could leave for Gibraltar shortly after dawn and be at the bank as it opened. He could telephone the Bank of Andalucia in

Ronda and get the money transferred to La Linea, bordering on Gibraltar, and pick it up there. Then armed with £180,000 he could fly to Madrid and then on to Buenos Aires. It was simple. But there were two snags. First, those meddling swine who were around the previous day and who might come back. Second, there were no flights from Gibraltar to Madrid. Gibraltar only had flights to the UK and Morocco. He would have to drive on to Malaga from Gib.

Collingson threw the garden cane into the flower bed in annoyance. Still, he could overcome the snags. The first thing to do was to establish whether the two intruders into his private life were still around. If they were, it was a heavy odds-on chance that they were staying at the Reina Victoria. He dialled the number from memory and asked the night porter to connect him to Mr Waterman, apologising for the early hour. There was a delay and then the sleepy voice of Bernard Waterman. Now he knew they were there. He replaced the receiver on its cradle and started to pack.

After ten minutes he strolled onto the terrace and gazed at a pillar with a crenated tile top. Yes, he would do it. A sharp tap with a stone brought the tile clear of the pillar, leaving a hollow area. Some valuables, he told himself, he couldn't leave behind. They had been with him for just too long.

* * *

It took a short while to close the current account in La Linea and Collingson then took a taxi across the airfield and into Gibraltar. Passport clearance was over in a few minutes and by ten thirty he was at the Bank of Gibraltar. He was quickly ushered into the manager's office and it was explained to him that as the money was on a month's deposit he would pay a considerable penalty if he withdrew cash that day. Collingson explained that his brother was very ill and needed the money for an operation. The expression on the manager's face told him that the story was not believed. Collingson became angry and pointed out that it was his money and he could do what the hell he wanted with it. An hour later Collingson left with a tightly packed briefcase.

The ABN proved simple. The deposit was on a monthly draw but was due that day. Luck was on his side and within a few minutes he was on his way. The taxi returned him to his car on the mainland. As the car crossed the airfield he took a long last look at the patch of sea where his life had changed all those years ago. It was changing again now and at the same site. History has a strange way of repeating itself, he thought.

19

As Collingson entered the N340 on the way to Marbella and Malaga, his mind ran over the events of the day so far – and it was now close on midday. He had the money, he had left Pilar a note saying that he was sailing all day, and no doubt that would be passed on to the two amateur sleuths when they turned up as they undoubtedly would. In his car he had brought a gold statuette, one of the few really valuable pieces he had retained from the original hoard. Somehow he had never had the heart to have it melted down like the rest of the stuff – it was too beautiful. He had taken a chance about ten years before and shown it to an insurance valuer, who had advised it was worth around £80,000 then. He suspected it could be reasonably easily traced even after all those years, and its value would be less in a melted-down state, but even then it would be worth quite a large amount. The question was how to sell it quickly. Then there was the car. Only one year old, it certainly must be worth two million pesetas even on a quick sale. The BMW agent near the airport would be closed for the afternoon when he arrived there. He swore loudly as he realised that his timing was out. Then he had an idea – that vulgar, loud-mouthed individual he had met at the annual money exhibition in Marbella last year – Rollason was his name – obviously at the exhibition sniffing out people with money and saying that he was always interested in a deal. He had said then that he acted quickly, for cash, and no questions asked. Now maybe he would put him to the test. He'd gone to Rollason's house for a drink and he was sure he could find it again. Rollason might be interested in a really cheap BMW, and he could even be interested in some valuables at the right price. And Rollason was a cash trader, no questions asked.

At Marbella Collingson turned off the N340 and drove into the urbanisation. He picked out the villa quickly – it was the one without traditional window bars and Rollason had explained that all his valuables were away from the house in the form of investments. He parked the car and hesitated about the briefcase of money. Should he risk leaving it in the car or risk taking it to the house of someone he hardly knew? He decided to take it with him but to keep it close at all times.

A ring on the bell brought the pretty Filipina maid to the door. He remembered her from his previous visit, she certainly was lovely. He explained that he wanted to speak to Mr Rollason and the girl reacted in surprise, her eyes filled with tears. 'Mr Rollason, he is taken away – he had bad car crash and people were killed – Mr Rollason is in prison with the police. The police they came here last weekend and take things away. Salvador and me – no work now – no money – we have to go.'

Collingson took her by the shoulders. 'What do you mean, police? What happened?' The girl started crying hysterically and Collingson pushed her gently into the room. 'I want to know what happened – tell me the whole story.'

* * *

'Do you think he has done a bunk on us?' Adrian asked.

Bernard lay back in the chair on the terrace at the Collingson home. 'I don't think so – his wife sounded very convincing, and according to Pepe he often takes off for Puerto Banus for a day's sailing when he feels like it. In any event we cannot stop him. If he has scarpered he could go by car – or change to a train or make for the airport, either Malaga or Gibraltar. We're not in a position to have him picked up. In the eyes of the law he's clean. It seems that all we can do is return to the hotel and then come back again this evening when he returns for dinner. That's apparently the usual deal according to Mrs C – or D, whichever name you choose.'

Pilar came onto the terrace with a tray of coffee. 'What is the name of your husband's yacht, Mrs Donnelly?' Bernard suddenly asked her.

'*La Vida Nueva* – the *New Life*,' she answered. 'But he will be at sea now so whatever it is you want to ask him will have to wait until this evening, I'm afraid.' She placed the coffees on the table and returned to the house.

'Well, he chose an apt name, no doubt about that. But it may be interesting to take a run to Puerto Banus and see if the boat is in its berth. That may tell us something. We can do it in an hour and a bit.'

Adrian sipped his coffee. 'Before that I'm going to ask to use the loo. I want to take a quick look at the house – may just see something which connects.'

A few minutes later he was back. 'You'll never guess, but I've a surprise. The statuette in the niche has gone.'

It was a few minutes before midnight that the Aerolinas Argentinas Boeing 747 left the runway on Madrid's Barajos airport on the start of its 12-hour flight to Buenos Aires.

Only a few hours previously Adrian and Bernard had realised that their quarry had given them the slip. *La Vida Nueva* rode peacefully at anchor in Banus harbour. Without discussing it, both knew that unless they could produce some concrete evidence, there was nothing they could do to prevent Wing Commander Collingson, DFC, alias Sean Donnelly from going where he wished – either leaving the country or moving within it. That evidence could be gathered but it would take time. They decided to join Betty and Lorna at Ella's Marbella villa only ten minutes' drive away.

Meanwhile the subject of their concern was enjoying a good champagne with his dinner some 39,000 feet over the Atlantic. The pretty young girl in the next seat accepted his offer of more champagne. 'I like it – I've never drunk it before.'

He adjusted his seat back – that was the best part of first-class, room to move. He had booked tourist-class from the travel agent in La Linea but with the new turn of events two first-class tickets seemed a good investment. It seemed a pity about the car but that couldn't be helped. Someone would take it back to Pilar.

He topped up his companion's glass. 'Beats you going back to the Philippines, anyway,' he smiled. Life has a strange way of changing direction. And he had a conviction that this direction was one he would like – and he had always fancied an affair with an Oriental.

Collingson breathed a sigh of relief as he cleared customs at Buenos Aires airport. No bags were opened – just a casual wave through so the story of his lucky charm which travelled with him wasn't necessary. The statuette certainly could pass for such a purpose, but he would rather not put it to the test. The ring he had on his index finger, with its tiny Star of David, would not have drawn the attention of any Customs officer; more likely they would have fastened on his Rolex Oyster and he had a perfectly genuine receipt for that in his wallet. Angie had worn the necklace but he didn't believe it was very valuable and it wasn't a high-profile item. Still, it was good to clear through without questions. Money wasn't a problem; Argentinian authorities were only too pleased to have wads of notes coming into the country and didn't want any reason, especially if they could have some small consideration – or so he had been told. Anyway, all was clear and all he needed now was an hotel.

The taxi driver recommended the Plaza and within an hour Collingson and Angie were being shown to their room on the sixteenth floor of the impressive building. He had made up his mind to have a break for a few days before calling Paco's parents. He looked forward to seeing them again but a few passionate days with Angie would be a pleasant interlude.

The voice on the other end of the phone showed considerable reaction. 'Of course we remember you – what a lovely surprise! You were so kind to Paco. He's so much better, nearly lost his limp and says he will be playing football again in a couple of months.'

Collingson explained his visit and his companion. 'Of course,' Erika replied. 'You must come and spend some time with us – no trouble at all. Father's been ill. In fact Alfonso had to cut short our European trip and come back to help on the ranch but now all is well and he would love to have someone to talk to. We have a little *casita* a few hundred metres from the house. Paco uses it when he comes over and friends who come out from BA for the weekend seem to love it – the two of you can stay as long as you like. What brings you to Argentina? Or let's leave that till we meet.'

Collingson took advantage of the pause in Erika's excited conversation to ask directions on how to find the ranch if he hired a car.

'Don't bother to do that. I come into town every Wednesday to shop at the supermarket. Just take a train to Rosario and we'll meet at the big supermarket in the Plaza Major at one o'clock this Wednesday, day after tomorrow. If we meet outside then we can take the weekly shop down to the car park, boys will take it actually, then off we go! Takes about an hour, just a bit over, to get to the ranch. Father will be delighted. We've told him about you. You can exchange wartime experiences – he'd like that. Alfonso will want you to come with him on the ranch, and your girlfriend – please tell me her name.'

'Angie,' Collingson put in quickly.

'Angie – what a lovely name. Does she speak Spanish or English?'

'Both. Incidentally, why are we speaking English? I may be Irish but I've lived in Spain most of my life.'

* * *

The old man roared with laughter as he tossed a steak onto the barbecue grill. 'I love it here, I love being out in the open, and now with your jokes, your sense of humour, I feel a new lease of life. You must improve my English. I used to speak it fluently but I've not used it for years – everyone here just speaks Spanish so I'm not the linguist I was.'

Collingson offered Angie a chicken leg from the grill. 'What other languages do you speak?'

'Well, my poor English, which you must improve with me – and of course my German.'

Collingson prodded another sausage. 'So you speak German?'

'My dear chap, I am German, but I've lived here so many years and spoken Spanish so long that I prefer to think of myself as Argentinian. Even Alfonso here, he looks on me as Argentinian, and Erika, well she was born here, although as you know she has made a trip to Europe recently – to Spain and England. She loved your England, especially the West Country.'

'I'm Irish,' Collingson interjected.

'Of course, I'm sorry – so many troubles between Ireland and England, as if the world hasn't had enough of war. I should know – war has no winners, my friend.'

Collingson smiled. 'We are peaceful enough here, it's really lovely. But your son-in-law, he was involved in the Falklands skirmish?'

The old man was prevented from answering by the telephone ringing and when he had finished the call Collingson remembered the question which he had been meaning to ask the old man. 'I have quite a lot of money which I want to put on deposit. I don't know anything about Argentinian banking or what I might expect in interest. Can you help me?'

'Of course, my dear friend, only too delighted.' The old man was flattered to be asked. 'I'll give you an introduction to my bank manager. We'll drive into town tomorrow – I have to get some veterinary supplies and your lady friend was telling me she wants to go riding, so we can have a real man's day out, have a nice lunch at a place I know which is famous for its steaks. You'll like Gonzales, the bank manager. He has looked after my affairs for years.'

* * *

"What do you mean, tampered with?' Collingson shouted in anger at the senior cashier in the tiny office at the back of the bank.

'I show you, señor – it is the third pack I check, the package should hold one thousand pounds sterling in twenty-pound notes. I count it three times and it has only eight hundred and twenty pounds.' The young man was flustered. 'Carmen here now, you see she has also been counting and her package has eight hundred and ten pounds.' The young man threw up his arms. 'Someone has paid short'.

Gonzales came into the room from his adjacent office on hearing the raised voices and quickly grasped what had happened. He held up a pack.

'See here Mr Donnelly, someone has slit the back of the cellophane and slid out some notes.'

'For Christ's sake count it – count every bloody quid and tell me the score, you can't trust the fucking banks these days.' He realised he had broken into English but his message was clear and the cashiers quickly went to work.

It was nearly an hour later that Collingson was handed a piece of paper in the manager's office and he stared at it in disbelief.

'Twenty-two thousand bloody quid and two hundred and fifty thousand pesetas gone – those bloody banks!'

'Mr Donnelly, you are asking me to believe that three separate banks, banks of considerable reputation, had staff commit the identical crime on the same day. I don't believe it – I do believe that someone has tampered with those packages whilst in your possession, a visitor to your house maybe?'

Collingson's hand was shaking as he took a cigarette from the box offered by the banker. Who? The old man, Erika, Alfonso, maybe one of the ranchers? But he had taken great care to hide the briefcase behind the gas stove in the kitchen so it would have been almost impossible to find, unless...

'Give me a receipt quickly – I want to get home and sort this out.'

An hour later Collingson threw open the lid of his suitcase – it was empty. 'The bitch – the double-crossing thieving bitch!'

'Where did you find the horse – tell me exactly,' Erika shouted across the yard, and the old rancher put down his bottle of beer and came across.

Collingson asked him the same question and the old man pointed to the south. 'Right by the main road, tied to an old dead tree she was – reckon Miss Angie was picked up on the road and taken off somewhere.'

'Today the road train came by on its way to BA,' Erika put in. 'Angie knows about it. When he came with the mail the other day she asked me when he returned, and I saw her talking with the driver. He usually comes by about midday so he will be in BA by now. I'll call the company and ask to speak to Juan.'

Six minutes later a pale-faced Erika came into the room and responded to Collingson's questioning look.

'Juan picked up Angie at the roadside and took her to BA – she gave him money to drop her at the airport so he went around that way.'

Collingson looked up from his chair. 'How did she pay – or should I say how did I pay?'

'I asked that,' Erika replied. 'She paid him cash – sterling. She told Juan she was going to England to look for a job and only had foreign money.'

"The bitch – she stole my bloody cash.' Collingson stared into the courtyard and looked at the sun. The new life hadn't started the way he had planned, not one little bit.

* * *

Unlike most supermarkets in Europe, those in Argentina and indeed most of Latin America have a number of young boys 'licensed' to carry heavy parcels to the customers' cars.

Erika was surprised. The chain of youngsters hanging around the door half an hour before had been spirited away. She paid, and pushed the heavy trolley along the pavement and down the steep slope to the underground car park.

On the second floor the supermarket manager said farewell to the three heavily built men who had occupied his office for the past two hours and turned over the thousand-peso notes. It had been easy money for the simple operation of establishing which day the family Fernandez normally visited the store. He had looked over the record sheets and then instructed his young checkout assistants to press the security button should one of them be presented with a cheque imprinted with that name. Apart from that the three gentlemen had wanted the use of his office and the opportunity to keep watch from his window. It wasn't a lot of effort and the financial reward would make a lot of difference to the type of holiday he and his wife could take that year.

Erika opened the tailgate of the Toyota and started loading the heavy purchases into the spacious luggage area. Not only did she buy weekly for her father, her husband and herself but several of the ranchers prevailed on her good nature to buy things at the large town supermarket which the small shopkeepers did not find economic to stock.

It was so sudden that she didn't have time to appreciate what had happened – she was gasping for breath on the floor of the large car while a dark-haired young man held her on her back with his hand on her throat. She felt the others – how many? – crawl past her and over to the driving seat. Her mind whirled as she tried to hand over her handbag. She knew the form – she had been mugged before and had got off relatively lightly. Or maybe this was rape. The young man's body was on top of her. God, she hoped it wasn't a gang rape.

'You answer questions and you'll come to no harm, I promise you that – we're not interested in you. We want to talk to your father.' The young man let go of her throat. 'Now talk.'

"My father, he lives with us at our, I mean his, ranch,' gasped Erika, still struggling for air and trying in vain to gain some composure.

'Get in the front and drive there and don't try any heroics.' His Spanish was poor and she wondered what he was.

The other two slid out of the front seats and opened the back door. Erika was propelled out through the tailgate and pushed roughly into the driving sear.

'What do you want from my father? He's an old man and he's not rich – what is it you want?' she asked, anger now rising to replace her fear.

'I'm asking questions – you're answering them. Now drive.'

She took a quick look at her assailant, about 25, with tousled jet-black hair, of medium height and slim build. He was of a very strong physique, there was no doubt about that. She could just see the other two in the driving mirror; one seemed much older, early fifties, and she could only see the top of the head of the last one.

She started the car and drove slowly out of the car park. As the big car approached the checkout barrier she felt the cold steel of a revolver at the back of her neck.

'Don't try anything. Here's the right money to pass the guard,' said the older man, who had said nothing until now.

As the Toyota crept through the main street, across the plaza and towards the highway the older man growled, 'How long will it take?'

Again, he wasn't Argentinian either. His Spanish was good but heavily accented.

'Just over an hour,' Erika croaked. Her mind ran on – how could she alert her husband and father back at the hacienda?

The older man grunted. He had expected longer in such a vast country. Anyway, things were moving now. He hated inactivity more than anything – the long waits, the endless watch which made up so much of his life. He was glad to have two youngsters along, fitter than he was, who could benefit from his experience. He was highly regarded by the Mossad back home and had become a national hero over the Eichmann affair years back. Now he had made his trace in just over a week and the two young men had worked well. He was proud of his team and proud of his job. He was a passionate Zionist and was happy to have spent his life in the service of his country and his country's justice. What a pity it was, he thought, that this young and vivacious woman was caught up in events which happened before her time – what was it the Bible said about the sins of the fathers being visited upon the children until the third and fourth generations?

He adjusted the air conditioning, which seemed to be malfunctioning – the inside of the car was unbearably hot. He longed for the end of the journey. Ikki seemed to have the matter well under control in the front and young Ibrahan, strong, small and silent as always, sat beside him – a man who had a keener sense of detection than anyone else he had met.

The car slowed down and turned off left into a narrow dusty track. The driver was obviously highly agitated knowing that the end of the journey was at hand. He pressed the barrel of his Smith and Wesson against Erika's neck. He didn't like treating women like this, but this was no normal assignment.

Collingson was surprised to see three men in the Toyota with Erika. Perhaps they were new hands on the ranch, he surmised. Alfonso had commented that they were short of labour, and that was why he had assisted his host all morning. Hard work for a 71-year-old but it helped to keep fit, providing he didn't overdo it. It also helped him forget the loss of part of his fortune and the way he had been so stupidly conned by a simple Filipina. Anyway, he felt better again after his afternoon siesta and now he was ready for a bath in readiness for the pre-dinner drinks. He took the gold statuette from under a loose floorboard and put it on a bookshelf. It made him feel better in two ways; it was lovely and it was valuable. At least he had saved that from her thieving hands. He ran the water and was getting into the bath when he heard a piercing scream. It came from the main house. It took him under three minutes to dry off and put on trousers and sandals. As he arrived at the house one of the men – a curly-haired and dark individual – appeared on the doorstep and stopped him entering. To his surprise the new arrival spoke in fractured English. 'I want you to take me to your room. I will search it. Tell me who you are.'

'None of your bloody business – what the hell's going on?'

The young man grabbed Collingson by the arm and led him across the yard towards the *casita*. 'This your place? You came from here, didn't you?'

Collingson took a half breath of relief as he remembered the money had been deposited in the bank. He pointed towards the dressing table. 'There's all the cash I have – a few thousand pesos, that's all.'

The young man opened the drawer of the dressing table and withdrew the Star of David necklace. His eyes gleamed, and he looked closer – a small ring. There was nothing else in the drawer except a watch and some money, which he ignored. On a bookshelf his eyes fastened on the gold statuette. 'You're going to do some explaining to my boss, my friend – he's cleaning up in the house but he'll be here in a moment and you'll have to do better than say you won it in a funfair!'

The old man took the key from the desk in the lounge and let himself into his study. Here he could be alone; no one troubled him here, no telephone and no visitors. This was his and his alone, even the flowers he replaced himself twice a week. Rows of books and a shelf of memorabilia, even his school report in a silver frame. The wall had a row of photographs covering his life: babyhood, childhood in Halberstadt, the army and his political career. Everything in the room was his or about him – indeed was him. He sat down at the heavy desk and started to write. Letter-writing was no hardship, he loved to stay in touch with old friends.

The old man had just completed the first line when he heard the car turn in the courtyard. He glanced out and saw Erika. Maybe it was his imagination but she looked worried and sad as she glanced around the yard. Perhaps on the journey she had been thinking of Paco; after all, Madrid was a long way off and the boy wasn't fully recovered. She worried too much. The old man sucked his pen.

The door opened and then was kicked fully open. The old man gasped as three men with revolvers burst in. One of them thrust him into a chair and he sat there for a few seconds, bewildered, as Erika stood by the door. He saw that she had tears in her eyes. The older man of the group held his fist to the old man's face and he saw the ring – silver Star of David. He knew the truth and his heart sank as he knew that this was the moment he had always felt was inevitable. He had done what his Führer demanded and had served his country before, during and after the war, but the newspapers from time to time had carried news of an ever-closing net.

The old man murmured, 'I'll come,' and rose from his chair. He took his military peaked cap from the stand and pulled the swastika from the wall. As he threw them into an open box he bent down to touch them for the last time. Perceptive though the three men were, they did not observe what the old man removed from the cap lining. No words were spoken as the old man made his way to the door and across the terrace towards the car. As he got into the front passenger seat he put his hand to his mouth and closed the door. A few seconds later he was in convulsions, and as the three Israelis watched in amazement the old man's eyes set in a mask of death. The big fish, as they called him back at the Mossad HQ in Tel Aviv, had perished in the net. Martin Bormann, friend and confidant of the Führer, one-time Nazi Party chief and the most wanted man after World War Two, was no more. The *in abstentia* death sentence of Nuremburg had been carried out – by his own hand.

* * *

Ikki Solomon listened intently to the young man. He had spoken for over half an hour but the elderly doctor's concentration showed no sign of flagging.

'Why did you bring it here, not direct to Israel?' he asked.

'You know – or rather perhaps you don't – the security checks on flights to Tel Aviv. They take your baggage to pieces. Questions would be asked and very difficult questions at that. Coming from Argentina was easy – we just wandered through Customs. Few people were stopped and even if we had been, Jacob had a business card on him, "Dealers in Antiques and Fine Arts", with an address in BA and another in Tel Aviv – we would have had problems but nothing we couldn't overcome.'

Dr Solomon smiled. 'It was as well. The owner, one of our people who doesn't live in Israel, will be here in a week or two so we can leave everything until he comes. I have little doubt he will be making a big contribution to the Zionist cause – he wants this back for sentimental reasons, he certainly doesn't need the money.'

'And what do we do with him?' Jacob turned to face the elderly man in the chair. Collingson shook his head without apparent reason.

'It is not our job to be military policemen – to bring deserters to the British courts even if there is a case against him. We set out to achieve an objective: the hand of justice to those who destroyed, who relentlessly persecuted our race, and we have done that. We have, on the way, restored much-loved treasures to one of our brethren. What else do we need – more trouble for no return? He is an old man who has lost his family, his fortune and, if he even had any, his honour. We will let him return to Spain. I have listened to his story – the story of a man from a fine family turned deserter and thief. My sons, justice has been done to him as far as I can see. We have no wish to carry this further.'

The two young men glanced at one another and Jacob nodded. 'You are right. Nothing further can be achieved.'

Dr Solomon took a key from his pocket and opened a small wall safe. Drawing an envelope he passed it to Collingson. 'That is enough to get you home. Your problems then are yours, your life in the future is not of our concern.' He opened the door and Collingson rose and walked out without a word.

The doctor paused for a few minutes, sipping at a glass of water. 'I have a telephone call to make to Italy to our brother who is the rightful owner. He will find all this so hard to believe.'

20

Franz shook the hands of the young couple and wished them every happiness in their lives together. He closed the shop door and smiled at his elderly assistant. 'In a way I was sorry to see that ring go – it really was unusual, but business is business, as they say and it was four thousand marks.'

Herr Blücher looked over his glasses. 'I didn't disturb you, Herr Grieb, but there was a telephone call for you when you were attending to those customers – a young lady from a public telephone. She said you couldn't call her back but she would call again in fifteen minutes. I had difficulty understanding her. My English isn't good, as you know, and she spoke with a foreign accent – kind of broken English.'

Franz Grieb looked out of the window as passers-by took occasional glances at the window display. It was good to be back in Hamburg, good to be running the business once again and to make decisions about advancing it. Herr Blücher had done a good job in keeping things turning over but his buying reflected his age and he had not come to grips with the jewellery requirements of the younger market. Now he was back, Franz was determined to cater for the affluent German youth market and had started to recruit a small panel of young people to express their views on his stock. Soon they would meet regularly at his flat to comment on different designs – market research on a small scale but nevertheless a good guideline.

His daydreams were broken by the ringing of the telephone and he crossed to the desk and picked up the receiver. For a second he greeted the caller enthusiastically then suddenly froze as he remembered her association with Rollason. 'What do you want, Angie?' he asked curtly.

'Franz, I must see you – I have so much to tell you. I've been to Argentina with someone who called at Mr Rollason's house. Oh, Mr Rollason, he's in prison in Malaga and some others are dead.'

'I know,' grunted Franz, who had heard the news from Adrian a few days before. 'And forgive me if I don't shed tears.'

'Oh, Franz, I know you think bad things of me – maybe right too, but I must see you. You remember when we stayed together you told me about you being a jeweller and how you looked for very precious things with your father, and you went to the desert? Well, my friend, Mr Rollason's friend, he had some things which he said belonged to Jewish people in the desert and now I have some of them – could they be the same? I don't know, I don't know how valuable they are. Franz, could we meet?'

Franz's brow furrowed. 'How did you know where to contact me in Hamburg?'

'You gave me your business card in Marbella, remember? I still have it. Yes, I'm in Marbella now. Franz, when can we meet so I can show you this beautiful jewellery?'

Franz paused; he needed time to think. 'Tell you what, Angie. You come up to Hamburg – there's a flight daily I believe from Malaga. You fly up here and come to my shop. If you bring the goods with you and they really are valuable then the fare will cause you no problem.'

Angie laughed. 'Oh, I took plenty money from him too, Franz, no problem about that. I come to see you tomorrow – I show you the lovely things and then maybe we make love again?'

'Maybe.' Franz smiled and returned the receiver to the instrument.

* * *

'How did you get them through Customs?' Franz turned the rings on the cushion as he spoke. 'I've no idea of their market value. This is a highly specialised field and I'm a high-street jeweller, not a specialist in this kind of thing. That they are valuable I have no doubt, extremely valuable. But didn't Customs question you?'

'I just wore them and no one asked me any questions, not when I came into Spain from Argentina or now, when I came to Hamburg.'

Franz whistled softly and picked up the necklace. 'You realise what this is?'

Angie gazed at the star with its ornate edging of diamonds and emeralds. 'It's pretty, isn't it?'

Franz sighed. 'Pretty! – it's exquisite and I bet it's very, very valuable. You shouldn't walk around with something like this. It ought to go into a strong-room safe at least. Any large city has its villains just looking out for young ladies with expensive tastes and possessions to match. Hamburg is no exception.'

'How much can we sell them for?' Angie held out her hand and touched Franz's arm across the desk. 'We can share the money, can't we, and have a good time?'

Franz shook his head. 'There are two things you must realise. First of all these goods are not ours to sell. I know the owner, or rather I know who he is and where he is. The second thing is that if we were involved in an illegal sale these goods would arouse considerable comment and word would reach the police, who would ask some awkward questions. In fact they would persevere until they had satisfactory answers. You could sell them through a fence – someone who buys and sells stolen goods – but the price you get would not reflect the true value. Count me out on that. I have a reputation in this business, a reputation inherited from my father, and I have no intention of spoiling it. Starting to deal with the underworld is easy; stopping is the problem. You deal with ruthless individuals like the one I told you about who broke into my flat. No, I want no part.'

Angie's face fell. 'You mean we have to give it all back, lose it all? No money and no precious things?'

Franz gave a wan smile. 'Yes, it does seem kind of unjust, doesn't it? All those years which father put in, combing the desert when the stuff lay hundreds of miles away, although I often wonder what action he would have taken had he located it. Anyway, all his work, the hassle which Mother and I have gone through recently, all for nothing. It could have been worse, I suppose. At least the stuff has come to light and some lucky sod will –'

'We have all wasted time,' Angie put in.

Franz put his head in his hands. 'We need time to think – let's put everything in the safe. It will be very secure there. We'll have dinner out tonight. You can stay at my apartment, and tomorrow – well, as they said in that great movie, tomorrow is another day.'

Franz chose the wine and Angie leant forward across the table and took his hand. 'Have a guess what it is all worth.'

He pursed his lips. 'As I told you earlier, what a fence would pay you would be peanuts compared with what its insurance value is. But let's assume we submitted it for insurance valuation, what it would cost to replace if replacement was possible. The rarity of the rings, necklaces and the statuettes are difficult for a retail jeweller to assess, but as you ask me I will hazard a guess. In pesetas I would be surprised if they were valued at less than thirty million, but that's what the Americans call a ball park figure. On top of that, the cash you have, shall we say acquired, is around five million when all turned back to pesetas. A total of thirty-five million, maybe more. A handy sum, to put it mildly.'

'Let's share it – sell it cheaply and get lots of lovely money. You could sell it, you're clever at these things, then we could buy a house in the country and live together in comfort.'

Franz laughed. 'I love your innocence – you really don't have much idea of money values, do you? It's a lovely sum of money but it doesn't mean retirement. As far as I'm concerned I'm not putting my reputation and the reputation of my well-established company on the line for that sort of money – don't forget, a fence would only offer you half of that, maybe less. But there is one thing you have overlooked...'

Franz broke off the conversation as the wine waiter poured the wine for him to taste.

'What is it? What have we overlooked?' Angie asked, and Franz raised his eyes slightly to indicate he would not speak while being overheard. As soon as the wine waiter left he continued.

'What you have brought to Hamburg is just a small part, a trifle, of what was originally stolen in Djerba. Remember how I told you in Marbella the story of the Jewish treasure we thought was buried in the desert? It must have been worth millions of marks, hundreds of millions of pesetas,' he explained, seeing the perplexed look. 'This is the tip of the iceberg. That's what we should think about – even if we had a small percentage of that it would be a huge sum of money and it could be legally obtained. Now let's enjoy our dinner and talk about it some other time. It's all too much for me to absorb at present – I'm a small retail jeweller, remember.'

As Franz and Angie approached the apartment they could hear the telephone ringing. Franz fumbled with the keys and rushed to the instrument. He was delighted to hear Adrian's voice and asked him where he was.

'Marbella,' came the short answer. 'We've been down here selling a boat in Gibraltar. Mr Carlucci's boat, in fact. We've been down here for three weeks tarting it up; the police had fouled it up a bit. We've been discovering a lot of things in the meanwhile, not least of all we've found the second Collingson, the author's brother, now called Donnelly. Anyway, Donnelly ran for it, apparently to Argentina, leaving his wife behind, but laden with some very nice goodies, property of the Carluccis. Dr Solomon's people got a trace on the Argentina family with whom he had been staying – the daughter had been over in Europe recently visiting her son in hospital. That was the lead which took the Mossad straight to the ranch in Argentina, just outside Rosario. There they found Collingson or Donnelly, who was holed up with – now you will never guess, so be ready for a big surprise...'

Franz stepped in smartly. 'I can, actually – indeed that person is right here with me.'

There was a long pause. 'I think you heard me wrong,' Adrian said in a hesitant tone. 'I said you'll never guess who was, or had been, there with him.'

'Yes I can. I can do better than guess, I know for a fact. It was Angie – she's here with me now.'

Adrian was obviously having difficulty collecting his thoughts for he croaked, 'I think – well...' There was a long pause. 'I don't understand – not a bloody thing. Anyway, let me go on. Donnelly, sorry, Collingson to you, was living with a woman and her husband who ran the ranch together with her father, an elderly man. Her father was Martin Bormann. Franz, did you hear me?'

Franz stared at the instrument as if he had been pole-axed, and his mouth dried. 'You mean, I, he...' His voice trailed. He looked at Angie. 'We had better go to Marbella again – there's been...' He ran his hands through his hair.

'Did you hear me – who I said?' Adrian's voice came through the instrument and a shiver ran down the back of Franz's neck. 'Are you there?'

'Adrian, I'm coming down to see you. Yes, I heard all right but I don't understand a thing, not a bloody thing. I can't get away for a few days, there's a hell of a lot on here. I'll come as soon as I can. Any news of Ian?'

Adrian hesitated. 'Well, I'll tell you all when you come.'

* * *

Captain Marcus Benjamin listened on the telephone link to the rear cabin. 'Put out a call for a doctor and keep me informed,' he told the purser. 'We have a passenger collapsed in a toilet, looks like a heart attack.' He told the first officer. 'Maybe we will have to touch down. See what the doctor says – if we have one on board, that is.'

In response to the passenger address announcement asking for a doctor, Hannah Rosenbaum raised her arm. The purser took her quickly to the toilet in the rear, where two stewards had removed the door. The patient was laid out on the cabin floor and Dr Rosenbaum opened his shirt and released his clothes. A flicker of surprise passed over her face as the opened shirt revealed a small swastika pendant on a gold chain.

'He has had a very severe heart attack – tell the captain that we must get him to a hospital as soon as possible and that we will need a doctor in the ambulance which meets the plane. It really is an emergency.'

Captain Benjamin heard the news and told the purser to inform the passengers that they would be making a short stop in Munich due to the illness of a passenger. 'With luck we will be on the ground for under an hour – I'll leave the announcement to you. I have to get clearance for landing.'

The purser made the announcement and returned to the doctor and the patient. He opened the jacket which had been folded beside the sick man and took out the passport. Robert Whiteman, aged 77. 'I guess he was travelling alone or someone would have come forward,' he said softly to himself. He walked back to the vacant seat. Two young men sat in the row where Whiteman had been sitting. In answer to Purser Cohen's question they said that they had just met Mr Whiteman on the plane. It crossed Cohen's mind that they were both more concerned than he would have thought – but that might be his imagination. He picked up the intercom to announce the landing at Munich and to request passengers to extinguish cigarettes and fasten seat belts.

It took little time for a crane loader to lower the stretcher to the waiting ambulance. As the ambulance pulled away from the aircraft Roberto Weissman died – five miles from the site of the Dachau Concentration Camp where he had engineered the deaths of thousands of inmates of B-Unit.

Captain Benjamin didn't leave the aircraft – there was no need, for all formalities could be done by the purser and he wanted an early clearance for take-off from the control tower.

He had another reason. He had no desire to set foot on the ground of the city, even the airport, where his parents had been arrested and taken to Dachau, never to return. It was all a long time ago and he had been a child at the time, taken by a gentile friend of his father. Ironically enough, the crematoria which took so many of his people had been used to dispose of the bodies of those monsters executed after Nuremberg. It was a long time, he mused – better to forget sad times. After all, life had been kind to him in the long run and if...

His thoughts were interrupted by the purser with papers for him to sign relating to the transfer of a passenger to hospital. He scanned through the form – passenger's name, Whiteman, Robert, British passport number 772176A, next of kin unknown, nothing of particular note.

'We have just been told that he died in the ambulance,' Purser Cohen commented. 'Poor sod – probably going on the holiday he has looked forward to for some time. Strange man, though.'

'Why's that?' Captain Benjamin looked up.

'Well, he had his flight ticket and boarding pass on him but he had another ticket also for today – to Buenos Aires. How come he is flying to Tel Aviv on one ticket and yet he has another ticket to fly the other direction to BA? Doesn't make sense.'

Captain Benjamin wrinkled his brow. 'Well, we're not here to sort those problems out, but I agree it's strange. Anything else?'

'Yes,' Purser Cohen replied, 'there was something decidedly strange – when the doctor opened his shirt he had a swastika on a gold chain around his neck.'

'Excuse me, captain, we have clearance to start engines,' the first officer chipped in.

Fifteen minutes later the big jet broke through the cloud and Captain Benjamin announced on the passenger address system that they hoped to catch up some of the lost time because of a tailwind. He switched off and turned to the first officer. 'It is strange what Cohen said – I wonder who that passenger was and what he was up to?'

* * *

Adrian wanted to discuss with Franz all the recent developments and asked Ella if he could use her telephone.

'Of course,' she replied as she worked away at the dinner. 'The meal will be a bit late tonight. Frankly, I'm not used to cooking for so many. Betty and Lorna have been a great help but I'm used to having just myself to look after.'

Adrian hesitated. 'Look it's going to be a long conversation in view of all that's happened and I should like to pay for the call. However, I have a better idea. How does the idea of a shared telephone account appeal to you?'

Ella stopped chopping. 'What ever do you mean? You cannot...'

'What I'm suggesting in possibly the most novel way yet invented is whether you would share your life with me?'

Ella laughed. 'I have just told you I'm used to being on my own – but I'm sure I'll adjust.'

As she put her arms around his neck and kissed him he gently pushed her away. 'Just put the knife down, will you? You make me nervous. And then I'll inform your new stepdaughter in the lounge.'

An hour later, Ella made the telephone call to Franz, who was delighted to hear from his mother.

'Your voice says all is well,' he remarked.

'Franz, Adrian has asked me to marry him,' Ella blurted out, and Adrian listened to the excited gabble of voices which showed the news had been well received. Ella passed the telephone across to Adrian. 'He wants to congratulate you himself,' she beamed.

'Hi, son!' Adrian exclaimed, and Franz laughed out loud.

'I can never really think of you as my stepfather after all our experiences in this strange affair – I'm so glad something good came out of it all. Maybe we are all on the road to finding Ian now.'

'Well, it's strange to mix news on a call like this.' Adrian's voice became serious. 'But I think we have all accepted the worst for some time now. The fact is that Ian died at Ronda some time back and his death wasn't natural nor was it an accident.'

Franz broke in. 'If you have known this before, why the hell didn't you call and tell me?'

Adrian's throat dried. 'Franz, I owe you an apology but, for Heaven's sake, things have really moved along so fast. I hope you can come down soon – there really is a lot, I mean a lot, of ground to cover. Why not come down to Malaga tomorrow so we can exchange news, views, congratulations and, I regret, condolences.'

* * *

Ella and Adrian greeted Raoul Carlucci at Malaga airport and assisted him with his luggage to the car park. 'You are no light traveller,' Adrian said with a laugh.

'That's to build your appetite,' Raoul retorted. 'I'll tell you what, drive me to a really Spanish restaurant away from the tourist trail, which does nothing for me. Find a real character place and I'll stand you lunch.'

Four kilometres past the airport Adrian swung off the highway and onto a small secondary road. Twenty minutes later they were running into the quaint market town of Alhaurin el Grande. 'The name, going back to Moorish times, means Garden of Allah,' explained Ella. 'When we first visited it not many years back the streets were packed with donkeys. Progress hasn't spoilt Alhaurin's charm; the narrow streets with whitewashed houses, the markets … it retains its character. Not many tourists come here and they miss such a lot,'

As they enjoyed a delicious lunch Adrian told Raoul about the engagement.

'I suspected he was a man who made good decisions when I asked him to join my company,' Raoul smiled. 'Now I know he's a man of good judgement. I'm so happy for both of you – so happy.'

As they walked up the steps Raoul took Adrian aside. 'And how is your lovely daughter taking the sad news about her husband?'

Adrian shook his head. 'She's stunned. She isn't distressed because I think she suspected something like this all along and she also faced the fact that even if Ian had been found alive he would be living on borrowed time. I feel she is upset because when he knew the future, Ian did everything he could to ease life for her, tearing around Europe and North Africa on a wild-goose chase. The pieces only started to come together after his violent death. That's the other thing which hit her badly, that he was actually murdered – it's strange how people react to that thought, because if you're dead you're dead, so is the cause important? She doesn't see it like that. Sam's father was actually pushed over a cliff; that's a dramatic end. She's worried too about her financial future and how it will affect Sam.'

'Adrian, you're not just a friend but a senior member of the company now. You are also my confidant, as, indeed, Bernard has been for many, many years. I would like to meet everyone involved today – I understood you have been kind enough to allow your house to be the rallying point, Ella. Then I would like the three of us, Bernard, you and me, to drive over to the gardens of the Hotel Don Carlos. It's not far away and it's peaceful there. I have some ideas and I need your input.'

* * *

One of the quietest places in southern Spain is the remote mountain retreat of El Refugio de Juanar. So tranquil is this small but lovely hotel that during the sixties Charles de Gaulle stayed there to write his memoirs.

Ella had suggested it when Raoul Carlucci said he would like 'an informal hotel away from it all, where we can all talk undisturbed'.

'I commend your choice, Ella,' Raoul said, as he walked from the bar onto the broad terrace overlooking the pine forest and in the shadow of towering mountain peaks. 'It really is lovely here. Who would guess that we are only half an hour's drive from the bustle of Marbella. This really is my kind of place.'

'Raoul, let me ask you a direct question,' Ella said. 'Why have you brought us all here? You have been so mysterious since you arrived – you took Adrian and Bernard off to the Hotel Don Carlos the other afternoon. Now you have booked us all in here. It's sweet of you but I must confess...' She waved her hand. 'Why is Pepe, Collingson's gardener, here?'

'You are puzzled.' Raoul replied and Ella nodded. 'I'll tell you after dinner.'

Raoul went on. 'Reluctantly I find myself centre stage in this drama – I was going to say "*tragedia*" but there has been an element of happiness in it all – like Adrian and you. By the way, I didn't ask, but I did fix you a double room. I hope I didn't offend.'

Ella smiled. 'We're grown up and both more than a little, shall we say, experienced.'

'You know, we Italians love romance. We are born lovers, I feel – perhaps the world's greatest, who knows?'

'I thought the French had already staked a claim!' Ella grinned.

Raoul grimaced. 'Anyway, I find myself, Raoul Carlucci, playing a role I do not like – a person to hold...' He sought a word.

'You are the pivot, the linkman, as they say in TV jargon,' Bernard put in.

Raoul nodded. 'Yes, I see – linkman. That's a nice English word. But I don't welcome the part, which came my way by accident. All that has happened, good, bad, indifferent, came as a result of my family treasures vanishing all those years ago.'

The conversation came to a halt as Pepe, Angie and Franz came onto the terrace.

Raoul suggested they took tea. 'I was going to say a very English thing to do, but Ella and Franz are German, Angie's Filipina, Pepe's Spanish and I'm Italian!'

'Don't forget I'm half English,' Pepe chipped in.

'And don't forget, I don't necessarily believe you.' Raoul's face broke into a broad smile. As Pepe started to speak Raoul went on. 'But there is so much ground to cover, so many i's left un-dotted and t's left un-crossed – an English expression

I like, Bernard taught it to me. No, we have much to cover and as the linkman I must, I suppose, pull all the facts together.' However, let us wait until everyone is present and then decide our future moves. May I suggest we meet up here in the bar at six? We can talk over dinner.'

Raoul took Angie by the hand. 'I have hardly had time to talk to you or to Franz. He was kept away from me in London, I guess because he's German and I'm Jewish. Franz my boy, I know the truth, I worked it out from what Adrian and Bernard told me. It was your father who organised the raid on my family home in Djerba all those years ago. But do not forget that he was acting under orders. I try to remember that. What I do know is that some – a little, of the original treasures are now back with me, thanks to the two of you. No, the real damage to my family was done by a Major Weissman. The North Africa campaign has been called a "gentleman's war". Your famous Field Marshal Rommel, Franz, saw to it. He was no bullying Nazi thug, he played the rules of war. Unhappily there are those who kill for the love of it, torture and torment, rob and rape, enjoy themselves at the expense of other people. Weissman was the one who organised the execution of my family – he was the one who murdered thousands of my fellow Jews at the B-Unit of Dachau – Solly, Dr Solomon, was there but he survived. Now Solly tells me Weissman is dead and I'm glad. Not just Weismann either, but a much bigger fish. All this has happened because of the action of everyone here. But there is more to be done on all sides. Tonight we have dinner here but I have invited yet one more guest.' He turned to Betty. 'Have you seen the view from the Mirador?'

Betty shook her head. 'I'd love to, but everyone wants to go there and in fact the road is closed for cars at the moment. Just in case you haven't noticed, I'm what they call "great with child".' She laughed. 'Makes a long uphill stroll a bit tough going.'

'I'll drive you there,' Raoul replied. 'I'm sure I am capable of cutting a tape to open the road, and furthermore I'm only too pleased to put a few thousand pesetas the way of anyone who objects – we Jews have a way of getting our way, so to speak. Come on, I've a hire car outside. You'll love the view and I want to talk to you anyway.'

A few minutes later Raoul slit the plastic band which crossed the unsurfaced road and the Opel went slowly along towards the well-known viewpoint or Mirador, as it is called locally. The two left the car and walked the last two hundred metres to the platform on the mountainside. Below, Marbella stretched out along the coast. Raoul pointed.

'That's San Pedro and further on you can see Estepona. The busy coast, sunbathing, noise and bustle. Hard to believe that life is so different up here; just a few kilometres and it's a totally different world. Life's like that, I suppose, one minute all is tranquil, total peace. Just around the corner, chaos reigns. I guess you have experienced some very dramatic changes yourself over the past few weeks. From what I am told you were working, until fairly recently, in the cosseted atmosphere of Harrods. Then off on a trip to Tunisia, where you saw your partner and boyfriend in company with Ian, the ex-boyfriend who had disappeared. That must have shaken you. Then you had the trauma of the phone call telling you your boyfriend was in your cottage with another woman. But I suppose the bombshell must have been your accidental discovery of the Nazi meeting at Cookham. You were alarmed but I guess you didn't realise the extreme danger you were in – not until Adrian put you right. Then you heard the background to the Nazi movement from Solly, Dr Solomon. Now after hiding in London here you are down in southern Spain, looking out over Marbella with an old Jew like me.' Raoul smiled as he ran his hands through his hair. 'Life is strange, don't you think, so volatile, so changeable and in many ways unfair – certainly unpredictable.'

'Father used to say that,' Betty chipped in. 'He really thought his last job was a winner, no fail, but he didn't see the tripwire, he said. You probably know he's in Dartmoor – the prison,' she added as she saw Raoul's face.

Raoul smiled gently. 'Yes, I do know, but one day he will be free again and may well go straight.'

It was Betty's turn to smile. 'Who knows? All I know right now is that in a very short time I'm going to give birth, and how I'm going to keep him or her I haven't any idea. Jobs aren't plentiful, whatever governments say about help for working mothers. There's always a chance I may get back with Roland, I suppose. After all, it was my hasty move without checking the facts which led to the bust-up. When Sara, my neighbour down in Devon, told me that she had been mistaken and that the girl in the cottage was Roland's cousin from Argentina, I could have kicked myself – so stupid to jump to conclusions.'

'We all do it,' Raoul interjected. 'It's human, I suppose.'

'But then there's the matter of those Nazis – I couldn't get back with him if he is one of those.'

'He isn't.' Raoul lit a cigarette, and Betty pointed to a sign warning of forest fire. 'I'll be careful, we've had enough forest fires lit, metaphorically speaking. Metaphorically – that's my new English word, sounds so impressive and strong. Yes, Roland got himself entangled in such a fire, lit by his father. Roland's father was one of the Nazi plants – got involved in Nazism in the late thirties when he was a young Member of Parliament. The world was in a mess and he saw how Hitler had pulled Germany together from 1933. Don't forget, when Hitler took over, the country was in a shambles, largely as a result of being squeezed beyond all reason by the victors of the First World War – although the American President Wilson, who engineered the Armistice, decreed there should be no victors. Oh no, the French and British forced Germany into abject poverty, with inflation running so high that a German's life savings could only buy a loaf of bread. That's no exaggeration. We Jews made capital of the situation and my father was no exception. We became easy targets for hate and Hitler needed an object for hate, someone to blame, and the Jews were obvious. Strange thing, hate; it binds people together more strongly than love. Germany in crisis needed to bind together. It had its leader, it had its target and Hitler achieved miracles. I lost my family because of the Nazis so I have a cautious attitude towards the Germans, although the

French also persecuted our race dramatically during the war. Having said all that, a new generation is here. Look at Franz – a nice young fellow who has grown up in a different world, different standards, new outlooks. It was different in the thirties. It is hardly surprising that many people, not just Germans, admired one man, the Führer Adolf Hitler who in six years brought a country from chaos to a situation where it could challenge the world – be feared by the world.

'Roland's father was one such admirer. On a visit to Germany he witnessed the changes, and he married a German woman. He secretly aligned himself with the Third Reich and, had Germany invaded Britain, he would have held high office in the Nazi party there.' Raoul Carlucci paused and sat on the wall of the viewpoint looking at the mountain. 'Yes, very high office indeed, for as an MP he had a position in society. But that is not all. He was well connected. We mentioned Martin Bormann when we discussed your father's neighbour.'

Betty nodded. 'Yes. I've learned so much more in the past few days, listening to Adrian and to Dr Solomon. Even Franz seemed prepared to talk, although he is a bit embarrassed. He was one of Hitler's key figures, wasn't he? That's what you said at Lorna's house.'

'Even more than that. Bormann was Hitler's right-hand man, a Reichsleiter, Secretary of the Nazi party, described as the "Brown Shadow." He was always with the Führer. Only Bormann was allowed to sign a document "By order of the Führer". He was very powerful and a possible new Führer. The reason that Roland's father was such a key figure is that his wife's sister was married to Bormann. Roland's Argentinian cousin who caused you so much concern was none other than Martin Bormann's daughter. Bormann is now dead and I'll tell you about that, or Solly will, some other time, but you gave the Israeli security force, the Mossad, the clue they sought for so long. You see, Roland's father was related to Bormann – they were brothers-in-law. There's no blood relationship with Roland. No doubt Bormann grew curious about how his ex-brother-in-law was getting on in

England, so had his daughter visit him. They had been close friends and dedicated members of the party. They had stayed in touch by letter and Davies senior had visited Argentina, presumably, and Bormann had changed his name and identity. He was also no doubt curious to know how the party was recruiting, for all the original members were old men. Next door to Mr Davies senior lived one of the most evil of men, the section leader of a block in Dachau and one of Bormann's closest friends – Weissman. You knew him slightly, you told us.'

Betty nodded. 'He was the one shouting at the meeting – I could hardly recognise him in that uniform.'

'They couldn't believe in the collapse of the Third Reich. It was their whole lives, a fanatical commitment which they could never give up. When Bormann disappeared to the Alps after the surrender, his task was to set up the foundations of the Fourth Reich. He believed Britain and France would unite with Germany against what they saw as the true enemy – the Soviet Union. None of these men gave up the cause and they recruited young men into the system, usually relations.'

'Including Roland,' Betty said softly.

'Not really. Son Roland only became useful when he became a highly skilled and qualified engineer. They needed funds and Weissman knew, or thought he knew, where an immense treasure trove was buried. His friend and neighbour's son had the knowledge and the equipment to unearth it. Here was the chance to pump considerable wealth into the movement to develop the Fourth Reich – the neo-Nazis. Roland was the professional seeker of goods which, by quirk of circumstance, belonged to my family. That's what brought us all together.

'Believe me, Roland isn't an *imbrolione*, as we say in Italy. Indeed, all he was doing was helping a group of old men, long gone to seed through lack of work and excess of booze – helping them to relive memories and make a future, however sketchy.

'Betty, when you weigh up Roland remember one thing – he is the father of your child and could bring up the child properly. Money is important, whatever the idealists say. As a Jew I believe in a stable background for a child. I don't try to advise you, certainly not to persuade you, because in the long run you must make your own decision. Think it over. Now let's drive back. I think you will find this evening interesting.'

21

Betty gasped. Now she understood. But why hadn't Raoul told her? Thoughts ran through her mind at breakneck speed. The man in the car park hadn't seen her, he was too busy unloading his car. Betty walked back into the coppice which adjoined the hotel.

So Roland had been invited. Why? And why hadn't Raoul mentioned it when he was talking at the Mirador less than an hour ago? He had mentioned Roland, of course he had. He had spent some time explaining that Roland was no criminal – even used an Italian word to explain it. She bit her lip as she remembered how hasty she had been in her condemnation of Roland, assuming the girl in the cottage was a – well, what did it matter now? She had learned the truth from Sara, who had called her – ashamed at her hasty conclusion. If there had been a telephone in the cottage Roland might have rung to tell her. Betty found herself assuming the blame for the break.

Roland had gone into the hotel and the reception looked free, so Betty crossed the small car park and entered the front door. Raoul stood by the reception desk. 'I know what you think.' He spoke softly. 'I'm a scheming, two-faced something-or-other. Not really. At the Mirador I told you what I felt was the degree of Roland Davies' involvement. I put the facts to you but I don't interfere. I never advise unless asked and then I only do so with caution. I've invited Roland here because I need him. Whether you two make up the relationship is up to you. No one can run your lives for you.'

'You may say that but you did advise me – you feel I should go back to him because of "junior" here.'

'Sorry, Betty, not true – I just said consider the baby and consider the point that Roland can provide for you both.'

Betty gave Raoul a wide smile. 'You're a strange man – I really don't know what to make of you.'

* * *

'You'll get used to it, Adrian.' Bernard Waterman sipped his drink as he spoke. 'Raoul's like this, he has a flamboyant style – the Rolls, the Claridges suite – and now he has booked the whole bloody hotel, although it is small, for this get-together. Raoul didn't want other people around, just those who have been involved in the saga of the jewels, as he puts it so casually.'

'Davies, the father of Betty's baby, has arrived. I saw him on the stairs,' Adrian replied. 'That I find decidedly spooky – he's tied up with those Nazi thugs and their cavorting around in Cookham. I would have thought that, as a Jew, the last person Raoul wants here is one of them.'

'Now you are working for him, you will have to come to grips with the fact that you will never completely understand him.' Bernard indicated to the barman that he would like another drink. 'He is shrewd, he is canny and indeed ruthless, for he built a considerable fortune starting with very little after the family fortunes dwindled. In spite of everything, he is an immensely compassionate man, very sentimental and basically very kind. I say that with the experience of years, yet I'm always surprised at some of the things he says and does.' Bernard stopped abruptly as Raoul entered the bar.

'Let's have dinner, shall we?' he said. 'I think we are all here except Betty and Roland. I believe they have a few things to discuss alone. They will be joining us.'

When dinner was cleared Bernard Waterman stood up.

'I know I've been pensioned off and my job taken over by my friend Adrian here, but Raoul has asked me to divulge how he sees the future. As I've been so involved in the past – ever since the incident of 1942, indeed – he thought it right that I should make my last job the revelation of where we go from here. It's a theatrical touch and typical of Raoul.' He laughed as he spoke. 'The straight truth is that less than fifty miles from the hotel, on the seabed, lies a considerable cache of valuable goods, measurable in millions rather than thousands of pounds. Everyone in this room has been instrumental in the location of that cache. Along the route over the years some of us have suffered loss, some have achieved happiness. Lorna has lost her husband, Adrian and Ella have found one another. In some way we have all had traumatic experiences because of those valuables. If I was a superstitious man I would say they had a curse on them but then I suppose it would be a strange curse which brought some people happiness. No, I think we just regard it all as the many-faceted sequel to a catastrophe which took place in Djerba during the war years. To some it has brought further catastrophe, to others happiness and to others troubles which have been resolved.' He looked at Roland and Betty, who sat next to one another, her hand on his.

'The central pivot, as he calls himself, is Raoul. His was the original loss but he does not want the goods returned because of their financial value – far from it. He's a rich man, and all he wants is the return of any items of sentimental value. To an extent, Angie has already obliged, albeit in a somewhat unconventional manner. The fact that the goods led indirectly to the identification and death of two of the most evil men who ever walked the earth is enough. All of us would like to be a bit better off than we are, and I say that with feeling. Roland is prepared to finance the recovery of the goods and to pay our expenses and living costs until we do. Once the goods are returned to the family they will be assessed by a firm of professional valuers. Raoul will purchase the goods back, less the expenses involved in the search, and I'm sure the tax people will want their share. The fund that creates will be split equally between everyone in this room. Obviously I cannot say how much that will be, for it depends on how much is recovered and how much the goods are worth at current prices. I should at this stage tell you that we have had a professional valuer flown out from London and the assessment he has put on the goods which Angie brought back from Argentina greatly exceeds what Raoul anticipated. If we could prove that they had been under the same roof as Martin Bormann they would indeed be worth more, I guess. Still, Angie may be able to sell that story – who knows?

'One thing I do know. This is a situation with no losers. If nothing is found, the present pile from Argentina is split and all expenses and living costs will be found for you. You will have a windfall but nothing dramatic. If we find the main bulk of the goods, then I for one will make Raoul an offer for his car. I've been its groom long enough. Roland tells me that in his technical opinion the goods could be located using modern-day sophisticated sonic equipment. To raise them we will need marine engineering experience, and in that we have to rely on Adrian, who has a long and successful track record in the field. Oh yes, between us we make up quite a team. You may think that covering the Mediterranean area miles and miles east of Gibraltar is like looking for a needle in a haystack. Not so. We have someone present who knows far more than he pretends.'

Bernard swilled the brandy around the balloon. 'Pepe, let me get straight to the point. You have been, as they say, economical with the truth with us. Half English, half Spanish – I don't believe it. You're as British as they come. We know your father was with Collingson – or Donnelly as he is now known – when the aircraft came down. Collingson made his way by dinghy to the shore. Your father was washed up, possibly wearing a life jacket, on the coast. Maybe the Spanish coast, maybe Gibraltar, who knows? Collingson had the goodies and almost certainly your father was unaware of their existence.

'When the war ended, some time after probably, they ran into one another. You told us your father was working for a marine company in Gibraltar. It's a tiny place. Not surprisingly, they bumped into one another if Collingson was living locally and conducting his search from Gib – the search for the aircraft from which they had both had a lucky escape. Collingson must have been worried. He was supposed to be dead – he was posted as "missing presumed dead". Yet here was someone who recognised him. Would your father put him away? But he had one point in his favour: he was very well off – rich, in fact. He could square your father one way or another. Your father, I'm sure, had no idea how Collingson came by his fortune. He almost certainly did not know the aircraft was carrying such valuable cargo and that Collingson had some valuables ready to hand. Why should he? The pilot, Wing Commander Collingson, had brought a tin trunk of secret papers aboard.

'How Collingson prevented your father from revealing his desertion we do not know. Maybe he made some financial arrangement. More likely your father regarded it as a sin of a long way back, best forgotten. Anyway, Collingson offered your father a slice of his self-made paradise, a job and a house in the sun. No doubt they went searching for the aircraft together. Why not? Two old comrades in arms seeking out a piece of their personal history, the wreck of their lost aircraft. One of them had the money to finance the venture. Your father may have seen it as a rich man's crazy whim. I doubt whether your father even had the faintest idea of what lay in the wreck or he would have involved you, a young fit man who could have played a vital role. Or maybe he kept you out because he realised the activity could be illegal.

'Collingson spent some time away from the house, either on his yacht at Puerto Banus or in Gibraltar on the search. After your father's death things must have slowed up a bit; maybe by then Collingson saw that the search was an impossible mission, especially alone. More and more of his time was spent in Puerto Banus. The guide in Gib told us he had abandoned the efforts off Gibraltar.

'Meanwhile you stayed at the *finca* doing the garden. With Collingson away, an intimate relationship developed between you and Collingson's wife – Pilar.'

Pepe stirred uncomfortably. 'I don't see what that has to do with anyone else – it has nothing to do with why we are here.'

'Forgive me, but it has,' Bernard went on. 'Adrian and I suspected some relationship when we came back to the villa after spending the night in Ronda. You were in a dressing gown on the terrace – unusual for a gardener. Pilar and you are of a similar age and we drew conclusions. I drew another conclusion; that Pilar, who knew of her husband's past, confided in you in a rash moment. You would obviously realise that was the reason why your father had sailed off Gib with your employer, to discover the aircraft.

'Now there enters a new player in this drama, one Ian Lacey. You made a big mistake at our first meeting, Pepe, when you said he wanted to be thought of as English even though he was Spanish, so you both spoke English. You spent a few hours together, surely you exchanged a few Spanish phrases, surely you were surprised at his very English accent? When he talked of Spanish place names, for example, he would have pronounced them in an English way. Ian didn't speak more than a few phrases of Spanish, Lorna tells me.

'When you were talking about Ian in the bar that day Adrian and I met you, you didn't, of course, know that we knew him. When you realised that from what we told you, you dropped your guard and reacted to the photo by recognising Ian. You knew bloody well he was English, didn't you?'

Pepe shuffled uncomfortably and muttered.

Bernard continued. 'Ian, I guess, was acutely depressed and talked to you. Two English chaps of similar age in a lonely house in the Andulucian mountains. Plenty to talk about. Ian told you of his condition and about his mission and it clicked. The search off Gib which Pilar had told you about, the one which had engaged your late father and your employer – Ian was talking of the same thing. Ian had read about the cache in the book. Now when Ian told you he had been to Switzerland to try to meet the writer, an English general called Collingson, you guessed that the general who came to the house in Ronda to visit his "cousin" – in reality his brother – was one and the same as the general who wrote the book. Ian's story of how he was shown a valuable necklace by the housekeeper at the general's house, one left to her in his will, that must have interested you greatly. There cannot be many retired English generals living in Switzerland; even fewer in the Geneva area.

'You agreed to work together to recover the goods, and you had the knowledge of the approximate position. Furthermore, Ian had a detection expert on hand.' Bernard waved his hand towards Roland. 'And Ian was prepared to take risks with his life for he was nearing the end of it.

'The two of you hatched a plan but it was thwarted. Ian pressed Collingson for money, I guess. You heard them arguing. Collingson probably suspected blackmail. Ian was desperate to finance the venture quickly. Whatever the circumstances, Ian was better out of the way, so he had a fatal accident. You must have been scared when you heard the news. Collingson made it clear that you must stick to the story of Ian Lacey being Spanish, or else. After all, he had no identity on him – conveniently. If you went to the police you couldn't prove anything, and you had a lot to lose – certainly your job, probably your life. You were in a spot.'

Bernard leaned across and filled his glass from the brandy decanter.

'Shortly after that Adrian and I showed up. In the garden you were ready, especially as Collingson told you to speak Spanish. I could pick that up even though I have only a smattering of the language. That evening in the *venta* we knew something was afoot. The carton of cigarettes which Ian smoked, the statuette in the hall, the menorah and especially the book with writing in the margin, the very book which Ian had bought. So in the *venta* we surprised you and we caught you off your guard. You spoke English and you also said too much, never dreaming of the connection between Adrian here and Ian. Perhaps you were so worried that you subconsciously gave this information, something for us to work on without actually spilling the beans – who knows? You were caught off your guard even more the next day when we saw you at the villa with Mrs Donnelly. You thought we would be later.'

Bernard paused and Pepe spoke softly. 'I had no part in the killing of Ian Lacey, none at all. Nor did Pilar; she was very upset when she heard about the – well – accident.'

'But you both knew about his nationality and you suspected – indeed were convinced – of foul play, yet you withheld information from the police,' Adrian slipped in.

Pepe nodded. His eyes went to the floor, avoiding Lorna's gaze. Tears were in her eyes. The details of her husband's end were proving too much.

Adrian took up the conversation. 'I guess we can overlook that. Maybe Collingson will tell all to the Guardia Civil, maybe not. That's a risk you take. But when Collingson vanished after Bernard and I paid our visit, the coast was clear. You could live in style with Pilar and you were free to search for the treasure without Collingson's knowledge. Fate had played right into your hands. The overwhelming snag was that you were virtually single-handed in a search which would certainly need several people if it was to have any chance of success. Collingson had abandoned it as a hopeless venture. You are not a skilled sailor, I assume, and you didn't have the funds to get the venture under way. Pilar could help a bit. But who could you trust as a partner? Now I confess I am baffled. The story ends as far as we are concerned, but one thing I am sure, you didn't just pack it in. Pepe, for a change, tell us the truth.'

Pepe rose from the sofa. 'Just excuse me a minute. I want to visit the toilet.'

No one spoke for a while and then Raoul broke the silence. 'I think Pepe may be a trump card – he needs to get over his surprise. I have an idea he will telephone Pilar, maybe someone else, to get approval. All I hope is he isn't told to say nothing more. Lorna, I know you are very upset, angry with Pepe, but he couldn't have saved Ian.'

'But he could have cut short the search, he could have brought justice to Ian's killer.' Lorna fought back the tears.

Pepe came back and stood by the window. 'OK, you obviously know so much there is no point in hiding anything. My name is Philip Baker and my father was Flight Sergeant William Baker. You are correct, he knew nothing of the stuff on the aircraft. He thought that Mr Donnelly – Collingson – had a bee in his bonnet about finding Alpha Papa, the aircraft from which they both escaped.

'I did not find out the truth from Pilar until after Dad's death – and it was only when Ian came and started talking that I pieced all the facts together. It seemed like a golden opportunity – literally golden. Then Ian was killed and with Collingson around there was little I could do. He had friends in Gib. One word that I was on the search and ... well, he had killed once and could do so again, I believed. He was too old by now to search and anyway he had given up the task as hopeless. But he didn't want anyone else to even have a remote chance. Newly developed technology was increasing the chance of success but it had come in too late for him. He was at the end of his life.

'Then you and Adrian arrived and he disappeared. There had to be a connection – there just had to be. He must have thought you were on to the find; certainly you knew his identity. You told me, in the *venta* the night before, all you knew about the search and Ian's death. So now the coast was clear and I could start prospecting but, as you say, I needed help. Pilar said she would provide some money. With her husband walking out on her she was angry. You know what they say about a woman scorned. She wanted to succeed where he had failed.

'Yes, indeed, I needed help. A strong man, an outstanding diver, an experienced sailor. Not just a hired hand. Someone who would not talk, but wanted a slice of the action. My search would differ substantially from that which you propose to conduct. If I read you correctly you plan to keep on the right side of the law. Not me. I planned to grab all I could, declare nothing and sell it to the highest bidder. Ian had talked to Henry Southon, his partner, but I hadn't any idea how to contact him. There was the detection engineer Ian had mentioned, Davey or Davis or something like that. I played with the idea of going to London and looking for him. But I did not know these people. They might be untrustworthy – they might want to work legally. No, it didn't make sense. Then suddenly I remembered the young medical student who was here in the summer. We had worked on the garden, building a rockery and fish pond. Mr Donnelly – Collingson – liked him a lot. I guess he wanted to earn money, not to depend on his family. His parents lived in Argentina on a ranch owned by his grandfather. He was fun and I liked him. When he left, Mr Collingson told me he had had a motorcycle accident and was in hospital. Mr Collingson was so upset he flew up to Madrid to see him, and met his parents, who had come over from Argentina.

'Before Paco left here he gave me his telephone number in Madrid. I reckoned he would be out of hospital so I called him. I mentioned the search that Mr Collingson and Father had done, just briefly, then I went on to tell him that Mr Collingson – of course I said Donnelly – had disappeared. You will never guess what he said. He knew – and he knew where he was: with his parents in Argentina. His parents had called him and said that he and a Filipina girl had turned up.'

Pepe stopped talking and looked at Angie. 'That was me,' she said, smiling.

'I know that now. But, Christ Almighty, I was stunned. What the hell was he doing there? I was so confused I forgot to mention Paco's possible involvement, the search of the sea bottom, it just went out of my mind. Now I've spoken with Angie everything is clearer, but at the time...' Pepe sat down abruptly.

'I decided not to tell Pilar until I knew more, and there was only one way I could make sense out of the situation. I telephoned Paco in Madrid again. Yes, he was interested in the diving side of the project; it would keep him busy in the vacation and the swimming would improve his leg. I told him only that we would be recovering valuables from an old aircraft. I also told him to say nothing. If I had summed him up correctly he would keep his mouth shut, but if he talked, so what? He knew so little that anyone hearing the story would dismiss it as a wild fantasy. I asked about Mr Donnelly in Argentina but he hadn't heard from his parents again so had nothing more to add. I asked him where his parents lived in Argentina as I wanted to speak to Mr Donnelly. After a bit of chatting he gave me the number.

'Late that evening, it would be morning in Argentina, I called the number he had given me. A woman's voice answered. She had a strong accent and confirmed she was Paco's mother, Erika. I told her my name and said I would like to speak to Mr Donnelly. She became very agitated, angry even. She asked me why I wanted to speak with him and I told her I was the gardener and had a problem. As I spoke she burst into tears and then a man's voice took over. He was very aggressive, asked me what I wanted to talk about. Frankly I was stumped, couldn't readily think of a reason. Then the voice said, "He's gone, caused enough trouble here", or something like that, and rang off.

'I couldn't think of a reason for the hostile attitude, but what I feared was that Mr Donnelly – Collingson – might return back home – he would be none too pleased to find that I had, well, I had really moved in with Pilar. He would also find the telephone call to Argentina on his bill and would start being very awkward, to put it mildly. Remember, I knew that he could kill to protect himself.

'I did nothing for a couple of days then I called Paco in Madrid to tell him what I had discovered and to suggest we delay the search until we discovered if the coast was clear. Then he told me that his grandfather had died – taken his own life, his mother had told him. He said he knew Mr Donnelly had disappeared.' Pepe looked straight at his captive audience. Matters were becoming very nasty. 'One so-called suicide in Ronda, a second in Argentina with Paco's grandfather, I don't know his name.'

'Martin Bormann,' put in Bernard Waterman.

'Well, it was just too much of a coincidence. Was Collingson some kind of raving...' His voice trailed. 'What name did you say?'

'Martin Bormann. You know the name?'

'Good God, of course, I've read books on Nazi Germany and the events of the war. Wasn't he a general or something?'

'No, not a general,' Waterman said softly. 'He was Hitler's right-hand man, a Reichsleiter – often called the Führer's shadow, a shadow more dangerous than the man who cast it, sentenced to death *in absentia* for war crimes at Nuremberg and never found. Some talk of a skeleton being his but it was never really proved. But you were right, Pepe, in assuming that he died because of some involvement with Collingson. He committed suicide because the Mossad, the Israeli security service, had been led to him, largely by the activity of some people present today. Betty here found a covert meeting of old Nazi leaders and their sympathisers in England. One of these sympathisers was Roland's father. Bormann's daughter, on a visit to England, called on the house with her cousin Roland here. By then the Mossad had the house under surveillance. It wasn't a difficult matter to follow her back to Argentina and then on to the house where Bormann had lived for many years as an innocent ranch owner. He was an old man by then but he knew he would be taken back to Israel and almost certainly suffer the same fate as his colleague, Adolf Eichmann, so he took his life. We had all the details from a Dr Solomon, an old friend of Raoul. Bormann's friend and Davies's next-door neighbour, another face which was absent from the war trials, was picked up in England and was en route to Israel when he had a fatal heart attack on the plane.'

'So Paco was Bormann's grandson,' Pepe said incredulously.

'Quite so – but little is gained by disclosing that,' Adrian interjected. 'He's a respectable medical student progressing well at Madrid University, and the horrors of the past were long before his time. I suggest we leave it at that and stay silent. You needed him when you planned to work as a small team, Pepe. Now we have assembled a real team with varying skills, we don't need to bring him into the deal at all.'

The silence which fell on the room was broken by Angie's

light voice. She held Franz's hand as she spoke.

'This man Bormann you have talked about. That must have been the old man, Erika's father, who lived on the ranch in Argentina, the one they called "Papa".'

Bernard nodded.

'I have never heard of him before,' Angie went on, 'but then I don't read much – I watch TV. From what you say he was a very powerful and bad man. This Paco you talked about, the student in Madrid, he must have been Erika's son. There was a picture on Papa's wall – Mr Bormann's wall, I mean. Paco was there, dressed in a uniform, very smart and good-looking he was. Erika pointed it out to me. She was so proud of him. He is studying to be a doctor in Europe, she told me, but he had a bad accident with his motorbike just after he finished working with Mr Donnelly. She told me that is how she and her husband met Mr Donnelly, at the hospital. She went on chatting about him. Oh, she was so pleased with him. Then Mr Donnelly, or Pip, as I called him, came into the room with the old man Papa. "He will be a great man in the new world," he said, and the old man said Paco would be a front-line commander. I didn't know what they meant but I just agreed. Then the old man said things about the need for real money to back up Paco. It all seemed strange to me because Papa had a big ranch and seemed to have a good life and Pip had brought a lot of money to Argentina. I know because I had seen it. I made up my mind to take some of it and go off – after all, Pip didn't want me for myself, just as a bed partner. All I had to do was to slit open some of the packets he had in our room and then take a few of the lovely things he had brought.'

The Filipina's face broadened into a smile. 'Payment for services, I think it is called. Anyway, with them talking of really big money I thought I could get more if I waited. So I asked them how they would make real money. Oh, their answer really surprised me. They chatted on about the money not being for them but for party funds – all for the party. Then Pip said Paco was a rising man in the party and said he had just joined. They told me Paco would one day be a leader, a *jefe* – a *caudillo*, as the Spanish people called Franco. It was all such strange talk. I thought it was silly; if you can make real money you keep it. Still, it was up to them.'

Raoul's voice spoke forcefully from the second row. It had a crack, a strong hoarseness in it. 'Angie, think carefully. You mentioned a uniform which Paco wore in the photograph. What did the uniform look like?'

'Oh, it was light brown and he had a red, white and black band on his arm – with a squiggle thing on it, like German soldiers wear in the war films.'

'A swastika,' Raoul groaned. The room was silent for several minutes; a dog barking in the woodland outside seemed to create a noise out of all proportion. Eventually Bernard spoke.

'If what I believe is true, then Bormann rang his grandson with the information gained from Collingson about the aircraft. Paco would relay it to other members of the group in Madrid. It may be passed on to the branch we know exists in Berkshire. Betty said that quite a few people were present when she stumbled across the meeting. Your telephone call to Paco, Pepe, just confirmed the information was correct. The neo-Nazis dream of big money for their big plan, the idea originally hatched by Martin Bormann in Switzerland in 1945, the creation of the Fourth Reich. They had their grandiose ideas, their brave new world, so to speak, but they lacked the money to advance. Organisations need money, and illicit organisations need to gain it covertly. Here was the opportunity they sought, to recover the property they believed was rightfully theirs.' Bernard's voice trailed off.

Roland's head was in his hands as he spoke. 'Don't forget I know these people, in England anyway. My father, as we all know by now, was a Nazi sympathiser from the late thirties. They will stop at nothing – they are fanatics. Some of them are grandchildren of top Nazis – oh yes, I remember talking to one Sepp Himmler. Need I say more? I wanted out when I heard his lunatic plans but they needed me and – well, frankly I was scared. Believe me, efforts to find that aircraft will be intense and ruthless.'

Raoul stood. 'I think we've said enough, heard enough for one day. One thing is for sure. This team will have to move fast, very fast indeed. And the first thing is for you, Roland, to lay your hands on some new equipment. I'll pay for it.'

22

'Welcome home, Mr Davies – and Miss Betty as well.' Mrs Summers arrived at her usual nine o'clock and started to clear away the breakfast things. 'I was so pleased when you called to say you would be coming back.' She hesitated. 'And together, too – I'm so glad. Would you like more coffee?'

She disappeared into the kitchen and Roland smiled at Betty. 'Funny old stick, she is. Notice she hasn't mentioned Father's death. Feels a bit awkward about saying it, I guess.'

When Mrs Summers reappeared, Roland Davies gave her a chance. 'Look, Mrs Summers, we are only staying here for the morning, then I'm going to drive down to Plymouth to pick up some technical equipment I need for a search near Gibraltar. It's a long story but we're involved in underwater exploring down there and I need to go west to pick up some machinery. We will stay at the cottage in Mary Tavy tonight then tomorrow morning we will be at the factory. Tomorrow midday we plan to drive back to Cookham to clear my father's house.'

Mrs Summers coughed. 'Yes, I'm sorry. I didn't like to mention it, such a nice gentleman, your father. It was a motor accident in Spain, wasn't it? Such bad driving, I'm told.'

Roland smiled. 'Well, it wasn't quite like that, Mrs Summers. No one was really to blame.' Mrs Summers shook her head. 'Then there was Mr Whiteman, died on a plane he did. Died a few days after Mr Davies. Two friends and neighbours going so close together, makes the area gloomy, doesn't it?

Roland stepped in. 'Don't let's dwell on it, Mrs Summers. Now we must get a few things together and then be on our way.'

As Roland and Betty left, Mrs Summers picked up the telephone and made a very short call. The recipient smirked.

* * *

It was dusk when the car left the M4 and Roland felt exhausted. Motorway or no motorway, the drive from the West Country is a long one, especially as he had driven down there only the day before. The tedium of motorway driving and the fact that Betty was asleep for a great deal of the journey did nothing to brighten his spirits. Ahead lay the prospect of entering his father's old home, now empty and uninviting. He reflected that the house next door, once the home of Robert Whiteman, would also be empty. Two old friends, his father and Robert, had both died within a few days of one another. Strange how things worked out. The Spanish police had asked for the house to be searched; presumably that would have been done by the local police, not that they would have found anything. Roland glanced at Betty, still asleep in the seat beside him. A look over his shoulder at the box secured on the back seat established that the equipment was in place. Last time he had travelled with such equipment it had been with his father. What a tragic effort that had been. They were crazy to have taken a thug like Rollason – why had they involved him? he asked himself.

As the car entered Cookham, Roland patted Betty on the knee. 'We're back – it's Cookham.'

Betty sat up and rubbed her eyes. 'Roland, look, I don't want to upset you but I wasn't asleep all the time. I was thinking. I don't really want to stay at your father's house tonight. Don't forget the last time I was there I had the fright of my life, and all I've learned since – well, I would rather stay at a hotel. Fact is, I'd rather not go into the house again. I have a book and I'll read whilst you get the basic clearing done. After all, you're just going to remove personal items, aren't you?'

Roland nodded. 'I see your point. OK, we can go to the Holiday Inn near the airport. The estate agent promised to come over around six. Once I've discussed the sale with him I'll leave him the key and he can do all his measuring, and notes. I don't have to be there. We can leave the car here – it can be part of the overall sale.'

Roland swung the car into the driveway and glanced at both houses before getting out. 'Odd, coming back like this,' he muttered. 'I'll be as quick as I can. When John Harrington, the estate agent, comes just send him in. He's a nice guy. It will be good to see him again.'

He took the key from his pocket and let himself into the house, then went to the telephone in the hall and dialled the number written in his father's hand on a table pad. The taxi would be there at six thirty, sharp. 'I'm sorry about your father,' said the local taxi driver, and Roland murmured his thanks. Everyone seemed to know what had happened. It would have made news in the local papers, perhaps the nationals. The house was cold, unfriendly. He looked around the hall, so strange without his father. He wondered if he had ever been in the house alone before; his father was always there in the past, rarely left the house unless to go to Robert Whiteman next door for a chat or one of those strange party meetings.

As he opened the door of the lounge his heart gave a leap and his throat dried. He stood still and tried to speak but managed only a whisper. 'You.'

Sepp Himmler rose from the desk, his uniformed figure framed by the large swastika on the flag hanging on the wall behind him.

'Good evening, Roland. I hear on good authority you have joined the other side – no room for the Fourth Reich now your father is dead.'

Roland tried to speak but Himmler waved him down. 'My grandfather used to say the only traitor to have around you is a dead one. As you know, he was a truly great man, a man devoted to the Reich and to his Führer.'

'How –' The blow which Roland received on the back of

his head silenced him and he slumped to the floor. A second blow from the iron bar splattered his skull around the room. His sphincter, no longer in control, opened and his body waste spilled out.

Sepp Himmer pulled a raincoat over his uniform. 'Good job, Heinrich.' He kicked Roland's chest. 'Did you really think we wouldn't know? Come on, let's get away. Use the back door.'

Betty woke with a start when John Harrington tapped gently on the car window. 'I'm sorry, I must have dozed off. I'm Betty Silvester. You must be the Estate Agent?'

'John Harrington. Yes, I've come to look around. Mr Davies called me yesterday.'

Betty smiled, 'Please go in. For reasons of my own I don't want to enter the house again, sentimental reasons you might say. The door is unlocked and Mr Davies is inside.'

A minute later John Harrington stood beside the car. His face was white and he was shaking, 'You'd better, you should... it's so...'

Betty knew. Of course! She jumped from the car and ran into the house. What she saw on the carpet caused her to run from the house and vomit violently over the rose bed.

* * *

Betty was waiting in the foyer of the Holiday Inn when the service coach arrived from the airport. Adrian collected the luggage whilst Ella walked swiftly to the pale-faced girl. Betty put her arms around her.

'Thank God you've come. It's been dreadful here, just dreadful. The police have been here. They were so kind but I had to tell them why we went to the house, what happened and why I stayed in the car. Then they asked what I saw when I...' Her voice broke. 'Anyway, they are coming back this afternoon.'

Adrian joined them. 'Sounds a bit trite, I know, but try to put it out of your mind for a bit. I'll speak to the police. Perhaps they will agree to us taking you up to Burnham

Beeches. It's so lovely there.'

A few minutes later Adrian returned from the telephone. 'Sorry, they're not happy about you wandering around the countryside until they're satisfied you are at no risk. They are sending two officers over straightaway so you can complete your statement. It's good to get it out of the way.'

That evening Adrian, Ella and Betty had dinner then settled into a quiet corner of the lounge. Betty broke the silence. 'I want to tell you what happened.'

'Just when you are ready. It can wait, if you like. Tomorrow will do,' Adrian said gently.

Without comment Betty started to recount the events. It was only when she came to entering the house – 'He was lying on the floor, blood everywhere and the flag, that flag' – that she broke down and sobbed uncontrollably.

Adrian brought a brandy and Betty soon regained her composure.

'You probably want to turn your back on all this, forget it ever happened,' Adrian said slowly. 'It's not like that. It is not an evil event which has come and gone. What you have witnessed is a brutal act of fanatical people who had been tipped off by their equally crazed colleagues in Madrid. Roland had been useful to them. Then they saw him as a traitor. They have an unsuppressible quest for world domination, bred into them by their fathers and their grandfathers, and anything – anyone – standing in their way has to be eliminated. We are intent to find that wrecked aircraft for the joy that the recovery of the contents will bring Raoul and his family. I don't deny it will bring us some more than useful financial gain. Their aims are different. They will stop at nothing, and I mean nothing, to finance and advance their crazy ambitions. They employ people of limited intelligence to create havoc, and these are the thugs the media tag "Neo Nazis". The reality is that the people behind the scene, the real fanatics, are faceless ... occupying senior positions in many walks of life.

'We need to get back to Spain and talk with Raoul. He is the most intimately involved member of our team. He is very much in charge. He must decide what we do now to prevent the maniacs getting their hands on his property.'

Betty dabbed her eyes. 'What you said a moment ago is true. I want to get out of this whole business. What good can I do?'

'I'm German and proud of it.' Ella spoke with feeling. 'The Nazis are part of our past. Franz and I live with that. We cannot forget it. But there is plenty we can do about it. The old Nazis, the Hitlers, Himmlers, Bormanns, Goerings and Goebbles may be dead but a new generation, equally brutal and fanatical, is surely and slowly taking its place in many countries. It is a legacy of evil. They have created havoc in your life, Betty, and they have killed the father of your baby. In three months your child will enter this world, a troubled world indeed. Enough problems without the activity of these crazed minds. They must be stopped, and in our own way we can defeat them. Demented phrases like "The Final Solution" and "The Purity of the Aryan Race" must be committed to where they belong – to history.'

AUTHOR'S POSTCRIPT

This book is a work of fiction but is based on fact.
    The events in North Africa are carefully researched. The synagogue did exist. The attack happened and I have interviewed witnesses on site. The crash on Gibraltar did occur. The train journey was recounted to me by Mrs Rommel. The events in Argentina are mostly factual and were recounted to me by Martin Bormann's daughter.

ACKNOWLEDGEMENTS

I would like to acknowledge the following people, who, in various ways, have all contributed to *Legacy of Evil*:

Joan Wright, Ramon Perez, Gabi Rey, the late Lucie Maria Rommel, Elizabeth Turnbull, Carmella Dight, the late Leslie Swift, the late D.A. Young, Tommy Frost-Hansen, the late Peter Norton, Erika X (née Bormann), the late John Habelin, Beverley Webb, D. Linton, B. Easterbrook, Baron Howard Strouth, A. Humber, P. Repetto, Nebil Abdul Mullah, James Blackburn and Colonel Rolf Schacht.